BOOM AND CHAINS

BOOM AND CHAINS

A Yiddish Novel Set in Israel/Palestine

Hanan Ayalti

Translated and with an
Introduction by Adi Mahalel

WAYNE STATE UNIVERSITY PRESS
DETROIT

ISBN 9780814351802 (paperback)
ISBN 9780814351796 (hardcover)
ISBN 9780814351819 (ebook)

Library of Congress Control Number: 2025931231

On cover: Hanan Ayalti, on right with the hat, working in Kibbutz Benyamina, ca. 1929–31. Courtesy of Daniel Klenbort. Cover design by Brad Norr Design.

Grateful acknowledgment is made to the Yiddish Book Center and the Bertha M. and Hyman Herman Endowed Memorial Fund for their generous support of the publication of this volume.

Wayne State University Press rests on Waawiyaataanong, also referred to as Detroit, the ancestral and contemporary homeland of the Three Fires Confederacy. These sovereign lands were granted by the Ojibwe, Odawa, Potawatomi, and Wyandot Nations, in 1807, through the Treaty of Detroit. Wayne State University Press affirms Indigenous sovereignty and honors all tribes with a connection to Detroit. With our Native neighbors, the press works to advance educational equity and promote a better future for the earth and all people.

Wayne State University Press
Leonard N. Simons Building
4809 Woodward Avenue
Detroit, Michigan 48201-1309

Visit us online at wsupress.wayne.edu.

CONTENTS

TRANSLATOR'S INTRODUCTION
Ayalti's Rebellions

Writing out of Liberty

The Palestinian problem currently occupies a large place in the Jewish world. One hears different opinions: on one side, there is the idealism of the *halutzim* and constructive socialism of the collectives; the other side is characterized by the reactionary Jewish organizations (seizing of labor and land). I wanted to show in my book how these contradictions are reflected in the soul of the individual and uncover the socio-economic roots of these phenomena.[1]

In July 1936, author Hanan Ayalti (1910–92) was interviewed by the Yiddish paper *Folksblat* prior to the serialization of his debut prose work in Yiddish, *Troymen un keytn* (*Dreams and Chains*), in the paper. When asked what motivated him to write his "Palestine novel," he gave the answer above. The tensions and contradictions Ayalti depicts in his novel, retitled as *"Bum" un keytn* (*"Boom" and Chains*, 1936), persisted in the years after he wrote them and, tragically, have continued to the present day. The significance of Ayalti's Yiddish debut lies in the unfiltered light it sheds on the realities of prestate Palestine and on the practices of the Zionist movement, particularly in its kibbutz form. Ayalti gives us a unique voice from within the Yishuv (prestate Zionism), recorded at a pivotal moment of Zionist-Palestinian history. Many of the tensions raised in the novel pertain to our present as well: the Israeli-Palestinian conflict, nationalism, struggles over land, indigenousness and migration, and the essence of progressive politics. Anyone interested in the history and complicated politics of Israel-Palestine will be engrossed in this sharp and gripping novel.

Toward the end of the aforementioned interview, Ayalti was asked specifically whether he had written his novel about "the recent occurrences in Palestine" (*di letste geshe'enishen in Palestine*), meaning the Palestinian revolt of 1936 to 1939, which had erupted in April of that year.[2] To that, Ayalti answered: "I finished the novel months before, but I permit myself to say that, analyzing the situation in Palestine, I predicted these occurrences, and I also portrayed similar occurrences [in my novel]."[3] The deep sense of injustice that Palestinians felt due to British policies in Palestine ultimately led to, in the words of historian Rashid Khalidi,

Ad in the Yiddish paper Morgn frayhayt *from July 29, 1936, announcing the serialization of* Troymen un keytn. *It mistakenly states Ayalti lived eight years in Palestine, rather than four. (Courtesy of Historical Jewish Press website, www.Jpress.org.il, founded by the National Library and Tel Aviv University)*

The 1936 riots between British police and local Arabs in Jaffa. (Wikimedia Commons)

"an unprecedented, country-wide violent explosion in Palestine starting in 1936." The uprising followed a six-month general strike of Palestinian workers, which constituted "a popular and spontaneous explosion from the bottom up that took the British, the Zionists, and the elite Palestinian leadership by surprise."[4] Consequently, "the Jews," notes historian Benny Morris, "realized that they were sitting on a volcano, that the Yishuv's growth could not but spark native resistance . . . the Yishuv would have to live by the sword."[5]

The change in the novel's title from *Troymen un keytn* (*Dreams and Chains*) to *"Bum" un keytn* (*"Boom" and Chains*) sharpened the contrast Ayalti wished to illustrate between the two groups, Zionist Jews and Palestinian Arabs, who inhabited the same geography. The epigraph explicitly states: "*Ertsisroel—in 'bum' / Palestine—in keytn,*" the Land of Israel is "booming," while Palestine is "in chains."[6] Ayalti's timely novel represented a unique and rare view *from the bottom up*. It sketched a blueprint for understanding the violence that erupted in Palestine just months after he finished his novel—and that he had predicted. Ayalti's explosive Yiddish novel, however, was not his debut novel. At the end of that same *Folksblat* interview, Ayalti says:

> I also had written a book in Hebrew about the life of the Zionist and *halutz* youth in Poland. That book was published in the Shtibl Press in Tel Aviv. But I had to stop writing in Hebrew. I think you can't write good stuff if you don't believe in what you write. The truth of the matter is that, what I wrote, they wouldn't have published in Hebrew.[7]

In his personal correspondence (in Hebrew) with Israeli Yiddish and Hebrew literary scholar Dov Sadan, Ayalti wrote that he was switching to Yiddish because "Hebrew is the language of one class among the Jewish People," meaning the elite class.[8] In another letter to Sadan, Ayalti expresses frustration that writings in other languages feature ideas from Communism to fascism and anywhere in between, whereas in Hebrew, you can only write in a Zionist vein. In such a limited environment, writes Ayalti, an anti-Zionist novel in Hebrew would never get published.[9] "But," Ayalti sharpens his point, "as Berdyczewski said: 'writing one can only do out of liberty.'"[10]

"One of the Most Important Storytellers in Yiddish Literature"

Bilingual Yiddish-Hebrew writer Hanan (Khonen or Chanan) Klenbort authored his first Yiddish novel under his pen name A-Yalti (later changed to Ayalti). Mordechai Halamish, the editor of an anthology of Yiddish stories set in Israel, published decades after Ayalti's debut, wrote, "[Hanan Ayalti] is considered today one of the most important storytellers in Yiddish literature, and his realistic style highlights, not seldom in a sober-minded, humorous tone, the ideological standing of the author toward the reality he aims to reflect in his stories."[11] Indeed, Ayalti's shifting "ideological standing" played a central role, arguably *the* central role, in his writing career. Therefore, comparing this Yiddish effort to his earlier Hebrew novel *Ba-mehilot* (*In the Burrows*, 1934) provides a strong indication of the evolution of Ayalti as a writer. From a young age, Ayalti had intended to become a Hebrew novelist, and throughout the rest of his tumultuous life, he contemplated returning to it. But *In the Burrows* became both the first and last novel that Ayalti wrote in Hebrew. Ayalti grew up speaking Yiddish, but it wasn't until his mid-twenties that he became familiar with its literature and textual culture. He nonetheless became a prolific Yiddish novelist and journalist.

Klenbort was born on November 15, 1910, in Sapotskin, Grodno region, then part of Russian Empire (now Belarus). It was a mostly mercantile town consisting of about two hundred Jewish families living in the town's center, surrounded by about a hundred Polish peasant families at the outskirts. During World War I, his family was forced to flee to Russia proper. In their Russian haven, Klenbort went to a Russian school and absorbed the revolutionary spirit of the time. His father was happy to go back to Sapotskin and send his son to a yeshiva to receive a Jewish education, after which Klenbort went on to study at the modern Hebrew

Hanan Klenbort (Ayalti), standing fourth from the left, with his classmates at the Hebrew school in Grodno, staging a literary trial of king Solomon. (Courtesy of Daniel Klenbort)

Members of the Hashomer Hatzair youth movement march in the May Day parade in Tel Aviv, 1946. (Wikimedia Commons)

high school *Tarbut*, in Bialystok; in the novel he includes a parody of a *Tarbut* teacher arriving to Palestine onboard ship. It was in Bialystok that he became involved in the socialist-Zionist *Hashomer Hatzair* (Young Guard) youth movement, founded in 1913 in Eastern Europe (Galicia), which he characterized as the most leftist Zionist movement of the time. He became a group leader, an experience he remembered as follows: "We talked about Zionism and about socialism and we sang, and we read stories, and we went . . . to the woods in tents . . . and educating that the only way of life is a kibbutz in Israel."[12]

His early life became the backdrop for his debut novel, the afore-mentioned Hebrew *In the Burrows*, which had a much more sympathetic view of Zionism than did the later Yiddish novel we have here. *In the Burrows* focused on young Jewish protagonists during the turbulent years in Eastern Europe during World War I and its aftermath. It shows these young people and the central character, Aaron, as they became refugees during the war, and it explores the influence on them of nascent Soviet Communism and the participation of Jews in labor unions and in the Jewish Labor Bund, as well as the theme of sex.

The novel contains many descriptions of sex between its young protagonists, of prostitutes as part of the urban human landscape of Eastern Europe, sexual violence involving soldiers, non-Jews, and Jews, and more, with various levels of graphic boldness. Ayalti had to respond to accusations that he was fabricating a sinful reality of Polish Jewish youth: "In regard to *In the Burrows*, I don't see that the protagonist there [Aaron] had sinned. . . . These things are accurate, and I could point to every deed and to any character. But I overdid it . . . in fact I did not overdo it, but I included too many sexual descriptions in a narrow terrain of other problems."[13] As we will also see in *Boom and Chains*, Ayalti's protagonists subscribed to the utopian socialist idea that the political revolution would not be complete without a sexual revolution as well.[14] An integral part of the revolutionary novel was the honest depiction of sexuality. The perception, imported from the Soviet Union, was that to "be an authentic proletarian . . . could mean abandoning self-restraint . . . it is ideologically superior to address one's sexuality frankly and with a minimum of fuss."[15]

The remedy for the troubled and idealistic youth in the novel was participation in a *hakhshara* program in Poland. Organized by the socialist-Zionist Hashomer Hatzair, *hakhshara* was a training commune for Jewish youth, intended to prepare them for a pioneering new life in the Land of Israel, working as agrarians in a kibbutz and finally becoming "productive" Jews.[16] Immigration to Palestine (Heb. *aliya*), termed "the other land" (Heb. *ha-adama ha-aheret*), to become part of a collective group, became for the Jewish youth in the novel the ultimate resolution to the contradictions of Jewish life in the diaspora, capable of bridging the gap between a particular Jewish identity and a universalist socialist agenda. As the book's title suggests, the diaspora youth spend the bulk of the novel in "the burrows," or tunnels, that is, metaphorically making the difficult shift to their new life in the Land of Israel. Then, by settling Zion and establishing a socialist utopia, they would help bring about the Messiah. According to the Jewish doctrine of *gilgul mehilot*, which is based on a midrashic interpretation of Ezekiel,[17] in messianic times, when the dead are resurrected, those buried in the diaspora will roll along underground tunnels toward the Land of Israel, where the resurrection of the dead will take place.[18] Add to this mystical backdrop the historical backdrop of World War I, known for its trench warfare, and Ayalti's choice of the title *Ba-mehilot*, which can be translated as *In the Trenches*, becomes clear.[19]

Ayalti, like his fictional Aaron, graduated from the *hakhshara* in Poland and arrived in Palestine in 1929, while still in his late teens. In 1930, his Hebrew manuscript, which he had already completed in Poland in 1928,[20] was accepted by a publisher. It was then that Khonen Klenbort adopted the pen name "Hanan Ayalti," which he drew from the name of the kibbutz, Ayelet Hashahar, that his brother Yehuda had cofounded. However, it took three more years until the novel saw the light of day as a book. Those three years were to be turbulent ones in the life of the young author.

In and Out of the Kibbutz

During the first two of those years, Ayalti lived on Kibbutz Binyamina, along with approximately one hundred other kibbutz members. Besides two shacks reserved for the sick, members lived together in canvas huts (tent-like structures called *badon* in Hebrew, or *baydl* in Yiddish; in the novel I refer to them as "tents") that could fit three people (the elitist "tent of five" mentioned in the novel is based on one inseparable group of intellectuals, three men and two women who squeezed into one single tent).[21] The tents were located at the outskirts of the Binyamina settlement, which was founded in 1922 by descendants of the Zionist settlers of Zikhron Yaakov. Zikhron was founded during the First Aliyah in the late nineteenth century, by settlers who had planned to base their economy on jasmine perfume production. The kibbutz members, who

Hanan Ayalti, on right with the hat, working in Kibbutz Benyamina, ca. 1929–31. (Courtesy of Daniel Klenbort)

perceived themselves as revolutionaries, refer in the novel to Binyamina and Zikhron as "the colonies."[22]

Kibbutz Binyamina was established under the leadership of Ya'akov (Kuba) Riftin (1907–78; likely Ignatz in the novel[23]), who led a line of leftist political radicalism, that resulted in quarrels both with the Binyamina settlers and the Histadrut (the union of Hebrew workers in Palestine). But despite the kibbutz's being considered more left wing ideologically than other kibbutzim and in favor of workers' solidarity,[24] its members were still expected in those years to participate in taking land and jobs from the *fellahin*, the native agrarian Arab populations (*kibbush ha-adama*, and *kibbush ha-avoda*, or the struggle for *avoda ivrit*, Hebrew [Jewish] labor).[25] The dissatisfaction by Ayalti and other Kibbutz Binyamina members' like Ruth Lubitsch (1906–2010) and Hanokh Bz'ozah (1910–64) with his Labor Zionist kibbutz, grew, particularly when they couldn't be in solidarity with Arab laborers striking to increase their wages.[26] To understand their resentment, it is necessary first to examine

Zionist settlers on the Zarka stream. (Courtesy of Zikhron Ya'akov Historical Archive)

what a kibbutz is (lit. "gathering" in Hebrew), and what role the kibbutz movement played in the evolution of Zionism.

In the 1830s, the French utopian socialist thinker Charles Fourier wrote about the need to restructure the economy according to principles of self-sustained cooperative communities (*Phalansteries*). These communes would not include Jews, however, for Jews were destined, according to Fourier's Judeophobic perspective, to establish their own experimental communes away from Europe, in Palestine. Fourier envisioned their being financially supported by Jewish millionaires like the Rothschild family, who famously would become involved, half a century later, in financing Jewish settlement in Palestine. He saw the Jews enjoying a national renaissance in Palestine and serving as an exemplary socialist society for the word.[27] The kibbutzim were not directly linked to Fourier's vision but rather were likely modeled on the Russian *artel*, a medieval cooperative comprising an elite of farmers, artisans, or workers, which in the modern era were mostly temporary "cooperative living arrangements" of workers from a common place of origin.[28] In any case, a century after Fourier, the first kibbutzim, in the sense of agricultural collectives, were indeed established in Palestine.

" בנימינה "

קבוץ השומר - הצעיר

– מיסודו של קבוץ-עליה א' בפולין –

Cover of the booklet "Binyamina" with the subheading, "Kibbutz Hashomer Hatzair, Founded by Kibbutz Aliya Alef in Poland" (Benyamin Pagi [Bolek], ed., "Binyamina," Givat Haviva: Yad Ya'ari Archive, 1986). (Courtesy of Yad Yaari Research and Documentation Center)

A Hashomer Hatzair kibbutz, like Kibbutz Binyamina in the novel, was composed of a small number of people who strove to be models of the "new man" and the "new society." Its members were influenced as much by Freud as by Marx. They strove to establish an insular "organic community" focused on *tikkun ha'adam* (repair of the human) and would develop a culture of lengthy nightly confessions in a group setting.[29]

Linguist Noam Chomsky lived for a short while in 1953 on a kibbutz associated with the Hashomer Hatzair movement (Kibbutz HaZorea, located not far from Ayalti's kibbutz) and agreed with Hashomer Hatzair's prestate positions. In a 1999 interview about the lessons learned from the history of the kibbutz, Chomsky observed that "Kibbutzim came closer to the anarchist ideal than any other attempt that lasted for more than a very brief moment before destruction. . . . I think they were extremely attractive and successful. . . . I probably would have lived there myself." "But," he continues critically,

They were embedded in a more general context that was highly corrosive. In part this had to do with the colonization/settlement project, which—undeniably—was taking away the lands of poor people, however the fact was concealed in ideological constructions, which I recall very well, having been part of this indoctrination system when I was a teenager leading youth groups. The doctrine was that Jewish and Arab workers should be pursuing common interests in opposition to rich Arab landowners and British imperialists; a fine ideal, but very far from the reality. . . . In part this had to do with other aspects of the ideology, in particular, the fervent nationalism. . . . Also highly destructive was the extreme Stalinism, even as late as Stalin's last anti-Semitic paroxysms.[30]

Indeed, as Ayalti remarked, Hashomer Hatzair accepted the Soviet ideology of dictatorship of the proletariat. It disagreed with Russia only on the question of the founding of a Jewish state (which the USSR eventually supported in 1947). Hashomer Hatzair members "became in Palestine more and more left until Stalin's story and now [in 1977] they are completely anti-Soviet. . . . Well, I wouldn't say completely, but they are anti-Soviet pretty much by now."[31] These "ideological constructions" that "concealed" the fact that the kibbutzim were "taking away the lands of poor people," which Chomsky mentions in his both admiring and critical take on the kibbutzim, arguably stand at the foundation of the kibbutz. Shafir and Peled argue that the origin of the kibbutz was not in realizing socialism, but as an efficient tool in taking over land as part of the Zionist national-settlement project. The model of ethnic settlement of the First Aliya (roughly 35,000 Jews, between 1882 and 1903), which consisted of Jewish land ownership and mixed Arab and Jewish labor, proved unsustainable for the national project. The Jewish settler employers preferred the cheaper Arab labor over Jewish labor. Therefore, the Second Aliya newcomers (1904–14, also ca. 35,000 Jews) demanded solely "Hebrew [Jewish] labor" from their First Aliya employers. As a result of the newcomers' failure to get their demands met, the kibbutz came to be seen as the pure form of settlement: land ownership *and* labor there were only Jewish.[32]

Thus, due to his growing objection to the dispossession of Palestinian Arabs, Ayalti, along with a number of other Kibbutz Binyamina members, became disillusioned with Zionism, even with its most leftist faction: Hashomer Hatzair was the only Zionist party to recognize the national rights of Palestinian Arabs,[33] and from 1927 until 1948 held a genuine binational vision for the land.[34] His move away from Zionism was part of a larger trend at the time, as Shmuel Dotan concludes. A significant number of *shomrim* (members of Hashomer Hatzair) made a similar move in the years 1929–32; out of the 1,500 *shomrim* who immigrated to Palestine, an estimated 400 left the movement (up to 700 according to other estimates), and most of these became part of the newly founded Jewish-Arab, anti-Zionist Palestinishe Komunistishe Partey (Palestinian Communist Party, PKP).[35] During those years, under a directive from Moscow, PKP was making efforts to implement a policy of Arabization of the party to better reflect the demography in Palestine; in the 1920s and 1930s, it was led mostly by Yiddish-speaking Jews.[36] One of the challenges of its being a Jewish-led party, according to Joel Beinin, was the inability of Jewish Communists to draw themselves out of their social milieu in the Yishuv[37] while trying to recruit Arab laborers with no common language.[38] Such challenges are examined in Ayalti's novel. In addition, the party, which was accepted into the Communist International (the Comintern) in 1923, adopted anticolonial language into its platform starting in 1928, as part of the struggle of urban proletarians.[39] The inclusion of the anticolonial struggle in the Communist platform had deep implications for the political reality in Palestine. It was at odds with the ways leftist Labor Zionist Jews cooperated with the British, and it motivated Communist Yiddish writers in New York and elsewhere to come out openly against Zionism.[40]

Ayalti would later claim he was a true Communist believer, although he did not become part of the PKP after leaving Hashomer Hatzair.[41] Yet, all evidence shows that in terms of activism and ideological conviction, Ayalti was in full agreement with the PKP and was part of the larger trend at the time of abandoning the Hashomer Hatzair movement in favor of the PKP.[42] Ayalti's good friend, Nyomke Gilai, described him as "one of the heads of the PKP in Jerusalem,"[43] together with PKP-Jerusalem leader Hanokh Bz'ozah, also formerly of Kibbutz Binyamina. Zalmen and Motke in the novel could be amalgamations of Ayalti and Bz'ozah.[44] Ayalti was also part of a pro-Soviet circle in Tel Aviv that read Marxist texts and Russian literature by Maxim Gorky and listened to reports from the USSR. Many of its participants became prominent in the PKP.[45]

PKP pamphlet in Hebrew addressed to youth and dated September 1934. The title reads, "Down with the Hooligan Conquest of Labor," and the bottom line urges youth to "organize together with the adult worker and as one launch a revolutionary war against the imperialist government—the main culprit to blame for your condition." Reprint: Shmuel Dotan, Reds: The Communist Party in the Land of Israel *(in Hebrew) (Source: Kfar Saba: Shevna Hasofer, 1991), 172.*

A significant number of members left Kibbutz Binyamina to join the PKP. At a certain point in the 1930s, ex-Shomrim became the dominant leadership in the PKP (75 percent),[46] a fact that both the movement's followers and its critics prefer to ignore.[47] Ya'akov Riftin, a founding member of Kibbutz Binyamina, referred to it as the "painful departure [*prisha makhiva*, that is, from Kibbutz Binyamina] of a group of young people to the PKP."[48] In 1932, working in concert with the Labor Zionist establishment, the British authorities initiated a massive anti-Communist

Palestinian fellahin crushing olives in Palestine, ca. 1900–1920.
(Wikipedia Commons)

campaign in response to their fears that local Communist activism was part of a larger Soviet, anti-British war effort. The crackdown led to the imprisonment and deportation of many of these defectors (many of whom would end up in Europe during World War II). That year alone, they arrested 210 people suspected of participation in Communist activity.[49]

On the run from the British due to his involvement in underground Communist activism (themes that would be explored in the novel), Ayalti was met with violence from his old kibbutz friends when he tried to seek refuge at the kibbutz. Nyomke Gilai recounts that the Haganah, a Zionist militia, found out about Ayalti's PKP activism with the Bedouins in Hawareth and pursued him. According to Gilai, Ayalti became part of the underground PKP cell in their kibbutz and went on to incite the Bedouins to prevent Zionist Jews from settling in Hawareth. He sought refuge in Gilai's chambers, but two kibbutz members demanded he leave, and he left while Gilai was not there.[50]

Kibbutz Binyamina was disbanded in 1931, largely due to the increasing number of ideological defectors like Ayalti. It first moved to Kibbutz Ein Shemer, where Riftin (who many viewed as responsible for the disbandment) and Zhenia settled with four other Kibbutz

---

FORCE MAY BE USED TO EVICT ARABS FROM WADI HAWARETH

JERUSALEM (J. T. A.)—Government officials have issued a warning to the Arabs now living on the Wadi Hawareth lands that unless they leave the land which was bought by the Jews, they will be forcibly evicted. These are the lands recently purchased by the Jewish National Fund with money contributed by Canadian Zionists.

A report from December 13, 1929, in The Sentinel *about the tensions around Wadi Hawareth. (Courtesy of Historical Jewish Press website, www.Jpress.org.il, founded by the National Library and Tel Aviv University)*

Binyamina families in early 1932. In 1933 the majority of its members joined Gan Shmuel.[51] On Kibbutz Gan Shmuel, the group from Kibbutz Binyamina became known as "Habenyimina'im" (The Benyaminites). They were featured in a special booklet issued by Gan Shmuel to mark seventy years since their arrival there. The booklet hailed them as "a group of young people, imbued with faith and ideals—who realized a dream, created a reality, and built us a home in the Land of Israel."[52] That many left Kibbutz Binyamina to join the PKP is left out of their authorized history, but visual evidence remains: In the cover photo of the "Habenyimina'im" booklet, from May Day, 1930, the one holding the red flag is likely Ayalti.[53] One of Ayalti's fellow kibbutz members in Binyamina, Benyamin "Benyo" Grinboym, became an influential high school teacher at Kibbutz Gan Shmuel, where he mentored famous Israeli dissident Udi Adiv.[54] Adiv summarized the dilemmas of his mentor, always a true believer in kibbutz life based on Communist ideals:

> The [Labor Zionist] leaders of [Ben Gurion's] Mapai were fearful by the attempt of the Left's youth movements to expand the youth's horizons and to give a socialist universalist meaning to the Zionist settlement. The fear was that the communist universalist ideal might weaken the Zionist faith of the youth movements' members and their readiness to sacrifice themselves and to fight for "the building of the nation," and "worst of all"—might take them closer to the Arab workers and fellahin.[55]

Ayalti left the kibbutz, after two years, around 1931 to become a construction worker, road paver, and miner in Tel Aviv and Jerusalem, where, for the next two years, he worked alongside Jews and Arabs. He was arrested due to his activism in the PKP by a British policeman, who framed him by planting illegal propaganda material in his pocket (which Ayalti did distribute on other occasions), and was imprisoned for a short while.[56] Knowing that the British were after him, he managed to flee to Paris by boat using false papers.[57] In Paris, he registered at the Sorbonne, which got him his visa, and, ironically, worked as a Hebrew tutor for Jews preparing to make aliya to Palestine, among them Hannah Arendt, who became his lifelong

Hanan Ayalti working in construction in Palestine, ca. 1931–33.
(Courtesy of Daniel Klenbort)

friend.[58] He wrote for local Yiddish Communist papers and became part of the local leftist-Yiddishist culture of the interwar years.[59] It was there that he switched to writing in Yiddish, changed the spelling of his Hebrew pen name (writing it phonetically according to Soviet Yiddish standards), and began to write, in his own words, a "sharp anti-Zionist novel."[60]

Switching to Yiddish, Writing *Boom and Chains*

Ayalti's move out of Palestine and to writing exclusively in Yiddish stood in contrast to so many modern European Jewish writers who, prior to moving to Israel/Palestine, were bilingual writers of Hebrew and Yiddish, but, in their new land, switched to writing exclusively in Hebrew. Such writers include Y. H. Brenner, Yaakov Steinberg, and Devorah Baron.[61] Ayalti stated that Sadan told him he was the only writer who did not return to writing in Hebrew after switching to Yiddish. In other words, according to Sadan, Ayalti was the sole writer who began in Hebrew, switched to Yiddish, and never returned to Hebrew.[62]

The novel *Boom and Chains* has a similar style and structure to *In the Burrows*: realist with touches of impressionism, and more polyphonic than hero-based. Loosely it follows the character of Zalmen, in certain ways the continuation of Aaron from the previous novel. Zalmen's close friend, Motke, also represents a continuation of the stories of the previous novel's characters, and his story echoes segments from Ayalti's biography, as we see in this passage:

> Motke had grown up during the war, under shrapnel and cannon fire, among Cossacks, horses' carcasses, mass graves, and blood. In the shtetl, Jews were hanged because of fabricated charges of espionage, accused of carrying secret telephones in their beards and signaling to the Germans with their tefillin. Afterward, the whole shtetl was deported deep inside Russia. Then the revolution broke out. The world turned upside down. Motke witnessed all of it. He traveled back with his parents to Poland, wandered through pogrom-infected Ukraine, and in his old shtetl encountered burned houses and an endless number of poor shop owners and artisans.

The trauma of growing up in war-torn Europe comes not at the center of the narrative here but, rather, as background information about the character's past prior to his settling on the kibbutz. The novel is thus divided into three major parts: 1. Kibbutz 2. Land and Work, and 3. God and Money. Over half of the novel is centered on the kibbutz, which makes it the first Yiddish novel to prominently depict kibbutz life, to be followed only decades later with one more such example.[63]

While the serial *Troymen un keytn* opened with a two-part prologue set in Europe, translated here in the appendix,[64] the novel *"Bum" un keytn* opens with Zalmen's arrival in Palestine. We read about life in the Zionist commune (part 1), about his and his comrade Motke's disillusionment with what they see as their kibbutz comrades' cooperation with the British rather than their uniting with the local Arab population in an anti-imperialist struggle (overall part 2, earlier for Motke), and his involvement in underground joint Jewish-Arab activism (part 3). Zalmen articulates their dilemma early in the second part, challenging the

Yalti

ח. א-יאלטי

(ח. קלענבּאַרט)

"Bum" and chains

‏„בּוּם" און קייטן

ראָמאַן

novel of Palestine

Y. 1179256

ערשטער טייל

ווילנע—1936

ווילנער פאַרלאַג פון בּ. קלעצקין

Cover page of "Boom" and Chains, 1936. (Kletskin)

intellectual leader Ignatz's tendency to conformity: "'But, what should we do about it?' Zalmen heckled [Ignatz], 'take over fellahin land, or join the fellahin in a struggle for an agrarian revolution in Palestine? I mean, we, as revolutionaries, what do we need to do . . . ?'"

Zalmen and Motke eventually pay a heavy price, including imprisonment, for choosing the revolutionary option. Along the way, we meet Palestinian characters from different social classes, from the simple fellahin like Rasheed[65] to the elite Effendis, the absentee landlords who sold the land farmed and occupied by the fellahin to the Zionist organizations, while simultaneously inciting the fellahin to violence against the Jews. Characters of PKP members would try to expose the Effendi's betrayal to the fellahin. We also meet young idealists on the kibbutz who wish to realize the ideals they absorbed in Poland and Russia of Zionism and socialism, which continues the story of the *In the Burrows* characters.

The novel echoes Russian literary works as well. Examples of similar works start with Nikolay Chernyshevsky's utopian Russian novel, *What Is to Be Done?* (*Chto delat'?*, 1862), about life in communes,[66] and continue with more direct sources of influence, like the novel *The Scorched Land* (*Opalennaia zemlia*, 1933–34; 2nd edition, 1937) by Russian-Jewish author Mark Egart (Mordechai Bugoslavski, 1901–56). Egart spent three years in Palestine (1923–26) and was part of the HeHalutz movement (a Zionist youth movement). He based the novel on his intimate acquaintance with the subject and his own personal story of disillusionment from Zionism and return to the USSR. It differs from *Boom and Chains* in being written in the first person, including parts set in Eastern Europe during the Bolshevik Revolution. The resolution of Egart's novel is the protagonist's voluntary return to the USSR; only there can his utopian aspirations be fulfilled, he now realizes, after having initially chosen Zionism over Communism due to anti-Semitism. Mostly set in a Jewish collective in Palestine, by the Sea of Galilee, the novel shows the hardships of the Zionist settlers and (intentionally or not) generates sympathy toward them. It includes characters active in the PKP, but the ethnic conflict is not as central in Egart's story as it is in Ayalti's.[67]

In Ayalti's novel, we step out of the kibbutz and read urban descriptions of Tel Aviv, Jaffa, Haifa at the time its port was being built, and

Jerusalem, including the anti-Jewish violence of 1929; chapters about right-wing Revisionist Zionists (founded in the early 1920s by Ze'ev Jabotinsky); working in quarries, paving roads, living underground; and like in his first novel—sex. A reviewer of his Yiddish works remarked that,

> Ayalti immediately succeeded in gaining a name for himself as a good novelist with both the Yiddish reader and critic, because he writes about eroticism without any inhibitions. . . . Ayalti writes about everything that is connected with eroticism and love in the simplest and most natural way . . . he paints the dynamic of a healthy eroticism, as a natural thing and it occupies a very large—maybe the largest—parts of his descriptions.[68]

Ideas largely based on Soviet models prevalent in early Zionist thought that are often referenced in the novel—the New Man, the New Family, and communal living on a kibbutz, away from "culture" and back to "nature"—brought with them new possibilities in the sexual realm.[69] In the kibbutz, there are no gender-segregated sleeping arrangements: "They slept pressed like herring, twenty people, on a twelve-square-meter floor. Boys and girls together. It was the 'revolution.'" And young women were initiating sex just as often as young men: "[Hanke] kept walking with quick strides and stopped near a big pile of crops. For a moment, she tapped the place with her foot in the dark and immediately lay down on the ground. Motke kneeled next to her and ravenously latched onto her warm body. The girl moaned like she was in great pain; he kissed her naked feet and breasts and comforted her in his arms."

As the Hebrew novel's honest depiction of sex was influenced by revolutionary Soviet literature, we see in this Yiddish novel how for some of these revolutionary Labor-Zionist subjects, the sexual revolution should be part and parcel of the social revolution. The pamphlet *The Sexual Revolution in Russia* (1923) by Dr. Grigorii Abramovich Batkis, a leading figure in the kabinet of sexology of the newly created State Institute of Social Hygiene in Moscow, was published soon before Ayalti completed the manuscript of *In the Burrows*. The pamphlet proclaims a revolutionary approach to sexuality in Soviet Russia compared with the previous czarist regime. Its agenda included the decriminalization of homosexuality and equal rights for women.[70] As it does with other aspects of revolutionary life, *Boom and Chains* depicts the presentation of an antiutopian element in sex, in which a couple's jealousy threatens to undermine the free-spirited joint sleeping arrangements:

> Avrom was away, so Ignatz slept in Avrom's empty spot next to Sara. At night he would kiss her fingertips and quietly whisper: "I myself don't know what's happening to me . . ." Every morning, Agda glanced gloomily toward the corner where Ignatz slept next to Sara. At night, she wandered lost for hours and would return with red, defeated eyes. Ignatz paced in long strides across the room between straw mats hanging his head and smiling sadly to himself. In the dark little rooms, people whispered: "It will end in tragedy! And hell is really going to break loose when Avrom gets back to the kibbutz. Oh-Oh, a tragedy!"

The charismatic Ignatz openly courts Sara in the joint sleeping chambers while her boyfriend Avrom is away, despite the presence in the room of his own newly arrived girlfriend, Agda. Romantic tragedy looms as the outcome for the people involved, likely stemming from their misinterpretation of the Soviet concept of "free love." According to Batkis, "free love in Russia is not some kind of rampant and wild self-realization but rather a relation between two free and independent human beings."[71] Ayalti's socialist Zionism was perceived at the time by its proponents as a utopian movement of erotic liberation. They believed that the kibbutz would create an erotic utopia by freeing sexuality from the constraints of property, and some went as far as to claim that on Hashomer Hatzair kibbutzim, scenes of wild sexual experimentation were taking place.[72] In that sense, and against the utopian aspirations of the idealists on the kibbutz, the novel can be read as an antiutopia, with the targeted utopia as Zionism with kibbutz life as its vanguard.

In the novel, the antiutopian realization for this group of young idealists on the kibbutzim stems from the reality they encountered on

The beginning of the serialization of
Troymen un keytn—*"a suspenseful novel
of Jewish life in present-day Palestine"—in*
the Yiddish paper Folksblat *from July 24,
1936. (Courtesy of Historical Jewish
Press website, www.Jpress.org.il, founded
by the National Library and Tel Aviv
University)*

the ground in Palestine. In this reality, the interests of poor Palestinian farmers were subsumed by the British imperialists, the Zionist settlers, and the Arab ruling class. These Jewish radical leftists found themselves on the wrong side of these clashes. "The genuinely anti-utopian is always driven by the passionate desire to disprove Utopia,"[73] asserts Jameson, and in the novel we see how an array of issues leaves its mark on the experience and daily life of these Labor Zionists, leading some to gradually arrive at their anti-Zionist realizations. These issues include the struggles over the swamps of Kabara, which used to stretch along the southern Carmel to the north of the Hasharon area, until Zionist efforts to drain

Members of the Arab al-ghawarna tribe, of which many were hired to drain the Kabara swamps in the 1920s–30s. (Courtesy of Zikhron Ya'akov Historical Archive)

it materialized in the 1920s and 1930s. Ayalti and his fellow kibbutzniks were among only fifty to sixty Jews out of the hundreds of workers who drained the swamp. The rest of the labor force was composed of laborers from nearby Tantura or members of the Arab al-ghawarna tribe. The tribe members lived around the swamps, and thus they might have had less reason to fear malaria than did the Jewish immigrants. They also had fewer employment options.[74] Ayalti's novel includes vivid descriptions of malaria and other diseases that caused suffering among the European newcomers.

Also prominent in the novel are struggles over labor in the orchards, such as the disenfranchisement of Arab labor by Zionist workers (*kibbush ha-avoda*), a practice strongly denounced by the PKP at the time for being anti-Arab and undermining workers' solidarity.[75] Ayalti's fictitious depiction of tensions echoes the real clashes of Nes Ziona in 1932 and Kfar Saba in 1934, during which some Zionist Jews termed their struggle against Arab labor in the groves as a "holy war."[76] Take, for example, this passage in the novel, when Zalmen and Motke hear the following speech by a Labor Zionist speaker:

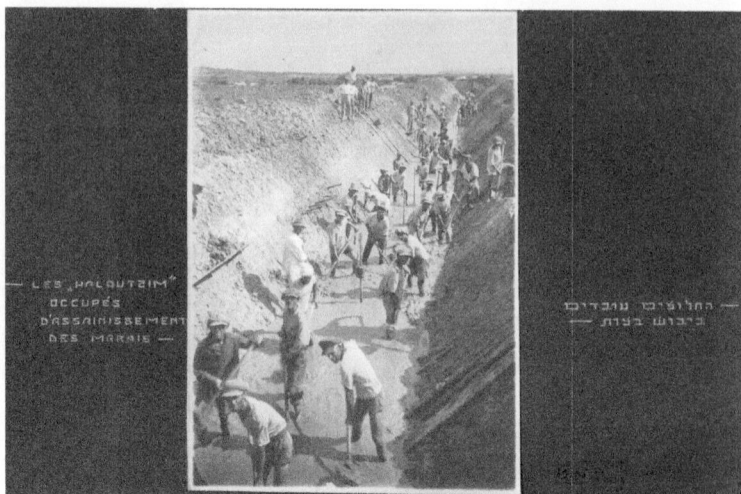

"Halutzim are working in draining the swamps." (Courtesy of Zikhron Ya'akov Historical Archive)

Water buffaloes at the Kabara swamp, ca. 1920s–30s. (Courtesy of Zikhron Ya'akov Historical Archive)

"Comrades! Controlling the workplaces is one of our moral principles. Today, this fight is happening in all across the land. Standing firm by hundreds of orchard gates, our comrades refuse entry to cheap Arab labor. The true class struggle is the struggle for one hundred percent Jewish labor. There isn't a colony, or a sector, or a city today where we are not in battle. And we will stand until victory."

After the speech . . . the crowd broke out in an enthusiastic hora dance.

Evident here is Ayalti's view that Labor Zionists had a distorted interpretation of socialism when they said that "the true class-struggle is the struggle for one hundred percent Jewish labor."[77] As noted by Morris, in the "conquest of labor," rather than meshing the social struggle with the national one, "the nationalist ethos had simply overpowered and driven out the socialist ethos."[78] The crown jewel of Labor Zionism, the kibbutz, functioned, in Zalmen's words, as "the vanguard of expelling Arabs from their work and from their land" Or, as Motke writes in a chilling letter to Zalmen, echoing the viewpoints he picks up from the kibbutzim in the valley, "there are only two options for how to resolve this situation: Either the Jewish Yishuv will give up its Zionism, in which case the antagonism between it and the majority population will cease, or, Zionism will eradicate the Arabs from the land" (*"Der yidisher yishev zol mevater zayn af zayn tsiyonizm, un memeyle vet ufhern der antagonism tsvishn im un der merhayts-bafelkerung, oder tsiyonizm zol oysrotn di araber fun land"*[79]).

Very important in the novel as well are the battles over the lands of Wadi Hawareth (*Khavarat* in the novel), known in present-day Israel as "Emek Hefer."[80] In fact, the much-publicized struggle over Wadi Hawareth during the first half of the 1930s is also considered a turning point in the history of PKP.[81] And it is where Ayalti's temporary kibbutz at the outskirts of Binyamina was originally supposed to establish a permanent settlement.[82] As Ayalti asked rhetorically in a letter, "how can one write a book with political tendencies without mentioning Wadi Hawareth and the guard shifts of Nes Ziona and Kfar Saba?"[83] Therefore, Ayalti devotes several chapters to exploring these struggles from different angles, with a

Kabara swamp, 1920. (Courtesy of Zikhron Ya'akov Historical Archive)

clear preference for the perspective of the disenfranchised fellahin. See, for example, this dramatic portrayal of a showdown between the Zionist Jews and the local fellahin over the right to work a piece of land, while Zalmen is torn between his national loyalty and his universal ideals:

> Fellahin with livestock arrived in the back. Both sides began plowing. . . . The Jewish guys finished plowing their square garden beds first and turned to the Arab ones . . . because plowing gave them the right of possession. A wave of shouting and cursing filled the air, bodies shoved, and fists clenched. A brawl erupted. Near the kibbutz's livestock, Sholem held the plow and Zalmen held the livestock. Zalmen was upset and thought it was a scandal, that he was about to rob someone else's land.
>
> The livestock . . . scattered. Zalmen and Sholem ran after them. Suddenly, somebody blocked their way. Zalmen raised his eyes and spotted Mustafa. His own blood smacked him in the face, and he froze in place. Mustafa leaned on a long stick and yelled: "Sons of bitches! Murdered the old guy and now you turn on us. A curse on your heads and on your father's faith . . ." He pulled ahead: "And you even spoke about brotherhood . . . about justice . . . Thieves, robbers . . . !"

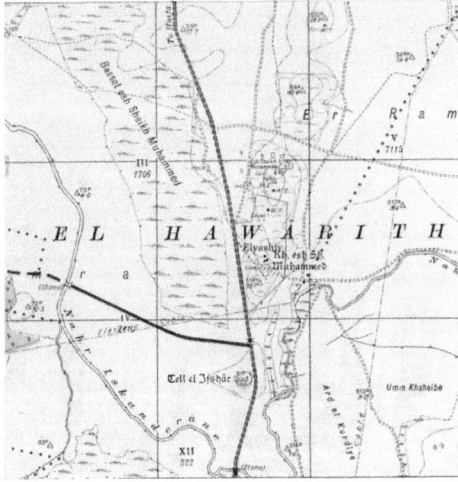

A 1940s map of the area of Wadi Hawareth from the Survey of Palestine. (Wikimedia Commons)

Here we see Zalmen, still part of the kibbutz group but already with doubts about its mission, confronted by Mustafa, with whom he was previously acquainted under different circumstances. Both Zalmen, the socialist-Zionist, and Mustafa, an Arab from a traditional agrarian background previously drawn to Wahabism, had been influenced earlier in the novel by the character of Milner, a Jewish Communist and anti-Zionist propagator (likely based on a real-life figure).[84] As a result, in the struggle over the Wadi Hawareth lands, Mustafa confronts Zalmen over those exhortations and beliefs. At the end of this sequence, Mustafa severely injures Zalmen's comrade Sholem, who urges Zalmen to fight. "'With whom?' asked Zalmen. Sholem looked at him, surprised: 'What do you mean, with whom? With the Arabs!'" (*"Vos heyst mit vemen? Mit di araber!"*).

Zalmen's question, which infuriates Sholem, indicates his change of loyalties, as his beliefs mandate that he stand with the disenfranchised fellahin, rather than with his comrades, whom he now realizes are involved in forcefully taking over the lands cultivated by the fellahin. This scene

*Zionist pioneers arrive at Wadi Hawareth / Emek Hefer.
(Wikimedia Commons)*

of the protagonist's "aha" moment of illumination illustrates the ideological turn at the heart of this thrilling novel. Zalmen articulates his turn after these incidents:

> "The Jewish question," Zalmen replied with conviction, "is a part of overarching injustices: exploitation, war, massacres, hunger, and enslavement. The Jewish question can only be resolved together with those other questions—through social change. And if you really want to solve the Jewish question, you can't fight through racism, chauvinism, or taking over workplaces from the Arabs—rather, in fact you have to do the opposite"

Now, Zalmen does not see Zionism as an answer to Jewish problems but, rather, as a movement that perpetuates some of the issues it seeks to combat. As he sees it, the path forward lies in the general struggle to repair the world of its ills. This new insight serves as the novel's ideological resolution.

Does solidarity with the fellahin include justifying indiscriminate violence? The debates in Communist circles at the time are echoed in the novel by Milner, who constantly contemplates this question in the aftermath of the 1929 anti-Jewish violence, asking himself: "Was this a pogrom or an uprising (*ufshtand*)?"[85] He is "beaten up and thrown out" (*tsepatsht un aroysgevorfn*) when the Arab patrons of a "cooperative restaurant" find out he is collecting money for both the Arab *and* Jewish "families of those killed in the riots (*far di mishpokhes fun di umgekumene in di geshe'enishn*)." Here and throughout, the novel explores the violence and its motives, never glorifying it.

On the Move

The evolution of Ayalti the writer clearly parallels that of his characters: from "good Hebrew Zionist pioneers" to "active Yiddish resistors" of, in Milner's words, the "colonization of usurped lands."[86] Ayalti, now a Yiddish writer, went to Spain during the civil war, where he wrote for a Yiddish Communist paper.[87] In Spain, he made passionate antifascist speeches in Yiddish, in which he credited the USSR for defeating both anti-Semitism and fascism and for being the only country where "the Jewish masses can become productive," and where Yiddish culture flourishes.[88] However, according to various sources, Ayalti's disillusionment with Soviet Communism actually began in Spain, when he realized that the Soviets would not send full support to fighters, and that they had arrested a close friend of his for involvement in POUM (Workers' Party of Marxist Unification, the anti-Soviet Marxist militia).[89]

Back in Paris, he married Charlotte "Lotte" Sempell, a German historian from a rich family, whom he had met through Arendt. In 1938, after finishing a second Yiddish novel, this time about the Spanish Civil War, he managed to visit his family in Sapotskin one last time, from which he wrote to Lotte that people in the shtetl were convinced there would be no war. He longed to be a writer in French but had to flee occupied France during World War II, and managed to arrive in Montevideo, Uruguay, with his wife, Lotte, and son, Daniel, in 1942. He spent the next four

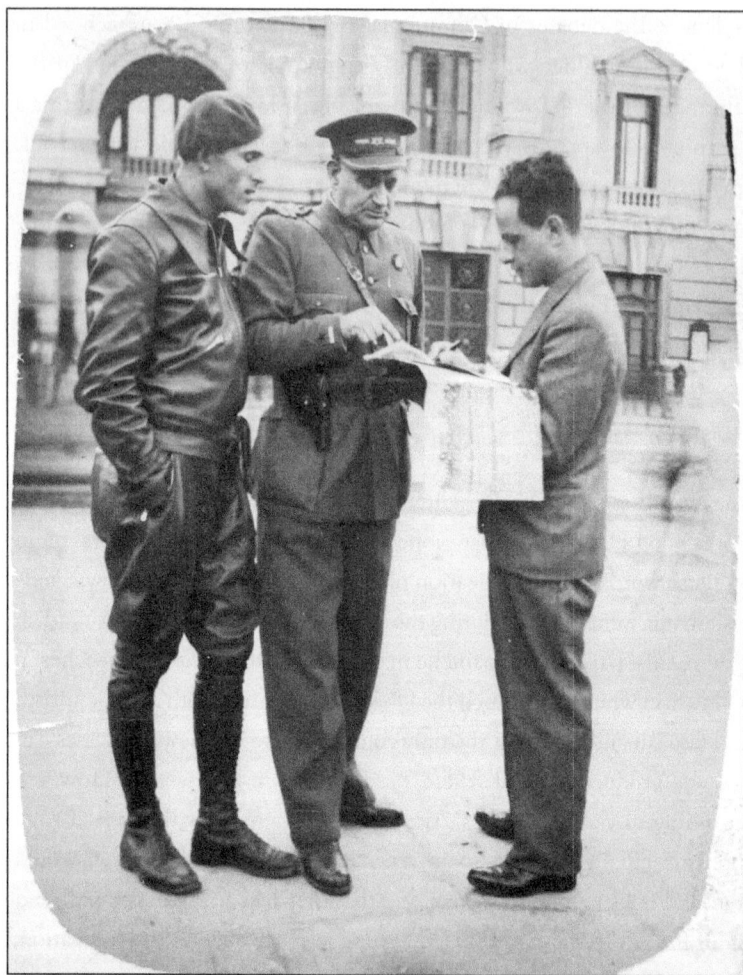

Hanan Ayalti working as a reporter in Spain during the civil war for a Yiddish paper based in Paris, 1937. (Courtesy of Daniel Klenbort)

Hanan Klenbort Ayalti, 1965. (YIVO Archive)

years there and participated in the local Yiddish culture.[90] In June 1946, the Klenbort family permanently settled in New York.[91]

In the later postwar years, Ayalti often omitted *Boom and Chains* from his bibliography.[92] By this time, he had become less radical, a family man, and a refugee. He also had aspirations to be employed as a Hebrew teacher (he also taught Yiddish at the Workers Circle) and as an editor of a Labor Zionist Yiddish journal in New York called *Yidisher kemfer* (Jewish Fighter), to which he also contributed translations of texts written originally in Hebrew. "I essentially renounced the novel out of ideological reasons, because I later changed my opinions again," he said decades later.[93] Not long after arriving to New York, he wrote the satirical short story "Messiah's Donkey," published first in *Yidisher kemfer*, in 1950 as a book, and later translated into Hebrew by Ayalti himself despite his insecurities about being a Hebrew writer.[94] This time the utopia under scrutiny was Soviet Communism and its blind followers, rather than Zionism. In this story, he returns to the kibbutz of two decades prior, to the swamps of Kabara, and general life in the commune. Here, the dominant tone is of sarcasm; gone is the struggle of replacing one utopian belief (in Labor Zionism and kibbutz life) with another (Soviet Communism and joint Jewish-Arab struggle).[95]

He writes: "Spring [on the kibbutz] brought with it not only sleepless nights, tragedies and melancholy—it also brought heat waves, malaria, and dysentery."[96] The decision in the commune to purchase a donkey, supposedly the beginning of their new independent, experimental cooperative economy, represents their trust in the false messianic promises of Communism. "'I have an idea,' called Aron. 'I'll sit up on the donkey and ride to Tel Aviv.' 'Like the messiah on his donkey!' Yenkl's mocking eyes grinned. . . . 'It's animal cruelty! What sort of an opinion would the donkey have of collectivism?'"[97] The ultimate existential state of these dreamers is encapsulated in its last phrase: "people are waiting for the Messiah, and only his donkey bothers to show up" ("*Men vart af meshiekhn un kumen kumt gor der eyzl*")[98]

Surely, Ayalti had a strong interest in suppressing his Communist past when he arrived in the United States in 1946, coinciding with the beginning of the Cold War and the newly coined term "Iron Curtain" to denote the separation between the West and the Soviet bloc.[99] He repudiated *Boom and Chains*, not even listing it in his bibliography attached to the story collection that included "Messiah's Donkey." As his son revealed "this was a novel that he never talked about, as it was very Communist."[100] Ultimately, Ayalti may have lost faith in Soviet Communism and become weary of big ideas in general, but he remained interested in leftist politics, such as the New Left movements of the 1960s. From personal correspondence with an Israeli friend, we learn that Ayalti showed interest in the Israeli anti-Zionist socialist group Matzpen, which operated in the 1960s and attracted young idealists to its ranks due to its uncompromising stand against the occupation beginning in 1967.[101] Ayalti was interested in reading their publications;[102] at least two of Matzpen's cofounders had their roots in Hashomer Hatzair.[103] Through his friendship with Arendt, Ayalti became acquainted with German leftist intellectuals like Erich Cohn-Bendit and his son Daniel ("Dani the Red").[104] Daniel visited Gan Shmuel in 1970, accompanied by his friends from Matzpen, to argue about Zionism and socialism, and admitted later to being profoundly shaken by meeting there with Holocaust survivors.[105] On April 4, 1968, Ayalti joined the enthusiastic Arendt on the first day of the student protests and takeover at Columbia University.[106]

Even today, almost a century after the events depicted in *Boom and Chains*, analyzing it remains challenging, particularly in terms of the sharp distinction the novel makes between pursuing egalitarian policies and implementing an ethnic-nationalist agenda.[107] Could one simultaneously reject inequality and call oneself a Zionist? Kibbutz Be'eri member and peace activist Vivian Silver (1949–2023), who was murdered by Hamas on October 7, replied in her own way: "I call myself a conditional Zionist. I believe in the right of the Jewish people to have a state, as long as we give the same right to the Palestinian people. This could be such a haven to both of our people here."[108]

On a personal note, my own family history is firmly entangled with the history of Israel/Palestine. Both my grandmothers managed to escape Europe (one from Germany and the other from Poland) after the Nazis came to power, arriving on the shores of Palestine in the 1930s. My maternal grandmother escaped Hamburg in April 1933 with her mother and younger siblings aboard what Ayalti describes in the novel as "the first ship of German refugees" that "arrived and with them began the big 'boom.'" Like Ayalti, my paternal grandmother attended the modern Hebrew Tarbut school in Poland and later became a Hebrew teacher in Haifa. Needless to say, I am grateful that my grandmothers had this safe haven to flee to. Their many family members (as well as those of my paternal grandfather who was born in Palestine in 1921) who were left behind in Europe were all murdered by the Nazis and their collaborators. Predating these arrivals, my maternal great-great-grandparents Avram and Aisha made the difficult trip from Morocco to Ottoman-ruled Palestine sometime in the late 1870s for Jewish religious reasons. Their daughter, Esther, born in Haifa in 1886, married my great-grandfather, Yitzhak Dana. He came from a prominent Syrian-Jewish family from Damascus that included the chief rabbi of Lebanon and Syria. Their son, my maternal grandfather, Michael Dana (1909–78), grew up in Haifa speaking Arabic and became a pioneer writer of Arabic-language textbooks for Hebrew speakers.[109] Moreover, the history of Hashomer Hatzair in particular has played a significant role in my family: my paternal great-uncle, David Emanuel Mahalel, an Ashkenazi Jew born in Alexandria, Egypt, in 1916, arrived in Palestine in 1919, was a Hashomer Hatzair counselor who was tragically murdered in Haifa in 1947 by his Arab coworkers during a period that many view as a civil war between Arabs and Jews.[110] My father, named David after his uncle, was born the following year and also served as a counselor in Hashomer Hatzair in Haifa and lived for several years in Hashomer Hatzair kibbutz. My wife, Laura, lived and studied on a Hashomer Hatzair kibbutz in Israel, and my daughter is now a Hashomer Hatzair counselor and had led its chapter in New York, where we live.

That said, the ideals of every movement ought to be examined critically, without fear of the scrutiny of identifying gaps between its ideals and its practices—certainly a brilliant achievement of this novel. In fact, it is an essential step on the path to true reconciliation, and for the realization of Hashomer Hatzair's stated goal of *akhvat amim* (solidarity of nations). After the Holocaust and the establishment of the State of Israel, Ayalti sought Israel's survival and prosperity out of fear of another catastrophe befalling the Jews. However, securing this goal, which I share with Ayalti, is conditioned on reconciliation with the past and its effects on the present day. Therefore, Ayalti's unique voice deserves to resurface and once again be heard, this time for a much wider, English-language readership.

Notes

1   "Vi azoy ikh hob geshribn 'troymen un keytn': A geshprekh mitn oytor fun undzer nayem roman vegn hayntikn Palestine" [How Did I Come

to Write *Dreams and Chains*?: A Conversation with the Author of Our New Novel About Present-Day Palestine], *Folksblat* (Kaunas), July 7, 1936, 5. All translation from Yiddish and Hebrew are by Adi Mahalel unless stated otherwise. "Halutzim" means Zionist pioneers, and "collectives" is "kvutses" in the original. "Seizing of labor and land" relates to the Zionist platform of *kibbush ha-avoda, kibbush ha-adama*. See Gershon Shafir, *Land, Labor, and the Origins of the Israeli-Palestinian Conflict, 1882–1914* (University of California Press, 1996). Ayalti signed his name in the novel as Ch. A. Yalti (יאַלטי .אַ .כ.), according to the norm in Russian literature at the time.

2 Rashid Khalidi, *The Iron Cage: The Story of the Palestinian Struggle for Statehood* (Beacon, 2007), 105–24.

3 *Folksblat*, July 7, 1936, 5. The occurrences portrayed in the novel took place at Clock Tower Square in Jaffa in 1933; see Tali Hatuka, "Negotiating Space Analyzing Jaffa Protest Form, Intention and Violence, October 27th 1933," *Jerusalem Quarterly* 35 (2008); 93–106.

4 Rashid Khalidi, *The Hundred Years' War on Palestine: A History of Settler Colonialism and Resistance, 1917–2017* (Metropolitan, 2020), 43–44.

5 Benny Morris, *Righteous Victims: A History of the Zionist-Arab Conflict, 1881–2001* (Vintage Books, 2001), 135. The revolt thus solidified the Yishuv's commitment to its overall goal of statehood; see Devorah Giladi and Yossi Goldstein, "'We Are All Ready to Fall': Creation of the Norm of Acceptance and Restrained Mourning in *Davar* During the Great Arab Revolt (1936–1939)," *Journal of Israeli History* 41, no. 1 (2023): 1–25.

6 See epigraph in Kh. A-Yalti (Khonen Klenbort), *"Bum" un keytn* [*"Boom" and Chains*] (Vilnius: Kletskin, 1936).

7 *Folksblat*, July 7, 1936, 5.

8 Hanan Ayalti to Dov Sadan, March 29, 1951, *YIVO*, RG 1337, Folder 197. Dov (Shtok) Sadan (1902–89), like Ayalti, was a member of the Hashomer Hatzair movement in his teens and twenties and remained identified with official Labor Zionism. See Dan Miron, *From Continuity to Contiguity: Toward a New Jewish Literary Thinking* (Stanford University Press, 2010), 50, 246–77.

9 Yiddish in the Yishuv was perceived as an obstacle to the implementation of a monolingual, Hebrew-speaking society that would replace the existing language diversity in the Jewish world, see Yael Chaver, *What Must Be Forgotten: The Survival of Yiddish in Zionist Palestine* (Syracuse University Press, 2004); Liora Halperin, *Babel in Zion: Jews, Nationalism, and Language Diversity in Palestine, 1920–1948* (Yale University

Press, 2015). For a thorough investigation of Yiddish literature in Palestine up until 1948, see Arye Leyb Pilovsky, *Tsvishn yo un neyn: yidish un yidish-literatur in erets-yisroel, 1907–1948* [in Yiddish] (Velṭraṭ far Yidish un Yidisher ḳulṭur, 1986), 251–357. For Yiddish's status post-1948, see Rachel Rojanski, *Yiddish in Israel: A History* (Indiana University Press, 2020).

10   "*liḳtov efshar rak mitoḳ ḥerut . . .*" (Hanan Ayalti to Dov Sadan, 1934, National Library of Israel, Dov Sadan Archive, ARC. 4* 1072 01 260). Micha Josef Berdyczewski (1865–1921) was a well-known European Hebrew, Yiddish, and German writer who advocated for the right of individual Jews to freedom from the dictates of rabbinic Judaism. See Avner Holtzman, "Mikhah Yosef Berdyczewski," *YIVO Encyclopedia of Jews in Eastern Europe*, August 7, 2017 (accessed January 18, 2023), https://yivoencyclopedia.org/article.aspx/Berdyczewski_Mikhah_Yosef.

11   Mordechai Halamish, "Hanan Ayalti," in *From Here and from Afar: An Anthology of Yiddish Stories in the Land of Israel from the Beginning of the Century Until Today* [in Hebrew], ed. Mordechai Halamish (Sifriat Poalim, 1966), 131. Dov Sadan participated in creating the anthology as well.

12   Hanan J. Ayalti, interview by Clifford Chanin, Wiener Library, New York Public Library, Dorot Jewish Division. Oral History Collection, December 15, 1977, transcript 52; Shmuel Niger and Jacob Shatzky, "Ayalti, Khonen," in *Leksikon fun der nayer yidisher literatur* [Biographical dictionary of modern Yiddish literature] (Congress for Jewish Culture, 1956), 1:43–44.

13   Hanan Ayalti to Dov Shtok, 1935, National Library of Israel, Dov Sadan Archive, ARC. 4* 1072 01 260.

14   For example, Kevin Duong, "No Social Revolution Without Sexual Revolution," *Political Theory* 47, no. 6 (2019): 809–35.

15   Gregory Carleton, *Sexual Revolution in Bolshevik Russia* (University of Pittsburgh Press, 2004), 28.

16   On the various projects since the nineteenth century to remake Jews as "productive agrarians," that were also promoted by Jewish socialists like the Bund, the Territorialists, and later in the USSR, see Jonathan L. Dekel-Chen, *Farming the Red Land: Jewish Agricultural Colonization and Local Soviet Power, 1924–1941* (Yale University Press, 2005), 26–29; and Jonathan L. Dekel-Chen, *A Common Camp? Jewish Agricultural Cooperativism in Russia and the World, 1890–1941* [in Hebrew] (Magnes, 2008), 38–42.

17   *Genesis Rabbah* 96:5.

18   In I. B. Singer's story "Taybele un hurmiza" [Taibele and her demon], the protagonist, Elkhonon, is buried with a twig (*ritl*) between his fingers, "with which he will, when the Messiah comes, dig a path through tunnels toward the Land of Israel" (*grobn a veg durkh heyln keyn ertsisroel*). *Mayses fun hintern oyvn* [Stories from Behind the Oven] (Farlag Y. L. Perets, 1971), 87.

19   Regarding the compatibility of Marxism and messianism, see Ernst Bloch's insight that "messianism is the red secret of every revolutionary enlightenment" (quoted in Adi Mahalel, *The Radical Isaac: I. L. Peretz and the Rise of Jewish Socialism* [State University of New York Press, 2023], 204).

20   Daniel Klenbort, "Afterword," in Hanan J. Ayalti, *The Presence Is in Exile, Too: Collected Stories* (Black Belt Press, 1997), 235–49; and Hanan Ayalti to Dov Sadan, 1934, National Library of Israel, Dov Sadan Archive, ARC. 4* 1072 01 260.

21   According to Zhenia Riftin in Interview with Goga Kogen (Givat Haviva: Yad Ya'ari Archive, 1986), 9. The five residents were: Zhenia Yunes (Riftin), Ya'akov Riftin, Genia Oshrovitz, Yisrael Rosenzweig, and David Rosenboym-Hanegbi (Yair Spiegel, *Against the Current: Yaakov Riftin; Biography* [in Hebrew] [Giv'at Havivah: Yad Ya'ari, 2022], 29). Mira in the novel, who "didn't want any women's work!" but prefers "to go with the boys on the hardest jobs," could be based on Zhenia Riftin, who "fought to work at the Orchard, and not do housework" (interview with Goga Kogen, 13). "It was the first feminist struggle, and as a result they later sent me to the Council of Women Workers" (interview with Goga Kogen, 8).

22   Morris notes that despite not being colonist in the usual imperialist sense, "the settlements of the First Aliya were still colonial, with white Europeans living amid and employing a mass of relatively impoverished natives" (Morris, *Righteous Victims*, 38–39).

23   Like Ignatz, among Kibbutz Benymina members Riftin gained a reputation as being more committed to his political career than to his leftist ideals (phone conversation with Reuven Shapira, October 24, 2024). As kibbutz member Sarah Haneni puts it: "[Riftin] visited our Ken [in Poland] and spoke very nicely in Yiddish. He really made an impression on me! In Binyamina I saw his two-faced appearance, and in my eyes he wasn't a reliable person. He wasn't honest. He had great persuasion power, but you could doubt the quality of his persuasion: he wanted to recruit people to his views" (Benyamin Pagi [Bolek], ed., "Binyamina" [Yad Ya'ari Archive, 1986], 44).

24   David Ben Gurion, who was then secretary of the Histadrut, met Ya'akov Riftin in the kibbutz and wrote in his diary that Kibbutz Binyamina "is the closest to communism of all Hashomer Hatzair kibbutzim in the Land of Israel, and nevertheless Riftin . . . made an impression on me of a good Zionist" (quoted in Spiegel, *Against the Current*, 32).

25   See David Zait, *Pioneers in the Maze of Politics: The Kibbutz Movement, 1927–1948* [in Hebrew] (Izhak Ben Zvi, 1993), 23; and David Zait, *The Shomer Dreams of Utopia: Hashomer Hatzair Youth Movement in Poland, 1921–1931* [in Hebrew] (Ben Gurion University Press, 2022), 359, 376–78.

26   A fascinating account of Kibbutz Binyamina members' switch to the PKP is given by Kibbutz Binyamina member Ruth Lubitsch, who left in 1931 like Ayalti to become a PKP activist, in Ruth Lubitsch, *I Chose a Life of Struggle* [in Hebrew] (Shahar, 1985), 17–57. Like Zhenia Riftin, she also fought for gender equality in the kibbutz. Even as late as the mid-1980s, Lubitsch chose not to use the real names of anybody in Kibbutz Binyamina. Unlike Ayalti, she remained involved in Communist politics in Palestine and later Israel for the rest of her life.

27   See Edmund Silberner, "Charles Fourier on the Jewish Question," *Jewish Social Studies* 8, no. 4 (1946): 245–66; and Shlomo Sand, *Imagined Race: A Short History of Judaeophobia* [in Hebrew] (Resling, 2020), 61–64. The term "Judaeophobic" is used by Sand over the more common "anti-Semitic."

28   Shafir, *Land, Labor*, 165–66.

29   Zeev Tzahor, *Shorshei ha-politika ha-yisre'elit* [Israel's Political Roots] [in Hebrew] (Hakibbutz Hameuchad, 1987), 46–48.

30   "Eight Questions on Kibbutzim," *Z Commentaries*, August 24, 1999. See also Mouin Rabbani, "Reflections on a Lifetime of Engagement with Zionism, the Palestine Question, and American Empire: An Interview with Noam Chomsky," *Journal of Palestine Studies* 41, no. 3 (2012): 92–120; and David Leach, *Chasing Utopia: The Future of the Kibbutz in a Divided Israel* (ECW, 2016).

31   Ayalti, interview by Clifford Chanin, 51.

32   Yoav Peled and Gershon Shafir, *Being Israeli: The Dynamics of Multiple Citizenship* [in Hebrew] (Tel Aviv University Press, 2005), 29–30; and Shafir, *Land, Labor*, 146–86. Sabbagh-Khoury claims in her recent study of three Hashomer Hatzair kibbutzim that "the kibbutz colony came to constitute a crucial pillar of settler colonial action."

Areej Sabbagh-Khoury, *Colonizing Palestine: The Zionist Left and the Making of the Palestinian Nakba* (Stanford University Press, 2023), 8. Sabbagh-Khoury takes as a case study the kibbutzim Mishmar ha-Emek (founded in 1926), HaZorea (1935; where Chomsky lived), and Ein Hashofet (1937). It was not until 2009 that the first Arab became a full member of a kibbutz, joining Kibbutz Ein Hashofet (Leach, *Chasing Utopia*, 190).

33 According to Joel Beinin, "Until 1941 this recognition was expressed in a vague call for a binational state in Palestine, one neither exclusively Jewish nor Arab." Joel Beinin, *Was the Red Flag Flying There? Marxist Politics and the Arab-Israeli Conflict in Egypt and Israel, 1948–1965* (University of California Press, 1990), 27.

34 Shlomo Sand, *Israel-Palestine and the Question of Binationalism* [in Hebrew] (Resling, 2023), 118–23.

35 Shmuel Dotan, *Reds: The Communist Party in the Land of Israel [Adumim, Hamiflaga Haqomunistit Be'eretz Yisra'el]* [in Hebrew] (Shevna Hasofer, 1991), 212; Spiegel, *Against the Current*, 274; and Zait, *The Shomer Dreams of Utopia*, 381–83.

36 Amir Locker-Biletzki, *Holidays of the Revolution: Communist Identity in Israel, 1919–1965* (State University of New York Press, 2020), 4–9; Avner Ben Zaken, "From Universal Values to Cultural Representations," in *1929: Mapping the Jewish World*, ed. Gennady Estraikh and Hasia Diner (New York University Press, 2013), 133–37; and Sand, *Israel-Palestine and the Question of Binationalism*, 123–29.

37 Joel Beinin, "A Century After Its Founding, the Israeli Communist Party Is at a Crossroads," *972 Magazine*, 2023.

38 Lubitsch recalls her first gathering of Arabs and Jews in Palestine, where the Communist speaker spoke passionately in Yiddish to a majority Arabic-speaking crowd. She wondered how they understood his words (even she had to focus hard to understand since Polish came more naturally to her), but then she noticed a translator whispering to them in Arabic (Lubitsch, *I Chose a Life of Struggle*, 18).

39 Amelia M. Glaser, *Songs in Dark Times: Yiddish Poetry of Struggle from Scottsboro to Palestine* (Harvard University Press, 2020), 87.

40 Ayalti's ideological shift had precedence in Yiddish literature, like that of the Yiddish proletarian poet Betsalel Fridman (1897–1941). Like Ayalti, Fridman was born in what is now Belarus, became a Labor Zionist who lived in Palestine (1920–22), then moved to New York and shifted his leanings to Communism. In 1929, he wrote the poem "Palestine," in which he denounced Zionists for standing against

the brotherhood of Arabs and Communists: "Arab and persecuted Communist / Against the Zionist!" [*Araber un farfolgter komunist / antkegn tsiyonist!*] (Glaser, *Songs in Dark Times*, 86–87). See also Lauren B. Strauss, "Kulturkampf on the American Jewish Left: Progressive Artists React to Events in the 1920s and 1930s," *American Communist History* 15, no. 3 (2016): 263–81; and Lauren B. Strauss, "'Dancing at Two Weddings': Radical Jewish Artists and Their Relationship to Yiddishkayt from the Popular Front to the Postwar Era," in *From Popular Front to Cold War: Celebrating the Interracial Left*, ed. Elissa J. Sampson and Robert Zecker (forthcoming, Cornell University Press, 2025), chapter 10.

41   His wife and son echoed this claim. See Lotte Klenbort, *Life in Interesting Times*, 177; and Daniel Klenbort, "Afterword," 243. Daniel acknowledged that his father probably didn't want to admit he was a member out of a desire to suppress his Communist past (author conversation with Daniel Klenbort, February 17, 2024).

42   Dotan, *Reds*, 165–56. One example is cofounder of the PKP, Joseph Berger-Barzilai (1904–78), who was in contact with Ayalti, and was a former Hashomer Hatzair kibbutz member. See his memoir *Shipwreck of a Generation: The Memoirs of Joseph Berger* (Harvill, 1971).

43   Audio interview with Benymain Gilai, Gan Shmuel Archive.

44   See his memoir Hanokh Bz'ozah, *Drakhim Rishonot* [Early Roads] [Hebrew] (Am Hassefer, 1965).

45   Dotan claims that those who didn't join, who would later become part of the Israeli establishment, preferred to remain silent about their past participation (Dotan, *Reds*, 208, 553n47).

46   Dotan, *Reds*, 212. Dotan's comprehensive book is one of the few books on the subject that thoroughly examines the Yiddish sources as well.

47   Sabbagh-Khoury admits to ignoring "normative tensions" among kibbutz members (*Colonizing Palestine*, 27). Conversely, Ayalti explores these contrasts throughout his novel. Also notably absent from her study are any discussions of the significant defections in the late 1920s to early 1930s from Hashomer Hatzair to the PKP, stemming from the resistance of its members to the very Labor Zionist policies she criticizes.

48   Ya'akov Riftin, *On Duty* [in Hebrew] (Sifriyat Po'alim, 1978), 15–16.

49   Locker-Biletzki, *Holidays of the Revolution*, 9. Two former members of Ayalti's kibbutz, Eliyahu Goldenberg and Plovitz, who joined him in the PKP underground, were deported by the British, only later to be killed at the Bialystok Ghetto uprising (interview with Goga Kogen,

11). The same thing happened to Rahel Fuks (Lubitsch, *I Chose a Life of Struggle*, 47). It is estimated that about two thousand Jewish Communists were deported by the British during its years underground, 1921–42 (Lubitsch, *I Chose a Life of Struggle*, 130).

50   The episode upset Gilai tremendously (Recording of Benyamin [Nyomke] Gilai [Gan Shmuel Archive]). About life in the underground PKP cell, including the term "connection" used in the novel, and her imprisonment with other women, see Lubitsch, *I Chose a Life of Struggle*, 61–231, in which she mentions feeling the need to improve her Yiddish in order to fit in with the PKP activists (Lubitsch, *I Chose a Life of Struggle*, 63).

51   According to Spiegel, Riftin's decision to stay in Ein Shemer and not leave with the majority to Gan Shmuel signaled a moderate turn in his politics (Spiegel, *Against the Current*, 34–37). Twenty years later, in 1953, Riftin stood at the center of another leftist Communist split in Mapam (the party Hashomer Hatzair became a part of) (Spiegel, *Against the Current*, 161–79).

52   Ofir Haneni, ed., "Habenyimina'im" [The Benyaminites], Gan Shmuel, 2004.

53   Haneni, "Habenyimina'im," 21. The conclusion that the person holding the flag is Ayalti is my own. The history of members leaving the kibbutz and joining the PKP is discussed in an older booklet edited by a former Kibbutz Binyamina member (Pagi, "Binyamina").

54   According to Reuven Shapira, kibbutz scholar and son of two Kibbutz Benymina members, Yaakov and Sarah Shapira (phone conversation, October 24, 2024). Udi Adiv credits Benyo as "the person who influenced me the most, and established my Marxist viewpoint" (Udi Adiv's autobiography in Hebrew, *ha-Mahapekhah she-lo hayetah* [The Revolution That Never Happened] [Pardes, 2023], 36). Adiv (1946–), who in his youth was active in Hashomer Hatzair, became the best-known example of the model socialist-Zionist sabra who turned to subversive and underground Arab-Jewish activism. Adiv's grandfather, Yisrael Adiv, had cofounded Gan Shmuel, and Udi became the first grandchild on the kibbutz (Udi's father Uri used to work alongside Ayalti's friend Nyomke Gilai). Adiv joined Israeli anti-Zionist socialist circles in the aftermath of the 1967 war, in which he had fought. Adiv's radicalization and subsequent cooperation attempt with leftist Palestinian factions in Syria led him to be put on trial and ultimately to serve twelve years in prison for treason (*ha-Mahapekhah she-lo hayetah*, 35–41); personal correspondence with Udi Adiv (email on January 2,

2024); and Lutz Fiedler, *Matzpen: A History of Israeli Dissidence*, trans. Jake Schneider (Edinburgh University Press, 2020), 240–51. Today Adiv does not identity as an anti-Zionist and rejects what he terms the "'essentialist' anti-Zionist discourse" of the present (Udi Adiv, "Under the Threatening Shadow of a Fascist Government: War and Occupation Are Not a Historical Imperative," [in Hebrew] *Zo Haderekh*, October 20, 2024, https://zoha.org.il/132955/). See also Adi Mahalel, "Anti-War Israeli Describes His Fascinating Life in New Book" [in Yiddish], *Forward*, December 2, 2024, https://forward.com/yiddish/678937/anti-war-israeli-describes-his-fascinating-life-in-new-book/.

55 Adiv, *ha-Mahapekhah she-lo hayetah*, 40.

56 Conversation with Daniel Klenbort, February 17, 2024. Similar episodes are portrayed in the novel.

57 Elisha Porat, "Hanan Ayalti: A Modern 'Ahasuerus'" [in Hebrew], *Khulyot* 11 (Summer 2008): 129–34. Porat, who interviewed kibbutz members who knew Ayalti, characterizes Ayalti's ideological turn negatively. He claims, with no evidence, that Ayalti was apparently involved in terrorist activity in 1932. He also mistakenly asserts that *"Bum" un keytn* is a Yiddish translation of the Hebrew *Ba-mehilot*.

58 Samantha Rose Hill, *Hannah Arendt* (Reaktion, 2021), 70; Elisabeth Young-Bruehl, *Hannah Arendt: For Love of the World*, 2nd ed. (Yale University Press, 2004), 118–19; Lotte Klenbort, *Life in Interesting Times*, 175–77. I thank Marina Touilliez for sharing Lotte's memoir with me, which Touilliez examines in her book *Parias: Hannah Arendt et la "tribu" en France (1933–1941)* [in French] (ECHAPPEE, 2024). According to Ayalti's son, with whom I had a phone conversation on June 12, 2023, Arendt tried to help Ayalti receive royalty payments for his first Hebrew novel, *Ba-mehilot*, but to no avail. He rarely actually studied at the Sorbonne but was registered there to receive the student visa (author conversation with Daniel Klenbort, February 17, 2024).

59 Young-Bruehl, *Hannah Arendt*, 123; Nick Underwood, *Yiddish Paris: Staging Nation and Community in Interwar France* (Indiana University Press, 2022).

60 On the evolution of Ayalti's pen name to match his ideological wanderings, see Sharon Bar-Kochva, "Some Reflections on Hebrew Pseudonyms of Yiddish Writers: Meaning of the (Seemingly) Meaningless," in *The Trilingual Literature of Polish Jews from Different Perspectives: In Memory of I. L. Peretz*, ed. Alina Molisak and Shoshana Ronen (Cambridge Scholars Publishing, 2017), 214–16. Ayalti referred to the novel as "a sharp anti-Zionist novel" [*a sharfer anti-tsiyonistisher roman*] in a

video interview with Itzik Gottesman from 1985. I would like to thank Itzik Gottesman for sharing the video with me.

61 On Steinberg's bilingual poetry, see Elazar Elhanan, *The Path Leading to the Abyss: Hebrew and Yiddish in the Poetry of Yaakov Steinberg, 1903–1915* (Columbia University Press, 2014). Another Hebrew novelist with a trajectory similar to Ayalti's early one (minus his departure from Zionism and Hebrew) was Yisrael Zarchi (1909–47). He also emigrated from Poland to Palestine in 1929 to join a kibbutz and displayed cynicism toward the imperialist presence in the Middle East in his novel *And the Oil Flows* [*Ha'Neft Zorem La'yam Ha'tikhon*, 1937]. See Nitzan Lebovic, *Zionism and Melancholy: The Short Life of Israel Zarchi* (Indiana University Press, 2019).

62 Interview with Itzik Gottesman, 1985.

63 Ayalti's *"Bum" un keytn* thus challenges Pinsker's assertion that Yossl Bishteyn's novel, *Af shmole trotuarn* [*On Narrow Paths*], published in 1958, "was the first and only novel in Yiddish about life on the kibbutz." See Shachar Pinsker, "*Choosing Yiddish* in Israel: Yung Yisroel between Home and Exile, the *Center* and the Margins," in *Choosing Yiddish: New Frontiers of Language and Culture*, ed. Lara Rabinovitch, Shiri Goren, and Hannah S. Pressman (Wayne State University Press, 2013), 287.

64 See *Folksblat*, June 24 and June 26, 1936.

65 The character of the fellah Rasheed could be based on Mustafah Ali Ahmed from Ṣaffūriya, who alongside two others was convicted of the murder of Yosef Yaakobi and his son David in the settlement Nahalal at the end of 1932. The three were executed the following year by the British. See Dotan, *Reds*, 84; and Dinur, Ben Zion [chief ed.], *Sefer Toldot Ha'haganah* [History of the Haganah] [in Hebrew], vol. 2, part 1 (Tel Aviv, 1964), 403. In their Yiddish pamphlet *Ibern yetstikn politishn matsev* (October 1933), the PKP protested that the government "*git aroys talyenishe urteyln kegn di atenteter af ya'akobi*" [issues death sentences against the murderers of Ya'akobi]. See *Sefer Toldot Ha'haganah* [History of the Haganah]: part 3, 1166.

66 Thank you to Michael (Moyshe) Lerner for the reference. The novel was published in Yiddish translation by *Literarisher farlag* in New York in 1917 as *Vos tut men?* (What Should One Do?)

67 See excerpts in English from *Scorched Land*, from the Russian of Mark Egart, trans. with Margarit Tadevosyan, in Maxim D. Shrayer, ed., *Voices of Jewish-Russian Literature: An Anthology* (Academic Studies, 2018); and in *The Posen Library of Jewish Culture and Civilization*,

vol. 8, *Crisis and Creativity Between World Wars, 1918–1939*, trans. Alexandra Hoffman (Yale University Press, 2012), 987–97. About the novel, see Maxim D. Shrayer, "Mark Egart and the Legacy of His Soviet Novel About Halutzim," *On the Jewish Street* 1 (2011); and Marina A. Aptekman, "To the Holy Land and Back: The Opposition of Two Zions in Russian-Jewish Literature of the 1930s," *Iudaica Russica* 6, no. 1 (2021): 5–27. Aptekman compares Egart's novel with another Soviet Russian-Jewish novel, Semyon Gekht's *A Steamboat Goes to Jaffa and Back* [*Parokhod idet v Iaffu I obratno*, 1936]. Among other differences, Gekht clearly contrasts Palestine against the "true Zion," Birobidzhan, the Soviet attempt to create a Yiddish-speaking autonomous region in East Asia. But in contrast to Ayalti and Egart, he never lived in nor visited Palestine and based his programmatic novel solely on secondhand accounts. See also Sasha Senderovich, *How the Soviet Jew Was Made* (Harvard University Press, 2022), 123–67; and Vladimir Khazan, "Russian-Language Literature in Eretz Yisrael (Basic Outlines and Authors)," in *Studies in the History of Russian-Israeli Literature*, ed. Roman Katsman and Maxim D. Shrayer (Academic Studies, 2023), 30–32. Historically, there were such cases, like that of the Elkind group that came out of Gdud Ha'avoda, and left Palestine in 1928 to form a Soviet kibbutz in Crimea, USSR (Dotan, *Reds*, 125–29).

68   Emanuel Fershleiser, *Oyf shrayberishe shliakhn* [On Unpaved Literary Roads] (Ha-Sofer, 1958), 188.

69   The "New Man" doesn't "refer to the individual, but rather to the working class and to society as a whole. The social body was supposed to be renewed according to new, progressive, communistic ideals" (Maja Soboleva, "The Concept of the 'New Soviet Man' and Its Short History," *Canadian-American Slavic Studies* 51, no. 1 [2017]: 68).

70   Grigorii Batkis, "The Sexual Revolution in Russia," reprinted in *In Defence of Marxism*, May 2, 2018, www.marxist.com/the-sexual-revolution-in-russia.htm. About Batkis's pamphlet, which made headway in its German version, in Susan Gross Solomon, "Soviet Social Hygienists and Sexology After the Revolution: Dynamics of 'Capture' at Home and Abroad," *Ab Imperio* 2014, no. 4 (2014): 107–35.

71   Batkis, "Sexual Revolution." Ayalti complained that the publisher wanted more sex and less politics and made drastic cuts to other parts of the novel ("shtark opgekirtst"), while leaving in the sexual parts (interview with Itzik Gottesman, 1985).

72 David Biale detects a dialectic in early Zionism of erotic liberation and asceticism (officially Hashomer Hatzair called for "sexual purity"), and he asserts that "the kibbutz movement captured the larger contradiction in the utopian Zionist attitude toward eroticism: the more explicit the discussions around sexuality, the greater the repression." David Biale, *Eros and the Jews: From Biblical Israel to Contemporary America* (University of California Press, 1997), 176–203.

73 Fredric Jameson, *Archaeologies of the Future: The Desire Called Utopia and Other Science Fictions* (Verso, 2005), 381.

74 Yehudit Elon et al., *Draining the Swamps of Kabara* [in Hebrew] (Bet sefer śadeh Ḥof ha-Karmel, 1985); Meron Rapoport, "A Classic Zionist Story" [in Hebrew], *Haaretz*, June 10, 2010.

75 S. A. Glazer, "Language of Propaganda: The Histadrut, Hebrew Labor, and the Palestinian Worker," *Journal of Palestine Studies* 36, no. 2 (Winter 2007): 25–38. According to Hen-Tov, the denouncement of these policies led the Comintern and the PKP to embark "upon a worldwide campaign to halt the Zionist immigration to Palestine" (Jacob Hen-Tov, *Communism and Zionism in Palestine: The Comintern and the Political Unrest in the 1920s* [Schenkman, 1974], 95).

76 Glazer, "Language of Propaganda," 28–29.

77 Ayalti's friend Hannah Arendt was famously appalled by Israel's then Foreign Minister (and Labor Zionist) Golda Meir's telling her, "As a Socialist, I, of course, do not believe in God; I believe in the Jewish people." Quoted in Young-Bruehl, *Hannah Arendt*, 332.

78 Morris, *Righteous Victims*, 51. For a comprehensive book on the subject, see Zeev Sternhell and David Maisel, *The Founding Myths of Israel: Nationalism, Socialism, and the Making of the Jewish State* (Princeton University Press, 2011). Gutwein sees the relevant contrast within Labor Zionism not between its nationalist and its socialist ethos, but between the "elitist" agrarian *halutz* and a prolabor socialist platform, which challenged the movement from within (Daniel Gutwein, "The Contradiction Between the Pioneering Ethos and the Socialist Ideology of the Israeli Labor Movement: David Ben Gurion and Yitzchak Ben Aharon, 1948–1967" [in Hebrew], *Iyunim bitkumat Israel* 20 [2010]: 211–13). For a compelling discussion of major Labor Zionist theorists Moses Hess, Nachmnan Syrkin, Ber Borochov, A. D. Gordon, and others, see Shlomo Avineri, *The Making of Modern Zionism: The Intellectual Origins of the Jewish State* (Basic Books, 2017).

79 A-Yalti, *"Bum" un keytn*, 177.

80   Battles that became "a national symbol for Palestinians dramatizing their fears of a Zionist takeover of the land" (Sharif Elmusa and Muhammad Ali Khalidi, *All That Remains: The Palestinian Villages Occupied and Depopulated by Israel in 1948*, ed. Walid Khalidi [Institute for Palestine Studies, 1992], 564). For the history of Wadi Hawareth, see Elmusa and Ali Khalidi, *All That Remains*, 563–65; and Roy Marom, "Dispelling Desolation: The Expansion of Arab Settlement in the Sharon Plain and the Western Part of Jabal Nablus, 1700–1948" (PhD thesis [in Hebrew], Haifa University, 2022).

81   Dotan, *Reds*, 181–84; Mūsá Budayrī, *The Palestinian Communist Party, 1919–1948: Arab and Jew in the Struggle for Internationalism* (Haymarket, 2010), 29. One can find endless news reporting and opinion pieces in various languages on the struggle over Wadi Hawareth in the online archive of the National Library of Israel. In Hebrew, from the point of view of the Zionist establishment, see, e.g., *Davar*, June 17, 1933; *Davar*, 27 February 1933; Moshe Beylinson, "Wadi Hawareth," *Project Ben-Yehuda*, January 18, 1932, https://benyehuda.org/read/7483. From the right-wing Revisionist Zionist leader Zeev Jabotinsky, see Zeev Jabotinsky, *Zionist Revisionism Approaching a Turning Point: A Collection of Articles from Rassvyet, 1932–1934* [in Hebrew] (Machon Jabotinsky, 1986), 36–39.

82   Yaakov Shiloni testimony, *History of [Korot] Kibbutz Binyamina* [in Hebrew], Yad Ya'ari Archive, File 3, 1986. Shiloni claims that Ya'akov Riftin and a few workers in Binyamina active in PKP were the main influences in shifting some members of Kibbutz Binyamina from Labor Zionism to Communism and the PKP. Riftin's wife Zhenia refutes Shiloni's claim, arguing that her husband never rejected Zionism (interview with Goga Kogen, 13).

83   Hanan Ayalti to Dov Sadan, 1934, National Library of Israel, Dov Sadan Archive, ARC. 4* 1072 01 260.

84   In her memoir, Lubitsch mentions Shalom Lustig (pseudonym), a Communist activist and agricultural worker in the Binyamina settlement. He talks kibbutz members into joining the PKP (Lubitsch, *I Chose a Life of Struggle*, 17).

85   On these debates, see Yehoshua Porat, "Revolution and Terrorism in the Policy of the Palestine Communist Party (PKP), 1929–1939" [in Hebrew], *The New East* 18 (1968): 255–67; and Budayrī, *Palestinian Communist Party*, 18–44. According to official Haganah history, in 1929 the PKP was prepared to defend poor and working-class Jews on a temporary basis alongside the Haganah against the Arab rioters.

But PKP soon changed course and came out the following year in their Yiddish paper *Foroys* against the Zionists' plan to establish an "army of Jewish fascists" (Dinur, *History of the Haganah*, 401–3).

86 Or "contra-revolutionary," in Ayalti's own words (Hanan Ayalti to Dov Sadan, 1934, National Library of Israel, Dov Sadan Archive, ARC. 4* 1072 01 260).

87 Gerben Zaagsma, *Jewish Volunteers, the International Brigades and the Spanish Civil War* (Bloomsbury Academic, 2017), 38–39, 197n54.

88 "Far der farteydikung fun der kultur" [For the defense of culture], *Naye prese*, July 17, 1937, 4. His speech was part of an Artists Against Fascism assembly, with speeches given in various languages.

89 E.g., recording of Benyamin (Nyomke) Gilai (Gan Shmuel Archive); Klenbort, "Afterword," 245; and author conversation with Daniel Klenbort, February 17, 2024. George Orwell, also in the Workers' Party of Marxist Unification (POUM), expressed his disillusionment with Soviet Communism following his involvement in the Spanish Civil War in *Homage to Catalonia* (1938), and I thank David Haziza for pointing that out to me.

90 Lotte Klenbort, *Life in Interesting Times*, 175–240; Gilles Rozier, introduction to Hanan J. Ayalti, *Attendez-Moi Métro République: Roman*, trans. Monique Charbonnel-Grinhaus (L'antilope, 2017).

91 The New York Yiddish daily *Der tog* wrote about Ayalti's visit to its editorial office a week after his arrival, likely in search for work ("Kh. ayalti, yunger idisher shrayber, bazukht redaktsye fun 'tog,'" June 10, 1946).

92 Abraham Lis, an Israeli Yiddish critic, supported this omission: "One book is missing from his bibliography, a novel which Ayalti stubbornly silences, as if it never existed [*farshvaygt akshonesdik, ke'ile loy hoye*] . . . And in his novel . . . with such a resonant title as *Boom and Chains*—he mainly portrays the persecutions that the Arabs endured from the Jews who came to the Land of Israel to build their new home and new life. . . . But if the author wants to forget this book, we will also forget it. In particular, because a few years later, he sobered up and truly saw the Jewish reality and the reality of the Land of Israel, and he turned his fictional eye towards the Jewish reality and to an all-Jewish thematic." (Abraham Lis, *In der mekhitse fun shafer* [In the Midst of Creators] [Tel Aviv: Farlag Y. L. Peretz, 1978], 228–29).

93 Interview with Itzik Gottesman, 1985. According to his son, later in life Ayalti returned to supporting Labor Zionism. His desire to see the State of Israel survive and prosper stemmed in part from his fear

of another catastrophe befalling the Jews (author conversation with Daniel Klenbort, February 17, 2024).

94   Ayalti's Hebrew translation appeared in Halamish, *From Here and from Afar*, 131–38. Ayalti's insecurities are evident when he asks Sadan at the end of a letter what Sadan thinks about the possibilities of his writing in Hebrew based on his Hebrew in the letter (Hanan Ayalti to Dov Sadan, March 29, 1951).

95   See "Meshiekh's eyzl," in Kh. Ayalti, *Der tshek and di eybikayt* (Reznikovich, 1950), 93–109.

96   Ayalti, "Meshiekh's eyzl," 94. The sentence first appeared in *Boom and Chains*, but in a short story its sarcasm becomes especially emphasized.

97   Ayalti, "Meshiekh's eyzl," 100.

98   Ayalti, "Meshiekh's eyzl," 109. Translation here my own; for a full English translation of the story, see Ayalti, *The Presence Is in Exile, Too*. Ayalti's ideological departure from Soviet Communism is apparent in his collection of articles *On a forhang* [Without a Curtain, 1962], following his visit to the Soviet Union.

99   Ayalti casually inserts the typical phrase used by those accused of Communism during the blacklist era, "I really need to plead the fifth" (*ikh darf nemen dem finf amendment eygentlekh*), when he talks about the Communists on Kibbutz Binyamina (interview with Itzik Gottesman, 1985).

100   Klenbort, "Afterword," 245. Daniel claims that Ayalti and his circle all lied on their US immigration forms by saying that they never had been involved in the Communist Party (author conversation with Daniel Klenbort, February 17, 2024).

101   Nitza Erel, *Matzpen: Conscious and Fantasy* [in Hebrew] (Resling, 2010), 244.

102   Moshe Gilboa to Hanan Ayalti, date unknown, *YIVO*, RG 1337, Folder 178. On Matzpen in English, see Fiedler, *Matzpen: A History of Israeli Dissidence*. Ayalti also wrote to Sadan, "If I had the means, I would have immigrated to Israel [*oleh artza*], settled in it, and written in Hebrew. And not necessarily out of idealism—I stress this fact, because there's so much false idealism in the world—but due to my profession [as a Hebrew writer]" (Hanan Ayalti to Dov Sadan, March 29, 1951).

103   Moshé Machover (1936–) and Meir Smordinski (1931–2012) began in Hashomer Hatzair in Tel Aviv, were ejected from the movement for ideological subversion, moved to the Communist Party, and then rebelled against the Communist Party in the 1960s to cofound Matzpen (Erel, *Matzpen: Conscious and Fantasy*, 29–30; Fiedler, *Matzpen: A History of Israeli Dissidence*, 34–35). Many others in Matzpen's orbit

had been previously involved in Hashomer Hatzair; see examples in Fielder, *Matzpen: A History of Israeli Dissidence*, 89–90, 115–16, 225.

104 Hannah Arendt and Heinrich Blücher, *Within Four Walls: The Correspondence Between Hannah Arendt and Heinrich Blücher, 1936–1968* (Houghton Mifflin, 2000), 330; Young-Bruehl, *Hannah Arendt*, 412.

105 Fiedler, *Matzpen*, 3–7 and 325–27.

106 Rose, *Hannah Arendt*, 186; Young-Bruehl, *Hannah Arendt*, 415–16.

107 For a historical exploration of a Zionism devoid of an ethnonational agenda, see Dmitry Shumsky, *Beyond the Nation-State: The Zionist Political Imagination from Pinsker to Ben-Gurion* (Yale University Press, 2018); for the possibility of reviving such a brand of Zionism, see Omri Boehm, *Haifa Republic: A Democratic Future for Israel* (New York Review of Books, 2021); and Hayim Katsman, "Hayim Katsman, an Israeli Murdered by Hamas, Envisioned a Democratic Israel/Palestine," *Jacobin*, November 9, 2023, https://jacobin.com/2023/11/hayim-katsman-gaza-war-zionism-israeli-left.

108 Bradley Burston, "For Vivian Silver, Whom We Failed—Remembering a Lighthouse of a Human Being," *Forward*, November 16, 2023, https://forward.com/culture/570135/remembrance-of-vivian-silver/.

109 My grandfather argued that Hebrew speakers should be taught colloquial Arabic by a native speaker, using Arabic script as it was taught elsewhere in the Arab world (Abigail Jacobson and Moshe Naor, *Oriental Neighbors: Middle Eastern Jews and Arabs in Mandatory Palestine* [Brandeis University Press, 2016], 111). The earliest example that I have found of my grandfather's Arabic textbooks is from 1946 (referenced in Yehoshua Ben-Chanania, "Sfarim Ivri'im Lelimud Ha'aravit" [Hebrew books to learn Arabic], *Davar*, January 10, 1947, 7). Ben-Chanania refers to Haifa as the "fortress of the Arabic language" (*metzudat hasafa ha'aravit*).

110 A., "Zikaron Lanoflim" [Memorial for the Fallen], *Ha'aretz*, January 27, 1949, 3. He was murdered along with thirty-eight other Jewish employees at the Haifa Oil Refinery. The massacre was part of a bloody cycle of violence between Jews and Arabs: Beforehand, Etzel (the Irgun) gunmen had thrown bombs into an Arab crowd by the gate of the Haifa Oil Refinery, killing six people and injuring fifty. Afterward, the Haganah raided the Arab villages in which many of the refinery's workers lived, killing about seventy, according to Haganah reports. Ya'akov Riftin, then representing Hashomer Hatzair in the Haganah's leadership (the Yishuv's "security committee"), criticized the indiscriminate nature of the Haganah's raid, arguing that

many of the refinery workers had not participated in the killing (a few actually had protected Jews) and pointing out Etzel's initial provocation. Ben Gurion supported the Haganah's action. Consequently, large numbers of Arab and Jewish workers avoided going to their mixed workplaces (Benny Morris, *The Birth of the Palestinian Refugee Problem Revisited*, 2nd ed. [Cambridge University Press, 2004], 101–2). Prior to the attacks, the Jewish workers' committee at the refinery, dominated by Hashomer Hatzair members, had maintained good relations with Arab leftists and union activists. See Zachary Lockman, *Comrades and Enemies: Arab and Jewish Workers in Palestine, 1906–1948* (University of California Press, 1996), 351–54.

BOOM AND CHAINS

The Land of Israel—in "boom"
Palestine—in chains

PART I

"KIBBUTZ"

Land!

Zalmen woke at dawn in the fourth-class chamber of the ship, shivering from cold. Around him, a couple dozen halutzim, pioneers, and young men and women lay on the floor, curled up in old coats and leather jackets. The ship rocked from side to side, as if hopping from one foot to the other. The young men snored, snuggling their noses into their warm garments. Zalmen raised his head and scanned the group with sleepy eyes. He shuffled to the wide-open door and looked out at the sea.

A thick cloud hung over the air and wrapped the surroundings like a thin water net. The waves raced, then opened their foamy mouths wide, before diving into concealed abysses and vanishing in an endless, foggy distance. The ship slid over the plowed sea, cutting a furrow into its blue-black body. A long, fat shark swam in front of the ship's beakhead, made strange jumps in the air, then dove deep to challenge the panting machine in a wild competitive chase. A wet chill blew into Zalmen's face. His teeth rattled in staccato. Suddenly, he heard a whoosh of wings overhead, and he focused his gaze toward the distance. He tore out a scream: "Fellas, land!"

No one moved. Zalmen stood alone, surrounded by the damp dawn amid the noisy sea. Gray mountains and foggy valleys slid slowly into view. Somewhere between cliff tops, lumpy white clouds lay like smoke from gigantic cigarettes. Remote little villages napped on deserted slopes. A pillar of smoke from a shepherd's belated bonfire rose to the sky, twirled in circles and blurred like a dream. A small red fire glimmered in the distance, clasped between mounds of rocks, and winked for a while before it faded, together with the dying stars in the sky.

Dawn's gray blueness poured over Zalmen, drenching him. He felt a gnawing in his heart as his lifelong dream appeared before him suddenly on the naked mountains and valleys, unclear and veiled, like all the surrounding world at that hour of dawn. Ideas rushed through his head like the waves in the sea: "Here, new life begins, the new man, the new family, the new society . . . people will build, and people will work and create . . . everything anew . . ."

A memory of his small town. In a flash, all kinds of images passed before his eyes: his father, a small shopkeeper, reading a holy book before a meal, constantly on a quest to find an interest-free loan . . . The tax inspector, coming for an audit . . . And everybody else walking around with their heads uncovered . . . Old Jews reciting Psalms . . . Mother complains: "Three stores in each building. The food is being torn out of our mouths!" Youngsters walk around the marketplace with nothing to do but whistle military songs . . . Single men still live with their parents and stand around for entire sunny days by the entrances of vacant shops with their hands in their pockets. Artisans stand on the bridge waiting for a carriage with harvested crops to pass, hoping to barter for a bit of money. Friday after market closing, when Sabbath candles have already been blessed, drunkards scream and yell in the streets, and the Jews shut their window shutters in terror . . .

A white light sprayed from behind the mountains. Everything cleared. The ship quietly slid on the tranquil sea, under a blue sky, along a desolate yellow coast. Along the wide door, the windows, and the deck railings, sleepy, semidressed fellows stood rubbing their eyes with dirty fists, and open mouths, staring in amazement. A laggard young woman ran across the deck, tottering on her feet and asking: "Is this the Land of Israel?"

The tense and pensive crowd gazed on the emerging coast. Above, in second class, tourists gazed down through opera glasses and spoke English. A sailor ran past, looking alert; someone began to sing and immediately went silent once he noticed no one joined in. The coast became clearer and clearer. The fog dissipated. White sands, green fields, and rocky mountains were now visible in the distance. A palm tree proudly rose in its tall figure. Electric poles flew by. Cattle herds, like tiny dots, were on the move.

It was still early, when it all came into view: a city with church spires, minarets, walls, building blocks, water reservoirs, and networks of alleys. The ship turned and headed decisively to the coast. A siren whistle echoed in the air and an anchor chain moaned heavily. The ship had arrived in the waters of Jaffa. It was quiet at the port. A couple of small boats bobbed between the stones on the coast. About a dozen broad-shouldered Arabs with white shawls over their heads rowed back and forth but didn't come close to the ship. A commotion erupted on deck. They asked themselves: "How come no one is getting off?"

At last, a person with an insignia in Hebrew—"The Jewish Agency"—approached the ship, came on deck, spoke with the captain, and then announced to the tourists: "There's a general strike in the whole country! The shipmen are striking too. It's a strike against the British and . . . against the Balfour Declaration . . ."

For a second there was quiet. Then at once, everyone started to yell, clamor, debate, and advise. The hours dragged on. The Arab boats continued circling around the coast on watch. The clearing revealed the movements of broad arms, paddles that poked holes in the water, and white shawls fluttering in the breeze. The crowd, worn out from their anguish and yelling, gradually dispersed into the cabins. Zalmen stood by the door and looked out at the Arab boatmen—and suddenly it struck him: these boatmen were the ones who weren't letting him in . . . He felt overwhelmed with sadness.

Evening fell. The tourists in second class invited the halutzim to their deck and treated them to chocolate. The yellow-bearded Polish businessman suggested the halutzim dance a "hora." The Americans smiled and felt comforted that they could see the Land of Israel from the ship. The halutzim danced a hora, stomping their feet, and enthusiastically shutting their eyes. The crowd beamed with joy. Zalmen took a lorgnette and looked through its lenses down below. Beyond his feet a city stood silent—walls, houses, and mosque towers. The silence alarmed him. Arab boatmen continued circling around the waters. Armed soldiers paced the coast.

The next morning, the passengers went down to the boats and swam to shore. The tourists were afraid to go into the city. A halutz comforted them: "Nothing will happen! It's nothing. Just last month Ben Gurion came and was driven around in a car with machine guns on its roof . . ."

A young stocky Arab stood nearby and, looking around to make sure no one saw, drew his hand over his neck like a butcher knife, as if to say: "Just you wait, you'll be slaughtered . . ."

In the car to Tel Aviv, five halutzim sat together with Zalmen, as well as three English policemen with guns. The car navigated through narrow dusty alleys. Flat roofs, donkeys, camels, and palm trees indicated they were in the East. Car horns mixed with the yelling of people and the howling of animals. Suddenly, as it slid out of an alley, the car stopped in front of a crowded mass of people. The driver grunted: "A mosque! Today is Friday." The English soldiers grabbed their guns, ready to shoot.

The street overflowed with masses of Arabs. Men in red fezzes and white shawls stood pressed together, listening to a speaker; every couple of minutes they let out strange, wild shrieks. On the top of the mosque the muezzin released quivering sounds. A tall Arab demonstrated sword tricks. He waved, slashed, threw a sword in the air, then stuck it in the ground. Worn-out workers sat cross-legged along the way and napped. By the houses, on both sides of the street, women stood dressed in black with black veils covering their faces. The car cut through the sea of people, who stared at the newcomers in anger and alienation. The soldiers sat still as ice with guns in their hands.

When the car exited the mass of people and rolled over an even street with relief, Zalmen came to his senses. In a moment of insight he smiled to himself: "How strange. I came to fight British imperialism together with the Arab masses, and here I am getting protected and escorted from the harbor by armed English soldiers! . . ." He bit his lip and uttered: "*Nu*, we'll see . . . we'll see what happens . . ."

The narrow alleys and old houses disappeared. A beautiful city appeared before his eyes: walls, shop windows, cars, unveiled women, European clothes. A young man strolling on the sidewalk gave a shout: "New halutzim, hooray!" A few gentlemen removed their hats and said "shalom." Children ran after the car and threw flowers through the open door. Zalmen looked out at the street, welcoming him with such friendliness, and tears gleamed from his eyes. Here he was in the first Hebrew city, in Tel Aviv.

The Tents Sink in the Swamp

The camp was sinking into mud and darkness. The peaks of the tents reached sadly toward the dark sky. Thick rain fell nonstop as if from buckets. Large, heavy drops slapped against the wet tarps, splashing into beds, and running into little streams all over the muddy floor. The corroded poles shook and sank into the soaked clay earth.

The rope howled and moaned. Somewhere nearby, a lonesome, hungry jackal howled in the soggy darkness of the night. A pack of jackals answered him from afar. The cries spread everywhere in the wet valleys, and through the cold rocky mountains. In one of the tents, a rope popped with a squeak and a whistle; soon another one popped. A pole tumbled. A shot of wind suddenly lifted the tarp completely up into the air. The tent leveled off for a moment, poked its white top into the black of night and fell in the mud with a lash and a splash. A sharp, female scream echoed over the camp. Thin white shadows ran through, tapping barefoot in the mud. Lightning slashed a stripe of sky, brightening the sleepy camp and the horizon's pitch-black mountains for a second. Then everything darkened once again.

Hanke ran barefoot. Her long nightgown tangled around her feet. The wind ripped around her naked body and stroked her face with a cold hand. She bent down, untied a small canvas door, and quietly shuffled inside a tent. By the light of the lamp that hung partially dying on the center pole, she spied three beds shoved together, a small table, and a couple of small boards that had been nailed together to serve as a closet. She looked closer at the sleeping forms and fixed her eyes for a while on the long body of Simkha, who was lying spooned, twisted in his quilt, with half-open eyes and a smile on his lips.

Outside, the wind ran wild and beat the rain about. Hanke trembled from cold. Her wet shirt clung to her body, revealing its attractive contours. She suddenly noticed her own body: her pointy breasts and narrow, roundish hips. For a second, she listened intently to the storm and pondered having been thrown into a *kvutse*, this Zionist agricultural collective, in the middle of nowhere, about her dreams of the New Man, and about her scant twenty-two years—and she felt her attraction to Simkha's warm body and strong arms. She wanted to feel somebody's protection on this stormy night. But she turned back, bit her lips, and ran off through the mud to another tent . . . A minute later she nestled in Sara's neighboring tent.

Shimon was the night guard that night. Although he was furred up like a bear in a long thick cloak with a raincoat on top, and in a pair of big boots, he was nevertheless soaked through to his bones. He was returning now to the big wooden tin-roofed barrack and its two rows of indoor benches. On the way, he stopped several times, pointed his ears like an animal, and gazed deep into the black darkness.

When he entered, he leaned on a table, lowered his head, and listened to the night music from outside: "It's been raining like this for three days now! When will it stop already?! . . ." Unlikely tomorrow, because otherwise they wouldn't have appointed Shimon as guard. Since winter began, half the kibbutz had been unemployed. That's why the intellectuals wandered around in the workless days, like communal he-goats, completely idle, striding around the muddy camp, brooding on the small beds, or fussing around the newspapers in the reading hall. These were the same fellows who had always been sent to work.

Shimon strolled around the barrack and a phonograph standing on a cupboard in the corner caught his eye. Somebody had dragged it from their mama's house in Poland. In his own small village, his shtetl, there had been only one such device, owned by the affluent Zalkind, and he turned it on only at the end of Sabbath to play cantorial music, or during the summer months, when Zalkind's daughters came home and played foxtrots.

The sight of the phonograph reminded Shimon of his shtetl, his childhood, and the mornings at home. His father was a shoemaker, a cobbler.

He could see him now, sitting on the low shoemaker's stool, with wooden nails in his mouth. Or he's pulling through a thread and humming this song: "We stand at the front as comrades, the red flag in our hand . . ." At home there was never enough bread to fill you up. There were many children, and it was always cold. Father always joked around, and mother was always cursing . . . If we ate potatoes with herring-brine—that was a reason to celebrate.

Shimon began to reminisce about how he had left to join the Shomrim—the shtetl's well-to-do kids—the sad songs, the incomprehensible words, and the angry eyes with which the shoemaker's apprentices looked at him. Thunder woke him from his thoughts. He stepped toward the door and suddenly heard steps among the tents. He grabbed his revolver: maybe an Arab . . . ? It was strange. In Poland, the Arabs existed as words, as difficult discussions, as "an Arab question." Here they suddenly materialized in the form of people. Riding on donkeys, running on foot, working, living in small villages far in the mountains, and getting jobs only in the swamp's worst workplaces.

He turned on the electric lamp and spotted Shloymke. "What're you doing here, Shloymke? Where're you crawling off to now, in the middle of the night?"

"I don't know . . . I couldn't sleep, so I dragged myself out for a bit. Some kind of barking fest all over, like the world's gone mad."

"Go in the kitchen and turn on the primus stoves; we need to get the coffee ready, before the cooks get up in an hour. You'll warm up your hands in the process." Thunder interrupted Shimon's words. A ribbon of light rushed through and ripped open a piece of the sky. Shloymke gazed mesmerized on the newly revealed world: Up on the hill stood the solid little bourgeois houses of the colony. A tall, slender palm tree raised its head in the distance over the silent Kabara Swamp, and the wind raged around freely, as if telling stories about yellow fever and rheumatic twenty-year-old invalids. A ruin squeezed itself into the black, clouded mountains. It reminded the kvutse that it had once been there, eventually collapsed, leaving half-ruined stone walls and a well, a well in which, legend has it, a young maiden from the kvutse who had fallen in love drowned. Now on hot days, lizards crawled out from between its walls and warmed themselves in the sun. Far off, down a mountain, an Arab village pressed against the rocks. Shimon disappeared in the darkness. Shloymke remained on the threshold of the barrack and looked for a while at the bare tables, the sandy floor, and the sadness that hung in the air. Then he opened a door and entered the kitchen. It was filthy, damp, and cold in the kitchen. Long-mustached cockroaches strolled around the walls blackened from smoke. Two chunky pots stood on the primuses. After a few minutes the primuses roared like tractors, silencing the outside wind.

Shloymke warmed his hands. His heart was heavy with sorrow. Loneliness choked his throat and reminded him of a poorly warmed house, somewhere thousands of miles away, in a shtetl, sinking in darkness and poverty; of a father, a former "manager" for a rich lumber merchant, who plucks the edge of his yellow beard, eternally silent and grim, or sits with a holy book humming a melody which makes his soul gloomy and his bones cold; of a mother with teary eyes and a wrinkled forehead . . .

The water in the pots boiled. Shloyme turned off the primuses and entered the barrack. The cold sadness still hung in the air. He crossed the sandy barracks, approached the gramophone, and placed a record from the cupboard on it. Meanwhile, Shimon came back. Through the open door, a gray dawn walloped into the barrack. Shloymke ran to the door and gazed outside. A pale light crawled from among the cloudy mountains and spread over the sky. The tall, green palm tree stood over the Kabara. At the nearby wadi, the water fell loudly. The camp lay silent in the gray early morning light. The flooded tents huddled together like soaked cats. The jackals snuggled in their holes and fell asleep. The gramophone record died. The needle scratched sharp, gratingly . . .

Almost like "A Night at the Old Marketplace"

The winter lay long and wet. It rained week after week. People lay around for entire days and nights on their small beds, in the damp, stale tents that smelled of drying laundry and sweaty socks, reading thick books and discussing imperialism, Jews, the Arab question, and the erotic for many hours. There was barely any work. Before the rain, the ground was too hard and didn't respond well to the plow. After the rain, the ground was soaked, and it was impossible to step on it. The old workers from the colony worked only two or three days a week. Even without the kibbutzniks, there were too many workers from the colony, yet new ones were sent to work anyways, because fresh halutzim continually arrived in the land.

Young men and women teemed like lively spring days amid the winter wetness, steadily arriving to the camp from overseas, exhausted from the long journey, but with beams of hope and enthusiastic amazement in their wide-open eyes. The youth brought tightly packed suitcases with large inscriptions: "Jaffa." Their clothing carried a smell of well-to-do houses and young women's wedding attire. Many of them brought certificates of eighth grade, high school, or years of studying philosophy. Among the young men and women everything got chaotically mixed up: redemption of humanity, October Revolution, religion of labor, anarchist freedom of the individual, absolute social justice, the ancient Christian communes, free love, and the new family. Great faith in the new life flourished at the camp. Here, between the mountains and the swamps, in the torn tents and deserted barracks, a new life had to be created to resolve all these questions.

Zalmen arrived with several others. From the train he stared at the muddy black fields, the colony's small brick houses, the sole baker's chimney, and the fragrant jasmine bushes. The group of fellows stepped in the mud and were silent. Only Ignatz, who had come to pick up the group from the train, smiled under his glasses: he shook the hands of the newcomers and said: "Nu, we're building a kibbutz . . . we're building this kibbutz . . ."

From downhill, Zalmen noticed the peaks of the barrack and the tiny footpaths—a hodgepodge of bricks and stones—in the mud between the tents. The unknown secret of life pressed again at his heart, a fresh animation all around him.

The kibbutz got closer and closer. Zalmen looked intently at the tents, as if wanting to take in everything at first sight. It was not, however, the first kibbutz he had seen. Straight from Tel Aviv he had visited the big kibbutz camp in Ness-Ziona, and from there he had written in a letter to his friends in Poland: "a big camp; dozens of tents. Young men in thin shirts and rolled-up sleeves. An odor of young, energized proletariat, as if the young petit-bourgeois Jews had drastically reinvented their lives. It is possible to feel the collective and the spirit of the new man at every corner. And I am eager to immerse myself as soon as possible in its powerful, growing body."

In the food barrack, the newcomers stowed their large suitcases in the corner and sat at a table. Sholem Bomshteyn brought in bread with olives, told the young men to eat, and took a bite himself. Little Bashke carried in two pillows, a couple of blankets, a novel by Ehrenburg, and a pile of laundry. Motke ran inside with a cry: "Zalmen's here? Hello, my friend! Nu, what's this? Here you are, really on a kibbutz!!" And right away he started pulling updates out of Zalmen.

They went outside. The camp was a mess of scattered small broken tables, gas tin pans, lamps, pillows, books, and beds. Shimon and Shloymke fussed back and forth, dragging things out from the collapsing tents, and beginning to raise their poles and tighten the ropes. Motke brought out a folded-up tent and consulted with Yanke, the job distributor, on where to set it up. Zalmen went out with the newcomers to the common room to give over their things.

Sara sewed at a machine in the common room. Khasye dragged out green blouses with yellow patches on their shoulders and handed them over for more repairs. People came in to take bundles of dirty laundry from the laundry room. Hanke sat in the corner, sewing and singing a Russian song, dragging out the lyrics:

Th-e-r-e on-ce wa-s a mou-n-tain, a mou-n-tain,
And under the mou-n-tain a che-rry tr-ee.
I lo-v-ed a gyp-sy wom-an,
But she ma-rrie-d one o-ther than mee . . .

Zalmen finished quickly. He handed over his things, which now belonged to the entire commune, and felt light and good: "I don't have anything private now; it all belongs to the kibbutz! Got rid of private property."

He went off to look for Dora. He stood and waited, leaning against a tent. Suddenly the thought struck him that, here at camp, it was a sure thing he would go all the way with Dora. He turned red from his own inner thought and said to himself: "nonsense!"

Dora arrived very late. They shook hands. Zalmen checked her out and assumed she was thinking the same thing—he turned red again. Dora began to speak: "Nu, here we are in the Land of Israel and here we are again: same old, same old! Remember how people spoke of women's liberation? And here too girls get sent to do the laundry and carry out the night pots. But what can you do? Come into the hut."

In the tent stood two beds, made up with white, quilted blankets. A picture and a couple of books sat on a small table. The floor was covered with yellow sand. The clothes in the corner were covered with a white bedsheet. "Are you living with somebody?"

"Yeah, with Genye. You'll also come and live with us? Many fellas don't want to. The position here at camp is that it's petit bourgeois . . . that it's the old family! Genye will also stay in the meantime, right?" She turned red with her last words: "Bring in your cot; I'll go search for bedding in the common room."

The night watchman grabbed Zalmen's leg and yelled: "You're going to the highway in Pardes Khana today!"—and disappeared among the tents. Zalmen peered into the dark empty space of the tent, his eyes wide open and surprised. Through the bare triangle of the door, he could see a strip of bleak sky and pointy tent peaks. Soaked, pale sheets hung above his head and water stood on the floor.

He felt his socks. They were wet. His shoes were full of water. Even his trousers, lying on the small table, had shrunk from the humidity in the air. He jumped off the bed. The cold rid his eyes of the remains of sleep. He quickly put on the damp clothes. The wetness crawled into his bones. His teeth chattered, but a strong joy cut through him: "We will build nonetheless . . . We'll build a new life right here, in the wasteland . . ." In the food barrack, people grabbed coffee and bread. Simkha ran inside with great joy: "Today he is going out to work with the cattle . . . for the first time in his life he will plow with cattle! He'll whip the beast and 'yeeha!' out to the fields. And then they'll go slowly along a straight garden bed to lift big, black heaps of earth . . ."

With a shovel on his shoulder, Zalmen set off with a bunch of others to Pardes Chana, to the new highway. He wanted to make solid strides, but his feet sunk into the sand. The journey lasted an hour and a half. He was surrounded by silence: the thoroughly soaked yellow fields, the blue-gray mountains, the small Arab villages on the horizon and, here and there, the few eucalyptuses. Light rain drizzled nonstop and created a desolate atmosphere among the group. The crew sat on a hilly spot, overgrown with thorns and roots. They needed to pave a path here. Zalmen pushed the shovel into the ground with all his strength, but the wet earth didn't budge and remained stuck to the iron. Every couple of minutes, Shimon blurted out: "Relax, this isn't hot soup! Don't rush—the work isn't a goat that's going to run away . . . !" But he was able to shovel like the ground was butter, and you could see how in a matter of minutes wild hills could turn into an even pit with smooth sides. Rain sprinkled from the sky like from a sieve. Shloymke grumbled: "Enough already! Is it raining or not?"

And the rain, as if to spite them, dawdled as if it had all the time in the world. It wasn't even really a rain, but more of a wet cloud that creeped into bones and glued clothes to flesh. But nobody stopped working; they threw their shovels into the ground and kept a gloomy silence. Finally, even Shimon lost his patience and ordered: "Guys, take down the rope!"

A few minutes later, they were walking on the sandy path home. They didn't work anymore that day. All soaked, Zalmen threw himself on his cot and slept for a good couple of hours. When he woke up, it was already dark in the tent. He took a walk around the camp. A dreary evening wrapped the tents and mixed the dark with sadness, staring out through triangular openings. Young women walked with lanterns, bringing kerosene to the kitchen. The gramophone screeched.

The bell rang: come eat. People came from every direction and every corner. Soup was served. But it was thin and burned and no one touched it. The kasha also remained on the table because no one dared put it in their mouth. The crowd nibbled bread. Nekhe the cook roared in a corner: "You can't cook with zero ingredients!" It was dark in the barrack. Eighty young people sat along narrow tables. They banged forks and spoons, increasing the despair even more.

It was raining on Saturday morning. Not until about eleven o'clock did people begin to crawl out of their beds and show themselves at camp. Khayim threw on a pair of patched pants, wrapped himself in a wool blanket, stuck his skinny feet inside a pair of boots, and went out to drink some coffee. Shaul yelled after him: "Bring something for me to drink too!" and shoved his head back in a book. "Crazy" Dovid showered under a prickly cold stream in a small open barrack, through which a cold wind blew, and his sounds carried over the entire camp. Zalmen sat with Dora on a bench near the reading room, reading a newspaper. Dora raised her head and said: "If there's a revolution in Germany, there will be a world revolution."

After a few minutes of silence, Zalmen said: "Ghandi is a British agent; he is leading the Indian masses astray!" They continued reading. People entered, looked around, rummaged, and left. Wild Arab dogs sniffed around the garbage cans for food scraps. Simme from Kamionka started burning the bedbugs from her bed; the singed smell spread over the camp. Shaul recited a poem in the "Tent of Five."

That morning, Sholem Bomshteyn had been fussing all around camp; he attached handles to the shovels, tinkered with the fence, and was very angry, it was obvious how he was unloading all his rage into his work. It pained his heart that the people in the camp were so impractical, the way they went around messing everything up with bizarre words, and forget about it when it came to the economy: nothing of value. Sholem dreamed of simple, healthy labor, of mules that stayed in their barn, a farm, raising rabbits and doves, and of improving the camp. His eyes sparkled when he talked about it all. But he didn't have time to ponder and get into an argument with Yankl the bursar: "What, then, can't these guys work a bit? May unemployment fall on their heads! Straight after eating they're in bed with their books, like a bunch of princes! They're so strange: talking and talking, guzzling books and newspapers, and yacking endlessly. But in the yard there's not a blade of grass or a sign of a tree—bleak as a desert!"

Sholem Bomshteyn was a simple guy. He hadn't gone to high school like most of the guys in kibbutz had, and didn't even know Hebrew. He came from Smocza Street in Warsaw. There hadn't been any grass or crowing roosters in the dark yard where he grew up. Early each day an old merchant cried out: "Deals! Deals!" Even then, Sholem had longed for farm animals and produce. And here on the kibbutz, among all this strange discourse, his longing had become even stronger.

Khayim Lilienblum had finished his coffee and was taking a little stroll. He was dark-skinned and thin, with a long nose, long fingers, and big glasses. He lived in the "Tent of Five," which stood like a sphinx in the middle of the camp. Simple people knew that the "intellectual elite" lived there—the light stayed on till dawn, while they read poetry, and discussed "important questions"—but no one knew for sure what was happening over there. People in the camp respected Khayim. In Poland he lectured about "revolutionary socialism"; here in Palestine, he had soon realized that if you wanted to build a Jewish State, you had to stop talking about revolution and see to it that Jews occupied all labor positions. Khayim was almost always sick: He suffered from anxiety, so he very rarely went to work.

Khayim's father came from the Radziner Hasidim, and although they were well-to-do, his father never ate with a fork, even when guests came over. Everyone in that home suffered from unknown illnesses. Once his mother woke up in the middle of the night and burst into tears. The children asked fearfully: "Mama, why are you crying?"

"It's nothing, my dears, I'm just weeping about death . . . the death that rules over everything. I'm just crying . . ." The doctor said it was her nerves. But the people who knew her knew she was not clear-minded . . .

People had talked about his grandfather, about how after seventy years of being a man of faith, he went up to the top of the church and screamed: "It is a lie that there's a God in the world. There are many truths—not just one . . . !" Khayim paced around the camp with a furrowed brow sipping drops of bromine.

* * *

By the evening, Zalmen received notice that he was on today's night watchman assignment. He ran off to his tent quickly and stretched out on his small bed to get some rest before the long sleepless night. He hadn't slept long when Motke woke him up: "You're still a green, brand-new halutz. We all meet up in the kitchen Saturday night after shabbes, and you're sleeping? Come on!"

People walked through the dense darkness from all the tents to the kitchen. A pale lamplight penetrated the thin sheets and cast a gray shine onto the mud. Rain fell thin and sharp. Fellows lifted small linen doors, peeked their heads out, draped their shoulders in the wet clothing, shivered in the night and made their way to the kitchen light.

Simme from Kamionka walked among the young crowd. She had solid breasts and thick lips. Her mother had written to her from home: "You're not a child anymore, so what is your plan? A girl is not a boy!" And her dad added something at the end in small script about "chuppah and good deeds . . . ," the traditional parental blessing.

In their home at the end of Wasilewich Street, all three older sisters worked as seamstresses. The machines banged from dusk till dawn. Her father was preparing to lead prayers in the main synagogue and was constantly practicing the High Holiday melodies. The oldest sister, Sorke, was already in her thirties. There was talk of matching her to some widower with three kids. Sorke saved money, made clothes, and bought cosmetic powder. She cried often at night and her mother moaned. Then, when the cow they needed for Sore's dowry died, sadness overtook the home. That's when Zalmen started talking about the kibbutz, the New Man, and free love. She understood very little of what he was saying: It seemed to her a distant dream.

Simme sat at the table with the carriage drivers. She felt their strong arms close to her, and the heat of her own body. At night, she felt the stirrings of youthful womanly longings and the romance novels she had read. And very late on sleepless nights, she pressed herself against her warm pillow unable to understand why none of the guys kissed her.

Tzipke and Nachman were on a walk. They were a "couple" and lived together in one tent. Like the rest of the kibbutz, Tzipke believed in free love. She wrote home: "Mama, I got married." Her mother replied: "Did you go to a rabbi at least? Stand under a chuppah? People here are saying that bastards are running around all over where you live!"

Shloymke walked slow and gloomy, stomping in the mud, and singing something in a strained voice. Hanke thought about going to the kitchen with the others, but she kept lying on the sofa in her tent, barefoot, reading a book under the cover of a leather jacket. Dina lay on the bed across from her with another book. Grinfeld, the student from Nancy, took Hanke's hand and played with her fingers. Hanke gazed briefly at Dina and reimmersed herself in her book. With Grinfeld sitting so close to her, she felt a heat in her body, quickly moved aside and hid her hand under her coat. When Dina left for a minute, Grinfeld hugged Hanke and kissed her lips. She tossed her head, swayed her wavy hair, and yelled half-laughingly.

In the kitchen, two big primuses roared as they prepared coffee for tomorrow's workday. The kitchen was dark. Only the fire that glowed from under the sooty pots lit the black walls. The young boys and girls stood densely around the tables, by the fire in the middle of the kitchen, and talked. Nekhe argued with Yanek that it was long overdue for her to be taken off kitchen duty: "Everyone is always talking about equality at work—and where is that equality?"

"Theory is theory"—says Yanek—"and practice is practice. There's no industry here, and even in the city the young girls are only working household jobs." Simcha pushed his way through the crowd, fork in hand, ready to snatch a piece of fried bread, and at the same time, caught Zalmen and Motke, who were standing in the corner, to talk to them about the forms of the new family and free love. Motke said that's how it used to be in the hakhshara collectives.

The oil in the frying pan began to bubble. The kitchen flooded with the smell of fried oil, burned onions, the commotion of the primuses, and human voices. Phrases echoed through the room: "imperialism," "organization of the Arab workers," "national movements in the colonies," and "consequential class struggle." Big black cockroaches appeared on the walls, crawling fearlessly out of their holes, apparently used to the commotion. They strolled around, tapping their long whiskers forward.

"Tea is ready," yelled Khayim. "Sugar! The proletariat demands sugar!"

"Sugar!!" echoed the entire rest of the crowd. But the sugar was locked away. A few weeks ago, a little wall had been erected in the kitchen, sealing away the meat cutlets, preserves, and sugar on the other side.

"Yankl the bursar starves the proletariat!" screamed Simcha.

Yankl the bursar was a skinny, cross-eyed, silent type. He kept his head shaved right to the roots. He maintained that the kibbutz was permitted to keep the people a little hungry, for the sake of saving money and building an economy. "When we grow tomatoes in the garden and our cows give milk—then the food will improve."

To that end, he ran around Haifa for days seeking out rotten dates, moldy gruel, spoiled milk, damp sugar, and stinky herring—all of which he would buy cheap and bring down to the kibbutz. That's why there was such fury in the kitchen against Yankl when people didn't have any sugar for their tea. But the little wall didn't reach the ceiling. Simcha climbed over to the other side and distributed sugar. Now people were lined up in front of the frying pan. Meyke dunked pieces of bread in boiling oil, let them toast for a while, and shared with the group. After they got their fried bread, people lined up for tea. They sipped loudly, gnawed their bread, and used their hands to wipe the oil that dripped down their chins onto the floor.

Boris left the kitchen to go to Hanke's tent. He was tall and slim with a smooth, pretty face and big sad eyes—pessimist's eyes—as Dina used to call them. Before Boris arrived at the kibbutz, Hanke and Dina chatted at the intellectuals' table: "Boris is in Berlin. Studies political economy and art. He's coming to the kibbutz very soon." And at the laymen's table,

Simcha described him too: "A young man who is always suffering! He's got that kind of soul, you know? A pessimistic worldview . . . always only got doubts, hesitations . . . inner unrest . . ."

Boris's parents, who had a dry-goods store in Poland, had gone bankrupt. They were no longer able to send money to their son studying political economy and philosophy in Berlin—so he landed here at the kibbutz. He was tall and walked around camp, his neck long like a giraffe. A long day's work, bending down under orange trees' short branches, broke his bones. In the kibbutz, people were cold, wet, and hungry; who had time to deal with Boris the pessimist?

Zalmen stayed awake the entire night. He surveyed around the camp. Everybody had dispersed from the kitchen by now. Some of the tents, where people were sleeping, were dark. Only a few figures, like lost shadows, were still walking to the food barrack and back. Zalmen got into a conversation with one person or another to help him resist his urge to sleep. He entered the dark and empty barrack. Only Moyshele and Dvoyre were there, sitting in a corner reading a book about individual psychology.

When Zalmen came in a half hour later, after a second round through the camp, the "individual psychologists" were no longer there; now Hanke and her friend, the almost-agronomist from Nancy, stood by the record player, deliberating about what to play. Hanke threw her head backward and looked at the filthy tin roof. Her eyes fogged over as if wandering somewhere in an abyss. The student stood leaning on the table. The gramophone played.

Zalmen left to do another patrol of the camp. A few minutes later, while stumbling in the mud near the wadi, he heard Vertinsky's voice pouring from the record player. Then silence. Zalmen's head spun. The camp, the barrack, the tents, people with their past baggage and vague futures, reminded him of Peretz's *Night at the Old Marketplace*. People come, go, play phonograph records, survive tragedies. He sat on a bench and began to analyze the situation according to materialism: The Jewish shtetl is dying. Foundationless occupations are going bankrupt. Poverty increases. The youth degenerates, both economically and spiritually. The only way out—is to become rooted in the land, be productive! He looked outside. The tent peaks scratched the sky. Everywhere was dark. Only one lamp was still visible through a tarp and it cast a pale shine over the camp. Zalmen looked inside, curious who was still up so late.

Odd people were in that tent: that was where the group of five lived, sleeping two to a bed. When it rained, water poured into their beds, because it was too crowded to shove the beds together. They were always writing poems and discussing elevated subjects . . .

When the bell rang at nine in the evening, Zalmen knew that a meeting was being called. That wasn't special: There was a meeting almost every night, and discussions till midnight. Today the smokers were calling for a meeting because Yankl the bursar didn't want to disburse any money for cigarettes . . . It was already after midnight when it was deemed necessary to tackle this question in principle, and every speaker started again from the beginning. Speakers brought evidence from Confucius, from the Hebrew Bible, and so forth.

A knock on the door interrupted the discussion. Sholem Bomshteyn entered with a triumphant expression on his face and dragged a young donkey with him into the barrack. A turmoil and an uproar erupted. Everybody surrounded the frightened donkey, which perked its long ears and didn't understand what was going on around him. Sholem brought a piece of bread for the donkey and looked very pleased at how he gnawed the crust between his big teeth. Simcha yelled: "Hanke, Hanke! Put on the record player! He is feeling blue—the poor thing has stumbled into an individualist kibbutz . . ." The donkey was the first step to a farmstead of their own.

* * *

At the end of winter, the kibbutz began to build a farm. One Saturday, as people crawled out of their beds late and made their way inside the barracks to drink coffee that had gotten cold, they saw Sholem Bomshteyn plowing the empty area that stretched between the tents and the wadi. He held the reins in his hand and smacked his lips with pleasure—"Giddy up, you lazy carcass, let's go!"—staring with contempt at the fellows who were just standing around. A few days later, people were shredding clods, making garden beds, and planting tomatoes, cabbage, and bean seeds.

On the same Saturday, they started building a new residential barrack. Shimon dragged out a couple of guys to help and began to lay out concrete blocks for the base. When the walls were up and standing, a lot of people came to take photographs. Young girls dressed in white blouses, with pants hiked high above their knees, climbed up the smooth walls made of wooden boards, and sat on narrow beams, screaming and wobbling in the air. Some girls had a guitar, others a harmonium.

At the end of winter, people also poured a cement floor in the big barrack. From then on, the boys clapped with their feet when they danced the hora, and the girls twirled like summer birds at the polka. On Friday nights people danced like that till dawn. They also hung an electric lamp. It gave such a strong light that people could see it in faraway mountains and in remote Arab villages. Every night, the lamp announced: "Eighty barefoot young men and women are building a new life here . . ."

Abu Khalil Also Wants to Live . . .

On a wet winter morning, Abu Khalil woke up in his hut, built of pegs, twigs, layers of dirt, and tin. He glanced at the gray mountains, quickly peeled the thick blanket off himself, and got up from his straw sleeping mat. He threw a lit match into the small branches that were piled between two stones in the corner of the hut and placed a small greasy pot on top. Then he lit his pipe with a red-hot coal, inhaled, and released a cloud of smoke.

The fire thrust its long, narrow tongues, and the pot hummed. Abu Khalil sat down cross-legged, released little clouds of smoke, and patiently waited for the coffee to start boiling. A bird squawked on a wild carob tree in the mountains. Abu Khalil didn't know when he was born—no one counted his years, no one recorded them. He only knows he is gray and very old. He had memories of the swamp from his childhood: The sun had always risen from behind the mountains and set, not far away, over the hills of white sand, into the sea waves. Between the sands and the mountains lay the black swamp, with small patches of sand in between the moldy still waters.

Abu Khalil strongly feared Allah and has been kneeling before him five times a day for decades now. And other than Allah, Abu Khalil feared the swamp. Oh, the swamp had gobbled up so many people! No wise man on earth could count them! Everyone near to him had died: this one from yellow fever, that one from regular fever, and the other one from Egyptian malaria . . . Others died plainly: starved, fell ill, and gave up their souls to Allah the Almighty. Only he, remained, alone.

At dusk and at dawn, he could see the black swamp covered in a dense fog-like dread; you could barely notice the tips of the rocks. He planted tomatoes, cabbage, and corn seeds. In the spring, sweet, watery melons grow here that cheer up the soul. And in wintertime, he could eat a honey-sweet banana from a green, branchy shrub—praise Allah.

Generations of history lay in the surroundings. Shattered walls and wrecked monuments. Here is where Roman governors had once lived. Through there, the foreign Roman rulers had come to the land. To the north—the fort of Atlit, built by the Crusaders, who came from Europe "to establish the holy kingdom of Jerusalem." Peoples and tribes had made their way over the land like storms and left behind traces: ruins, wrecked sewerage canals, and a mix of foreign blood.

In the religious school, the *kitab*, where he had studied for a short period as a child, Abu Khalil was taught a little reading and writing and a lot of praising the Lord's name. Accordingly, he lived calmly, with a deep sense of faith that everything comes from Allah, the bad as well as the good. There was a time he even dug canals with other *fellahin*, the Arab peasants, to channel the water into the sea and drain out the swamp. However, he never believed it would be possible to dry out the swamp completely. In any case, the water streams from the mountains into the valley, feeding the swamp and spreading malaria and trachoma. That's how this way of life has to remain.

The "Ingleyz" (English) and the "Yahud" (Jews) had recently arrived. Abu Khalil still remembers the first Jews, from when they came fifty years ago and settled in these mountains. In the village, the tales began immediately: "They are rich like the Calif from Istanbul, and they come from 'Moscobye' (Moscow), where gold, packs of tobacco, and pretty women roam the streets. They call their sheikh 'Baron,' and he owns fields and gold all over the world, and if he wanted to, he could purchase the whole of Palestine. . . ."

The water in the little pot set on the rocks began to boil. Abu Khalil ground a handful of coffee beans, mixed in some milk with great dedication, and hummed an old song. He poured the ground coffee into the little pot. A dense crusty layer formed to cover the boiling water and released a nice smell. With deep pleasure Abu Khalil breathed in the smoke from the pipe, the coffee aroma, the smell from the black swampy earth, and the wild muddy grass around him. He prepared himself to drink. A sharp whistle cut through the silence. A long train ran by, banging and knocking. This iron beast that has been roaring through for many years now, every dusk and dawn, between the swamp and the rocky mountain, awoke sad memories in old Abu Khalil of the day when the Zamarin farmers left their village.

That was a hot, summery day. The sun burned on the filthy streets. Below, on the mountain slope, the dreamy sea cast its blue colors to the midpoint of the horizon. The Zamarin farmers packed their bits of belongings onto a few donkeys, poked their beasts with sharpened nails, and went on their way with a long-expanded cry: "Ya-l-l-a!" Behind them followed families spanning three generations: old dark-skinned fathers and white grandfathers, black-eyed children with filthy faces, and women wrapped in black clothing, with tiny children in their arms. The women cried, calling on Allah the almighty and merciful for help. The youngsters walked quietly, biting their lips, only occasionally poking the lazy donkeys and letting out their long "ya-l-l-a!!"

The path led down the mountain. A tree, rooted in a tiny piece of earth between craggy, wild cliffs, grew sloped, as if bowing its head, constantly latching to the earth with its final energies, and crying into the hot terrain: "I want to live!" On the horizon, a fellah farmer from the village of Al-Sindiyana was plowing, holding his wooden plow nail in his hand, and following a tall humpbacked camel, which continually grabbed mouthfuls of thick cactus leaves from the side and chewed the long, spiky needles with pleasure. Somebody in the caravan sang softly:

Beladi ya beladi
Ana bidi rukh biladi

Village, my village
I want to go to my birth village

The crowd joined in the singing. The sad, trilled melody wafted over the surrounding mountains. Abu Khalil poured himself a small cup of coffee and drank slowly, sip by sip. He also thought about how, slowly, step by step, the Yahud village had been growing. The old village of Zamarin had vanished. The stones from the wrecked walls were being used to build new, pretty little houses; only the name remained. Even now, people in all the Arab villages call it "Zamarin," even though it's been forty years already since the Yahud started calling it "Zikhron-Yaakov . . ." And as the years drifted on, the vineyards grew, the big winery was established, and the village of Timsakhi had been erased from the face of the earth. Like a bird of prey, the newcomers had been tearing off pieces of the area, sticking their claws deeper and deeper into the surrounding villages. Throughout the entire valley, only Jewish settlements were visible—the Arab villages had been shoved into the stony mountains. And now they have their eyes on the swamp . . .

"Shukri Effendi from Khaldia came to visit us," a young boy interrupted his thoughts with a tiny shrieking voice. "He says you've got to come in to the village!"

Abu Khalil put his little pot of coffee away in a corner of the mat. Shukri Effendi again? What does he need him again for?

He had no love for big shots. Whenever they show up, it's a sign something bad is going to happen: an order to pay taxes, give a "portion" for the land, go to war, or simply to work for no pay. That's how it's always been: whether under the Turks or under the Ingleyz . . . Nevertheless, he put on his coat and went outside.

It was drizzling. Abu Khalil walked one step at a time, looking for dry trails while pondering: "Surely they're calling me again about my piece of land . . . but what do they really need my little field for in particular? That rich Baron doesn't have enough land?!" The Effendi had already sent for him a few times and launched the debate: "Sheikh Abu Khalil, you'll get a few additional pounds; so sign it, already!" Son of a bitch—he even called him "Sheikh" to get him to sign. But it didn't work. A delegate of the Baron himself even came from Zamarin and offered him more money. But he didn't give in!

Because what would he do after that? The whole village had been sold. They had all gone mad, run away to Haifa and pressed their black-inked fingers on white papers. And that was it. Poof went their field! You're not even allowed to work in the swamp anymore. They brought some foreign boys, a group with ready-built linen tents, like soldiers have, and laughed in your face when you asked for work . . .

Shukri Effendi greeted him with a good-hearted smile and served him coffee. "Well, yes, Sheikh. You have figured it out! The Baron is offering another fifty pounds . . . ! Abu Khalil will become a rich man . . . and in his golden years buy himself a young little wife—Ha-ha-ha!" Effendi smiled under his thick mustache.

"What do they need my land for, Effendi? Where will I rest my head in my golden years?"

"For that money you'll live better than you do in your stinking hut. Not everyone is so lucky. It's just that the Baron wants to dig his canal through your land. This situation is sent from Allah himself; by the life of the Prophet, I swear to you, it's a sin to pass on such an opportunity." Nevertheless, Abu Khalil did not agree.

"In any case, your land will be handed over to the Yahud. Before he died, your grandson, the sole heir, signed in the Registration of Land Ownership, the *Tabu*, that the Yahud will receive the land for free— Don't you understand this will just be easier for you, you fool?"

"My grandson can do what he wants; I will not leave that place . . ."

"That's silly, ya-Sheikh. With money you can set yourself up anyway you want . . . What good does it do to get your old bones wet in the swamp?"

Abu Khalil stayed in the village until dusk. He went back to his hut after the sun had set. He stared into the dark without seeing anything; only feeling the big sleepy swamp. Before going to sleep, he lit a fire between the rocks. Red tongues lashed into the darkness. Sadness pressed Abu Khalil's heart: He was alone . . . His first and second wives had passed away . . . and in the end, the swamp will belong to the foreigners . . .

His grandson Rasheed had already left the swamp. A portion of it had been dried out and plowed. So Rasheed moved around, somewhere far over the sands of Wadi Hawarit, among the Bedouins. They were hard times for the poor, simple people. Effendi says they are going to bring in machines and dry out the swamp, that there won't be any more mosquitoes and no more ague. But where will he and his grandson Rasheed lay their heads? No, he will not leave this place peacefully . . .

"Lying in the Mud and Barking at the Moon"

The "Tent of Five" already had a few years' history under its belt. Its roots started a few years back in Poland, in Mosh's *kibbutz-hakhshara*, when they founded their collective to train in preparation for life in Palestine. It would even be possible to begin its history with that evening when Mira arrived at the hakhshara.

Mira stormed like thunder into the small, packed room and immediately created a fuss around her. Later that same evening, she took off her coat, her dress, her sweater, even her blouse, leaving only a pair of shorts and a thin, tricot shirt. She wandered around dressed like that until she left. She never entered the room through the door, but always jumped through the window, her bare feet first, then full hips, followed by her impressive, somewhat compressed breasts, and lastly—her head covered with a wave of hair, out of which peeked a pair of laughing eyes.

Once she arrived and changed her clothes, she immediately began talking about tomorrow's work: She didn't want to work in the kitchen or in the laundry—she didn't want any women's work! She wanted to go with the boys on the hardest jobs. As she spoke, she stared at the distraught crowd of young men.

The room was filthy. Half-dressed girls, tired after a long day's work, napped on the floor. In the corners, among dusty bags, torn work clothes, and stinky socks, boys lay on straw mats and blankets, scratching themselves. No one remembered there was water there, and the ability to bathe . . .

Early the next day, Mira ran to the men's jobs: She pumped water and mixed clay. In the evening after work, she rushed into the house with

an emergency, like an unslaughtered hen: "Oy, my heart, my heart . . ."
She flung her head, with half-open lips, and shut eyes, and threw herself
on the straw mat in the middle of the room. A noise, a stampede. The
boys brought water, rolled up her pressed tricot shirt, and poured water
on her snow-white breasts. Their eyes followed Mira's naked feet to the
relaxed movements of Sara's elastic, slightly full figure. Almost all the rest
were small-town types, rugged, with rough hands, exhausted faces, and
tired eyes. At night, however, all the girls were upset, and after lights out,
the small suffocating room filled with moaning, repressed weeping, and
whispering.

They slept pressed like herring, twenty people, on a twelve-square-
meter floor. Boys and girls together. It was the "revolution": In small
towns, for months earlier, Ignatz had spoken about cleanliness, asceticism,
the art of the body, and the spirit of the new man. The girls gazed at him
in those days with dreamy stares and sang heartfelt songs.

Masha was chubby and a bit clumsy. She knew about petite bourgeoi-
sies and free love. But Mira's figure, which attracted the boys' stares during
daytime, tortured her. The dense air clogged her throat. Desire flooded her
body with pain, and she felt like crying. People came and left. Students
arrived from the University of Warsaw, as did graduates of the Bialystok
Hebrew Gymnasium and children of shopkeepers in small towns. No
one knew how many people were there; no one counted the number of
arrivals and departures.

They worked, carrying blocks and laying bricks, but it didn't feel like
working to anyone. At night, there were lectures. Zalmen walked like a
drunkard on the twisted scaffolding. At night, his head spun from the
masses of flesh lying on the floor. Avrom arrived in the middle. He had
been a teacher somewhere in a small town and suddenly decided to turn
his life entirely upside down; "a drastic change," he said to Ignatz, who
picked him up from the train. He wore glasses and was balding. From the
first day, his presence stirred the young crowd: What is a man with a bald
spot, a former teacher, doing here? He was sent away to some workshop,
where he scrubbed polished tables with a rag all day.

He returned from work in the evening. As usual, the tiny room they
called home was filthy, unkempt, and dark. On the bed in the corner—the

only one, reserved as a sickbed—lay Lotte with an upset stomach, and Yitshok Raykhl, who had a fever, because of an unknown illness. Lotte—a long, skinny girl, who wore a pair of glasses on her pointy nose—was clad in a white nightgown that glimmered like a light beam in the dark room. Yitshok Raykhl—a chubby guy with red hair, freckles, and foolish eyes—lay wearing a filthy green shirt with epaulets and ragged dark blue trousers, all covered up in a white bed sheet. When people passed by, they remembered that sick people were laid up in this room and whispered: "sh . . . sh . . . sh . . ." scampering on their tiptoes. "Nu, how do you like it here?" Ignatz asked Avrom.

"Well, I hadn't really thought about how it would all look. I'm getting a picture of it now."

"Outward appearances shouldn't frighten you. We carry within ourselves a great human message . . . We're going to fulfill a great historical task—the redemption of our people and society! We must always reveal the points of light in the darkness—the sparks of light, which illuminate and lead us to our goal . . ."

Sara sat on a duffle bag and gazed, entranced, at Ignatz. It seemed to her that he had descended into an abyss and carried out the true meaning of life. Khayim also sat nearby, and Mira stretched out on a straw mat. They were in the spiritual chamber of the "spark," which hosted discussions and singing almost every evening. Ignatz spoke passionately and at length. His eyes glimmered, and sparkled. He gestured with his hands and gazed into the distance, as if over the heads of a great mass of people. Ignatz was a known figure in the movement.

Ignatz had grown up in turmoil: The small-town poverty and the hunger in the neighboring Belarusian village had taken a toll on him. He devoured life with a strong drive and wanted to swallow up everything he could. He passionately read Bialik's poem "In the City of Slaughter," weeping in secret over the Kishinev pogrom. For weeks he recited Jasienski's lyrics about the peasant uprising to his friends. When he was still spending Yom Kippur Eves in synagogue listening to the sad singing of the Kol Nidrei prayer, the shoemakers were already doing time for subversive activism. A great mishmash governed Ignatz. He started his career at the hakhshara in Kilnica. Then he became a "Yiddishist" and spoke with a sharp "r" about deep Jewish folksiness. He was able to express his thoughts clearly, and he quickly became beloved by the masses.

Late in the evening, when the crowd lay half asleep on the floor, listening to Khayim's lecture, Sara felt Avrom's gaze sliding across her body. She bent her knees, pulled her skirt way down, turned red, and ran out of the room. Those were cold nights and everyone slept together.

Everything spun in Sara's head like a nightmare: the small, dark, packed room, the bodies squeezed together on the floor, the assemblies, Ignatz's talks about revolution. Khayim's lecture about hunger and love. And then it suddenly occurred to her: "I'm nineteen years old," and she touched Avrom. Avrom woke up, unsurprised. He remained calm for a minute and then pressed his body to hers, calling her endearing names. She surrendered herself to his hands. It was quiet in the barrack; only a snore pierced the dead silence.

The entire hakhshara collective knew Ignatz was waiting for "his girl," Agda. By communal labor, a shirt was cleaned with a small standing pitcher. Mira found a pair of intact women's stockings somewhere and made them into socks. They even made a clean handkerchief for Ignatz. In the evenings, he paced around his room on the narrow strips of earth between the straw mats and sang with starry eyes. Life in the hakhshara was going his way.

Agda arrived. She was thin and flexible, like a sapling, and had green, catlike eyes, which lit up at night, and tiny, solid breasts that suggested green, unripe apples. Ignatz walked slowly beside her, as if she were made of glass, spoke softly, and gazed at her dreamily. In the evening, he sat next to her on a straw mat, his head held low in fervent silence. He dragged several blankets together and made a place for her to sleep while he went off to the other end of the room to lay down. Every morning, he jumped up from his bed, wrapped himself in a bedsheet, entirely shivering from cold, and gazed at the sleeping girl.

Avrom was away, so Ignatz slept in Avrom's empty spot next to Sara. At night he would kiss her fingertips and quietly whisper: "I myself don't know what's happening to me . . ."

Every morning, Agda glanced gloomily toward the corner where Ignatz slept next to Sara. At night, she wandered lost for hours and would return with red, defeated eyes. Ignatz paced in long strides across the room between straw mats, hanging his head and smiling sadly to himself. In the dark little rooms, people whispered: "It will end in tragedy! And hell is really going to break loose when Avrom gets back to the kibbutz. Oh-Oh, a tragedy!"

And, indeed, soon after, Mira told the whole group: "Sara is depressed . . ."

Ignatz spoke one evening among a crowd of exhausted friends: "We're living in a nerve-racking century. There are thousands of streams traversing our souls . . ." At that, Zalmen interrupted him and said: "People are lying in mud and barking at the moon . . . !" And that idiom lasted for years on the kibbutz.

Orchards Crawl . . .

1

To the right, on the shore of Crocodile Stream, grew a small young orchard. It was the first orchard in the colony, and it belonged to the young colonist Ben Asher.

Years ago, Ben Asher had been a halutz. When their small groups met in his city, he sang, "In der sokhe ligt der mazl-brokhe" (In the Plow Good Fortune Is Found) and "Dort vu di tseder" (Where the Cedars Are) and spoke about the reconstruction of the impractical Jewish *Luftmensch*, and about "the ancient Jewish peasants on the land of the Patriarchs." In the early years, he had even been an active member of the *Histadrut*—the Labor Zionist union, lived in a kibbutz, and dreamed of communal socialism.

Recently though, he had left the kibbutz, became a colonist in Zikhron, married, and had two children. "The joy and agony of creation"? That's what halutzim are for. In Petah Tikva the colonists already had plantations that earned a couple of thousand pounds per year, so how is he any worse than they are? He's got an orchard now and he's his own boss. Following his example, other colonists also planted orchards.

It provoked an uproar. A few older colonists objected: "What are you doing? You are ruining our whole ideal! Now it's not even an agricultural village but the same small shtetl like in Poland: little shops, tradesmen, a few artisans, soda vendors—and now even the plantation owners have arrived—indeed, all we are missing is Jewish landowners! . . . And where is the productivization?" The crowd of colonists looked from afar at the olive trees in their own orchards turning green and black and grinning under their mustaches: "nothing serious, just chumps, irrelevant!"

2

Shukri Effendi Latif is an Arab national, a religious person, loyal to the tradition of his parents. He loves "Palestine," hates the foreigners, wears a red *tarboosh* (flat-topped, brimless hat) on his head, and eats very salty and peppery fatty foods. Shukri Effendi Latif stems from a respectable family: His lineage traces back to the times of the prophet Muhammad and begins in the holy city of Medina. His father was the richest man in the village of Khaldia and the greatest Effendi in the whole area. He owned lands stretching from the yellow Wadi Hawarit to the black grounds of Caesarea. His herds pastured far into the mountains and in the wide valleys of Wadi Hawarit.

His fields grew rye, corn, and watermelons. Hundreds of Arab farmers slowly followed the cattle with their long whips, steered the nail plow, pleaded to Allah to give rain, hurried on the lazy donkeys and the long-necked camels, and paid, every fall, a third of what they had stored in the barn to the Effendi.

When little Shukri was born, his father celebrated with a big feast. Many guests came from the surrounding villages. The crowd sat in a circle around a fire, under a clear sky, and in the center, placed a whole roasted lamb with a full belly of cooked rice. The servants hurried around offering salted olives and sheep cheese. The Effendis cut pieces of meat from the whole lamb and packed piles of rice inside their mouths.

Around them stood the fellahin from the village, clapping when the holy songs were sung and staring with hungry eyes at the fatty legs of lamb and white rice. There was horse racing, and young Effendis in long *abaya* cloaks demonstrated all kinds of tricks. Until the gray dawn, people danced enthusiastic *dabkes*, kicking their legs, clapping their hands, and singing sacred verses. Old folks reminisced over their childhoods, when they had fought in the army of Sultan Abdul-Khamid with the Ingleyz and the Muscovites. Veiled village maidens peered out through their windows. That was many years ago. Shukri grew up. The senior Effendi died before his time, and Shukri had come to possess his father's entire fortune as an inheritance.

For the land as well, much had changed before its time. People started trading in shares of the Chemical Society of the Dead Sea, completed the construction of an airport in Gaza and a military port in Haifa, and planned a railroad from Haifa to Baghdad. All this while the British colonial clerks played golf and drank whiskey in expensive restaurants. The land's people began to wear European clothes, drive cars, and adore white women. Shukri Effendi Latif was not left behind. His beautiful palace gazed with pride at the valley at the foot of the mountains of Jerusalem.

3

The Jewish colonist Khavaja Musa came from Hadera to visit Shukri Effendi. Shukri showed him everything: his big barn, where the fellahin lessees brought their share after the crop, the stores of wool and the specially bred sheep, the barrels of marinated olives, and the buckets of date honey. While they sat on a white divan, which a servant had spread on the ground, and leaned on soft little pillows that another servant brought in, Khawaja Musa asked: "And how is business, ya-Effendi?"

"Thanks to Allah, we're satisfied!"

"People still plow with the nail?"

"That's the way our fathers and grandfathers lived . . . and this is how we live . . . People feel secure with their piece of bread!"

"Yes, but crops are becoming cheaper by the day . . ."

"Masbut, ya-Khawaja—agreed Effendi—you're right. Bread is getting cheaper, also meat, and the same for wool . . . Only Allah in heaven knows why . . ."

The coffee was ready. Shukri Effendi poured it into tiny pots. Later, the servant brought a piece of roasted lamb on a porcelain plate. Khawaja Musa ate a small piece of meat, wiped his mouth with a white napkin, and said in a friendly voice: "When you sell a couple thousand dunam of the croplands, for that money you'll be able to dig a well, put in a diesel engine that will pull water from the ground, and plant a couple hundred dunam. Hell, what you can get from a dunam of sand . . . and the oranges—a few

years will fly by, like wind over a field, and every tree will bring in pounds!"
Khawaja Musa bade a friendly goodbye, set up a second meeting, and left!

Many years had passed since those tranquil times. Shukri sold hundreds of dunams of land and planted hundreds of dunams of oranges. He moved out of the village and built a palace with electricity and water pipes, just like the Yahud in Tel Aviv. Shukri Effendi sees all the villages in the area with a broker's eye. He always comes at the time of need . . .

When the lands of the village of Khalsania were about to be auctioned off, because the Arab farmers owed debts to the government, to the Effendis, and to the loan sharks, Shukri Effendi rushed to save them. He told them: After all, you're selling to one of your own, not some stranger . . . and he bought cheap. Afterward, he rushed in his own Chevrolet to Jerusalem for a long conference at the King David Hotel, with the director of the Jewish National Fund. A couple weeks later, halutzim with tractors were already plowing the land of Khalsania, and at a meeting of the Arab Executive, Shukri protested along with all the other nationalists against the Yahud, who are usurping the soil of the Holy Land.

By the door of his palace, Shukri placed two lions made of stone. Their price—his brokerage fee for the sale of a village. At the garage, his driver scrubbed his Chevrolet for two hours a day. At night, he didn't feel like sleeping with his two old wives any longer; he decided to purchase a youngster, a sixteen-year-old. And in the area, remote villages continued to plow with the nail and continued to live in their wretched clay huts. By this time, it was Shukri Effendi's secretary who oversaw their accounts.

4

The young fellah Saeed walked home from Hadera. He had circulated in the groves there for an entire day inquiring about work. But no one wanted to take him. Whole swarms of people from the surrounding and farther off villages lay on the small paths between the fences and waited; maybe someone would hire them. In many groves, the young guys whom he asked about work scanned him from head to toe, accompanied by an angry smile. Those smiles pierced his heart and awakened angry thoughts.

As he stepped barefoot on the white sand, many questions floated around in his head, intertwining and tangling. He didn't understand why once, when he came to work in a grove, a group of boys from the Yahud blocked the gate against him and didn't let him inside . . . Maybe it's written there in the Yahud's Torah that Arabs are not permitted to work for them—so then why are they buying land from the fellahin?

And another strange thing: The young Yahud constantly talk about a *jamia*, an organization of workers. While talking, they interlace their fingers and say "Yahud u-Arab sawoa-sawoa"—so if sawoa-sawoa (friends), why don't they let people work?

And people say—even our own boys say it sometimes in the evening, sitting at the kawa (café)—that there's a country where you work only six hours, everybody eats together, there aren't any rich people, and you don't pay a third to the Effendis . . . that's something Saeed doesn't fully grasp!

Earlier, Saeed had been a herder. He would spend the whole day between the fat sheep and the quick goats. On occasion, he would wander far off with the herd, to Wadi Hawarit. For those times, he would take food with him for the entire week: several thin pitas, a bundle of green onions, and a sack of olives. He understood everything then: The billy goat goes ahead of the herd and Khadj Ibrahim Tadji heads the whole village. This is the way of the world, and this is the way it will always be . . .

But then, Shukri Effendi began to sell his lands. One dunam after another, the land was handed over to the Yahud and was cultivated. Like a snake, the strip of orchards crawled and swallowed one section after the other. The territories plowed with the nail shrank. Saeed wasn't a shepherd anymore. The wide fields disappeared—only narrow meadows, between barbed fences encircling green groves, remained. And now, it's hard to get a job in the young orchards, and when you finally manage to get something—they don't let you work. Indeed, only Allah above knows what will happen in the end!

Saeed approached the village. From a distance he noticed the tips of the palm tree that cut the darkness with its edges. Then, he walked between the spiky cactuses that spanned both sides of the road. A few more steps and he was home. Saeed passed the yard and entered his room, where he lived with his old father Farris, and his old mother. The two other married brothers lived with their many small children in a side room. It was hot and stuffy in the little room. From the naked walls, pieces of unplastered clay stuck out; a couple of sooty pitas lay on a shelf; in a corner, between a few stones, warm ash was still smoking—a sign that his mother had cooked dinner not too long ago.

Walking in the colony, he had looked through the windows of the little walled houses and scanned the furnished rooms, glass cabinets, white divans, and white beds—and now he felt sad and constrained among these smoke-blackened walls.

"Where can I go now?" he asked himself. "In the market, old people sit cross-legged telling miraculous tales: how Muhammad flew up into the sky that night, how the calif Harun El Rasheed disguised himself as a stork, and how the thousands of faithful from the entire world circle around the holy stone, Kaaba, in Mecca, and immediately become Khadji, with white shawls around their turbans. And the young people stand by the little tobacco shop and tell of a horseman, a Jeddah of the mountains, who stole his beloved at night from her parents and carried her off to a faraway land, or about an old sheikh who noticed that his wife, whom he had purchased young, was, not, in fact, a virgin . . ."

A sad song interrupted his thoughts. He looked out the window and spotted a large group of girls with jugs on their heads. He immediately forgot all his worries. The scent of the ripe oranges from the mountains, which he smelled every day this spring, and the sound of the streams in the wadis, fully intoxicated him. He continued gazing out the window, transfixed.

The village girls looked pretty, as they walked to the well with jugs on their heads: Tall and slim, like the palm trees on the horizon, they marched step by step, not moving their bodies; only their feet were in motion. Under their thin shirts, their breasts jiggled like waves on spring-time rivulets. Saeed gazed through the dark evening at the girls, listened to their quiet song, and eerie thoughts flooded his brain. He knew that you needed a lot of money to get one of these women. How many years do you have to work to save up a hundred pounds for a pretty girl?

5

"Salam Aleykum, you're as deep in thought as if you were reading the Koran!" a voice sounded, and Saeed trembled. He turned around and recognized Rasheed. A bit embarrassed, he mumbled: "Welcome, Rasheed! How are you?"

"Pretty girls in your village," laughed Rasheed. "It warms your heart looking at them, exactly like after Ramadan . . . Were you in Zamarin, maybe? How's your sister, Khadija?"

Rasheed had been in love with Khadija for several years and came by often. But he was poor, and old Farris had sold Khadija to a servant from Zamarin who had worked for a Jewish colonist there since childhood and had been saving money to buy a wife. Saeed noticed his confusion and changed the topic: "And how's your grandfather, dear old Abu Khalil?"

"He's still living in the swamp but there's no space there anymore. The Yahud, may their house be destroyed, have taken over . . ."

"But they say they want to give your grandfather an additional fifty pounds to take his piece of land . . ."

"The fellahin are like animals, selling their land. What did you sell your land for?"

"What sells, who sells?" shouted Saeed, disquieted from anger and fury. "Who told you we've sold? Don't you know it's the common land of the entire village?"

"I passed by your place and saw for myself that they're drilling a well. The Yahud were working there like demons! Yesterday I was walking there with my herd and saw them digging a well with a machine."

They ran outside and told the story to a couple of men they found. A bunch of people gathered. The old fellahin didn't want to believe it at all. Old Farris assured them: "Nonsense! You know Effendi will not sell our land!"

Nevertheless, Saeed ran off with a couple other guys to see if a well was or wasn't being dug on their land. The village land was located not far from the Jewish colony. Nearby, young orchards encircled by fences raised their little green heads. Near the groves a sandy piece of land stretched over mountains, hills, and valleys and awaited its fate silently.

When they reached the place, the men spotted a pyramid in the middle of the field and a hole in the ground with an open black mouth. A machine stood by its side, covered by a thick sheet. Rasheed touched the machine with a finger and said: "A week from today, water will be sprouting from the ground. Planting in the spring and afterward . . . and afterward everything will be lost."

"They won't dig anymore!" shouted Saeed, running back to the village. Rasheed ran after him. And running into the village, they shouted into every hut: "They're digging a well on our land!"

From their clay houses, men, women, and children poured out into the street. Old folks walked around, shaking their heads at this sinful generation. The youth were furious: "It's time to chop off their heads and put an end to this already! Who sold them our land?! We won't sign! Let's go to Shukri Effendi!" Everybody shouted, everybody roared.

At night, when the entire village was sleeping, a group of young people assembled near old Farris's yard and left from there, going along the fields to the place where the well had been dug. They held pieces of metal in their hands: shovels, and thick pipes, and in the pockets of their broad pants—long daggers.

A Well

On the kibbutz, there had been long arguments about who should be sent to dig the well, because work was scarce, and most of the healthy men were idle. But since Motke insisted that he of all people wanted the job, they obliged and assigned him to do it.

At dawn, Motke sat on a wagon among a dozen workers from the colony. The horses dragged themselves around slowly, the wheels sunk deep in the sand, and the group lurched and snoozed. But Motke couldn't sleep any longer. He was anxious and turned his head in every direction gazing into the distance; wide plowed fields surrounded the area. Here and there stood a lonely shack or a pump. Young, freshly planted groves spanned the mountaintop. Thoughts floated in his head: "They will lower the drills deep into the ground; it will create a stream of water that will soak the thirsty earth. After that, people will plant and build . . ." He felt fresh and healthy.

Motke had grown up during the war, under shrapnel and cannon fire, among Cossacks, horses' carcasses, mass graves, and blood. In the shtetl, Jews were hanged because of fabricated charges of espionage, accused of carrying secret telephones in their beards and signaling to the Germans with their tefillin. Afterward, the whole shtetl was deported deep inside Russia. Then the revolution broke out. The world turned upside down. Motke witnessed all of it. He traveled back with his parents to Poland, wandered through pogrom-infected Ukraine, and in his old shtetl encountered burned houses and an endless number of poor shop owners and artisans.

Meanwhile, a gray, slow life dragged on: a suburb, factories, textile villages, poverty. In the evening, people discussed Idealist and Marxist ideologies as well as social revolution and the Jewish question. But he never considered joining a professional union, or spoke about those questions with simple workers. Motke wanted to travel the world, but in his small Zionist circle people spoke of the new man, and about collectives that were building a new way of life in our time. Evenings were depressing. In the local branch, people danced horas and sang sad, moving songs. He decided to leave for Palestine and join a kibbutz. Reminiscing like this, Motke fell asleep in the wagon. By the time he woke up, the wagon had halted. The boys jumped down to the ground and ran across the field. One of them screamed: "Look at this: It's all been destroyed!"

Motke ran to the spot where they had begun digging the well the day before. Everything in the pit was a mess. Even the tents that they had set up yesterday were smashed and laying in the bottom of the pit. He exchanged glances with the boys. Shmaria, the group's leader, pointed his hand to a bunch of clay huts not far away in a valley and said: "This is their work! Always the same story!"

"We have to go over to the colony to call the police!" one said.

"We have to teach them a lesson once and for all!"

"We need to call the English," yelled a couple of them, hopping on horses and rushing toward the colony. "Only the English! The Arab police officers respect them!"

The English bewildered Motke. He closed his eyes: "The English . . . ? They, who are spread out to all corners of the world, in the streets of Bombay and at the Fortress of Singapore, in the concessions of Shanghai and on the battleships of the Hong Kong seaport . . . they, who are enslaving a world . . . English soldiers? Against whom . . . ?" He looked down at the little village. Its clay huts grazed the downward slope of a bare mountain and lay scattered in the valley. Motke was not upset: "Here is a part of the East, a part of that great East that stretches from here till Shanghai and struggles for bread and land . . . and he, Motke—so many years he's been dreaming about revolutions and barricades, and today he's sending people to call English soldiers against the fellahin . . . ?"

The group stretched out on the wagon and took a nap. The boys quickly came back from the colony and delivered a message: "They won't allow plowing for now. The fellahin claim it's their land!"

"But the Jewish National Fund bought it!" They began to harness the animals and headed back.

Spring, Depression, and Malaria

1

Spring arrived. Grass began to grow in the tents. It became green everywhere: under the bed, under the table, and in the clothing corner. Bedbugs also came from somewhere and wandered around. They occupied the bed, the pants pockets, and the sheets of the tents. During the day they disappeared; at night, they crawled around over the warm, reeking bodies. Between the mountains and the sea, the swamp turned green, hiding its stagnant waters under blooming bushes. In the evening, mosquitoes flew from the swamp to the little fires near the tents. Their buzzing informed the world that malaria was coming.

A fat American passed by on the highway. She had traveled to inspect the Jewish collectives, which "instilled justice without the wild Bolshevism." A Jew from Lemberg traveled with his wife to visit the land of his fathers and while he was at it, to do some business. In Tel Aviv, he was impressed by the police officer who spoke Hebrew; near the mountains and Binyamina he shouted out to his wife: "Yentl, this is the Carmel!" He picked a little flower, put it in an envelope, and inscribed it: "a gift to my youngest from the mountains of Zion and Jerusalem."

At the kibbutz meeting, people spoke of job prospects. Dora said: "This is becoming unendurable. The people are becoming idle." Yanek, the job distributor, spoke of a shiny jobs future: People will go out to drain the swamp, build an additional two kilometers of highway, and plant trees on the coastal sands so the dunes won't spread out and encroach the groves. Shimon however, was a pessimist. He said that people wouldn't plant so fast . . . On the contrary; planting is unlikely. The Bedouins, who pasture their cows on the wild grass of the hills, won't let us plant; they will probably oppose it by force. Motke teased: "Nu, we'll organize together with them in the struggle against imperialism . . ."

The crowd smiled. Zalmen however, became a bit flushed and began to speak in a serious manner: "It's not surprising: The Bedouins won't have any place to pasture once the sands are cultivated! The skinny Arab cows will die of hunger—and after them their children too—why would they want these groves?"

There was a moment of silence. Everyone examined Zalmen, who sat in the corner, sliced a piece of bread, and began to chew. Khayim Lilienblum leaned with both hands on the table and uttered: "What does that even mean? Bedouins? Arabs?! There are neither Bedouins nor Arabs in the Land of Israel . . ." Ignatz weighed in as well: "We must build and overcome all difficulties."

Spring continued. Nights of white moons. The kind of nights described in fundraising speeches by the Jewish National Fund. Yanek was busy with job distribution. Tzilye had come to the land by herself. She was the cobbler of the kibbutz. She walked around with her hair short and wearing a filthy cobbler's apron. By day, she patched torn work shoes and by night she dreamed of music and love. The kibbutz nicknamed her "the enchanted soul." She had a rich father in Warsaw. He had given her sister a dowry of a hundred and fifty thousand kopecks. Tzilye was not interested in a dowry, nor in a dry-goods store on Nalewki Street—she dreamed of a new life—so she came here.

Together with the spring, guests began to arrive at the kibbutz: sunburned, backpacks on their shoulders, guys who wandered from village to village. On the kibbutz, no one asked them who they were or where they came from. Bread and olives were brought out from the kitchen and offered to eat, and then, iced tea. At dusk, they ate together with everyone at the tables, and late in the evening the night watchman showed them a place to sleep. The next morning, they left and new ones came. One morning a young German Jew named Theo arrived. He stayed on the kibbutz for a few weeks, working, dancing, playing the harmonica. But he was attracted to the snaky roads—and went off wandering after Tzilye.

2

Simme from Kamionka was stuck in a depression, even though blue sky peeked inside her tent, white nights visited the camp, and the mountains blossomed with red flowers and green grass. The spring roared in her body, filling her breasts with agitation, with life, but her heart was sucked up in sadness . . .

Mad Dovid became melancholy. Out of nowhere he would suddenly start screaming wild sounds, right in the middle of the food barrack. Even Shloyme, who was built like a water buffalo and nicknamed with the animal's Arabic name "Jamus," became melancholy, though he didn't know why or how.

A roasting sun burned, casting everything in yellow light. Hot, shiny sand stretched all around. The boys watched the farm animals avidly, and with a sparkle in their eyes. A donkey tied to a fence near the highway spotted a female donkey, screamed loudly with bitter sounds, and yanked himself from the fence with all his strength. When they released him, he threw himself at the female donkey with a whiny shriek. She stood and waited, calm and subjugated . . . At dinner, Shloymke sat at the table across from Simme. He looked at her full figure and trembled with desire.

On Saturday, Hanke strolled around in thin, short pants, folded high above the knees. Her wide, black, fluttering pants covered up snow-white, well-formed hips and tanned-brown, smooth feet. Small, round, pointy breasts jiggled under her white blouse. She ran through the camp, from the barrack to the reading hall, and then disappeared into her tent.

After dinner, she mingled with the group of broad-shouldered swamp and road workers. The boys surrounded her and wouldn't let her leave. She laughed with half-open eyes and tugged herself this way and that. Nobody touched her—but she felt punctured by the hot lust of the broad-shouldered, tanned boys, and a stroke of heat ran through her body.

At dusk, Motke left to wander across the highway toward the mountains. He was desperate. Hanke seemed like an incomprehensible dream. He was certain there wasn't a force in the world by which he could have her. He thought of her blue eyes, which shifted like life itself: At times they beamed out lively light beams, and at others they looked sad and pensive. When he returned to camp, it was already dark. Berele raised the "lux" light high. Fires had been kindled in every tent.

Motke went to Hanke's. She raised her head and registered him with amazement: "What are you doing here?" Her eyes were opaque and cold. Motke's spirit cooled and he quickly ran away. On exiting, he thought to himself: "What did I crawl in there for? When I didn't even know what I was going to say to her . . . ?"

The next morning Motke was impatient at work. The workday couldn't end soon enough. When he got home, he quickly took off his work clothes and ran off to shower. The cold stream turned his body all red and the blood rushed into his veins. His impatience grew and became even stronger. He bit his lips from joy and tore whole bundles of hair from his head by combing too quickly. He changed his clothes and ran off to Hanke. She was sitting and reading by the tent opening, facing the mountains, which were golden from the last sunbeams. Her wet hair fell down her neck, dripping on the sand. The red sky reflected off the blackness of her eyes. She examined him for a second like a stranger. In that single moment, Hanke's glance shut down his urgency. His impatience turned into a deep sadness.

At night, Motke went out with Simme. The evening was a bit cool, and she threw a coat over her shoulders. Behind the colony, close to camp, lay the barn—big mountains of unthreshed crops. They walked another couple of hundred steps and lay down under a tall mountain among the prickly fresh stalks. She lay with closed eyes as if she had fainted. Motke became entranced by the smell of her body. He couldn't believe that a woman lay before him who wanted to give herself to him so willingly . . .

A bit later, she got up and asked: "Say, how do you really feel about me?"

Motke still felt a bit sheepish. All around, it was already beginning to smell of summer. Between the scented mountains of crops a pale light flashed from the tents nearby in camp. "You know . . . the way you feel toward a girl . . ." he answered.

They walked quietly back to camp. By then, there were several official families on the kibbutz, who lived—he and she together—in a tent or in a small room of a barrack. The "free" boys didn't want to live together like that; it seemed petit bourgeois. Simply to live as man and wife like they do in the old society . . . ? What about the new family, and the new man?

3

The end of spring was hot. Dry winds blew and covered the tents with warm sand. After work, people found their laundry and clothing covered in layers of dust. The sand crawled into their beds as well. The commune worked hard and changed the bedsheets every three weeks, but it didn't help—the beds were always filthy. Diseases spread throughout the camp, and the most widespread one at the end of spring was boils.

Many people had boils—but Aaron Rosenkrantz had more than anybody. They grew everywhere on him: on his neck, on his face, on his shoulder, wherever they could. Aaron was given shots—didn't help; he avoided eating meat for a few weeks—the furuncles only spread more. The doctor, desperate, finally said: "It's from blood . . . It's spring . . . Aaron needs a wife! Aaron Rosenkrantz absolutely must fall in love." And that is where the tragedy began . . .

Aaron went up to Hanke, perched on an empty tin pan of kerosine, and sat silently. He sat like that for a few evenings. On the fourth evening, Hanke was away and arrived very late, when he wasn't there. That's how it went with Hanke, same with Dina, with little Shulamit—with all the girls of the kibbutz. The tragedy erupted in its high point when Sara arrived at the kibbutz. Aaron knew her from back when, and for weeks he wouldn't stop trying to make sure she would be his girl. He prepared to pick her up from the ship: he spruced himself up in a white shirt and a pair of tight blue pants with a leather jacket and a flower in its lapel. He had a sparkle in his eyes.

Sara arrived, tall and full-figured, with full breasts and the gift of gab. On her first night she pressed Zalmen to her chest in the middle of the food barrack so brazenly that he got all red. Khayim started telling people right away: "It's fire! Not blood, just red hot fire."

The following evening, Sara ran off to the mountains with Simcha the tall one. They came back down around midnight, covered in grass and hay. There were many such "tragedies" on the kibbutz. Little Shulamit left many victims. The first victim was tall Boris, a grumbler and a downer; he would walk around silently for days on end. He also suffered from fever and pessimistic moods. Shulamit rushed to get him a doctor, brought him food, and climbed on him like a high tower. The second victim was Dovid. But two did not suffice, and she looked further. In general, Shulamit loved sick intellectuals.

4

With spring's arrival, the "Tent of Five" shook up. Khayim was the first to move out. "This is boring," he said. "The whole thing is a bluff. There's no holiness here."

The ideological discussions began all over again. They prepared for a conference of the left-wing kibbutzim. Their kibbutz had to decide on its direction and send delegates. Khayim was one of the first to speak: "In other countries, maybe they do need to make revolutions. We need to build. And that talk about us organizing together with the Arabs isn't anything other than empty dreams. We want to bring as many halutzim as possible to this land and, therefore, we must control the workplaces for ourselves—not for the Arabs."

The crowd gaped: Khayim was one of the most left-leaning ones, and suddenly such words! It was hard to find alignment on the Arab question: News came from all corners of the land about a major campaign to take over workplaces. The Histadrut sent Jewish workers to all the colonies as watchmen to guard the gates and not let in any Arabs.

In the kibbutz, nobody believed in organizing the Arabs anymore. They spoke of it only out of habit. Ignatz and Zalmen left for the conference. The long discussions till midnight ceased. Life went back to normal. Khayim hung around the tents. He didn't want to go to his own room: It was filthy and empty there, and his work clothes were all over the place. He didn't go to work either; he was unemployed. Sara lay alone in the Tent of Five. She looked out through the open triangle at the tops of the other tents, and at the wide fields—and suddenly the camp seemed to her like incomprehensible rubbish, and she couldn't grasp how she, Sara, had come to be here, and what she was doing here. The mishmash began in Mosh at the hakhshara, the training camp in Europe. Ignatz spoke there about "redemption of the individual and the religion of work." She didn't understand it all but liked the words and the inspiring tone. He spoke calmly to her, lying in a corner, on a straw mat—and she let him kiss her. But here in this tent it is gloomy and boring. This is no kind of life here. Something hovers around like shadows. And suddenly it becomes clear to her that she's wasting her life here—she must escape as soon as possible.

The delegation returned from the conference. Zalmen was silent; Ignatz reported back. "We dwelled too much on discussions and politics," he said. "We need to build; we need to create a life." Sara examined Ignatz. She saw now that he had a lot of gray hairs and a toothless mouth, and she wondered how she was able to live with him . . . At night, Ignatz wanted to embrace. She blew him off. At the end of spring, Avrom came to the kibbutz. Ignatz immediately took him for a long conversation in the mountains. He told him: "We're building a kibbutz. We're building a family. Well, about Sara . . . It's hard to say. I don't know! But, as you know, we have always hoped to create a new family. . . ."

People said on the kibbutz: "t-ra-ge-dy!"

Sara couldn't endure being in camp any longer: She left with a group of fellows "to help" a collective in the valley that needed more people for crop season.

5

The spring didn't bring only white nights, tragedies, and melancholy— It also brought heat waves, dysentery, and malaria. Once at dusk, when Zalmen was walking home from work, little Shulamit met him at the edge of camp and cried: "The first case already happened!"

"What case are you babbling about?"

"Malaria . . ." And she began to recount: Shimon collapsed today in the middle of work. The doctor came and firmly declared: malaria . . .

Zalmen, sunburned and filthy with sweat and dust, stood and listened with complete indifference. The next morning, little Bashke got sick; the morning after next—Aaron Rosenkranz. The doctor came, inquired, listened, tapped—but it was only for appearance's sake. Everybody already knew it was malaria. The mosquitoes were spreading malaria. They propagated in the Kabara Swamp, in the standing water of the wadi, and in the gutters, which drove the filthy kitchen slop across camp and into the valley. At night, the mosquitoes, attracted to the light, flew in swarms and buzzed inside the open tents. Later, in the dark, they bit the sleeping youths, and forty days after getting bitten they became ill.

In the nearby colony, there was no malaria: Those houses were enclosed, made of bricks, and their windows were covered with dense nets, so the mosquitoes couldn't enter. The doctor told Shulamit: "You all need to eat better! The colonists eat meat and butter, so their blood has an immunity against the malaria." Shulamit reported his advice to the kibbutz.

At a kibbutz meeting, a sanitary committee was selected. The committee installed nets on the windows of the barracks. As a result, it became hot and stuffy in the barracks, but the mosquitoes flew in through the doors. In the tents the nets still couldn't be installed at all. Shulamit announced in the name of the sanitary committee: "No one is allowed to sit at the small tables at night. You must lie under the mosquito nets!"

After the conference, Zalmen became very quiet and spoke very little at meetings. He crawled under the mosquito net with a thick book. A *khamsin*, a dry desert wind, was blowing, which made the air suffocating. The mosquitoes came buzzing around, attracted by the light. In their buzzing, Zalmen heard a story of the fellahin lying not far away in the swamp, hungry and sick . . . Forty days later, Zalmen became ill. The doctor declared: malaria.

The khamsin didn't rage like a winter storm—it was still and subdued. The air glowed hot like burning steel. The grass and the trees lay subdued. The flowers on the mountains died out. Arab dogs walked around panting with outstretched tongues; people said that they had gone mad. So Berele Pfeiffer grabbed the hunting rifle and shot a couple of dogs on the bridge of the wadi. Their carcasses stank, and the dry wind carried the rotten odor into the camp. Even the camels were tired and looked for shade to hide in.

Only a few healthy people were going to work. On the highway, the dust crawled into people's throats; rivers of sweat pouring from the bodies. Shloymke drank sixty cups of water a day. A couple of days later, he came down with dysentery. The dysentery spread like the hot khamsin waves . . . The khamsin lasted three days and didn't even let up at night. The hot bedsheets didn't cool off at night. People slept covered up and couldn't shut their eyes. In the middle of the night, they crawled out of their tents and rushed to shower in cold water, but the pipes of the waterline were also hot. A couple of weeks after the khamsin, most of the kibbutz was sick with malaria.

6

In the spring, the jasmine bloomed in the garden near the camp. The wind blew the smell of the flowers into the tents and mixed with the smell of sweaty work clothes and dead bedbugs. The jasmine belonged to the Baron. The Baron also owned the factory at the edge of the colony, near the Georgian neighborhood. The factory produced an extract from the jasmine and sent it to Paris where they manufactured cologne. The Georgians lived behind the colony in a separate neighborhood. They came from the Caucasus and had strange names, which all ended with "shvili."

Khayim Shvili didn't have a house; he lived in a tiny barrack, near the jasmine garden. He had an extraordinarily big belly and fourteen children. The Georgians called him "Baron"—maybe because he had such a big belly and maybe because all fourteen of his children—including the four-year-old—worked in jasmine.

After midnight, when the small flowers opened wide, he pulled the rags off his children, who lay, all fourteen of them, beside each other on the floor, and talked to them in a foreign, Caucasian dialect. The kids opened their little eyes, like the flowers in the garden, scratched themselves, yawned, and got dressed. The smallest "shvili" cried his lungs out—and the Baron helped him put on his little pants.

The Baron's kids arrived first to the garden; the other Georgian children had an additional three-quarters-of-an-hour walk in the sand from their neighborhood to the garden. A large group of women and children entered through the gate and immediately started working; every child had a basket hung around his neck to collect the flowers.

The youngsters flew like bees from bush to bush and quickly plucked the little open flowers. The work had to be done by dawn, because when the sun shone the juicy little flowers wilted and lost their valuable fluids, from which the perfume essences were made. To earn any money, you had to pluck a couple of kilos, and the flowers weighed very little.

The sky under the mountains began to gray. The jasmine gave a nice smell at the crack of dawn. The children wanted to sleep and rubbed their tired eyes with their fists. In the morning an employee weighed the baskets of flowers and paid a couple of piasters.

Motke went to Hanke and invited her for a walk in the jasmine field. She lifted her head from the sofa, pondered for a minute, and agreed. Hanke, in general, went on very few walks now. She would run through camp with a song, grab a little book or a newspaper, and disappear into her tent. Hanke believed that she didn't have time for that now. Overall, she didn't even know what she needed this time for. Her twenty-one years pressed upon her shoulders, and she constantly thought: My days and my years are slipping away like water through my fingers . . .

In her mind's eye she constantly saw the white Neman River in Eastern Europe and the green vases on her balcony. In her childhood they spoke Russian at home. Her father worked all day in the luxury-goods business, and her mother read the works of Pushkin, Lermontov, and Dostoyevsky and was unhappy. Later, when the businesses ended badly, and she had to fire the maid and cook and clean the rooms herself, she was even more unhappy . . . Hanke read the same books as her mother. Books in which a wind blew from lonesome train terminals and from longing souls. Where young women wanted to live but didn't know how. It weighed on her: her father's bustling businesses, her mother's sadness, and Soborna Street, where bands of boys and girls strolled back and forth all evening, yawning, talking about books, and reviving their souls with a little cup of coffee and a piece of cake at "The Turk's" bakery.

Lying that evening on the small sofa, the thought occurred to her that she's living that same kind of life now.

They left the camp, followed the sandy path, and entered the jasmine garden. They sat close together under a dense bush. Hanke pressed on him a bit. Motke felt emotional and didn't know what to talk about. He just managed to blurt out: "Many of our people don't know how to live!"

"And you do know?"

"I feel life's crossroads and that gives me a sense of it."

Hanke was silent. Motke took her hand and kissed it. She didn't pull it away. He spoke choppily: "You have a strong life force; but you can't squander it . . . You don't express your own power . . . You get caught up under the wave of forces that are roaring inside you . . ."

Hanke leaned on him. Her warm hand stroked his fingers, as if she sensed them only now. Motke went silent. After midnight, they got up and returned to camp. It was quiet in the garden; only the wind amused itself with the blooming flowers.

In the Swamp

1

A gray dawn had just opened its muddy eyes and peeked out from behind the mountains when a small little Arab drove a herd of water buffaloes out from Seven Miles village to the far-off corner of the swamp, which was not yet completely dried out. The water buffaloes stretched out their long necks, raised their heads, poked the grayness of dawn with their twisted horns, and mooed. The little man shivered from the cold and hopped from one bare foot to the other.

When the sun began to shine, the water buffaloes entered the swamp. They submerged themselves up to their necks in the thin mud, and only peeked their heads out to catch a breath of air or a bit of grass. When they crawled out to warm themselves up in the sun for a minute, they licked their noses with their wet tongues, swung their long tails to drive off the packs of flies that immediately attacked them back, and sank again into the thin swamp.

In the morning, Zalmen left with a group of "jamuses"—they referred to swamp workers from the kibbutz as water buffaloes—to work. That day, the group included only Shimon, Dovid, and Zalmen; the other "jamuses" had dropped out recently one by one: This person had a malaria attack, that one got sick from dysentery, another lay ill with rheumatism . . .

They passed Abu Khalil's shack and inspected the canal they had dug out a couple of days before. They lay flat on the ground and waited. A couple of minutes later, Ben Dor came, marked the points, and gave the measurements. The fellows took off their shirts, socks, and shoes, until only their tricot shorts remained. They walked to the marked points.

The swamp was cut through with a deep, wide canal that reached the ocean and led the water there. From both sides they had dug *siniyen*, narrow canals, which absorbed swamp water through their walls and led it to the wider canal. Then, they placed long perforated pipes on the canals' covers, covered them with earth, and finally planted eucalyptuses. In a couple of years they would begin to plow.

Zalmen and Dovid were set up to dig a *siney*. Shimon, with a group of workers from the colony, were down in the wide canal. Dovid pulled the rope, spat in his hands, and flung out the first shovelful of dirt. He warmed up right away, pressing his entire body into the shovel, flinging out clods of earth, laboring and sweating until his entire body trembled. He shouted: "Zalmen, keep digging!"

At the thirtieth centimeter, the ground became soft. The shovel slid in and cut it like butter. Their feet sank. Dovid chopped long thin chunks, hurled his shovel, and watched the pieces fly off with pride. "Don't stamp your feet!" he yelled to Zalmen. "You'll thin out the mud and we won't be able to fix it later!"

They went down another couple of layers. The earth became muddier and their feet sank deeper. From the swampy depths a stream of water burst out, soaking their entire bodies. The thin mud splashed after every shovelful and covered their naked bodies in large dark splotches. The sun rose in the sky and smothered their backs in fire. Dense sweat poured from their faces, streamed down their necks, and created sticky mud.

Zalmen was a stubborn laborer. He constantly demanded to be sent to work in the swamp, even though he already showed signs of rheumatism. He kept up with Dovid and quickly chopped the strips of earth. Dovid wiped his head, gazed a while at the sun, and screamed: "The fellas at the canal are breaking for lunch already. Let's go!"

They lay down in the shade from a small tool shed. All the workers were lying around and eating. The kibbutzniks had very little for lunch: a couple slices of bread, a few tomatoes, and a bowl of pudding. A worker who had come from elsewhere said: "Boy, they starve you out there on the kibbutz! How much longer are you going to hold out?"

"But we're shock workers, and shock workers don't worry about their strength: They work and that's that. Main thing is—to dry up the land and build! Haven't you heard of shock workers?"

"Some comparison! There, in the Soviet Union, shock workers are building a socialist economy, so it is important to build, but here we're working for the capitalists!"

It was Milner who said that. He was a tall blond guy, who was lying and eating off to the side of the group. The entire colony knew him and knew he was a lefty, so they kept their distance from him and avoided talking to him. The labor clerk persuaded private colonists not to hire him, but the agronomist from Kabara, a silly German with principles, did hire him. That was the only reason that this character, who hung out with Arabs, remained in the colony.

"And the kibbutz is not socialism?" Dovid spoke up after pondering for a while.

"No!" said Milner. "Aren't you exploited like all the workers of the world? You are starving badly here, and instead of simply demanding work and better salaries, you muddle your minds with hora dances and a fake building of socialism. It's not for nothing that the kibbutzim are set up as the first spots in the swamp and in order to work the newly acquired fields, where death comes easy . . ."

Someone raised his head and yelled: "Again with the discussions! Give us a break and let us sleep!"

In the afternoon, they got up to work again. Shimon climbed down below with the other workers. The canal was five meters deep and descended gradually. They worked standing deep in the mud. From a distance, a strip of water snaked and neared the holes; the canal there was complete. Dovid bent down and stroked the side with his hand—His eyes sparkled as they did when he stroked a lover's hand.

Suddenly, Shimon yelled, lost his balance, and fell in the mud. Two guys grabbed him and dragged him up to ground level. He lay with his eyes shut, breathing heavily. His broad chest rose and fell rapidly; his thick, muscular arms lay powerless at his sides. After he had rested a few minutes, Dovid propped him up and yelled to Zalmen: "Crawl inside the canal; it must get finished today! I'm just going to help Shimon, and then I'm coming right back."

On the way home, Shimon could barely drag his feet. The hard, dry path was uneven. The sun burned their heads. Shimon trembled and stopped many times. When they arrived at camp, Dovid yelled: "Hey, somebody come right away; take Shimon!" And then he ran back to the canals.

2

Friday evening, Shaul stood by the small door of his tent and gazed at the sunset. He thought about the downfall of Europe, humanity, about life and death. He'd been thinking about these topics for years now. He'd also been thinking of the dry yellow clay in the surrounding fields and how sad the orange trees seem in the evenings.

Warsaw. Genshe Street. Papa and Mama are in the shop, and he sleeps till eleven. The maid opens the door to his room: "What will the Herr be drinking: milk or coffee?"

There is a bustle in the street. A few sun beams manage to penetrate his thick curtain. Below, masses of people, trams, more people, and automobiles are running around. The daily hoo-haa roars. In the kitchen, pots are scrubbed and meat is fried. In Poland he was in the hakhshara. The farmworkers, clumsy, virile gentile men, hurried their horses with whips and firm Russian curses. At dusk, the gentile girls filled the sky with loud shrieks.

Shaul stood for a long time by his tent, gazing at the setting sun. Meanwhile, people started to come back from work. The highway crew came by car, which remained in the middle of the camp. Then, the plantations crew came back. They arrived from all corners, blackened, sunburned, with tired strides and bowed heads. Shaul almost never went to "outside work"; he was usually assigned housework: washing dishes in the kitchen, doing laundry, cleaning up the barrack, or watering the camp's small trees.

That Friday too, he hung back with the "unemployed," dragging himself around the tents all day, as they stood as usual, thrusting their peaks into the wilted space. An Arab walked by with two laden donkeys and burst out in a songful voice: "*Yalla ya, tomati* . . . Hurry, tomatoes! *Yalla ya, bri-n-di-zhi*! Hurry up, vegetables!"

A warm wind drove sand into the beds and into the books. Dogs emerged from behind the fence, emaciated, beaten down, with fearful eyes and disheveled hair. They looked around carefully, sniffed the air, and slowly engaged with the garbage can.

He waited for the mail. No letters arrived. He went into the reading hall, looked at a newspaper and went back out to the yard, where a few sick people and several chronically unemployed were roaming. Toward the end of the day, Ignatz entered the barrack with a briefcase under his arm. The crowd greeted him with a long "haaaa," surrounded him, and pressed him for news. Ignatz also rarely worked; his name was always in the "traveling" column. He would travel to Jerusalem, to conferences of the kibbutzim. After each trip, he recounted news from the world at large, behind-the-scenes politics, and gossip from the kibbutzim.

Minneh came back from work. She washed herself quickly, changed her clothes, and ran to Shaul. They walked out together toward the wide field and strolled quietly. No one else was around. She quivered with a desire to embrace Shaul and kiss him, but Shaul gazed ponderously into the distance. She bowed her head and strode beside him sadly and silently.

At around ten o'clock, people began to gather in the barrack, feeling sleepy. The semidark emptiness of the barrack squeezed people's shadows, merged their voices and their dreamy gazes, and told of loneliness, youth, and extinguished dreams.

Shaul didn't go into the barracks; he wandered among the tents and looked through the wide-open doors and windows at moving shadows. Later, when a white moon up in the sky showered the camp in a silver light, he went to the window, pressed his forehead to the mesh, and gazed out with foggy eyes. After dinner, someone played a harmonica in the barrack. Several couples broke into dance. Quickly it turned into a hora. The crowd jumped from the tables and benches, stretched out their hands, and began to swivel in a circle. They stomped their feet and banged on the cement floor.

A steamy, massive crowd of half-naked bodies filled up the barrack. Shaul still pressed his forehead to the increasingly wet net and gazed out at the world.

The Death of Abu Khalil

Abu Khalil set the hoe on his shoulder and went out to the garden. These were hot days. The sun roasted and dried the earth unmercifully. The tomatoes and bananas were thirsty. The spring pounded from beneath the mountains. The water splashed between the stones and loudly streamed down the mountain. For hundreds of years now, this brook had been making its way to the narrow bed, not far from Abu Khalil's garden, and then falling into the Zarqa River. Abu Khalil dug out a narrow canal and directed the water into his small garden.

Abu Khalil paced slowly. He was thinking about his only remaining grandson. Suddenly, he froze in astonishment—The brook had disappeared! He focused his gaze: The riverbed was there, but without any water. The "bed" lay dry, its top split by the sun, covered with smooth pebbles and trampled roots.

Abu Khalil shuddered: What happened? What's going on here? Had Allah punished him and deprived him of his sanity? He quickly set off along the culvert, climbing the mountain toward the spring. The spring was pounding happily like on any other day. But the water was falling on the right side, into a canal. How did a canal suddenly show up here . . . ? There had never been any canal here before . . . !

Suddenly a thought raged in his head: the Yahud . . . ! The Yahud had dug this canal to take away his water! That's what they had been so busy with the last couple of days near the spring . . . Abu Khalil bent over, tore out a couple of heaps of earth, and threw them into the canal. He wanted to clog the hole, so the water would flow in its old path and water his garden's bananas and tomatoes. But the canal was deep. The heaps fell with a plop and sunk onto the cover. The water continued to stream into the canal, and the flat bed of the brook remained dry and cracked from the heat. He lowered his head and slowly walked back. What was he to do now?

The rocky mountains gazed silently; the swamp lay still. Abu Khalil paused by his garden and examined the thirsty plants. The long, green leaves of the banana bushes had begun to fade. The tomato branches drooped to the ground. The young cabbages shrunk in exhaustion, tucking their heads between their shoulders to hide themselves from the sun. Abu Khalil felt how the heat sucked the vitality out of every little piece of grass . . . but the spring was far away, and the garden was fading and dying.

"That's how Zamarin ended, Sindani and Timsakhi ended this way too, and all our villages in the valley will end like this . . . ! The spring will continue to flow from under the stones, but the water will irrigate the newly planted grove of the Yahud, which stands on the coast of the blue Zarqa stream . . . Abu Khalil's garden will die of thirst . . ."

The sun burned and roasted Abu Khalil's head. All of a sudden, he felt dizzy, and fell to the ground, landing on his face. His few remaining teeth buried themselves in the land. His feet quivered one last time, and then lay calmly on the dusty ground. The little branches and leaves in the garden lowered their heads even further and stared with tired, dry eyes at the immobile old man. Not far away the green leaves of the orchard were nourished by the cold humidity of the earth and warmed their tips in the sun. On a plowed piece of land on the dried-out swamp, a translucent stream of water irrigated the long garden beds and a recently planted mint bush.

When the sun set, and the sky darkened, a large rat came out of a hole in between the roots of a tree and went to look for water. He followed the dry culvert to the spring and sipped cold water for a long while. Afterward, he gazed between the garden bushes. His tiny eyes noticed the prone dead body. He lifted his jaw and sniffed the air intently. With slow, careful strides he approached the corpse, smelled it, and stuck his sharp little teeth into the flesh of its uncovered stomach.

PART II

LAND AND WORK

About the Holy City and the Sinful Man

1

Jerusalem is the holiest city in the entire world. There are holy places on every corner, and on every sacred spot a church, synagogue, or mosque. Throughout the holy city circulate Russian Orthodox priests, Catholic cardinals, Jewish rabbis, Muslim Muftis, and black Abyssinian priests. The stone cloisters of the monasteries are closed off, and by day a cemetery-like stillness dominates the area. The crosses, crescent moons, and sloping walls of the crumbling Jewish study houses all cry out to the heavens.

The Yemenite and Bukhari Jews who arrived later built narrow streets and produced many children. High above, laundry dries on ropes hanging between dark, dusty walls; below, youngsters play raucously in the filthy alleyways. In the summer, the water in the foul-smelling wells dries up, and old women and small children stand in long lines for a can of water from the city pump. Tourists—who have come to see Christ's grave or the collectives in the kibbutzim—photograph the lines by the pumps and sip mineral water, which they brought in small bottles from abroad.

The grand new buildings around the market are adorned with signs reading "Iraq Petroleum Company," "Shell Company," and "Barclays Bank." English military camps surround the city. In the high commissioner's palace lies the Bible—the New Testament—and a map of the Imperial Air Communication points: London–Cairo–Palestine–Iraq–Persia–India–Hong Kong. The high commissioner is responsible for the cradle of the three religions, and for the oil pipelines, which extend from Mosul all the way to Haifa. The high commissioner of Palestine is indeed a man of the Bible, but he also wants to have a strategic path to the pearl of the English crown, that is, to India. Therefore, on the strategic map of the Empire, Palestine is marked with a thick, black dot.

2

Since childhood, the fellah Salim, from the village of Shlil, had heard about the floating rock and Buraq, Muhammad's holy horse. Salim came to Jerusalem by foot. By the gate of Al-Aqsa, he removed his torn shoes, washed his feet, and entered after paying the muezzin a couple of piasters. The muezzin showed him the stone of the patriarch Abraham and of Samuel the prophet, explaining to him: "In the past, the stone hung entirely in the air! Only in recent generations did it get these small walls beside it added on."

The Jewish Temple, as was well known, had burned to the ground, and only one wall remained intact. But Soreh, the shopkeeper from the Old City of Jerusalem, never gave much thought to the veracity of those stories. Only when she realized that income was scarce did she go to the Wall, where she wrote a note to the Master of the Universe, asking him to take away a couple of customers from her neighbor Rokhl and give them to her. Rokhl was also a shopkeeper in the Old City. She also went to shed a tear by the Western Wall and beseeched the Master of the Universe to take away a few customers from her neighbor Soreh and give them to her.

People placed their little notes between the stones of the Wall. The sexton (called *shammes*) came, took a bit of money from the women, and threw their notes into a pot to burn. In addition to the shammes, a tall English soldier with a telephone also stood by the holy Wall. The soldier did not think about the holy rock or Muhammad's flights—he knew you could fly from Jerusalem to Mecca or Bombay by airplane. When something happened, he made a telephone call and soldiers came. And things did happen. One case involved a Jew who dreamed of a Jewish state with police, soldiers, airplanes, and uniforms; unable to wait any longer, he took a shofar and blew it by the Wall, and so he was arrested.

A second case concerned Rabbi Buk, an old Jew with a respectable white beard. The leaders of the Histadrut were on their way to consult with this particular rabbi on how best to lead this sinful generation away from its wicked path and persuade it to cease hiring Arab workers. On the way, in the taxi, the editor of the socialist newspaper said: "The religious emotion is the mightiest of human emotions; it dwells in the depths of the soul . . ."

Ben Hillel, the secretary of the Histadrut, looked out at the small Arab villages settled throughout the surrounding mountains and answered: "Oh, yes, deep in a person's soul lies religion, in particular in this country, where every rock reminds you of fiery speeches by the Hebrew prophets about justice, equality, and truth; where the dream of world peace was woven; when lamb and lion will graze together . . . Yes, it surely will help . . . If Rabbi Buk issues a ruling on this question the colonists will surely expel a thousand Arab workers from their groves . . ."

This same rabbi maintained that even on the holiest day, Yom Kippur, in the holiest city, by the holiest Wall, there was still a chance men might stare at the women and come, God forbid, to sinful thoughts, even though the worshippers were already in their eighties . . . Therefore, a *mechitza*, a partition, must be built to separate the women from the men.

Satan the Destroyer intervened in this affair in the form of the Mufti of Jerusalem, who knew that Muhammad's holy horse, Buraq, had stood by this Wall. And sacred objects, knew the Mufti, bring in significant revenue, and so he cried out to his followers: "Save us, believers! The nonbelievers want to take away the holy Wall!"

3

The Wall was in Jerusalem, amid its ancient fortifications. Hasan's little house, however, was located in Ein-Kerem, not far from his fields. When the foreign Yahud came and began to tear apart the stone walls of the little house and cut down the old olive tree, Hasan's younger son, Ismael, asked, "Papa, why are they cutting down our tree? Its salty olives are so tasty!"

He couldn't get an answer from his father because the whole situation was too complicated. Some Zionist company had begun to build a new quarter of villas near Jerusalem. They had turned to the greatest Hebrew poet, Malkin, and he came up with a name for them: "To Mountain and Valley." The name was both marketable and biblical; the only thing missing was a lot to build on. That's when the manager of the company, Ben Amram, read the following notice in a newspaper: "Due to outstanding taxes—twenty pounds and eighty-five piasters—an auction of the household of Hasan Ibn Muhamad from the village of Ein-Kerem. The property contains 6 dunams of land, a small stone house, ten olive trees, and five rows of grapevines, five-and-a-half years of age. The auction will take place at 11 King George Street, second floor on the right. Signed: Judge Thomson."

Hasan's property had been purchased lawfully. But when the Jewish bricklayers began tearing the bricks from his little home, Hasan showed up with a whole gang of fellahin ready to fight. His youngest son and his wife, Fatma, swore dark curses and stirred up the fellahin. With tears in his eyes, Ismael gazed at the healthy olive trees that had been cut down. In the end, police dispersed the gathered fellahin. Hasan left to live in the nearby village of Khadra, and the socialist Hebrew paper ran an article that asked, "Why are the authorities silent when peaceful bricklayers are being disturbed at their work? Where are their promises of fellowship among nations and all humanity?"

4

Milner had been living in Jerusalem for the last few years. During that time, the Mosul oil pipes had been laid and fighter jets had been quietly sent through Palestine to India. The city around him was old and petrified; it moved slowly. Its stashes of discarded holy scrolls had been accumulated over the span of generations. But, Milner had moved forward from the city's history in just two decades. By his twentieth year, he had already attempted to leap into the future. It had begun back in childhood, when he read the Torah passage with the binding of Isaac and all its intricate details. Later he dreamed of rebuilding the Temple and reviving King David's glorious dynasty. More recently he looked around and realized that an empire is ruling now, complete with colonial slavery and a massive espionage operation, the so-called Intelligence Service. That's when he took a leap into the future and accepted the latest Torah: *Imperialism Is the Final Stage of Capitalism.*

The workers and the farmers would need to bring an end to this "Final Stage." Instead of destroying Hasan's home and sawing his olive trees to the ground, the Jewish workers had to become his comrades, had to shatter that last temple—that of the high commissioner—and distribute the land among the fellahin. Milner went to several villages and discussed these matters with the fellahin. But in the holy city, such heretical words were not permitted to be spoken out loud. Milner was arrested and put in prison.

Hasan went off to work at a quarry, where he hewed simple square stones as well as ornate cornerstones and sold them to the To Mountain and Valley company, which was in the process of building villas on the mountains around Jerusalem. Ben Hillel, Rabbi Buck, and the Hebrew socialist paper were successful, however, in their campaign against the building blocks: Since the To Mountain and Valley company was buying from the Arabs, the rabbi threatened to boycott. The bosses got scared and shifted to buying genuine Jewish stones. Hasan lost his job.

Having neither land nor work, the fellahin from the village of Khadra gathered in small circles in the marketplace or sat cross-legged and discussed politics. Speakers came from the city and described horrible things: The Yahud want to usurp the holy Buraq and the Omar Mosque! The speakers delivered speeches in the mosques and called on pious Muslims to protect the holy sites. The fellahin secretly winked and whispered: "There will be war! By Allah the Almighty—there will be a great war!"

Hasan listened to the speakers and their calls, and everything became clear to him. His house and land had been taken away from him, then they took away his work . . . He sharpened his crooked *shibriya* dagger and prepared dried *nabuts*, cudgels, from firm eucalyptus branches. Arabs from the city, in addition to the holy messengers, began to come to

Khadra. They snuck inside the houses as if they were passing by to drink a bit of water and quietly confided: "The British authorities are with the fellahin—the Jews must be slaughtered!"

5

It was the end of summer 1929. Milner was released from prison and returned to his old apartment in Mahane Yehuda, where he found his belongings scattered all over the place. In the alley nothing had changed: dark walls, children filthy with dust, and wet laundry hanging from ropes that stretched from house to house. Suddenly a panic erupted: Shop owners abruptly closed up shop, shutters were latched, people grabbed their children by the hand and disappeared into their narrow, enclosed stone yards. Everywhere people were yelling: "Run, the Arabs are coming!"

From all the surrounding villages, large numbers of Arabs flocked into the city. Dark-skinned women with children hanging off them stood in their doorways, drumming on their puffed-up cheeks with their fingers and wailing bitterly. Young Arabs with gleaming eyes ran ahead, seeing in front of them white women on the ground, and shattered shop windows filled with gold and silver. The crowd had scurried quietly over the twisting trails from the surrounding mountains, tapping their way through the stones with their eucalyptus sticks. Their loose, wide pants whooshed like inflated bellows, and their shawls fluttered like flags in the wind.

Near the Old City the marching mobs were joined by porters, carriage drivers, café-goers, and the unemployed. By an old mosque, a Hajji held a talk about the holy sites that the Jews wanted to seize. Young Effendi sons waved their little swords. The mob grew by the minute and foamed like a stormy sea. Here and there people shouted: "The authorities are with us—slaughter the Jews!"

Singing holy songs, the masses began to stir, finally spilling over into the scattered Jewish neighborhoods and alleys. The first shots rang out.

For three days the slaughter lasted, extending deep into remote corners. In the city, horrible news rushed from one person to the next: "A Bukharan family was slaughtered." "A fifteen-year-old girl was raped in the Yemenite quarter." "A man was killed while on guard duty in the Old City!"

Armed Jewish men left the city center at dusk, heading toward the fortified Jewish quarters.

Srulik, a young quiet fellow, wrote a proclamation in broken Arabic in favor of workers' solidarity and collective struggle against imperialism. One evening, he left with the proclamations and never returned. A couple of days later, the police brought back his corpse with a deep gaping stab wound in his shoulder. In his clenched fist, he still grasped tightly his proclamations about workers' solidarity.

A week later the city had calmed down. The fellahin transported their wounded and dead back to their villages. Hasan was sentenced to ten years in prison. A large funeral took place for the murdered Jews. Milner watched the caskets as they were followed by weeping, wrinkled old women and whole herds of starving children. The whole time he was contemplating the question: "Was this a pogrom or an uprising . . . ?"

All around, the churches, mosques, and ruins of holy temples raised their heads. Hatred and a thirst for revenge grew in the poor quarters, fortifying a wall between the nations. Milner struggled against the frothing wave, which, armed with the strength of millennia, could carry him away and drown him. One evening he went to the cooperative restaurant to collect money for the families of those killed in the riots. The crowd in the restaurant knew him, so they asked with surprise: "For which families?"

"For the Arab and Jewish . . ."

He was beaten up and thrown out.

Zalmen Discovers
Arabs in Palestine

1

On Sunday, only Zalmen and Dovid went to the Kabara swamp. When they passed "the Baron's" small barrack they looked inside through the open door: On the ground, dressed in rags, lay about fourteen young people, who snored with lengthy whistles. The tin roof glowed over their heads. They were fast asleep, tired from the nightly toil, and felt nothing. From afar, you could see the camp: several rows of tents; under the hot sheets lay those sick with ague and dysentery. A couple of semihealthy youths rotated among the tight ropes, carrying cold compresses for the newly sick.

Dovid and Zalmen worked till dusk. When the sun began to settle, they dunked their feet in the freshly dug siney and turned back toward home. On the way, they met Milner and the three of them walked in silence. Small pieces of dirt from the hard, dry earth got inside their shoes and scalded their toes. The swamp was covered with a layer of mist. At the Zamarin train station, a train whistled. On the sand beaches, an Arab swayed on a tall, humped camel. The trees on the mountains were dressed in black.

They had reached the tall palm tree by the outskirts of Kabara when they noticed a soft crying and moaning from between the bushes. "A jackal, probably," remarked Dovid.

Milner listened closely for a while and began walking down from the path. "It's a kind of human voice," he said, "not a jackal." The guys followed Milner, winding down the little path between the bushes, and approached Abu Khalil's shack. They spotted something among the weed grass. Next to dry tomato bushes and tall, snaky bean grass lay an old dead man in torn clothes with big holes in his stomach. At his side, bent over, was a young Arab, about nineteen or twenty years old. He pulled the old man along the ground, stopped, wept, and continued to pull. "It's Rasheed, the old man's grandson," said Milner quietly.

Young Rasheed, wailing, mumbled something to himself: "killed off the old man . . . ! A curse on the faith of their father . . . Took away his water, the vegetables died, and the person died . . . May their house be ruined . . ." He lifted the old man a bit, brought him closer. The corpse lay on his shoulder. He was entirely chewed up and emitted a foul odor. The young Arab held his head with both hands and wailed: "Oy, grandfather, grandfather, grandfather! . . ."

The surroundings in Kabara had grown dark. The Arab on the hunched camel disappeared below the horizon. The train from Zikhron ran by with lit windows, making a great racket; the projectors flashed red beams at the mountains, illuminating them for a brief second, after which they immediately darkened again. Everybody was quiet.

Milner was the first to make a move. He approached the shack, broke down a couple of rough pegs, shoved them under the dead body, and with his eyes signaled the guys to come over. The four of them bent down and carried the dead body into the shack. Rasheed tore down a filthy sheet from the wall and covered the dead body. Milner lit a match and threw it into the chips that lay near the shack between a couple of rocks. The dry little twigs clicked, shot long tongues of fire into the darkness, and cast a red shine over the withered banana leaves, over the shack, and over the men bowing their heads.

They stood a while longer, then walked slowly away. After cutting across the path to Caesarea, they stumbled on scattered pieces of wood and tin. "Where did we crawl into, Goddammit?!" said Milner.

"They're building a bridge here over the canal that we recently dug," answered Zalmen. "That was a plan Shantov the engineer devised: Dig out a canal from the fountain to the Zarqa stream, so Abu Khalil wouldn't have any water and would have to leave this area!"

"And now," Milner replied with irony, "you will establish your kibbutz—the prototype of the new society, and thus you will lead, together with the Arab masses, the struggle against British imperialism . . ."

Zalmen was silent. Dovid burst out: "Well, don't you work in Kabara?"

"Workers work anywhere they can. But I'm against the land theft, and you go and implement the colonization of usurped lands. You position yourselves in a struggle against the expropriated farmers—not in the same camp with them."

2

Zalmen listened closely to the discussion. In that moment, all his fundamental principles started to waver, and he found himself mixing up his youth and his path to the kibbutz in his head. Images from past years surged and haunted him: They forced Shmuel the fisherman, with his son, out of the city. Just like that, taken from the street and driven away. Two days later, a gentile reported: They were forced to dig a hole and crawl into it. Then they were shot. Later, he saw the rotting bodies with bullet holes and Shmuel's beard, which had been torn out.

Nobody dared leave the shtetl. They were plundered and beaten . . . beards torn, tossed from moving trains, and whipped to death . . . ! He came here, to his only safe haven. But was it, indeed, the only one? The correct one? Or does he need to rethink everything all over again . . . ?

It was quite late when they arrived at camp. A group of people, some sitting and some standing around the tables, discussed imperialism, Arabs, the English.

"The imperialism is showing its teeth," some argued. "We've always said that we have to unite with the Arab masses in the struggle against the English . . ."

"The English are uniting with the Effendis against progressive Jewish colonization."

"The English are going with the Arab Effendis, and we have to go with the workers . . ."

"And the workers are going to hand us their villages, as long as we're establishing kibbutzim . . . ?"

Zalmen slowly ate cold soup with dry kasha and listened to the discussion with one ear. After eating, he left the camp and went to Milner's tiny barrack. He heard noise from a primus coming from inside. The barrack was stuffy and messy: Newspapers, books, food, and clothes all lay on the bed; heat from the warmed tin roof attacked him. Milner smiled: he hadn't had a guest for a long time. No one from the colony came: Everybody knew that he mingled with Arabs and spread calls against Zionism. He had even been thrown out of the restaurant several times. He lived alone, with only books and newspapers, and . . . with hope for the socialist revolution.

"If you want, could we go check out Kabara?" Zalmen said, somewhat ashamed, right as he entered.

"Have you ever been in an Arab village?" Milner asked him.

Zalmen pondered: He'd been discussing the Arab question in Palestine for six years now and had never spoken with Arabs. In fact, all he knew of Palestine was Tel Aviv, a couple of kibbutzim, and that's it. The hundreds of Arab villages didn't even exist for him.

"Was once," he answered, "I mean, no more than passing through. Not long ago, our boys photographed themselves under a palm tree with some Arabs."

Milner smiled and quickly drank his tea. Stepping out of his room he said: "Nu, Zalmen, we're going to discover Arabs in Palestine . . . !"

3

The summer evening was overcast. Young couples strolled and strayed from the path to the trees and bushes. Thousands of new jasmine flowers opened their buds and filled the air with their scent. A white moon crept from behind the mountains and lit the way. Milner and Zalmen trekked quickly and got to the palm tree in fifteen minutes. A humid breeze blew from the swamp.

Around a fire next to a cabin, a group of Arabs, elders with one youth, sat in a circle speaking and gesturing with their hands. Rasheed lay by the door, with his head to the ground. When they noticed the guests, they stopped talking. Milner grumbled under his nose, something close to a "good evening." An older Arab answered, "welcome," and pointed to a spot by the fire. They all sat silently and listened to the dry twigs crackling in the fire. The silence became painful. Milner smoked a cigarette and offered some to the Arabs. Little by little, a conversation developed. The Arabs complained that the faith has weakened; allowing the Arab people to become enslaved and made subservient to foreign rulers. The urban youth are dressing European and learning foreign ways . . .

"It has always been hard for poor people, whether under its own leaders or under foreign ones," interjected Milner.

"The Koran also looks out for the poor people," said the young Arab, Mustafa. "When the religion is upheld, it will be better for everyone."

"And if all Muslims uphold Muhammad's faith, then the English won't rule the land anymore?"

Mustafa, who until now had expressed his opinions only to fellahin, felt his confidence grow and continued developing his ideas: "Ibn Saud re-established the old traditions and the true faith—and now the foreigners don't rule anymore in Hejaz. The Asuan live as Muhammad's knights of the past. They began a holy war and spread the pure faith in the surrounding lands. This is the path of redemption."

The crowd of old Arabs surrounding him listened but didn't understand the conversation. They enjoyed watching young Mustafa, who could speak with such wisdom even with an educated Jew. One of them stood up, rubbed his hands, and said: "It's getting cold, we need to make some coffee!"

He went in the shack to fetch the tools. Mustafa half stood up and gestured with his hands. His long shawl fluttered in the wind. He spoke with passion: "In Hejaz, Muhammad's laws are the official rule: When someone steals—his hand gets chopped off; when someone doesn't come to pray in the mosque—he gets whipped, and for smoking or drinking wine, there are large fines. You can leave a camel there in the middle of the field, and you'll find him the next morning!"

The crowd in the nearby circle cheered enthusiastically. "But in Palestine, as we know, the Ingleyz rule and the People must obey," Milner responded. "What good will piety do here?"

An old Arab poured coffee into two little pots and served the two guests. Afterward, the little pots made their way, by turns, across the entire circle. The crowd sipped silently. Mustafa got up and said that he had to go home. And clomping with a long stick over the hard ground, he disappeared into the night's darkness.

On the way home, Milner said to Zalmen: "Their faith in Allah blinds them. But the English hate them." Zalmen reflected on the situation: "You know, we are indeed funny people; we're always talking about: revolutionary masses, turbulent East . . . Our newspapers write long articles, but when it comes to what is really happening all around us, that's what we don't want to see. Everything gets brushed off with one word: 'The Mufti is a pogromist, and the Arab fellahin are being incited' . . . How are these fellahin of Palestine any worse than the Chinese farmers who defend themselves against foreigners? Why do we call the Chinese 'revolutionaries,' and the fellahin, who don't want to leave their land—'pogromists' . . . ?"

By the time they got back, the camp was quiet. Only the gramophone played in the barrack, and a couple of boys were sitting nearby. Zalmen found Motke in the kitchen and immediately delivered an entire speech to him: "Here they are, still playing! Instead of thinking, they're dancing horas. Tell me: why are our people so impressed by the national liberation movement in India, but they see the Arab nationalist movement as a band of pogromists? Huh?"

4

Mustafa didn't remember exactly when he had started going to the kitab, or when he had learned the first chapter of the Koran by heart. Mustafa's father was not a rich man, but he had his own land and so he hadn't needed to pay a third to Effendi. His father would say to him: "Learn, Mustafa, well and fluently! When you know the entire Koran by heart, we'll buy you a new coat, and you'll become a sheikh."

Mustafa learned fluently and quickly knew the Koran. When summer arrived, the khamsins began to blow. They dried up the wells, burned the grasses, and also brought whole bands of spirits, demons, and ghosts in from the desert. Mustafa's teacher prepared long strips of paper and boards, wrote on them in ornate letters, and carried them across the village to sell. You only had to swallow nine such strips of paper, and you would be safe from all kinds of illnesses, particularly eye inflammation, which was spread by the swamp and clouds of dust. Every family had a couple of blind children, so people did indeed purchase the teacher's amulets, paying him with colored eggs.

In the evenings, Mustafa loved to listen to the village singers, who would sing lengthy songs recounting various stories of heroes and tribes that wandered in remote deserts seizing new cities and lands. Their melodies were trilled and sad, and their heroes were always rewarded with sweet pretty girls and endless gold and silver.

A bit later, when Mustafa got older, he ran around with groups of guys in the nearby fields and mountains and ended up having wandered all the way to Caesarea. Near the coast stood a big building with a golden cross on top. It was a Greek Orthodox church, which once had lots of land, gardens, and livestock. Nuns lived in the chambers, doing nothing but entreating God for the health of the holy "little father," the czar of Russia. After the revolution there was no more czar. But here, they only learned that news many years later, when they realized that they lacked enough money for the big crowd of worshippers. The nuns quickly scattered; the fellahin began plowing the church's land. Across the empty yard, only an old Greek Orthodox priest hung around, leaning on a stick and accompanied by a big hairy dog.

The fellahin told all kinds of stories about the past riches of the church and about the bad ending of its czar. He had a lot of land, and so his slaves murdered him and took it all . . . Once, a red star appeared in the sky, and the spiritualists said that the world would turn upside down in one month's time. The village roared in an outbreak of turmoil: People were afraid to sleep in their houses, wives cried for their children, and men pleaded with Allah for mercy. The month ended, and the world didn't turn upside down. But a short time later, the war broke out. At first, people said that the foreigners, the heretic Ingleyz, wanted to seize the holy cities of Mecca and Medina and force the faithful to kneel to a foreign god. At that time, everyone here respected the Turks, although they hated them for sucking the blood of the population. A bit later, people began taking the opposite view: The foreign Ingleyz actually intended to protect the holy cities, and to liberate the Arabs from the heavy taxes and bribes.

5

The war ended but Mustafa didn't become a sheikh. A few months later, his father announced that his mother was sick, there was no one who could work, and it was probably the will of God for him to travel back home. Mustafa put aside the holy books and wandered the streets of Jaffa to observe how people lived.

He wandered for days across the city, at every step encountering the tall figure of an English soldier, who rose stiffly and coldly on every corner: in the port, in the marketplace, and at the intersections. He went around to the cafés and listened to the conversations about politics, the strength of Britain, the impotence of Allah, the English spying operation and their famous English spy Lawrence—who disguised himself as an Arab and wandered across Palestine, showing up in one place or another—the quarrels between the Mufti and the dominant Nashashibi family, and the land speculators.

Mustafa took up reading newspapers and even found an old book in Arabic, which explained world politics and was full of strange tales about Karl Marx's *Kapital*, the ten lovers of Napoleon I, and the ape origins of humans. Mustafa didn't understand much about how all those things were tangled up together, but nevertheless, this book revealed new worlds to him, and he began thinking about all the nations that, up until now, he had only labeled as "infidels."

He decided not to travel back to the village until he understood what was going on in the world: "Why do the Ingleyz rule the world? What is the source of white Europeans' strength? And did people actually derive from monkeys?" He wandered across Jaffa with a half-empty belly, reading, listening, and searching for an answer to the thousands of questions that suddenly swirled in his imagination.

During this time, the legend of the ruler Ibn Saud slowly took shape in his mind. The figure of this hero was engraved in his fantasy by newspaper articles, café conversations, and his own concealed desires: He lies like a lion in the desert and protects the holy cities against the Ingleyz, he behaves according to the true Muslim faith, and he denies entry to the alien machinery, which brings heresy and foreign rule. He is as cruel and as merciful as the desert which surrounds him . . .

Mustafa adopted the traditions and laws of Ibn Saud's teaching, which was called Wahabism, as he understood it himself. He became a partial recluse and took upon himself the task of spreading the true faith to the People. When he returned to Khaldia, he preached the new practices to the fellahin. They heard him out with a smile and nodded their heads, as they would listening to stories from *One Thousand and One Nights*.

Hanke Decides to Live

1

This khamsin heat wave was one of the last of the summer. It was also one of the very hottest. Waves of glowing hot air moved across the cloudy grasses, dusty trees, and dry wadis. At the laundry, they didn't light fires because the tap water was hot enough. Near the camp, the jackals wailed at night because they didn't have anything to drink. Only the swamp had inexhaustible underground springs and sent swarms of young new mosquitoes into the world.

Hanke had malaria and suffered from a high fever. She woke up in the middle of the night and looked around: The sheets of the tent were rolled up, so the bed stood uncovered, as if it were in the middle of the open camp; outside was a silver-white night, with visibility as on a clear day. Hanke noticed talking and turned her head. Boys in short tricot pants and girls in nightgowns lay in the grass along the barrack. The burning tin roofs and the warmed-up tarps had driven the entire kibbutz outdoors. By the barrack, they laughed and spoke loudly, but she couldn't hear clearly about what.

She got bored and tried calling out loud. But her voice was weak and no one could hear her. She remained lying in bed, desperate, gazing into the night. A couple of hours passed and she still couldn't fall asleep. Near the barrack, she noticed a tanned, half-naked boy bending over a girl. He pulled her by the hand, and she stood up and followed him. The girl was full-figured, with long, messy hair. Her long nightgown, which revealed bits of flesh under her neck and on her back, got tangled over her feet. Hanke strained to look closely and recognized Motke and Simme. She was very surprised they were going together.

Motke and Simme walked slowly toward the mountains and dis-appeared among the tents. Hanke was struck with a desire to follow them. She placed a foot on the ground and immediately fell down in the sand. With great effort, she made it back to her bed. Worn out, she stayed in bed, looking toward the sky. It was quiet all around. People dozed near the barrack.

She lay like that for a while. The stars dimmed in the sky. The air darkened and cooled. A gray dawn immediately began to suffuse the air. Hanke heard steps from behind and turned around: Simme walked through the tents, hunched and wrapped in her nightgown. She looked ahead, her eyes wide open and her feet bare, searching for a path on the dry earth. A couple steps behind her walked Motke.

2

Hanke was still alone. The morning cooled her naked body. She embraced her own body with her hands and stroked her breasts and hips with her fingers. She cried quietly lying there, powerless, embraced by her own hands. When she woke up, a hot sun burned above her head. The malaria fever had dropped; she could see the images from the past few hours clearly. She felt fresh and easy, and a firm decision arose in her: "Enough! We've got to start living; why waste your days and years for nothing . . . ?"

She patted her forehead. It was cool, but weakness permeated her organs, and her head felt dizzy. In the daytime, her bed got moved to a small room in a barrack that had been freed up for her and Dina. She lay there in a long, white nightgown. In the evening, Motke came after work. He crossed the room on his tiptoes and sat on the bed by her legs. Hanke placed her white hand on the blanket. He took her hand and stroked it. She looked at him with gentleness and touched the sturdy palm of his hand with her fingertip. In her starkly pale face, her eyes became even deeper and bluer.

Hanke lay at home for another couple days because she was so weak-ened from the malaria. In the evening, Motke raced home from work like a madman. He quickly shaved, showered, changed his clothes, and ran, with his hair still wet, to Hanke's room. Hanke lay on the bed under a mosquito net and read. When Motke entered she put her little book to the side and moved over, making room for him. The thin web of mosquito guard separated them. She grabbed the net, threw it over his shoulders, and pressed herself against him.

Motke felt her warmth. He was surprised: He expected passive consent from her but not an active advance. He had imagined Hanke giving in to his will as a reward for his strong love for her, not as her own independent striving for him. He hugged and kissed her. Hanke held him close with her arm and pressed him to her.

3

That summer, the kibbutz rented a vineyard. Half the kibbutz hung out there in the evening, because aside from thin soup and dry bread with radishes, there wasn't much to eat in the barrack. Still hungry after dinner, they rushed to revive themselves with some grapes. One evening, when Hanke had regained her strength, she went there with Motke. A large crowd was in the vineyard. Hanke was lively and in good spirits; she was close with everybody. She laughed a lot, sang, and wandered around with guys and was unrecognizable from the previously closed-off lonesome girl.

A large group of them walked back. Motke followed from behind, pensive. Suddenly, he felt a sharp pain in his hand. He turned around: Hanke pressed his finger into her hand and pushed him backward with all her strength. Her eyes seemed wild to him, and her face contorted from the effort. The group walked away, but he stayed back beside her.

It had already turned dark, and an enflamed sky reddened over the green mountains. Jasmine bushes huddled in the nearby fields. A stream of water poured loudly down from the high concrete reservoir on the colony's hill. Suddenly she burst out: "Come on, let's go!"

Hanke ran quickly ahead on the sandy path as though driven by a hidden force. She was wrapped up in herself and didn't see Motke at all. She came out at a vacant field, full of thorns and recently shorn prickly little stalks. Hanke's naked feet got scratched and bled, but she kept walking with quick strides and stopped near a big pile of crops. For a moment, she tapped the place with her foot in the dark and immediately lay down on the ground.

Motke kneeled next to her and ravenously latched onto her warm body. The girl moaned like she was in great pain; he kissed her naked feet and breasts and comforted her in his arms. Only much later, when the night began to brighten, did they rise and begin to shake off the straw that stuck to their bodies. Hanke's body was completely scratched and bloody. She gazed at the distance, over the Kabara swamp, and said: "I would want to stay with you like that the whole night . . . hundreds of nights . . . !"

The next day it happened again. After dinner she waited for Motke by the gate. She took him by the hand and quietly pulled him to follow her. When they stepped out of the camp, she leaned on him, laughed, and gazed into his eyes: "It's a pity about the time, right . . . ?"

Right away she left the path, entered the jasmine field, searched around with her eyes, and lay down under a bush. All her movements irritated Motke: her odd, almost animal-like manner of sniffing out a quiet corner, her impatient running, the way she threw herself on the ground.

They returned to the barrack during a meeting. Hanke combed her hair outside the door, wiped off the dust, and sat at a table in a corner. Her face turned serious and determined. She leaned on her hands and looked the speaker in the eye, hanging attentively on each word. Again, it seemed weird to Motke: This same girl, who's sitting here so seriously, clothed from head to toe, listening to a talk about politics, and making sure not to reveal even the smallest part of her body, was recently rolling naked in the sand and submitting entirely to his desire . . . "Is that the boundary between people and animals, which I don't understand"—he asked himself—"or is it simply the influence of her years of education . . . ?"

Shukri Effendi Worries About the Arab People

1

At dawn, Ali the driver shivered in the cold. He slept in the small garage covered in a tattered coat. Once, when Shukri Effendi found him sleeping in the car, he smacked his feet and almost fired him from his job.

At six in the morning, Ali jumped off the straw mat, oiled up the machine, washed off the dust, and tested the wheels and brakes. At eight o'clock, Shukri Effendi Latif hopped in the car and yelled: "Jaffa!" Three women looked out their bedroom windows. Zefire, the youngest, who had recently been purchased, smiled: To spite her rivals, her mister had spent the night with her again and had promised to bring her a gift from the city . . . She would surely have a son, and who could match her then? She sensed the hateful stares from the other wives, who stood by the windows and then quickly ducked their heads back inside.

The Jaffa streets were lively with braying donkeys, honking cars, the ringing cymbals of lemonade vendors, gramophones that wept trilled melodies, old Arabs grabbing boxes of tomatoes from their carts, and amid all the commotion, a little Arab running about and hawking the names of Arabic newspapers in his sad, twisted voice.

Ali drove to the editorial offices of the *Muslim Voice*.

The *Muslim Voice* was a newspaper that was "concerned" for everybody: the landowners and fellahin, the deported farmers from the village of Qalansawe, Shukri Effendi, his driver, and his workers.

Shukri was greeted at the editorial office with great respect. Everybody knew him. Not only was he the editor's cousin but he also had a nice car, even nicer than the Ingleyz had, a bigger orchard than the Yahud, and money in the bank. Everyone shook his hand. Shukri Effendi greeted each person separately in the name of Allah, asked about their wives and children, and then stepped into another room to speak with the journalist Ibrahim Tadji.

"How are you?"

"Blessed be Allah. And how are you?"

Shukri Effendi took out a box of English cigarettes and offered one to the journalist. Ibrahim glanced at the brand, smiled, and offered Effendi a light. Shukri leaned back in his chair, threw his head back, released a cloud of smoke, and asked: "And how's it going in our beloved country, Palestine?"

"Badly. Wherever the soil is fertile, it's handed over to the foreigners. Soon Palestine will no longer be an Arab country . . ."

Shukri Effendi considered his new house, with the stone lions at the door, and the grove of young trees that he intended to plant, and moaned: "Yes, yes! The foreigners are snapping up everything . . ."

"They say," Ibrahim commented, seeming disturbed, "the *Sayoni* (Zionists) are in negotiations to purchase Wadi Hawarit: Thirty thousand dunams of plantation land will fall into the hands of the Zionists with one stroke of a pen! And your Khaldia," he looked at Effendi, "will drown amid the Jewish 'companies.'"

"A delegation will be sent to the high commissioner about it," Ibrahim continued. "The Higher Committee communicates with the most important people in the country. But . . ."

Ibrahim fell silent for a moment, coughed, inhaled the smoke from his cigarette, and spoke a bit softer: "The whole world knows there are people on the Arab Executive itself who sell land to the Zionists . . . The British governor Johnson said officially: 'Why do the Arab Effendis complain about the Zionists when they themselves are selling land?' We'll shame them! All the newspapers will publish their names."

The young journalist went on and on. Finally, Shukri Effendi said: "You work hard for our beloved country. You need to relax a bit, Ibrahim! My car will be available in a couple of days; you can take it for a drive across the country. You could even stay with me for a couple of weeks; my house is very spacious . . ."

They parted. Shukri Effendi raced down the steps and glanced at his watch: 10:30. He has to meet with the Al-Thani and the cursed Yahud, what was his name? Oh, it's hard to be an Arab Effendi: The religion and the People must be protected, but the village has brought in so little income that you must sell the land to the Yahud . . . "Ali! Hotel George!!"

Ali, having been left on his own, bought an Arabic newspaper and dug in on reading the Palestinian news: The Yahud have bought a thousand more dunams in the south, another six hundred dunams near Safed, seven hundred dunams near Beit She'an, they're negotiating about Wadi Hawarit and Wadi Qabbani, and they're sending brokers to Ber Sheva . . .

Ali was extremely tired. He hadn't slept the night before because he had been with Effendi in Jerusalem. While he rested his head on the newspaper napping, the previous night spun in his head: an English bar. Blond soldiers drinking whiskey and singing. A gramophone playing. Effendi coming out with a white woman. Laughter over his shoulder. Effendi and the girl disappeared down the hotel corridor. Outside, the starry sky. The night going by. Effendi coming out, throwing himself into the soft back seat. The loud engine, tires screeching against the highway gravel, Effendi snoring. The highway winding . . . faster . . . faster . . . the faces of Effendi's three veiled wives whirling by . . .

Shukri's yell woke him up. He rubbed his eyes, honked the horn, and began cutting through the alleys of King George the Fifth.

2

A quarter of an hour later, Shukri Effendi was sitting in the dark bar at the Hotel George. A short, dark-skinned Arab sat next to him and yelled to the server, a young black man in a white suit: "a piece of cheese, Ahmed! A bit of veal! A glass of wine, ah, Ahmed!"

Ahmed ran back and forth, bringing small plates of cheese and meat. Shukri, tall and broad-shouldered, extended his hand, took the tiny slices with his fingertips, and tossed them into his wide-open mouth. The pieces slid down with a smack and a slurp. The short Arab didn't touch a thing and didn't stop screaming: "a piece of Swiss! A piece of honey cake! Where have you gone, Ahmed?"

The young, dark-skinned man was gritting his white teeth and sweating. Shukri Effendi swallowed everything and looked contemptuously at the short Arab by his side. The short man, frightened, looked at Shukri and asked: "Well, can they go out and plow?"

"Certainly, they can. Tomorrow even . . . The Khawadja won't come himself?"

"No, he won't come. He told me to organize everything. Is it all set in 'Tabu,' ya Effendi?"

"It's all set, all set . . . So, another piece of land sold to the Yahud and it doesn't bother you at all?"

"What are you talking about, it doesn't bother me . . . ? But what can you do . . . ? Everyone is selling, the rich and the very rich too . . . even Musa Kazim Pasha! It happened in the village of Tira. Musa Kazim bought three hundred dunam of orchard land from the Tira fellahin and sold them to the Yahud. Half a year later, his son comes in a car to Tira, again to buy land. The fellahin surround him and ask what he wants, to buy land? And now where are those 3,000 dunam? Well, they won't do for an orchard . . . 'Ah, they're no good for an Arab orchard' the fellahin laughed, 'but they'll be just fine for a Jewish orchard . . .'"

"Good, well said," Shukri Effendi exulted. "Hey, you, son of a dog!" he yelled at the server. "Two more coffees and a chicken leg for the Mukhtar Subhi Effendi! . . ." "Well, everything is set," he said to Subhi. "They can go out tomorrow to plow; all the managers are with us, and part of the fellahin lessees too. The roosters won't even crow."

Shukri got in his car. He felt relieved after eating and listening to Subhi's stories. He smiled with satisfaction: "Now people will go to the high commissioner to protest, and the land will become more expensive! The Yahud will get scared and grab more land! And if selling land really became forbidden? Well, we'll think of something . . . !"

He slouched in the soft back seat of the car and began to calculate where he still needed to be that day: He still needed to finish a land transaction; he had to talk with the sheikh regarding the delegation to the high commissioner. And later . . . later he would go to Tel Aviv and buy a nice gift for M. . . . She was worth it . . . A big fat smile lingered on his face, and he slowly dozed off.

The Kibbutz and the Village

1

In the village, adamant rumors spread that the Yahud were preparing to plow the southern piece of land. The poor shepherds who leased that land discussed it at length. Fathers discussed it while drinking coffee in the *madhafahs*, and mothers scared children with it: "The Yahud are coming!" The youths, known as *shabab*, dried clubs of eucalyptus and sharpened their *shibriya* daggers.

Mustafa raised his plow while working in the field, turned around to his father, and asked: "What do you say, Papa, will the shepherds really be driven off their land?"

"It's not our concern, son! We don't have land to sell and we're not shepherds. Allah gave us a small piece of land, and when He so desires, He'll give us enough rain and food will grow. We don't need to get involved in foreign affairs, son!"

"But then the Yahud will turn to our land next!"

"No reason to be scared. The land is in our name, and I don't have big debts. As long as Allah gives rain . . ."

After work, Mustafa left for the spring, which flowed in the valley near the shepherd's huts. On the way, he met Kamel, the son of Khadj Ibrahim, and they walked together. Kamel's father was rich, and he financed Kamel's studies in the big city. He walked with pride, dressed in a new silk jacket and a colorful shawl on his head, as if to say: "Look at me; I'm already an Effendi!" They approached the spring and sat on a rock. Saeed came up from the side, greeted them, and sat down as well.

The Arab girls approached, with pitchers on their heads. The boys ran after them, their eyes glistening. Kamel searched among the girls and finally pointed at one of them: "See her? my father will bring me that very girl! She is pretty as a young camel."

"But her father wants a hundred pounds for her," responded Saeed.

"Well, so what? My father will have a lot of money. Soon enough, we'll also plant a grove. You make a lot of money off a grove . . ."

Saeed lowered his head. His bright eyes grew sad and he bit his lip. He loved his village very much, and when guests came, he would always point to the fields in the area and say: "There isn't a village like ours in the whole of Palestine; its lands stretch from mountain to mountain, and we have as many people as the sand of the shore . . ."

And at that moment, it all suddenly became clear. The village was not his, and the land was not his: The land was being sold, groves were being planted, wives were being bought, and nobody was asking him. He leaned over to Mustafa and said: "Soon, there won't be even a third of the land left to plow, if Effendi and his bullies don't stop selling it!"

"The Yahud pay well," Kamel snapped, "and everyone has the right to do what they want with their own land."

"We're all brothers," Saeed spoke softly, "when we pray, or when the muezzin calls us to fast on Ramadan, or when we dance at celebrations. But when it comes to planting groves and selling the land—no more good brothers."

Kamel fixed his new shawl on his head, straightened his silk jacket, and left without saying goodbye. Saeed followed him with his gaze: "They buy silk clothes and young wives for themselves while we die of hunger." It occurred to Mustafa that Saeed spoke like that Yahud Milner. That was surprising.

2

He walked home in the dark and passed the Khadj's *madhafah*. The scent of delicious coffee assaulted his senses. He looked through the *madhafah*'s window and spotted a couple of landlords from the south side sitting in a circle on a mattress, leaning on pillows, and drinking coffee from little pots. To his surprise, he spotted Sami, one of the poorest lessees, in a corner: what was he doing here among the landowners? He pressed his ear to the window and got wind of their talking: "The government will not stay silent," he recognized the Khadj's voice. "Tulkarem and Jaffa have large jails!"

"Hankin is rich; the Baron sends him money. They can buy up the whole of Palestine," said another one.

The Khadj served Sami, the lessee, a small glass of coffee and pushed an open pack of cigarettes toward him. "So, what are people saying in the village?" he asked.

Sami gulped down the glass in one sip, coughed, wiped his lips, and spoke at length: "The *shabab* want to beat you up. They're saying that blood will flow . . . and Mustafa conspires with them in secret for days on end . . ."

"You can say to the village that if they come in good faith they'll make out better. Each of them will receive a couple of pounds. For us it doesn't make a difference, but I mean for them, they're our brothers after all," said the Khadj, shoving half a pack of cigarettes into the lessee's pocket.

The lessee left, and the remaining men began to talk softly. Mustafa was only able to catch a few words: Tabu . . . Kushans . . . Tomorrow . . . Very early . . . Still dark . . .

The thought occurred to him that the Yahud are going to come out to plow tomorrow morning, and he turned around and ran to the lessees' huts.

He could hear yelling and commotion from afar. When he approached the village, he found upheaval. Everyone was yelling: the men, the women, the children; even the donkeys were braying and scaring the barking dogs. The whole village was on the streets. He wanted to run over to them and deliver the news. But they already knew.

Suddenly Saeed came up and yelled: "The Yahud are coming out tomorrow morning to plow our land!" The entire mass of people swayed. Rasheed stood up and glared at them with stony eyes.

The entire crowd, including women and children, old people, and even donkeys, lunged forward and marched through the narrow alley toward the part of town where the landlords lived. The front line of the crowd got there first. They all congregated at the market and the mosque. A couple of young men snuck under the Khadj's window and made a racket. The wives and children reacted from all directions with shrieks and curses.

The Khadj emerged, pale, with a white shawl on his head. Voices arose from all over:

"The land belongs to the entire village! You've sold our land!"

"Go yell at the land registry, the Tabu!"

"Shukri Effendi gave a *bakshish*, a bribe, at the Tabu!" Mustafa shouted.

"Effendi does business with the Yahud!"

"He lives well and we're dying of hunger!"

The Khadj stood fearfully and pleaded with the older fellahin: "Don't sin against Allah! No one loves the Arab People and holy Islam like Shukri Effendi, God protect his health! The youngsters these days are insolent and they jump like goats!" "He's right," intervened the lessee Sami from out of the crowd. "What can the Effendi do against the machinations of the Yahud? The Khadj will plant a grove and give us work too . . ."

"Search his pockets and you'll find the Khadj's cigarettes," Mustafa yelled to the guys.

The crowd of young people approached Sami. Khadj ran inside the house and slammed the door. Outside, a brawl broke out. The women and dogs wept their hearts out. The young men pulled knives from their wide pants and screamed: "Son of a bitch! Our land! Our land!"

A couple of hours later the crowd of fellahin slowly dispersed to their homes. Mustafa left the village with the young people and piled heaps of stones next to the southern part. Late at night, the young people went from house to house knocking on the little windows: "Be ready . . . At dawn the whole village is going out . . ."

3

Zalmen spent entire nights by a tiny little lamp perched on a stack of books and brochures, studying, making calculations, and ultimately concluding that if the land of Palestine were divided among the fellahin, each family would have fifty-eight dunams, when a family must have, at minimum, a hundred dunams! How could there be Jewish colonization, and how could there be fellahin . . . ?

The next morning, a general gathering was called in the barracks, to decide whether to go plow the purchased land of Khaldia!

They discussed the matter vigorously in the barracks. Ignatz defended two points: "First, Lenin also said that when village land concentrates in the kulak's hands it brings class war into the village, and second—if we won't buy this land, someone else will. In any case, the primitive fellahin economy must crumble."

"But, what should we do about it?" Zalmen heckled him, "take over fellahin land, or join the fellahin in a struggle for an agrarian revolution in Palestine? I mean, we, as revolutionaries, what do we need to do . . . ?" The meeting lasted till late at night, and at the end it was decided by a majority vote that they would go out to plow.

In the dark before dawn, Sholem Bomshteyn drove the livestock while riding a horse; his whip whistled through the air, and he smacked his lips and bounced in the saddle. He had sat in the barracks all night long, listening to the discussions, and hadn't understood a thing. He was confused why people had talked for so long: "Obviously they need to plow"—he thought to himself. "Does a greater pleasure exist than following livestock as they plow, and watching the black clods of earth spread out?" He dozed off in the middle of the meeting and woke up when it was almost time to go harness the livestock.

From the back and front stretched a row of wagons with people and plows. Zalmen was sitting there, sleepy-eyed and shaking. The path became softer, the wheels sunk deeper, the horses sweated, and the carriage drivers let go of their reins. From atop the carts, boys whistled horas and the socialist anthem "The Internationale."

They parked the wagons on a hill. Not far from them hid the silhouettes of small, tightly packed village huts, a dense fence of cactuses, a tall palm tree, and a white stream of water. It was dark and quiet around them. Only dogs barked somewhere in some yards. The crowd held its breath and went to work in the stillness.

People began to drag the plows down from the carts. A worker rolled a barrel of water down from a wagon and poured the water into buckets. Several guys offered water to the horses and began harnessing the livestock to the plows. Suddenly, a racket broke through the stillness. The crowd straightened up and looked down at the village. A multitude of old and young fellahin ran toward them. Long shadows leaped wildly over the field. When they neared the hill, the fellahin stopped and stared at the foreigners. Both camps stood still for a while, each quietly observing the other.

Mustafa had run up with the first to arrive. He stopped and breathed heavily. Silent, naked mountains slept, wrapped in fog. Villages stood on the slopes, hanging their heads low. There, Khaldia was also getting pushed aside: to its hunger, to its death, to its downfall . . .

Fellahin with livestock arrived in the back. Both sides began plowing. Every plower established a square garden bed and walked around and around over yellow clods of earth that had been turned over. The livestock walked with their heads lowered, oblivious to what was taking place. The Jewish livestock, stronger and well-rested, pulled firmly. The Arab camels and donkeys, skinny and exhausted, inched along slowly. The yelling and whistling of their riders didn't help. The Jewish guys finished plowing their square garden beds first and turned to the Arab ones. They wanted to plow as much as they could, because plowing gave them the right of possession. A wave of shouting and cursing filled the air, bodies shoved, and fists clenched. A brawl erupted. Near the kibbutz's livestock, Sholem held the plow and Zalmen held the livestock. Zalmen was upset and thought it was a scandal, that he was about to rob someone else's land.

The livestock, sensing a weak hand, tore the plow out of the ground and scattered. Zalmen and Sholem ran after them. Suddenly, somebody blocked their way. Zalmen raised his eyes and spotted Mustafa. His own blood smacked him in the face, and he froze in place. Mustafa leaned on a long stick and yelled: "Sons of bitches! Murdered the old guy and now you turn on us. A curse on your heads and on your father's faith . . ." He pulled ahead: "And you even spoke about brotherhood . . . about justice . . . Thieves, robbers . . . !"

Rasheed jumped. His big black eyes flickered in fear. White, clenched teeth peeked out from his wide-open foamy lips and his loose shirt revealed a sweaty, hairy chest. Not uttering a peep, he pulled a *shibriya* knife out of his wide pants and aimed it at Zalmen. The white blade flashed in the gray dawn. Zalmen kneeled. The *shibriya* slashed through the air and hit Sholem. A stream of blood burst from Sholem's shoulder and poured down onto the sand. Sholem yelled and fell down.

Meanwhile, one of the Jewish boys ran to the wagon, pulled a hunting rifle out from under the seat, and fired. The Arabs ceded for a moment, unleashing curses and wild screaming. A couple of Arabs ran to the piles of rocks they had prepared and began throwing them at the Jewish boys. In another corner, people fought with *shibriya* knives, *nabut* sticks, and boards from the wagon. Moans of the injured filled the air.

Zalmen was on his knees next to Sholem, trying hard to control the bleeding. He put his hand on Sholem's shoulder and felt a warm, sticky fluid. The blood continued to pour out and streamed through his fingers. Zalmen felt unhelpful and raised his eyes, looking for a solution. The fellahin barraged them with stones. The frightened livestock ran all across the field. The Jewish guys hid under the wagons. From the village a new group ran up. Ragged, barefoot children jumped up and shrieked. Women covered in black screamed like a pack of crows, drummed their cheeks, and gave rocks to their men.

4

Dawn blanched the area. The sky cleared. Zalmen shivered a bit in the cold. Sholem lay on the ground and groaned with pain. Stones rained down over his head. In his ears rang the words: "Son of a bitch, you spoke of peace and brotherhood . . ." He grabbed Sholem and carried him far away, where no rocks could reach them. His bleeding slowed a bit. Sholem raised his pale face and uttered: "I'll stay here by myself; you can go fight!"

"With whom?" Asked Zalmen.

Sholem looked at him, surprised: "What do you mean, with whom? With the Arabs!"

And Zalmen understood his own question. It was all suddenly clear to him: Sooner or later, one must fight! It's only a question of with whom . . . And it's a shame about the kibbutz, the camp, the tents, the doleful nights, and the smoky kitchen with the long discussions. He's got to leave it all . . .

Police arrived: tall, blond Englishmen, dark-skinned Arabs, and white Jews. They dashed across the field on horseback. The Arabs retreated.

Half Hallel, Oil, and Fate

1

Late at night, Zalmen drove the wounded Bomshteyn in a wagon from Hadera to Binyamina. Bomshteyn lay in the cart on a couple of sacks of hay. Over the journey, various memories from Zalmen's youth passed through his mind.

In San Remo, they divided the oil of Mosul, solidifying the creation of the Jewish national home.

He remembered when he came home for the holiday and chatted with Simme about celebrating the Balfour Declaration in the shtetl. Simme's father, Moyshe Berl, who had a resonating voice and bleated like a lamb, was preparing to pray from the pulpit on the High Holidays. He let out sad, pleading notes, which reverberated all over the few huts that had survived the burning of the synagogue alley.

When the uproar over the Balfour Declaration happened, a club of youths hung a picture of Dr. Herzl up on a study-house wall and went out to collect money for the Jewish National Fund. Jewish women cut out Balfour's picture from the newspaper, hung it up on the wall, and pointed: "What a fine Jew, that Mr. Balfour! A gray beard, like our rabbi, may he rest in peace; may we all live long and prosper . . ."

Zalmen gave a passionate talk in the study house preaching fiery words. Simme stood in the women's section wiping tears from her eyes. On the Sabbath, Noyekh-Avrom son of Aron, a young man from the senior pioneers, who already had a wife and three kids and worked very hard, thumped on the lectern in the study house and unleashed a yell: "Fellow Jews, in honor of the Balfour Declaration, today we pray a half Hallel!"

A passionate turmoil erupted. Old Jews banged on the lecterns and tables and screamed: "Insolents!"

Moyshe-Berl stood there, confused. He didn't know that the oil of Mosul and control over the Arab peoples had been divided at a meeting in San Remo. What did he know about oil back then? During the week, people went to sleep early without lighting any fires at home, or they burned thin pieces of tar. But on Shabbes, they had to fill their lamps with kerosene to illuminate the meal!

A bundle of memories arose in his mind, and, being very deep in thought, he got a bit lost and arrived back home around two in the morning.

2

It was still bright in the big barrack, where a group was holding a kumzitz campfire. A "kumzitz" was a kind of feast with revelry in the middle of the night. They were starving, and from time to time in the middle of the night, they broke a lock to raid the food storage, snuck out a couple of herring, little cans of sardines, or a piece of sausage and sat around the tables in the food barrack.

When the wagon arrived at the huts with a screech, people ran out of the barracks to see what had happened. A couple of minutes later, they carried Bomshteyn out of the carriage and into Boris's small barrack. The entire crowd clamored for updates all at once. Girls naked but for their nightgowns and guys in torn underwear jumped out of their tents and ran over to check out Sholem. Only Motke stayed next to Zalmen. He said with a smile: "Well, you've become a national hero!"

"For the first and last time," Zalmen replied quietly, "what kind of devil united us to brawl with the Arab fellahin?"

"What do you mean?"

"We are just small pawns in the hands of the British: They want to build their strategic base here, so they need to have a force that will always resist the local liberation movement . . ."

"But what about Jewish poverty? Do you think the Jews from Kamionka and Pitshich are running here to protect the Suez Canal?"

"Jewish poverty made all these things possible! I am not denying that the Jewish masses find themselves in a dire state, but Zionism is a seductive dream on one hand and a base for imperialism on the other. England will only let in a few Jewish men here, in order for them to combat and defeat the local uprisings. You can see it happening here: Now the fellahin are going to believe that we are their enemies and will constantly fight with us!"

"So you mean we're here for nothing; we only think that we're doing something, but in reality, we're only doing the bidding of supernatural forces?"

"Not 'supernatural,' in fact, entirely real, reactionary forces . . ."

In the kitchen, the kerosene stoves burned as always, and a small lamp smoldered on the wall. Empty cans labeled in three languages—"Shell Oil Company"—rolled across the floor. In a frying pan, onions boiled in oil, prepared for the kumsitz but forgotten amid the big rush. It was quiet in the area; only the tent peaks cut through the darkness of the night.

The camp, the music, the twisted Arab letters on the gasoline cans, and Zalmen's words all swirled around in Motke's head so forcefully that he started talking to himself: What? This means that the whole story with the "ancient communes" is only so the English can have good protection for the Suez Canal . . . ? And the tragedy of the new family is also a delusion? The most important factor is their need for the Haifa–Mosul oil pipeline . . . ?

Outside, a group of people surrounded Zalmen and badgered him. "If that's how it is, then what are you even doing here? You need to pack up your stuff and go home!"

As they walked to the tent, Motke asked Zalmen quietly: "Tell me, Zalmen, even with all that, how will you solve the Jewish question? You don't deny the economic abnormality of the Jewish masses, the anti-Semitism, the persecutions, the pogroms!"

"The Jewish question," Zalmen replied with conviction, "is a part of overarching injustices: exploitation, war, massacres, hunger, and enslavement. The Jewish question can only be resolved together with those other questions—through social change. And if you really want to solve the Jewish question, you can't fight through racism, chauvinism, or taking over workplaces from the Arabs—rather, in fact you have to do the opposite . . ."

A Colony Gets Built and People Get Overworked

1

"For how many people?"

"For eight!"

"One and half cutlets per person," ruled Nekhe the cook, "and one and a half tomatoes. But no more! Otherwise, there won't be enough for the water buffaloes."

Shimon picked out the best shovels from the tool shed in the small barrack. Bashke placed small loaves of bread in baskets. They set off on the path. The morning became whiter and the earth sandier and softer. Their feet sunk deep and they had to drag them out. After fifteen minutes' walking, the group began to sweat. Shimon, who walked ahead of the rest searching for solid trails, took off his sweater.

They were all as quiet as the morning in the surrounding empty fields. The path led up the mountain and their breathing got heavier. It still was an hour until they would reach the work site.

At last, the tops of Pardes Hanna appeared. There were two houses on the mountain so far. But the plan was bigger: plant hundreds of dunams of oranges, build houses and water reservoirs, dig paths, install sewers, and settle hundreds of families. Even the plan for each block was ready: on the left—the colonial homes for 800 pounds; on the right—the ones for 500 pounds, as well as the officials from the Palestine Jewish Colonization Association (PICA); and down the mountain—on the side of the Arab villages—the workers' quarter. Pardes Hanna should become the center of all the surrounding colonies and export tens of thousands of cases of oranges all over the world every year.

Shimon panted by the big old tree and said: "They'll make breakfast now, so we won't need to break in the middle of work, not till lunch."

Bashke spread out a couple of newspapers and placed the food on top of them. The guys sat in a circle. A short conversation erupted: What to eat now and what to leave for lunch? It was decided that everyone should eat up to half a cutlet and a tomato, and leave the whole cutlet for lunch. Bashke cut the bread. The group began to eat.

"It's made of meat, you know, the cutlets, I mean," Motke interrupted the silence with irony.

"Oh sure, at least, they were laying next to the meat," Simcha roared out with a full mouth.

"How is it the cooks' fault that Yankl the bursar doesn't them give any money? Two pounds of meat for thirty people . . ."

2

They went to work. The area was desolate: hills, valleys, wild bushes, tree roots, prickly thorns, and hard-clay ground. The men needed to pave a road by digging out hundreds of cubits of earth, dumping it in the valleys, and pulling out the roots.

Two fellows laid rails and placed carts that had holes poked on both sides on top of them. Mad Dovid—an expert in using these carts—pushed a metal plate between the wheels in order to be able to brake. Down the mountain, he whistled through an empty sack, sounding like a real locomotive. In a second corner, they dumped the earth into wheelbarrows and moved it along a long path of wood boards.

Hands went up and down. Carts came and went. They quickly removed the layer of sand and reached the hard clay. Shimon assigned two boys with mattocks to crack open the ground. Motke threw off his shirt and started knocking. The mattock jumped up and cut his hands, his muscles became sore, and his heart ached. The brown clay stared with stubborn eyes. Motke raised his mattock even higher and dropped it with momentum and all his strength.

The work was scorching hot. They took off everything except their hats and shorts. Rivers of sweat poured from them, dripping onto their necks and shoulders. The sun burned mercilessly.

Gnat clouds came from a distance. They filled the air like a dense fog, leeched onto each fellow's naked body, bit him, sank in his sweat, and slid down inside his pants with the thick drops of sweat. Bashke found a preventive tool: She smeared her face with oil. The bugs got stuck and died, so that after work, Bashke's face shone like a scoured copper pot.

At lunchtime, they lay under a tree to rest. The gnats flew after them, encircled them from every direction, and wouldn't let them sleep. Motke ran off to get a look at the road they were building, and the path the boys had already completed.

Along heaps of boulders, girls and boys sat hammering big rocks into pebbles. The hammers slammed at a fast tempo. The stone splashed in their sweaty eyes. Tall Simcha, leaning over a hill, panted heavily and worked as hard as the devil. He wanted to be the best stone smasher, and regularly did three cubic meters a day. But, a couple days ago, as they were pouring the pebbles under the steam roller, they found three large rocks hidden under a mound. The supervisor was furious and threatened to deduct it from the measurement. All the boys yelled that it was Simcha's work . . . that he could never do three cubic meters a day . . . and that's why he sits so bent over, with bitten lips, black glasses, and a sticky wet shirt on his body, banging and banging, never wanting to come down for lunch.

A bit later, the steamroller drove on. The wide stone rollers moved slowly, settling with cold certainty. Zalmen ran in front of the steamroller and spilled water on the bare rocks. The broad wheels and the midday sun quickly dried out the water. The pebbles were poured together and became cemented.

Motke crawled up on the steamroller and looked around: A long white road snaked down the mountain, becoming indistinct among the yellow sands in the distance. From the front, he saw a straight path, checkered in yellow-brown-black, like layers of earth, with fancy holes and ornamented slopes on both sides. In the distance—curved hills, valleys, thorns, holes, roots . . . He stood and gazed for a while, and suddenly an extraordinary happiness took hold of him, swirling in his head. He felt the joy of creation, both around him and in him: the two rows of guys bending over under the hot sun, the naked, sweaty bodies over the blunt shovels, the battle with the stubborn brown clay and the flashing hot rocks. The joy of building boiled up in him: Many houses will be built, enormous amounts of cement will be poured, the road will stretch far, far away, and high, ten-story water reservoirs will rise up and provide water for thousands of greening groves in the sands all around.

By now, all the stone smashers were lying under a tree. Shimon snored, covered in a filthy tablecloth. Zalmen was immersed in a newspaper. Little Bashke loaded the tools. In the middle of all this, the supervisor, Ben Dor, a short, broad-shouldered guy, twenty-seven years of age, with a pimpled face and crooked shoulders, approached them, singing part of a hora, and threw a lustful look at the girl's naked feet. As soon as he sat down in a corner, he interrupted the boys' conversation: "Ay, kibbutzniks, kibbutzniks, you're still set on living on the kibbutz? We played that move already . . . The years of Gdud Ha'avoda are gone . . . The Labor Battalion had forty-four divisions, from north to south, from Metula to Beer Sheva. People worked in wood and metal, in leather and mining, and in whatever else you'd want. Forty-four divisions! Then, they spoke of forming one collective of the entire country, one big commune, building socialism straight up, without revolutions and without 'dictatorship of the proletariat,' as you call it . . . But, what ends up happening is that the commune is really a commune, and meanwhile, the colonist Smilanski plants a few dunams of groves, and Greenberg establishes a nice cement factory and drives around in a car, while the battalionists still run around barefoot . . . Nu, people dispersed and that was that."

The supervisor, Ben Dor, started swaying, immersed in memories, and shook his head: "Ay, those were the days! Yeah, they used to run around barefoot, not giving a damn! Ay, that was living . . . Nowadays, all that dancing, with the singing till midnight . . . and the romances in the Battalion . . ."

Shimon awoke, jumped up, and yelled: "Boys, back to work! It's late already!"

The group made a move. An Arab rode a donkey over the newborn road, leading a camel that followed behind. Ben Dor leaped over, untied the camel, pushed him back, and smacked him. The Arab got scared and began to plead: "Sir, I didn't know I'm not allowed."

The Arab turned back. The supervisor came back to the tree and spoke, out of breath: "I can't stand them, the blacks, enough already! It's okay, we'll build the new colony, expel them from these fields, together with all their huts—for once and for all! And you, fellas, you need to make sure that not even a foot of an Arab worker should step here." The group bit their lips and were silent.

3

Avrom had long since left the kibbutz and become a teacher in some collective. Sara stayed with Ignatz, but the estrangement between them grew every day and living together became more and more difficult.

In the evenings, if she spent them alone with Ignatz, she would fall into a depression. Ignatz sensed the girl's sadness and feared her distance. To ease her sadness, he read books and newspapers out loud to her. She sat next to him, looked at the dense lines for a while until her eyes would start to close, and then it took great effort to keep herself from falling asleep.

Tsille, the "enchanted soul" of the kibbutz, sat in the cobbler's house, bent over on a low stool, trying to set a patch between two rotten pieces of leather on an old shoe. At night she slept very little. She would run around with Theo in the mountains and return home only when the last stars were visible. Yanek walked around sad and gloomy. Zalmen had become extremely serious. In one conversation with Motke he stated very clearly: "We have to look the truth in the eyes; the kibbutz must be destroyed . . ."

Motke was surprised: "Destroy the kibbutz . . . ? That would definitely mean destroying our own lives . . . It's connected with everything here: the saplings, the donkey, the mules, and with the dark, sad nights that have accumulated in the large barrack over a two-year period—and to destroy all of it . . . ?"

Zalmen didn't speak. His gaze alone said: "It's hard for me too; This is the life in which I grew up . . . But we don't need to have illusions . . ."

Meanwhile, discussions in the large barrack proliferated, and the new opinions spread like an epidemic. People were still talking about social revolution and the solution to the Jewish question, as they leaned on tables, encircled by long shadows. The simple crowd swayed their heads toward Zalmen and didn't even want to hear out Ignatz's outdated words. Only one thing weighed on them like a heavy load and didn't let go—the kibbutz. Where would they go if the kibbutz crumbled? What kind of life would they be able to start?

Doubts and uncertainties spread like winter wetness over the camp. The intellectuals exchanged whispers in the corners, looked with real pain at how the crowd was losing faith—and didn't know what to do about it.

The Wild Arabs

1

The donkey jumped and jerked his behind; Ben Dor swayed but stayed immersed in his thoughts. He poked the donkey's neck with a nail and decided to make his way to Khadija, the dark Arab beauty, early in the morning. "Just got to make sure Arish doesn't come."

Arish got up at dawn and led out the mules from their stall. He lived with Khadija and their four children in a tiny room, which the owner had fenced off from the stall. Previously, he had lived there by himself; then he bought Khadija, and later on their children were born. For six years he'd saved up all he could, till he bought his wife. Now, he lives reasonably, thanks to Allah: The owner, Khawadja Yusef, provides an apartment in the stall. The owner's daughters give away their used clothes so his wife and kids have enough.

When he left the yard, everybody in the house was still sleeping. Arish glanced for the last time at the small door to his room where Khadija lay, at her warm, sweet body, and went on his way to the field.

Khadija was born in Khaldia. She didn't wear a veil like the urban women but she wasn't allowed to meet with Arab guys. When she went to the spring she could feel the men's eyes on her. But she never replied to their winks. Zefira, the neighbor's daughter, was once spotted in the field at night with Zuhudi's older son. Zefira's brother, Kamel, stabbed his sister and her lover to death. He's in prison to this day. Khadija knew that they pay less for a girl who had already "loved"; an important bachelor wouldn't buy her at all, other than as a kind of slave.

By the time she turned thirteen she started longing for a man and sang songs about the pretty Zaniba, whom a wealthy, foreign man had kidnapped.

That's when Rasheed used to visit her brother and look at her with hungry eyes. But she knew Rasheed wouldn't buy her; he didn't have any money. One day, Arish came and offered seventy pounds. Her father, and especially her brothers, were reluctant, but Arish offered another ten pounds, and the match was settled.

At her wedding people sang and danced a lot. Afterward, she was led inside to a separate room. A stranger approached her and knocked her down on the floor mat with a smack to her shoulder. That smack signified that she must be subservient and loyal. From then on she began to bring a child into the world every year.

The first to come to her was Khawadja Yusef, who was already an old man with a long beard. He was one of the old colonists in Zikhron Yaakov, with a wife and two daughters Khadija's age. He came and said: "Go up to the attic and throw down hay for the donkey!" Khadija had worked with fellahin and knew you don't give hay to donkeys—they don't like to eat straw or grass—but, when Khawadja Yusef himself says so . . . She didn't run quickly up the ladder. The Khawadja walked after her, probably to make sure she didn't throw down too much—she figured.

In the attic, the Khawadja approached Khadija and hugged her around the waist. She got very frightened and didn't know what to do. The fact was, everything belonged to the Khawadja: the house, the stall, their room, the cows, the livestock . . . Everybody works for him. When the children grow up, they will also work for him . . . Maybe she belongs to the Khawadja too? He must be obeyed . . .

She didn't have much time to think; she lay on a mountain of hay, a couple of hands fussed with her clothes, and a prickly beard scratched her face . . . It was sometime later when Ben Dor came. He gave the children a coin and told them to go buy candy. When they were alone, he went up to her and carried her to the corner.

Khadija got scared; she was in general fearful of the "newcomers," the Yahud, and was constantly in awe of their tricks and magic. The Yahud drove around on whining "iron carts" and harvested grain with big machines that moved across the field with the power of the devil.

She kept her eyes shut and gave herself over without resistance.

That day, Ben Dor arrived in the early dawn hours for the sake of safety. And afterward, as he rode to the highway, he thought it over: It's all pretend: the kibbutzim, the Labor Battalion, the whole ordeal . . . At the end of the day, a person needs to get married, to get serious at some point . . .

Saeed came to Jaffa when the summer ended. There wasn't much to do in the village, so he took a stick in his hand, packed a couple of pitas with zaatar in a sack, and took off along the sandy dirt road, through Tulkarem and Qalqilya, into the big city. In Jaffa, he put a big sack on his shoulder and walked around like a porter, across the market and at the port. At night he slept on an empty spot near King George Avenue, on a soft bed of small paper sacks. During the day he made coffee on a fire between stones and nibbled on cheap dates or semispoiled tomatoes. From the buildings under construction in Tel Aviv, he carried off empty paper sacks and wood chips for the fire. And so, he generated profits from the establishment of the "national home" and lived well under the blue sky of the Land of Israel.

Once, he took a long walk across Tel Aviv. Small children, who knew that Arabs are thieves, turned away from him on the path. Then a group of foreign journalists, who were also on a walk to observe the Jewish city, stared at him as if he were an amazing sight, deriving pleasure from the original, which appeared before them serendipitously.

Saeed hadn't noticed any of it: He walked along General Allenby Street down to the sea and was quite amazed by the pretty shop windows, the cars and businesses, the immobile mannequins, and the loud radios.

With the first rain, Saeed left for the nearby colonies. Golden oranges sparkled among green orange-tree leaves, spreading intoxicating aromas across the entire area. Between the wet fall days, a happy sun shone and dried the fruit. Hope shone in Saeed's heart: He would earn enough for bread, olives, and a wife. By the groves, however, there were picket lines, denying Saeed entry. He wandered around the Jewish colonies, but the picket lines followed him and monitored his steps. Desperate, he went back to the city.

The paper sacks got soaked and thinned out like Saeed's hopes. The rain extinguished the fire between the stones. The stands with the tomatoes and vegetables, from which you used to be able to steal something or get spoiled leftovers, disappeared. The chairs on King George Avenue and from Salahi Market were also gone; the fat Effendis, who had sat on chairs drinking cold lemonade in the summers, moved to the big cafés, sipped warm coffee, and listened to the ringing, attractive melody of the gramophone:

Yama—i-n-ti, o-kh-ti—ay-ni (Mama, you're my sister, you're my eye).

2

Saeed didn't have anything to do. He decided to return to the village, and on the way he visited his sister, Khadija. In the field near Zamarin he noticed a girl. With one hop he stood next to her, and a little while later the girl lay under a dense cactus tree. It didn't go as easy for him as it did for the old Khawadja Yusef or the young Ben Dor. This girl bit, scratched with her nails, and kicked with her feet. She screamed horrendously. But, with violence, Saeed got what he wanted. Afterward, he ran away to the mountains.

A roar broke out in Zikhron Yaakov: "They're raping Jewish girls . . . !"

They started to arrest Arab fellahin; they lined up all the Arab suspects, old and young, in the police corridor, for a confrontation. Shulamit passed by with modest, lowered eyes and searched for her rapist among the young Arabs.

Ben Dor, who just had traveled through the colony of Binyamina, stopped at the kibbutz camp, entered the big barrack, and said: "Nu, what are you going to do now? Organize the Arabs . . . ? Lead a class war with them . . . ? Make an International . . . ? They're a wild people, and you know it; that's what they are . . . !"

At the Mother of the Jewish Colonies

1

Winter began. It was impossible to go out to work in the cold swamp. The young plantings in the groves bent over from the cold and drank rainwater. The road was complete. There was no work in the kibbutz. A cloudy sky hung over the camp. The wind blew into the torn, raggedy, semifallen tents and whistled through the couple of barracks where they had packed the aged, the rheumatics, the invalids, and plain old intellectuals. In the food barrack, the soups became thin and the coffee more bitter. They stopped serving meat altogether. The old, used-up needles screeched and scratched on the gramophone records and there was no money to buy new ones.

Motke lived by himself. His tent flew around in the wind, bent over to the ground, and whistled and whined at night. The water poured through the leaks and flooded his shoes, socks, and satchels.

One night, Ignatz came and told the boys there would be work. A meeting was convened right away. Ignatz gave a report from his trip: The Zionist Executive Board promised to donate another barrack. The Labor Bank will give a loan to plant a larger garden plot, and the Labor Center issued an order to send a group of twenty men for work.

Zalmen sat in a corner and kept silent. Since his anti-Zionist declaration, he did not take part in any political discussions. Ignatz addressed him with a smile: "Well Zalmen, will you go?"

Ignatz always smiled, even on the damp evenings, when jackals cried in the surrounding fields and Sara disappeared somewhere till late at night.

Ignatz also announced, with a serious expression, that the negotiations regarding the purchase of Wadi Hawarit were about to conclude and the kibbutz would likely go there to settle.

Aron Rosenkranz's heart warmed on hearing the news. He circled the crowd and said quietly to each one separately: "In spite of everything, we still have a unifying idea, eh?"

Late at night, they gathered to select twenty men to work in Petah Tikva, the mother of the Jewish colonies. Among the eighty men, it was hard to find twenty healthy ones. Finally, a list of men was released, and people dispersed to go to sleep.

The next morning the girls stitched, sewed, and banged on the machine until they had repaired several blouses and shirts, adorned front and back with yellow and green patches. Sholem walked by like a shadow. He continued to suffer from malaria attacks, was severely weakened from the stabbing near Khaldia, and he was extinguishing like candlelight.

2

The group of twenty men arrived at the colony of Petah Tikva in the evening. They quickly set up their tents near the camp of a neighboring kibbutz. It was muddy and dark. The kibbutz group was young, newly arrived to the land, and the boys—simple boys from small Polish towns—were extremely bored in the evenings. Zalmen spoke with one of them: "How's it going at work?"

"First of all, you've got to have work! We've been sitting at home like this for three weeks now. The individual workers grab a day's work wherever they can on the black market, but us kibbutzniks can go to hell."

"But aren't they saying there's a labor shortage?"

"If they would send away all the Arab workers from the plantations, there'd be even more of a Jewish labor shortage!"

"Why does the Center send new people here, when there are so many more senior people hanging around without work?"

The "greenhorn," who was no more than a couple of weeks in the country, looked at him with surprise: "When there's high unemployment, the masses won't let the Arabs work, and will take their jobs. The work belongs to us, because we're the local labor here and the Arabs are the foreigners!"

The next morning no one worked and they all slept till noon. They hovered around camp all day and in the evening, went for a stroll in the colony. The market was reminiscent of a shtetl: soda-water stands, movie theaters, shops in every entrance, newsstands, and lazy middle-class kids on the sidewalks. In the center of the market, a couple hundred workers hung around, dressed in work clothes or leather windbreakers; they smoked, spat, chatted, and joked around. One worker complained that you can only get hired in a grove for one or two days—so you need to run to the Labor Exchange every night to try to find a new day's work. It takes an hour to walk from the grove to the colony, and then right after supper—you've got to go over to the Exchange. It means everyone is wandering around for entire evenings . . . And when it rains, there's no work at all. In winter, you work at most four days a week . . .

A couple dozen supervisors wandered around among the dark-skinned masses of workers, examining the crowd, weighing their strengths, and searching for the strongest ones to hire for work. Near a soda stand an older man stood leaning on a stick. He was a colonist, observing the workers from afar, like horses in the marketplace, awaiting the supervisors' rulings.

3

On the third day Zalmen and Motke went to check out the Arab Labor Exchange. It was still very early. They spotted a large mass of people when they were still far away.

A couple hundred Arabs in rags and sacks, some sitting and some lying down, squeezed together like herring on the sand, behind fences, in ditches, and on empty barrels. A cloud of flies and bugs hovered around, buzzing in the crowd. Hearing steps, heads rose and immediately lowered—they instantly recognized them as unimportant people's steps. The humming of the flies and gnats and the curses, grunts, and yells combined to create one garbled symphony. A few people busied themselves with breakfast: They pulled filthy napkins from under their shirts, unwrapped a couple of pitas, broke off a piece, and dunked it in minced grass. Then they wrapped the remains back up and shoved them under their shirts. That was their food for a long day's work.

Several supervisors and colonists arrived from the colony. Zalmen recognized the chubby colonist, who had chosen workers on the Jewish Labor Exchange the day before. He paced slowly, measuring his steps, and held a tallis bag under his arm. When he neared the mass of people, he stopped, leaned on his stick, and directed inquisitive looks at the crowd. A couple hundred hands raised toward him and dozens of mouths yelled and pleaded.

Many Arabs displayed their proficiency in Jewish sayings, like: "Yishakeni . . ." (Let him kiss me), "Shema Yisroel . . ." (Hear, O Israel), "Parnose . . ." (livelihood).

The colonist just stood in place and cast his eyes from one to the next, measuring their strength and suitability. At the end, he took a step forward, touched a broad-shouldered Arab with his stick, and jerked him forward. The young Arab jumped up. A wide smile spread out across his white, jagged teeth. His eyes sparkled. The rest of them gazed at him with envy.

4

During the day, an assembly of workers was called in the colony's workers' house. Portraits of Karl Marx, Dr. Herzl, and Trumpeldor hung on the walls. Motke unfolded a flag with a large inscription: "Workers of the World, Unite!"

Young men from various kibbutzim came. The local branch was packed. A short, skinny young man, dressed in an urban suit, crawled up on a bench and yelled: "Comrades! Controlling the workplaces is one of our moral principles. Today, this fight is happening all across the land. Standing firm by hundreds of orchard gates, our comrades refuse entry to cheap Arab labor. The true class struggle is the struggle for one hundred percent Jewish labor. There isn't a colony, or a sector, or a city today where we are not in battle. And we will stand until victory."

After the speech the girls raised up their hands. A circle immediately formed and the crowd broke out in an enthusiastic hora dance. When the group calmed down, the speaker Grabelski divided the crowd into groups, appointed leaders, and sent them off to different groves.

Zalmen and Motke left with about ten guys altogether. They walked for half an hour, the entire time in the sand, and remained silent. Several workers passed by with spades. Finally, they arrived at the designated grove. The group leader placed the boys along a path, between acacia trees that led to the small door. A couple of guys smoked cigarettes; others sat absentmindedly fiddling with stones. Some were off to the side telling jokes and laughing out loud.

A quarter hour later, the first Arab workers arrived. They ran quickly, fearful of being late. Recognizing the group of Jewish "Khawadjas," they halted, uncertain and startled. One of them, a tall man in wide Arab trousers and a European jacket, took it upon himself to go first. The others followed him, their eyes lowered and terrified. A group of Jewish workers blocked the path. Their leader screamed out in Arabic: "Mafish Tariq! There isn't any path!"

"But the Khawadja told us to come for work!"

The guys in the area stood up and surrounded the few Arab workers. Another couple of Arabs arrived at the work site. Jewish boys ran over from another grove. The back rows pressed forward. Some Arabs were pale and scared; the others were sullen, with bitten lips and glowing eyes. Zalmen's heart began to beat hard: Here comes a brawl . . .

But they didn't brawl. The Arabs retreated. They sat down along the prickly fence and waited. A few of them rolled cigarettes. A couple unwrapped filthy cloths and ate breakfast: pitas with salty olives. A couple minutes later, the broad-shouldered Arab tried again to enter the grove. The guys immediately rose and blocked his path and he sat back down among the Arabs sprawled on the ground.

Zalmen was fed up with sitting in one place. He grabbed Motke and they went off walking. On the way he said: "We've always regarded the kibbutz as the exemplar of the new society; it turns out, it is actually the vanguard of expelling Arabs from their work and from their land . . ."

They meandered between groves. Oranges winked between green leaves. Loaded automobiles moaned in the soft sand. Workers bent on their knees in the wet sand, crawled up ladders, cut fruit, and carried heavy baskets on their shoulders. The groves were speckled with gold. Not far away, by the gate of a grove, they encountered a second picket line. It was the same scene: Jewish workers with short pants occupied the footpath, while ragged Arabs waited patiently by the fence; perhaps they will be able to earn money for food nonetheless.

Zalmen stopped dead in his tracks, terrified: He recognized Mustafa, with whom he had brawled over the land in Khaldia. Mustafa was lying down with a bunch of Arabs by the grove and Saeed was next to him. The Jewish workers weren't allowing them entry. Recognizing Zalmen, Mustafa grew pale and raised his hand, as if to shield himself. He quickly said something to his neighbors.

"How are you, Mustafa?" Zalmen came closer, trying to smile.

"Thanks be to Allah." Mustafa immediately became bolder, although he was unsure about Zalmen's geniality.

"So we meet again . . ." Zalmen mumbled, not knowing how to begin.

"Yes, when there's no land, we meet by the groves . . . So, you came out here to keep us from working . . . ? In Hadera too, they don't let an Arab set foot inside the groves. You know, it was our land . . ."

"Let's take a walk," Zalmen called to him. Mustafa hesitated for a while. He looked around hesitantly and stood up. A young Arab, who was lying next to him, also got up and followed him.

"This is my friend; goes by Saeed," said Mustafa.

"What happened in the end with that piece of land that we plowed?" Zalmen asked.

"What could happen? Nothing happened. It set off a series of trials and investigations. Wasting money over and over: for lawyers, for travel to the bigger cities. And how could we even get any money? Every day they dragged half of the village to the judge. The Khadj and the Effendi got money for a lawyer from the Yahud. Well, it's all over; we lost the land. And after the first rain, they were already planting there—and over here, they don't even permit us to work . . . !"

Zalmen and Motke quietly parted ways with Mustafa and his friend and left, ashamed.

In the evening Zalmen went to Dovid and announced: "I came here to work and I won't go to any more picket lines."

The next day at dawn, Zalmen ran over a deep, sandy path to a far-away grove where he found work. Other workers arrived out of breath and stretched out on the ground, tired from the long, difficult road. The supervisor arrived right away and commanded: "Well, fellas, get up! It's time . . . !"

In every four-meter-wide row, he placed four men with spades in their hands; it took several of them to plow up a meter-wide strip all along the row. Once the first of them made a move, the others started chopping the clay ground one after another, taking short breaks throughout.

Zalmen was the second in his row. The spade—a broad, thick iron one with a short wooden handle—was heavy and ripped at his body from below. He had to bend over constantly. The upper layer of ground was soft when hit with the spade, which made it even harder for him. But the deeper, drier clay layers were hard as rock and pushed back on the spade. Zalmen grit his teeth and banged with all his strength. His spade jumped back and tore at his hands and arms. "Hey, dig deeper! The supervisor is going to measure . . ."

He heard heavy panting from behind him. He turned around and noticed: An older, gray-haired Arab was in the row, banging so hard with his spade that his eyes bulged out of their sockets.

In the afternoon, the focus turned to fertilizing the ground. Two guys raked manure from a big mountain into their sacks and the rest carried it on their bare shoulders. Zalmen walked bent over under the heavy sack of manure. The path became more and more difficult to navigate. The stooped, low branches stretched over the entire width of the row; the boys in the front got on their knees and began to crawl on all fours.

A hot vapor emanated from the wet manure, warming his bare shoulder. A yellow fluid streamed out of the sack, mixed with his sweat, and flowed down his pants. The branches scratched his uncovered body and poked his eyes. The supervisor stood by with a stick and urged: "Hey, keep it moving!"

The afternoon hours passed slowly. The deeper the workers dug into the mountain, the hotter the manure became, and the stronger it steamed onto their shoulders. Zalmen spun back and forth like a blind horse, with the full sack and the empty sack, and tried to abandon his filthy, aching body, so he wouldn't sense the stench of the gooey fluid in which he was totally drenched.

5

It had already turned dark when people started leaving the grove. The group walked back, hanging their heads down and barely dragging their legs. When Zalmen got to camp his steps were slow and weary. The tents were empty. In the barrack, there were only a couple of fellows back from work, who were gulping thick soup. Zalmen asked in the kitchen: "Where the heck is everyone?"

"They're off picketing."

"Now? At night?"

"Yep! They found out the colonists are going to bring Arab workers into the groves at night."

Zalmen was upset by the events of the past few days and couldn't sit still. He slurped up some soup with a bit of bread, took a bite of smoked kasha, and left for the colony. He wandered around the market for a bit, where, as on every evening, a couple hundred workers stood around. Later he went into the side alleys, where he could hear the sound of a whiny Arabic gramophone singing.

Along an alley, cut off from the general marketplace, was a long stretch of cafés. Arabs sat on the stoops, on little benches, drinking black coffee and smoking hookahs. Old-fashioned gramophones with long needles scratched, producing long, throaty squeaks. The water in the hookahs boiled; cigarette smoke and a sharp smell of coffee spread through the nearby alley. Ragged workers who had not had the privilege to work that day, stood across from the cafés, extending their heads and noses toward the fragrant vapors and gazing enviously at their fortunate friends. A Jewish passerby, noticing Zalmen, stopped him and launched into a conversation, apparently wanting to pour out his heart to someone: "Well, what do you say about that? This is what it's come to in our oldest colony. Arab cafés in the middle of the village!! Why, there's even colonists who rent out their stables as apartments to the Arabs . . ."

In the middle of the night, sounds and shrieks woke Zalmen up. He got up in a fright and asked around: "Who is it? What happened?" Nobody answered. The sounds came from the food barrack. He wrapped himself in a blanket and trudged through the mud to the barrack. All the guys stood in a circle, hollering. Mad Dovid sat on a chair in the middle and a girl tightened a bandanna on his head. When he saw Zalmen, Khayim Lilienblum grumbled from a corner: "There's your Arabs for you! They've split open our heads . . ."

Motke told Zalmen the whole story: "We stood by the grove gate. When the Arab workers came, we wouldn't let them inside to work. A brawl erupted in the dark. The Arabs yelled and called for help. There was a Bedouin camp nearby. A large group of men and women lashed out at us with sticks and wild screams: 'Get the Yahud!' Several guys got their heads split open and barely got out of there alive."

Motke was silent for a while; and then he declared: "Enough, I'm not going to picket lines anymore . . . !"

"Tomorrow the papers are going to print," Zalmen said quietly, "that the Arabs attacked peaceful young men . . ."

The next evening, a demonstration took place in the colony. A couple hundred kibbutzniks walked the streets chanting: "Bread and work! Down with foreign labor! We demand a hundred percent Jewish labor!" When they passed by the home of the colonist Mangel, they shattered his window. On the same night there was a meeting in the kibbutz's camp.

A heated discussion blazed about Jewish capitalists, Jewish workers, and Arabs. Zalmen spoke and for the first time clearly expressed his opinion: "First of all, where did these Jewish capitalists get their money to plant groves? From the sky?—No, they earned it from Italian, American, Polish, Russian, and various other workers. So what kind of exclusive right do Jewish workers have here to work on these plantations? Second, it's not even a question of rights. The pickets create a chasm of hate between the workers of two peoples. The conscious Jewish workers must show solidarity with the Arabs and reject the picketing. But, if you're a

Zionist—then you do have to go to the pickets and you must occupy the land. Because in this country there are enough unemployed without the Jewish aliyah, and landless fellahin are also in abundance here. So it's only with the 'conquest of labor' and 'conquest of land' that you can build your 'national home.' Whoever is against that must also be against Zionism altogether!"

The gathering lasted until late at night. The exhausted guys occasionally dozed off at the tables or dragged themselves out of the barrack.

With a Bowed Head

1

In the "red barrack"—that's what they called the barrack where Zalmen, Motke, and many other left-wingers lived—a big group of simple folk sat together and spoke from the heart: "Ach, if only I had a cigarette right now . . . !"

"Y'think there'd be any harm in having something to eat?"

"I get hungry again straight after dinner . . ."

"And me—right after lunch . . ."

"All over the world the jobless are protesting; we should also have a hunger march . . ."

A demonstration took place at camp. Tall Simcha dipped a dry rag in kerosene, tied it to a pole, and lit it up. He marched with the burning torch at the edge of the crowd. Behind him, a group banged on empty gasoline cans with thick poles. Half-naked girls and boys, wrapped in winter coats, jumped out of the tents and mixed in among the marchers. The crowd grew larger—in five minutes almost the entire kibbutz was on its feet.

The demonstrators marched across the narrow paths between the tents. Mad Dovid lifted the flaps and pulled naked people out of their beds by their feet. The torch fires illuminated the edges of the sleeping tents and the desolated fields around them. The banging made its loud sound in the silence of the night and woke sleeping people in the nearby colony.

The crowd halted near the reading hall. Berele Pfeifer dragged out a pack of volumes of the socialist newspaper *Davar* and lit it on fire. Moyshke roared with a hoarse voice: "Down with the liars! We want work and bread!"

Ignatz didn't go to the demonstration. He was extremely upset: His whole life he had been one of the most leftist ones in the movement, always creating oppositions; he spoke of joining the pan-Arab movement and fighting against imperialism, establishing the first joint union with the Arab workers, and so on. But it didn't help: They regarded him as all talk and attacked him for nonetheless supporting redeeming the land and capturing the workplaces.

He sat in Yekhiel's room and lowered his head in silence. Yanek, Yankl the bursar, and Shaul sat around him with worried faces. Khayim Lilienblum lay on the bed staring up at the ceiling. Khayim felt drawn to the loud crowd in the barrack and embarrassed to be sitting with these moralists when the whole younger crowd was over there. He resented the "old guard" of the kibbutz.

Shaul spoke first: "The leftists are multiplying among us like rabbits," he said.

"Someday soon you'd need a lantern to find a Zionist on our kibbutz!" Yekhiel shook his head.

2

The next day, in the evening, the bell called the kibbutz for a gathering. The crowd crawled from their tents lazily and slowly, rubbing their sleepy eyes. Everybody knew: The discussion about working for the colonists would continue.

Yanek lectured: "We can get five jobs for stable workers with the colonists. They will pay one-and-a-half pounds plus food. I think that in the present moment the kibbutz needs to take on these jobs." From the corner, Simkhe yelled: "This is wage suppression! The Histadrut wants us to force the wages down to the level of Arab wages in order to expel the Arab workers from the colony."

Zalmen spoke along the same lines. The guys around the tables were angry. The labor distributor's offer had been discussed five times by now and was rejected every time. No one wanted to speak any more. And then Yankl the bursar crawled out of a corner and, with furrowed eyebrows, roared: "The deficit is growing . . . We don't have credit anymore . . . In a few days there won't be any food left, not even for the sick! They'll have to starve . . ."

He went back to his corner. Everybody was silent and the secretary put the question to a vote. A majority of the kibbutz voted for Yanek's proposal. But when it came time to offer candidates for the work, everyone abstained. The atmosphere in the barrack became painfully still. The crowd sat with their heads bowed. Suddenly the door opened and Sara entered the barrack. She approached the first table, sat down, and quietly said: "I'm letting you know that I'm leaving the kibbutz . . ."

No one reacted. The only sound was the deep breathing of the eighty people in the barrack. They sat like that for a couple of seconds. Ignatz looked around, frightened. He sensed a deep emptiness in the barrack, as if Sara weren't there. Suddenly he stood up, hunched over a little, and began to speak: "This business of not going working for the colonists, and yesterday's protest, they are symptoms of collapse. We must save the kibbutz, our constructive creation! The kibbutz—that's our last lifeline, the only shore where our wandering ship of life can find a harbor . . . We've burned all the bridges behind us—we don't have a path back! All around us, out there, there is a horrible loneliness lurking . . . An empty world . . . We are all alone . . . Alone . . ."

By his last words his voice had broken and he had begun to stoop like he was about to faint. Leybl, the nurturing type, ran out to bring water. Around the tables, guys and girls gazed around with terrified eyes.

3

Zalmen received frequent letters from Motke. He was traveling around the country and visiting various kibbutzim and cities. Zalmen would read these letters out loud to Dora and Hanke. Motke wrote:

Dear Zalmen,

Today, I arrived in the "Emek." From the top of the mountain, the entire Jezreel Valley had already been laid out before my eyes:

plowed fields, scattered little villages and collectives, herds of live-stock, and harvested vineyards. Nevertheless, my heart thumped: here's a valley where Jewish farmers live, plow, sow, plant, and build, where there are young Jewish men who don't live on commerce and air. They follow the plow, wait for the rain, and teach their children to ride horses—And we're really supposed to tear it all out by the roots because it's tied to imperialism? I'm against land theft and conquest of labor, but what are we actually supposed to do with all of this that already exists?

You say that the Jewish workers need to join in the struggle of the Arab masses for their freedom. That means that the small farm-ers of the Emek also need to join in the struggle. But it's also the case that the anti-imperialist movement opposes this very Emek, which was recently built on the ruins of the Arab villages! So how can these Jewish villages—even the poor ones—join the Arab revo-lutionary movement?

*   *   *

Alfa collective. Jezreel Valley.

Dear Zalmen,

I've passed through many collectives. People have greeted me every-where in a friendly manner, given me food and a place to sleep, and haven't asked who I am. I'm living with a fellow by the name of Nyomke. He's a shepherd, works from morning till night. In winter, he goes with the herd to the field and stands there under the pouring rain from 4:00 AM till 4:00 PM. Then, he milks the sheep till 7:00. At 8:00, he falls like a sheaf onto the bed, warms up his drenched organs, and sleeps till 3:30 AM. Then he runs back to work. He asked me: "Look, I work all day long. I don't wrong anybody. Why are you saying I'm a fascist?"

Alfa.

Seriously, what are we supposed to do?—In Poland, Jewish towns are dying of hunger, in Germany, anti-Semitism rises, in Romania there are pogroms to this day—Where should the Jewish youth go? Aren't there enough of them packing the prisons of Poland?

Nyomke is in the field now. His girlfriend, Rokhl, is working in the garden. What would Nyomke have done there in the Polish shtetl? Do you remember the hundreds of guys wandering around there, neither dead or alive? Here, as long as the Jewish Yishuv is Zionist, and for as long as there are Arabs in the land, every Jewish man must strive to keep the imperialists in the country. Because the moment they leave, it'll mean an end to their Zionist dreams. There are only two options for how to resolve this situation: Either the Jewish Yishuv will give up its Zionism, in which case the antagonism between it and the majority population will cease, or, Zionism will eradicate the Arabs from the land . . .

4

Friday night, they still danced the horas and polkas. Tall Theo played harmonica, tapped his feet to the beat, and gracefully bowed to the short girls. In the barrack area, girls and boys sat on the tables and chairs. Hanke laughed loudly. Sholem Bomshteyn brought in a couple of radishes and sliced a few pieces of bread.

Zalmen didn't dance. Neither did Shaul. He placed a ladder against the window of the barrack and climbed up it. A white moon drifted in the sky above his head. Minneh stood by his legs holding his hand. The night was humid and fragrant. They gazed at the mountains in the distance, and at the dancing circles in the barrack, and to them, the world seemed enchanted.

At eleven o'clock at night, when the crowd in the barrack thinned out, Shloymke turned on the gramophone. A pleading voice spread over the camp:

Gey—ni—sht—a—ve—k, Don't go away,
Zog—az—bist—nokh may—ne, Say that you be still mine.

Everyone had left. Dora was left alone and feeling sad. She tossed her head, half-closed her eyes, and sank, under the sound of the gloomy melody, into a sea of thoughts. She saw floating images: Yanka, her younger sister, a very pretty girl whom all the boys adore, while she, Dora, is almost always alone. Zalmen is strong and smart but the new work swallows him whole, and he has no time for her. Zalmen says one has to be strong; one has to work for the "cause."

* * *

Zalmen came in very late, almost at dawn. But Dora recognized his steps and sat up sleepy-headed on the bed. She called him: "Come here? What time is it? How are you?"

Zalmen sat down on the bed and took her hand. The room was dark. Dora didn't see Zalmen's eyes; she only felt his hand trembling. He sat next to her on the bed for a long time. He spoke softly: "I feel like I'm finally on a path, after long wanderings. I've found my faith again and I know what my purpose is in the world. You've read *The Life of Klim Samgin* by Gorky? It describes a similar group to ours. They're constantly talking: Narodnaya members, barefoot types, longhaired poets, liberals, coiffed intellectuals, all they do is talk and talk nonstop—and all it adds up to is a bunch of bourgeoisie that you should just take a broom to, and sweep them all out with the garbage!" He paused. Dora lay her hand on his shoulder and searched for his eyes in the dark.

"And it's just like that with us," he spoke on. "We're not only sinking in a political swamp, with things like 'conquest of labor,' driving the fellahin from their land, and such, but we're also sinking in a spiritual swamp: The entire so-called new culture of ours is nothing more than a continuation of bourgeois decay and sentimental romanticism. And it's not a coincidence that phrases like 'new man,' 'new society,' and 'model collectives' are used to disguise acts such as keeping vigil against workers, whose sole sin is that they're not Jews. There's a rot and a spiritual 'boom' reigning here . . ."

"So are people leaving the kibbutz?" Dora asked in an anxious voice.

"At the moment, not yet. They are actually workers here as well."

Dark-skinned Yisrulik, who'd been snoring on the other bed, woke up, wiped his eyes, and said in a sleepy voice in the dark emptiness of the room: "Zalmen, oh, Zalmen . . . Can you hear me . . . ? It is actually possible to be a good Zionist and a good socialist at the same time. For example: say you organize all the Arab workers! So what? Would that harm the Jewish aliyah? No, just the opposite! If the Arabs are organized to get equal pay with the Jews, then no one will take Arab workers, only Jewish workers. Everything will work out: The Arabs would be organized, you wouldn't have to go picketing, and only Jews would work in the groves . . . ? What do you say to that, Zalmen?"

5

The kibbutz was in turmoil. One morning, Communist pamphlets were found in all the tents and barracks: "Support the Arab Liberation Movement."

They didn't know who had distributed the pamphlets. Ignatz ran from one tent to the other, gathered up the pamphlets, and burned them.

Zalmen regularly disappeared after work. He met Milner somewhere in the mountains and talked with him at length. Often, in the evenings, there was a group that disappeared from camp. No one saw them—not in the colony, not in the reading room, and not in the barrack. They only came back in the morning to drink coffee and run to work.

It was confusing for everyone: They all looked at each other with suspicion and didn't know who was "out" and who was "in." Tall Theo chatted for a long time with Zalmen. Yanek walked around with Ignatz and had a serious expression on his face. Tsille ran between the two of them and completely lost her senses in the general turbulence. She decided she must live on her own, so she moved out of the camp and rented a room in the colony. But she wasn't permitted to be on her own. At night, Yanek and Theo took turns running over there. The situation caused a lot of bad blood in the kibbutz.

Amid this commotion, Motke returned from the Jezreel Valley. Right away, Zalmen took him off for a long walk in the fields: "Are you're still struggling?" he asked him.

"Yeah, I'm in this 'movement.' But many questions are still unclear for me."

"We'll discuss all those questions later; meanwhile, I just want to tell you that there are many."

"How did you get ahold of them?"

"It's a long story. It started when I heard that a group in our kibbutz, the simplest guys at that, who don't discuss anything, were planning to leave for Birobidzhan. Get it?"

"Ho-ho, that's no small distance: from the Jordan to the Amur River! That's so interesting: How's that going to work? It would mean having two Jewish Peoples: One to guard the Soviet border against Japanese imperialism, and the other—guarding the British empire against an Arab uprising . . . ! There were," he continued ironically, "two regions to where Jews hadn't spread yet: the Middle East and the Far East; and now, they're gonna spread Jews to those two places as well, ha-ha-ha . . ."

Straight after eating, Motke went off to Milner's. He laid out on the cot and prepared to listen. Milner began a long lecture on the history of Jewish colonization, Arab movements, and English politics. Motke was listening at the beginning, but then he plunged into thoughts of Hanke and dozed off. He woke up several times and saw that Milner was still talking and wasn't looking at him at all so he fell back asleep. By the end, he heard Milner talking about the occurrences of 1929 but didn't understand anything. When Milner finished, Motke asked him with a sleepy voice: "OK, but you can't call it an uprising when they attack yeshiva students in Hebron and slaughter them!"

"I'm not saying it's an uprising. But you do have to understand the entire evolution of this situation . . ."

"Here-an-evolution, there-an-evolution," Motke rubbed his shoulder on the wall. "I don't get anything at this point." It occurred to him that it must be late already and ran off to camp.

It was dark in the large barrack. Hanke stood there waiting all alone. She looked serious but wasn't angry that he had come so late.

"Come!" She took him by the hand and led him outside. Her hand was warm and pressed his wide palm. Outside was dark, and a thin rain had been falling. Not a soul appeared in the muted camp. A silence spread out far, reaching through the empty fields; only the water in the wadi made a sound. They crawled slowly past the tents and onto the wide path leading

to the mountains. Hanke took him by the hand and silently walked forward. Soon the muddy land of the camp disappeared; their feet sunk in
soft sand and their shoes got soaked. They were alone in the wide, black
outdoors. A cloudy sky hung over their heads, and they fixed their gazes
on the misty mountains, which stretched all around along the horizon.

On the way, they found an old, wrecked car and crawled into the
driver's seat. Motke embraced her and drank the water from her wet hair.
Hanke trembled from the cold; she shoved her hands under his shirt and
stroked his warm, naked chest. Motke whispered: "Do you like being here
with me like this . . . ?"

Motke was intoxicated by her warmth. After a bit of silence, Hanke
straightened herself up, shook him off her, and asked softly: "Nu, what,
did you talk with Milner?"

"Yeah, we talked. You think he had any answers?"

"And what are you thinking of doing now, staying on the kibbutz?"

"No, not that, I have to move on, even with these doubts . . . It's hard
for me to leave the kibbutz . . . What is there waiting for me outside the
kibbutz? A wife, kids, a furnished apartment, a servant in the kitchen . . .
a regular bourgeois life . . ."

Outside, the rain got stronger and made pinging sounds on the small
tin roof. There was a damp cold blowing in the air.

They walked back slowly. Suddenly Motke raised his hand and pointed,
in a fright: "Look over there, something's burning!"

She looked out and spotted a fire not far off, rising to the reddening
sky. They heard a few shots: The guards were waking up the colony. Suddenly, the windows lit up. Doors creaked. half-dressed, confused people
ran here and there, asking what had happened. The dogs barked and
wailed. On the water tower, the bell rang, full of dread . . .

Who Ripped Out the Trees?

1

Rain soaked the clay earth, surrounded the village with sticky mud, and streamed through the perforated roof into the cold hut. The wet branches between the stones in the corner refused to burn. They were scorching and filling up the room with smoke. By the wall, old Farris lay on a mat, wrapped in rags and coughing nonstop.

"Give me some warm water!" He raised his head to ask of Saeed.

Saeed carried the little pot over to him from where it stood on the stones. The water was cold, smoky, and covered with a dense film of soot. Farris fell back down on the mat and shivered from cold. Saeed left to go to his sister Fatma, for some warm water. There were five dirty, half-naked children scattered on the small room's floor. Skinny, scratched bodies peeked out of their torn shirts. Through the thin little wall, a child's cry snuck in from another room: His brother Ali had lived there, but he was still in jail after that big brawl on the southern land.

Fatma, a tall slim woman, was busy with the fire, shoving in little branches, blowing between the bricks, and placing wood chips to dry. Then she set to kneading dough and shaping it like a thin matzah. "Where's Musa?" asked Saeed.

"At the market, looking for work. People say that the Jewish supervisor is going to come for workers—so he's standing out there in the rain all day."

She put the dough on a half-domed, sooty baking tin. As the hot baking tin roasted, the thin sheet of dough turned brown from the heat and ash, and the smell of smoked bread wafted over the fumy room. The children immediately stopped fighting, ran to the fire, and reached out small, filthy little hands to their mother: "Yama, a piece of pita . . ."

The mother pushed the children to the side and put the baked pitas on a high shelf so they wouldn't be able to reach them. Saeed left with the empty little pot. In the yard he heard a "meh" from a little lamb and stopped. The gate opened and Rasheed entered the yard with a lamb on his back.

"Markhaba, Rasheed, welcome!" Saeed yelled.

"Alekum salam. How's your old man?"

"Sick . . . he's surely going to die soon . . ."

"It's good I came. At least he'll taste a warm piece of lamb before his death and not go hungry to the next world! We'll slaughter it soon and make a feast."

A house full of people came to the neighborhood feast. Rasheed made a declaration from the middle of the room: "Be happy, be happy, dear children; soon there won't even be any more sheep!"

"Why?"

"The land of Wadi Hawarit has already been sold and the machines of the Yahud are going to come to drive out the shepherds soon."

There was an uproar in the little room. Saeed gave Rasheed's sleeve a tug: "Is that true?"

"Solid truth. If people don't help the Bedouins, in a few months there won't be any trace of them left in the wadi."

They left to talk things over with Mustafa. When they walked back, the street was dominated by dead silence. The clay huts swam in the mud from both sides of the path. Smoke drifted from the tiny little windows. In the empty yards, hungry dogs clung to the wet walls and shivered from the cold. And groves bloomed on the surrounding hills. Saplings stood lined up in straight rows drinking rainwater. On a faraway hill lurked a couple of tall, fortified houses—the new colony of the Yahud.

"We can't let them go on planting," Rasheed said sharply. "That's the most important thing—not to let them plant!"

"You're right," responded Saeed; "all the fellahin need to rise up and tear out the orchards."

2

At night there was a large crowd at Farris's. The smell of the roasted lamb brought in women and children from the entire street. The men sat cross-legged in a circle in the middle. The children wandered in the back. The women stood in a corner near the door.

Suddenly it got quiet. The door opened and two hands presented a large baking platter. A brown, smoked whole lamb lay on the platter with its head and feet attached. White rice peeked out of its open belly. All eyes were fixated on that brown and white object.

Dozens of hands immediately moved to the lamb: people tore and shredded pieces of meat, cupped heaps of rice in their hands, and packed it all in their wide-open mouths. The cracking of the bones and the smacking of lips aroused their appetites.

The children's hungry little eyes gleamed. They brought their little heads forward. Several fellahin threw them pieces of meat. The little ones nibbled and smeared their hands and faces with fat. When a couple of old folks stood up and wiped their lips and mustaches with the laps of their robes, the kids jumped into the empty spots. The cluster of little bodies, pressed together, extended their little hands toward the torn lamb.

The children, who hadn't eaten fat for a long time now, fell asleep right away. The unusual satiety and cigarette smoke muddled their heads. Stretched out on their tummies, they lay on the clay floor and snored. In the second room, the women sat around the dish of leftovers. The men continued to smoke and while waiting for something, spoke quietly to one another. At some point, Rasheed came in and said, right at the threshold: "The Jewish guards are walking around in the colony. The gates are locked; we must think of something!"

Saeed stood embarrassed in the middle of the room. The crowd was silent, pondering. "You're all children," a voice interjected from a corner, "if you can't accomplish such a task!"

It was Camal, whose nickname in the village was "the Turk," because he had served in the Turkish army and always recounted miracles and wonders from faraway cities and lands. In the other room, the women were still licking their fingers and chattering. The crowd of fellahin stepped outside and dispersed in two directions: The older ones went off to the mountain, and the younger ones hid behind the village's last houses.

A fire flared on the mountain. People waved shawls and yelled wildly. A cloud of smoke rose up to the sky. The voices carried over the silence of the night and awoke the surrounding villages. The lights turned on in the high concrete houses. The guards blew their whistles, gathered together, and ran around, dazed, afraid to climb up the mountain.

Rasheed crawled over the fence with the rest of the Arabs. He leaped, ran over to a sapling, and pulled it with all his might. The sapling didn't budge. Rasheed grabbed it with both hands and twisted it to the side. The sapling bent with a whistle, made a cracking sound, and got its green crown stuck into the mud.

The wind whistled. Rasheed was jumping like crazy from one tree to the next, bending, breaking, and stomping his feet. The thin tree trunks cracked under his hands and fell like slaughtered bodies onto the ground. His hands bled from the prickly little branches, but he was drunk with vengeance and didn't feel any pain . . .

3

At nine in the morning, two large automobiles drove up the twisted mountain path between the village's little clay houses making panting noises. The whistling frightened the dogs in the yards and the children in their houses. Mothers stuck their heads through the windows and said a quiet prayer. The men put on innocent facial expressions and continued to warm their feet by the smoky fires, as if it didn't concern them. In the market, English soldiers and Arab policemen slid out of the cars. An Arab officer went straight to the head of the village, the Mukhtar, and asked: "Who ripped out the trees?"

"I don't know, Effendi. By Allah, I don't know!"

"We'll punish the entire village; tell us who tore them up!"

"Not me, Effendi, not me."

The officer spoke quietly with the Arab police and then, with guns in their hands, they headed straight off to the shepherds' neighborhood and scattered among the houses. A couple of minutes later, they returned, steering a group of fellahin; old and young, male and female. There were even small children straggling behind and crying. The English soldiers stood quietly by the automobiles and gazed indifferently at the gathered crowd.

"Who ripped the trees out last night?" Silence. No one responded.

The officer's eyes scanned the mute faces of the rounded-up men and women and pointed out several young Arabs: "Take them to the car."

Policemen surrounded the Arabs. A few women burst into tears. Small children jumped on their mothers and wailed. The soldiers pushed away the women, shoved the Arabs inside the cars, and pulled the curtains over the windows. The cars drove away. The crowd dispersed home bitterly, holding their heads low.

Several days later, the arrested Arabs returned. Almost all of them had been beaten and could barely stand on their own feet. Rasheed had two chipped teeth. The market filled with circles of people talking nonstop: "It's like this everywhere . . . The prison is full of fellahin . . . They're fighting for the sold land . . . ! The fellahin in Infiat village had a shootout with the Yahud . . ."

Soon after, a document from the government arrived addressed to the Mukhtar: the village must pay a 500-pound fine. The Mukhtar officially announced it to the whole village. That's when the real outcry began.

"Oy, children, my dear children," moaned an old fellah, "there's no playing with the devil . . ."

The next morning, something unexpected occurred and the news spread through the village like lightning: "Trees are still getting ripped out in the groves nearby . . ."

The village feared new fines. The elders placed lookouts around the village to prevent the hotheaded youngsters from uprooting any more trees, and at a meeting in the mosque, the fine was distributed among all the farmers who could pay. They wrote out IOUs, Shukri Effendi lent money, and a delegation traveled to the city of Tulkarem with the sum of money.

But the situation didn't quiet down. Over the next few nights, trees continued to get torn out. Again came divisions of soldiers from the city. The police rounded up the entire village in the marketplace and started an investigation. Next, they drove the livestock out of their stalls. Barefoot fellahin, hunched old people, and wrinkled, weary mothers stood in one corner of the market; in another—meager cows, bald donkeys, and disheveled goats. The officer announced: "If you don't pay a new fine of one hundred pounds immediately, we will confiscate your livestock."

An elderly fellah stepped out from the crowd; leaning on a stick, limping a little, he approached the officer, dragged a key out of his pocket, and extended it to him: "Here you go, Effendi! Here, have my key. You can take the whole house . . ."

The women wailed, with the children's assistance. The uprooting of trees continued. In Khaldia, the police rounded up fifty young Arabs, shackled them in chains in the middle of the marketplace, and drove them away to prison. But the identity of the uprooters remained unknown.

After All Is Said and Done

1

Ignatz ended his speech with a concrete proposal: The kibbutz should send guard units to protect the groves. "We, the Labor Zionist movement, and we alone," he added, "are bringing about the establishment of the Land of Israel. The rich plantation owners have never wanted to sacrifice their interests for the building of the country. So therefore, the obligation to protect the Jewish economy lies with us."

"But that means protecting the rich landowners' plantations!" Zalmen interjected. Zalmen argued against sending guards and addressed the heart of the matter, declaring: "I don't think that uprooting trees is the right combat strategy, but it's foolish to present the fellahin as bandits and robbers. It's only the fellahin who were expelled from their lands who are resisting with guerrilla tactics."

That's when the discussion heated up and went up to the wide dirt path. Simkhe the carriage driver stood up and asked: "Does that mean the Arabs can do whatever they please, because they're conducting a war of defense with guerrilla tactics? Go tell them to do some pogroms too while you're at it!"

"Pogroms? When you're standing at the groves like guard dogs to keep hungry workers away from their jobs? When you're snatching the poor fellahin's last dunams of land with the help of the English police?—That's just how to provoke pogroms! Only the struggle against the Jewish conquest of labor and land can stop pogroms!"

The meeting lasted late and decided nothing. The discussion was postponed until the next day. Zalmen and Motke left right after the meeting to look for Milner in the colony. But he was nowhere to be found. It started to drizzle. Exhausted from treading in the sand, they veered to the large tent with the old tractors. Searching for a place to hide from the rain, Motke suddenly noticed the silhouette of a person who was startled and looking around fearfully. Motke had an impulse to scream, but the other man leaned to him and whispered: "Shush, it's me!"

Motke recognized Milner and asked with great astonishment what he was doing there. But Milner didn't answer. He pulled both guys to the ground and, holding one hand to his lips as a signal to stay silent, he held them down with the other hand. They shut up and listened to a low conversation between two people: "So we gotta call off the action completely?"

"I think so. It's becoming suspicious. The fellahin are losing their grip."

"All right, so let them lose their grip. Then they can let 'er rip, but for now, we have to do the ripping . . ."

"But all the youth of Khaldia have been arrested. The old folks don't want to rip out trees, and one Arab guard has found some clues and begun to chatter . . ."

"What a shame! The mood in the country right now is so opportune . . . Everyone is in favor of a Jewish legion . . . ! For us Revisionists, this situation is a perfect opportunity . . ."

"We have to wait for directives from the Center . . ."

The voices became quieter and distant. Milner led Motke and Zalmen out to the main road and turned to them urgently: "Did you hear? The Revisionists themselves did the uprooting. . . . The Arabs from Khaldia told me so too . . . The first or the second time it was Arabs, but then they stopped. But the Revisionists liked the idea: They could take advantage of the situation and demand a Jewish legion. What's more, the impoverished fellahin would have to sell their land to pay the collective taxes . . . So they started ripping out the trees themselves . . ."

"But how did you get here?"

"I got lost and wanted to wait out the rain here . . . That was a consultation from the Revisionist leader . . . I know them . . ."

"The Arabs from Khaldia, you say . . ." Zalmen replied with his body trembling, "they've got to hear about this . . ."

2

By the time Zalmen and Motke returned from Khaldia to camp, the entire colony knew that what they were saying was indeed true: The kibbutz was no more than a "nest of Communists who are helping the Arabs rip out groves full of trees." They stared at them through the windows mumbling: "spies for the Arabs . . ."

The local Histadrut summoned Ignatz, talked with him for an entire evening, and made it clear that the whole kibbutz would be expelled from the Haganah military force until it kicked out the Communists. And before leaving, they added: "The colonists won't give work to the kibbutz either . . . and they're right . . . !"

Very late that same night, a kibbutz meeting expelled Zalmen and Motke and allocated one-and-a-half pounds for their expenses. Simkhe moaned in a dark corner: "The best fellas! Who's gonna be left here?"

At the next day's meeting, Theo got up and declared: "I'm letting you know that I'm leaving the kibbutz . . ." One evening later, Shimon announced: "For ideological reasons, I'm also leaving the kibbutz . . ." Now, everyone dreaded the evenings: "Who'll leave today? Who will stay?" The members wandered like ghosts around the camp mumbling: "The kibbutz is falling apart . . . falling apart . . ." The departing members, however, remained in the camp for the meantime, because the bursar didn't have any money for their expenses. Simme from Kamionka gave them some things: three shirts, two blouses, and a torn winter coat. And then one evening Simme also announced: "I'm leaving."

3

The camp was empty, even though no one had left yet; the tents drooped, raggedy as ever, and the guys restlessly paced around the barrack, not knowing what to do with themselves. The farm work had been neglected and the garden was covered in tall, prickly thorns.

Since announcing she was leaving the kibbutz, Hanke had the feeling of tears poking at her throat. At dinner time, she got up from her bowl, spilling soup, and ran out of the barrack. For the rest of the evening, she wandered around the little pathways in the fields behind camp.

Zalmen left the next morning. Simkhe occupied himself with the mules for longer than usual, unable to properly fasten their collars. He grumbled incomprehensible words in fury and kicked the donkey's behind in anger. Everyone emerged from the barracks and tents, lined up around the wagon, and said goodbye to Zalmen. Ignatz smiled bitterly, as he usually did in such moments, and held Zalmen's hand for a long time. Hanke climbed up on the back seat and clung to Dora. Zalmen took a look around: at the open tents, the unplowed garden, and the crouching donkey, but avoiding the glances of his sad friends. Simkhe pulled the reins and yelled with a desperate voice: "Heigh-Ho, dead-beats! I'll be your undertaker! I'll drive you to the train one at a time . . ."

4

Khomme traveled to the city to get her teeth fixed. She got work at the house of a manufacturer named Kalmanovich and lived in a small attic apartment. In three months' time—she calculated—she would be able to start getting her first fillings.

By day, she scrubbed the eight rooms' floors, rubbed the bronze handles with Sidol, and cooked thick soups. In the evening, she lay in bed in her little room thinking about the kibbutz. When boys came from the kibbutz, she grilled them for the latest news and listened eagerly to everything that had happened there.

Once, they told her Ignatz would come. That day, the Kalmanovich family ate burned cutlets and the handles in the hall didn't shine as usual. In turn, Khomme's eyes glimmered and joy bubbled in her heart. A couple of weeks later, Ignatz arrived. In the evening, they went to the cinema together. On the way back, Khomme walked close beside him and heard her own heartbeats.

Ignatz was silent. She found his silence understandable. She walked next to him and waited: certainly they'd start talking at home.

Ignatz stood still in her small attic room, leaning against the wall and looking around with a gloomy smile. Suddenly, he took her by the hand and sat her down on the bed. He played with her fingers and gazed across the room to the dark corner. They sat this way for a while, as the small lamp began to burn out. Khomme got up, poured gasoline into it, spilled a lot on the floor, and sat back down, with her head bowed.

Ignatz dragged himself up, stepped into the corner and started to undress. "A body needs to sleep," he mumbled. Khomme turned her head and examined him: He stood barefoot, pulling down his pants. His underwear was white. Despair seized her: "Already? That's all there is . . . ? No, no, no!"

She threw herself on the bed, buried her face in the palms of her hands, and burst into tears.

Ignatz ran over and hugged her: "What's the matter? What happened?"

She sobbed and didn't answer. He felt the tremble of her body and began to comfort her: "We'll build a new family . . . a new life . . ." he bent over her. "We'll have a baby . . ."

"A baby?"

She raised her head. The tears on her eyelids sparkled in the lamp's glow. Ignatz soothed her and calmed her down. He stroked her hair. Her body trembled all over. He got up and turned off the lamp.

PART III

"GOD AND MONEY"

Mustafa Learns About Women—and Capitalism

1

When Mustafa came to Atlit, hairy Mahmud gave him a long interrogation—Where is he from? What do his parents do?—and at the end he asked him: "So, you got a wife?" And, as Mustafa didn't have a wife, Mahmud gave him a look of contempt and returned to scraping out the larger stones of a tall pile of gravel with a mattock.

Throughout the four deep stone quarries it was loud as hell and the earth trembled. Above, on the mountain, air compressors banged with a groan and a clamor, long chisels drilled meter-long holes in the stony boulder, and hammers raised and lowered with a bang. The echoes reverberated in the faraway villages and mountains surrounding them.

Mustafa worked down below. He poured gravel into wheelbarrows that came and went nonstop. The whistle of the locomotives merged with the ambient sound and drilled into his ears and into his bones. Mustafa pressed the long shovel into the gravel and poured it into the wheelbarrows . . . Clouds of dust rose and choked his throat. For a time, an image passed through his eyes: a green field, a tall camel slowly walking, a laden donkey driving away flies with his tail, a fellah singing a trilled, sad melody. It seemed like a dream to him, like a picture from a different world. When was that?

A scream of "Barud! Rock explosion, barud!" woke him from his thoughts. Around him, all the workers threw down their tools and went running up the mountain. He ran with them and pressed himself, like all the rest, against a high wall. A little red flag fluttered on the mountain.

A worker lit a match, touched it to a wick, and ran away. Immediately it thundered, and a well of stones, earth, and dust sprayed in the air. Large hunks of stone rose very high and fell with a crack. Pieces of earth fell right at their feet.

When he returned to his hole, he didn't recognize the place. A two-meter-wide wall had fallen down to a depth of eighteen meters along the quarry and completely covered it. The large crane smoothly twisted its hook and lowered it into the ditch. Workers tied a large rock to the hook with thick chains. The crane made a cracking sound and lifted a rock of approximately ten meters cubed into the air. A drowsy man in a cap sat in the crane; he was smoking a cigarette and operating it by slowly turning a wheel. The large rock also turned in the air, as if guided by a holy incantation. Up high, electric air compressors continued to bang iron chisels into the mountain rock and prepared holes for new dynamite explosions.

2

It was loud from dawn till dusk. Throats choked with the smell of dynamite and stone dust. The supervisor, an older Arab in a long-striped coat and a white shawl on his head, stood leaning on a stick yelling nonstop: "Yallah, fellas! Yallah, ya shabab!"

A hot sun burned overhead. Filthy clothes glued to hot bodies. Small, pointy pebbles crawled inside torn shoes and poked naked feet. Locomotives whistled, long rows of wagons stood in their arrangement, the crane raised and lowered, shovels poured gravel, full wagons rolled off with a creak and a shriek, and new walls exploded, flew in the air, and fell to the pit. The wagons transported the rocks to Haifa and dropped them into the sea. The waves covered the rocks. The sea devoured nonstop.

The echo of dynamite explosions reached the faraway villages. It was from building the port of Haifa. Some of the Arab workers lived nearby and spent the night in their villages, but the workers from faraway villages stayed and slept over in Atlit.

In the evening, Mustafa sat on the white sand at the seacoast. Along the coast, hundreds of workers lay stretched out on rags and crumpled

coats. A row of bonfires blazed with coffee brewing on them. The workers untied their sacks—sooty pitas, olives, tomatoes, and onions—and
started eating. After supper, the older ones left, because it was too
cold for them to sleep on the beach. Tired from a long day's work, they
dragged themselves to the quarry, crawled into the torn-out holes, scrambled inside the warmed gravel, covered themselves in rags, and fell
asleep like rocks. The younger ones remained on the clean white sand,
sang for a bit, and chatted. Then, one by one, they fell asleep. The echoes
of their snoring drowned out the sound of the nearby waves.

Mustafa felt dizzy from all the machine noises, and it was hard for him
to hold up his head. He soon fell asleep, but rough dreams haunted him,
like heavy nightmares, and he woke up frightened, with a shriek. In the
moonlight he could see the forms of people lying wrapped in coats and
snoring. The fires were out. A cool wind blew in from the sea, bringing
the roar of waves. Nearby, someone moaned. A jackal howled somewhere.
He lay gazing for a while, until his eyes shut and he fell back asleep. He
woke up to the holler: "get up for work!" which engulfed the entire beach
encampment.

3

They worked seven days a week, but got off early on Sunday. One Sunday,
Muhammad said to Mustafa: "You've got some pocket change already!
Let's go to Haifa."

Mustafa agreed. He wanted to see the city. The recent events in the
village, the coerced land sales, Effendi's close friendship with the Jewish
land buyers, and the work in the quarry weighed on him bitterly, and
he wanted some diversion. The city attracted him with stories of a great
unfamiliar life.

The train traveled along the seacoast and stopped near the port that
was being built. The city welcomed them with a rain of nighttime light,
which flooded from all over: from high poles, from large glass windows,
and from a faraway ship in the heart of the sea. A cold wind blew on
sweaty Mustafa, and he covered himself with his jacket. "You're cold?"

asked Mahmud. "Come with me; you'll warm up." And he pointed with his eyes. Mustafa understood, felt his blood boil, and lowered his head, so Muhammad wouldn't see his eyes.

They went into one of the cafés by the coast. It was a large room, fully furnished with little chairs and tables. In the corners were booths decked in greenery; at the front, a curtained stage with a piano. A fat Arab approached them, asked what they wanted, and yelled in a crude bass voice across the entire room: "Two coffees, ya, Salim!!"

Soon the curtain opened. A girl started banging on the piano. Onto the stage came a chubby, half-naked dancer with a shawl thrown over her breasts. She snapped her fingers, tapped her left foot, and sang her heart out:

Zanuba, Zanubatna
Rachat, vaazavatna!

Zanuba went and left us!

A couple dozen young Arabs and several older fishermen were sitting in the hall on low chairs. A couple of rich Effendis with tall tarbooshes sat in the booths leaning on the walls. As soon as the dancer stepped out, the old fishermen settled in their seats, half-closed their eyes, and glimpsed the dancer from under their lowered brows. After singing for a while, the dancer began twirling in a circle, tapping her feet and wiggling her whole body simultaneously. Her dress flew up and revealed hips and little gray shorts. Next, she stayed in one place and began belly dancing: She turned her belly back and forth with quick movements, shook her hips, jiggled her breasts, hurled forward, bent over with outstretched arms and closed eyes, and finally fell on her shoulder, as if she had fainted from desire.

Silence dominated the hall. People breathed heavily and excitedly. All the young Arabs gazed with twinkling eyes on the prone woman. The curtain closed. The music played again. A slender young woman with long hair and sad eyes came onstage. She wore a long, black dress buttoned up to her neck and two little bells on her hands. She stood at the edge of the stage, set her posture, and began to sing a sad song of longing. Mahmud, excited, pulled Mustafa by his sleeve and uttered: "Come on, it's taking too long here."

They walked around the narrow streets, leading from the downtown Arab city to the new Jewish neighborhood, Hadar HaCarmel. Mahmud surveyed the houses, searching and peeking in the windows, and finally went into a stone courtyard, and from there, into a house. From a side room came a chubby Arab woman, about forty years old. When she walked, the goiter of her triple chin shook. From under her baggy dress, her full, sagging breasts, chubby belly, and thick, heavy feet hung out. She spoke quietly with Mahmud. He followed the woman into a little side room.

4

They both climbed a narrow road up the mountain to the Jewish neighborhood, Hadar HaCarmel. Mustafa's mind raced nonstop: "Is that really love? Is that all there is . . . ? And Shukri Effendi's youngest wife, whom he bought, is she also like that . . . ?"

The streets on Hadar HaCarmel were lively. The cafés were full of people. Young couples, men and women, strolled with their arms around each other, radio music echoed everywhere, advertisements sprayed light from windows. The street buzzed. Movie posters called out from the fences: "The Love Parade" and "I Love Only You."

Large, illuminated letters announced: "The First Girl." Mustafa gave Mahmud a pull, and they went inside and sat on the first free bench near the screen. The film was already playing; the pictures and captions ran at a blinding speed. Before their eyes spun ornate palaces, automobiles rushing by on wide streets, beautiful women smiling splendidly and kissing gently, eyes laughing, wine pouring, diamonds sparkling, rich gentlemen in top hats smoking thick cigars . . . A wave of beauty and wealth poured from the screen and baffled them.

As the film ended, the crowd rose quickly and made its way to the door. Mustafa left with the stragglers. The street swarmed with young couples embracing and rushing home through various alleys. A couple of cars made loud noises as they drove off with well-groomed ladies and gentlemen. Mustafa scanned the streaming masses and thought: "Surely, a house with a clean bed and a wife awaits them . . . and where are we going to sleep . . . ?"

"Let's go walk back," Mahmud urged him. "We'll get to Atlit by dawn."

Mustafa tapped his pocket and noticed he didn't have any money left. Even so, he didn't feel like walking to Atlit. After the palaces, women, and dance clubs that had just passed through the scene, he dreaded the quarry. "Let's spend the night somewhere here."

"OK, let's go up the mountain; we'll snooze in the trees there."

They left the city and climbed up a rocky mountain with sparse vegetation. Overhead shone the villas from Mount Carmel and the stars from the great Allah. The day and night buzzed in Mustafa's head scrambling dozens of images: the large ships and the breakwaters at sea; camps of displaced Bedouins and fellahin in Atlit and at the port; the glamorous women and golden palaces in faraway worlds. To whom does it all belong? It was all one long twisted ribbon, and he couldn't locate its end. Suddenly he heard a sound in the bushes and stopped. Their long, black shadows walked parallel to them, lay flat, and dispersed in the shine of the moon over the bushes and stones.

"Probably hashish smokers," said Mahmud quietly.

From behind a tree suddenly peeked a head with eyes. Then another one and another.

Mustafa looked and cried out with joy and astonishment: "Zalmen, what are you doing here? You don't have anywhere to sleep either . . . ?" They all sat down on the grass. The two workers who were with Zalmen parted ways with him and went off quickly, over the rocky path. Mahmud leaned on a tree and fell into a deep sleep.

"It's hard to understand this world," Mustafa began. "My head is spinning and I can't make sense of everything I've seen. Why are the English so strong they can take the entire world for themselves? And who owns everything here? All of this?" He waved his hand at the port. "Who's actually the boss?"

Zalmen thought for a while and began to speak quietly: "There isn't one boss; there's an entire class, a class of the wealthy . . . That's who's the boss . . . For thousands of years, there's been a war between the poor class and the wealthy class . . . It's hard to understand, but it is ultimately understandable."

"And among the Ingleyz there're also two classes?"

"Yes! But the rich Ingleyz oppress and rob many peoples, and they throw little bones to their workers, so they won't rebel and instead help to rule over the disenfranchised peoples."

To the right, on a mountaintop, a lighthouse was spinning and throwing light into their faces every few minutes. Far off at sea stood gigantic ships spraying the coast with dark light: concrete storehouses, white oil reservoirs, stone breakwaters, and a few remaining palms. Mustafa looked down and shuddered, sensing the power of the "foreigners," who rule over the coasts of the entire world. It seemed they had an incomprehensible, superhuman strength. He abruptly interrupted Zalmen: "So the rich are really going to rule forever?"

"Forever? No. We, all the workers, need to unite, then we'll free ourselves."

"But the Ingleyz are so powerful!"

"The workers can overcome everything! In one country the workers liberated themselves. Now, everything there belongs to the workers: the factories, the ships, the ports . . . everything! There was a person who lived there, people called him . . ."

5

Rasheed dashed like a shadow through the narrow twisting alleys of the Haifa suburb, walked a few minutes along the sea, and arrived at a tall mosque's door. It was dark inside. Through the window, in the weak outdoor light, he could only see ornate Koranic phrases on the walls. He leaned on the wall and waited.

At sea, the digging machines rattled. The three-story city rose opposite it. The villas from the mountaintop reached the sky and spread wide bundles of light. The illuminated church steeple spun, showing the way to the distant ships. Lower down, young Hadar HaCarmel lay with its wide roads, lighted shop windows, and noise from the cars and radios.

Way below, sunk in darkness, slept the Arab old city. In its alleys, only a few cafés shone. Old-fashioned gramophones scratched with long needles, ending their melodies in a tremulous squeak. Plump female dancers showed their naked feet. English soldiers bargained with pimps against dark gates: "I swear by Allah, a golden girl, a 'Francoise.'"

"You're lying like a mercenary! That's an old Arab corpse . . ."

Rasheed was impatient: Why don't they come . . . ? A storm of hatred rampaged in his heart: Every day the sirens blast in the port. English soldiers and young Yahud keep coming into the country. The two stone walls jut into the ocean like sharp-edged horns of a monstrous animal and create a calm refuge for the foreign ships. They build warehouses and kerosine boilers. New Jewish blocks clasp the Arab city by force and strangle it.

From a distance, quiet steps approached. Several shadows passed and asked: "Is the sheikh already here?"

"No, not yet . . ."

Again it was quiet. Finally, an old man in a tall fez arrived, wrapped in a white shawl. He opened the door. A couple fellahin in wide pants and a couple young urban Arabs entered. They sat down in a circle on the ground. The old man examined each one separately and began singing prayers. Everybody swayed quietly. When the old man finished, one of the fellahin said: "The Sheikh in our village says there will be a big gathering in Jaffa, where people will protest the Ingleyz and Yahud."

"People have been protesting for years now and it's not helping," said Rasheed in a hoarse voice. "We are dying out and the foreigners multiply. We've got to do something immediately . . . !"

The old man shook his head: "As it is written in the holy Koran: Muhammad's faith is in the sword . . ."

"And where will we get weapons?" asked the fellah.

"We'll get weapons, and dynamite too . . ."

For a time it was quiet. Then Rasheed turned to the fellah: "Do you fear death? Look, in any case we're going down . . . ! The foreigners' colonies bloom and our villages get demolished one by one . . . No reason to be afraid though—we're getting thrown into the sea one way or another! Their machines make loud noises and destroy our villages . . ."

"And what about the Ingleyz with their soldiers and ships?" a fellah pointed his finger through the window.

"If they kill one of us—thousands of us should launch a holy war. There are few foreigners, and many of us . . ."

The old man rose: "morning is coming. It will be light soon. Today we will swear loyalty to our brotherly bond. Next time, we'll devise a precise plan."

It got quiet. The old man pulled two candles out of his pocket and placed them in the middle of the circle. He rocked and read the oath aloud. They all shut their eyes and repeated quietly: "I swear . . . to defend . . . the holy faith . . . and the holy land . . . to my last drop of blood . . . to fight with blood and sword . . . against the foreign enemies . . ."

Darkness lurked in the corners of the mosque. The tallow candles alone threw their gloomy shine on the fellahin's long robes, the closed eyes and stern silent faces of the rocking people, and on the holy ornate verses on the walls.

*   *   *

"It's late already and we have to go to work today," Mustafa interjected and began to wake Mahmud. "We won't sleep here in any case!"

"Where do you work?" asked Zalmen.

"In Atlit!"

Mahmud woke up and started to scratch, curse, and expectorate. Angry and surprised, he looked around and didn't understand where in the world he was.

"Let's get to work; the machines will begin to crow soon!"

"They ought to crow for my death already," cursed Mahmud, lifting himself from his spot. "How much longer will they work us like donkeys . . . ?" Zalmen stood up, said goodbye, and they went their separate ways. Mustafa and Mahmud went down a narrow path through trees and bushes. They swayed from fatigue and their feet thudded on the stones.

6

For the entire lunch break, Mustafa and Zalmen circled the large crane, which was standing with its hook lowered in the middle of the quarry. It was impossible to do anything, because the machinist was constantly staring out of his cabin smoking cigarettes. It was only a couple of minutes before going back to work that the machinist dozed off. Mustafa quickly scrambled up on a rock and tied the stack of papers to the tip of the hook with a thin rope. He jumped down and tapped Zalmen: "Now scram . . . ! We'll meet in Haifa at eight."

A few minutes later the machines whistled. The crowd lazily rose to work. The whirring started up, and a cloud of dust covered the sweaty people. Mustafa banged a mattock on the mountain of gravel and looked out one eye at the crane's hook, as it spun back and forth, lifting large rocks, and hurling them magically into the little wagons. Suddenly, the bundle ripped. A wind blew in from the sea, lifted the pages up and spread them all over the quarries. For a couple of minutes, all work paused. The mass of workers and fellahin sprung to the leaflets and grabbed them in their hands. A few literate people read them aloud. A clamor broke out. An engineer ran out from the office. The supervisors pounced on the workers and dragged them back to work. At dusk, when it started to get dark, Rasheed snuck into the quarry where they kept the dynamite . . .

Children and Camels
in the First Jewish City

1

The gramophone stood on a small set of shelves of black, polished wood. Ben Yishai wandered across the room, his hands in his pockets, humming the melody that the gramophone had been playing:

Camel—my—ca-m-el, ca-mel my ca-me-l,
You're a f-rie-nd to me in Zif-Zif!

Meanwhile, he glanced with pleasure at the furniture, which they—he and his wife Shulamit—had purchased a couple weeks earlier; it was square-shaped, and from the same polished wood. Thick curtains hung on the windows and, on the walls, a large portrait of Dr. Herzl, a group of halutzim in a swamp, and a gray Jew in a yarmulke: Shulamit's deceased grandfather. The pink lampshade and the embroidered pillows on the divan perfected the mélange of office and boudoir. Upon visiting for the first time, Shulamit's friend, who years prior had graduated from a three-year Russian pre-gymnasium program, declared: "*Ochen' kharasho*, very nice! It's both intimate and comfortable. All you need to hang up is a landscape . . . Nowadays landscapes are very modern . . . !"

2

Ben Yishai thought to himself:
Back in the days before the city of Tel Aviv existed, and the youth lived in tents on the seacoast, people ran around barefoot, hatless, and in

shorts. In the evening, they danced in the streets and sang: "Am Yisrael Chai" till the walls trembled. Friday evening, the circles stretched from Allenby to Jaffa Street, and after dancing they stole bread from bourgeois shelves and went to sleep on the sand by the ocean. What a life—free as birds! In "those days," people dried out the swamps a bit! The group of friends got ague, rheumatism, and other chronic diseases! But those days are long gone.

With the first money he earned, he built a small one-story house and then sold it during the period of the Great Aliyah in 1924. Later, when the crisis began, and people flocked back from whence they had come, leaving their houses in the midst of construction; he built, for the same money, a small two-story house. And then he sold that house during the next housing-construction "rush." And Ben Yishai carried on like that: selling houses at a time of aliyah and building them at a time of crisis.

Once, he went to Herzl Street, polished off a glass of cold lemonade, and tugged the sleeve of a middle-aged Jew, who was passing by in a rush: "Adon Har-Zahav (Mr. Goldberg)," he began in Hebrew but quickly transitioned to Yiddish, "do you have a little plot of land for me? Nothing large—no more than six hundred square feet!"

Ben Yishai's dream was a house on Balfour Street, with front windows directly facing Ohel Shem, where the great poet Malkin celebrates Oneg-Shabbes every Friday night. Goldberg, a Jew with a pointy little beard and an unbuttoned jacket, under which snaked a thin gold chain, stopped and, short of breath, began to wipe the sweat off his face: "What heat, what heat, like a coal oven."

Goldberg didn't have much time: lots rose up by the minute like yeast, and then were grabbed up by the handful. And preparations were underway for the real boom: Hitler himself had one foot in the halls of power, so everyone expected a large emigration of German Jews, and the land speculation was only just beginning. But Ben Yishai was an old client and pulled him in closer: "Come inside Café Geulah; we'll talk with my partner and figure it out."

Café Geulah was smoke-filled and steamy inside, like a small-town bathhouse. For the first minute, Ben Yishai couldn't see anything; he only heard voices cutting through the dense cloud ringing in Yiddish, Arabic, Hebrew, English, and German: "Thirty franks for one square foot of rocks? Do I stammer?" yelled a deep voice in German.

"If you don't want it, never mind!"

"Petah-Tikvah is just the same as Tel Aviv!" Screamed someone in another corner.

"What could be more important than having a house in our own land—I ask you?"

Soon Ben Yishai's eyes adjusted to the fog and he started to distinguish different faces. Old and young people, men and women, dark Arabs and white Jews, sat on wide, white sofas, around small polished, glass-covered tables, arguing with one another and gesturing with their hands and with every body part. An Arab with a long mustache, sipping black coffee, spoke half Yiddish, half Arabic, and half Hebrew: "*Bikhyat Allah, ikh zol azoy zoykhe zayn tsu hobn nakhes, mafish migrash kazeh bekhamishim funt!*" (By the life of Allah, I should be honored to have the pleasure, but there isn't such a lot for fifty pounds!)

A dark-skinned, older couple stood in a corner and argued in an incomprehensible Caucasian dialect. He, the man, a pot-bellied Jew, forty-five years of age, with small eyeglasses on his nose, wandered around waving a thick cane and interrupted a young German man: "*Yekkes*, the German Jews, don't have any faith! We buy, we build, we sell, and that's it. The wheel turns, and the Jews make a living."

The deal was completed that same day: Ben Yishai bought the empty lot in Balfour Street. On Saturday, Ben Yishai strutted home along Allenby Street to enjoy Shabbes lunch, half of which was leftovers, reheated on a quiet primus, from the previous day, and the other half of which was cooked on Shabbes—a kind of fusion between cholent and regular food. Afterward, he lowered the shades and reclined on the wide divan to take a snooze.

He woke up exactly on time and headed straight away to the Oneg-Shabbes. The large hall was already full of bourgeois Jews, young people, and tourists. The poet Malkin spoke about how "Jews are in exile and the Shekhinah is in exile." He made hand gestures, dropped countless quotations from scripture, mixed in flashy ideas, and brought examples from poets, prophets, and philosophers. The audience licked their fingers and hollered with enthusiasm. Ben Yishai listened as well for the first few minutes, but then he couldn't overcome the temptation, and started looking out the window. He imagined the blossoming of the house he would build directly facing the windows, and he quickly calculated: three floors with three apartments—nine apartments. An apartment of three rooms and a kitchen—six pounds. The upper apartments—five-and-a-half pounds. So how much does it all add up to?

He glanced through the window and caught a glimpse of the tall menorah on the water tower. His enthusiasm increased even further: a trifle, thousands of Jewish children go to that very menorah at Hanukkah to light candles! Where can you find another city in the world with a menorah on its water tower? And his, Ben Yishai's, house will be directly facing the menorah!

*   *   *

Today, Ben Yishai is a model homeowner of the first Jewish city. He has a three-story house and owns, with two partners, a small brick factory by the name of Geulah (Redemption) Partnership. He is a member of the Histadrut, never buys vegetables from the Arabs, and smokes cigarettes secretly on the Sabbath. He sends his father-in-law an etrog for Sukkot every year and reads the socialist Hebrew newspaper. During the High Holidays, he goes to the large synagogue and is extremely pleased that the Histadrut has implemented the laws of kashrut in its cooperative kitchens and is very observant of kashrut in its private kitchens. In his youth, he was militant and had more of a temper. He had even broken windowpanes at a meeting hall, where, out in the open, in the heart of the Jewish city, people were speaking Yiddish. But recently, having reached his thirties, he had settled down.

Tel Aviv is proud of its resident, Ben Yishai, and Ben Yishai likewise is proud of Tel Aviv. It is a city where the poor little Yemenites, who work a whole year for five piasters a day, have the right to dance in the streets on Purim, where people pray in the middle of Allenby Street, and the mayor officially kisses the Queen Esther chosen at the Purim ball.

3

The record *Camel, My Camel* died out and the needle scratched at the end. Ben Yishai removed the arm and set in Sirota's "Rosh Chodesh" and, after that, Yossele Rosenblatt's "Umipney Chatuainu" (Because of Our Sins). A knock on the door interrupted Ben Yishai's reminisces about the bygone days. He opened the door and recognized Zalmen: "Oh, Zalmen, how are you?!" he yelled.

Zalmen entered the room and cautiously examined the furniture and the pictures. He had known Ben Yishai for many years. Because he hadn't been working lately, he had come to ask a favor. "Well, say something, Zalmen!" Ben Yishai nudged him. "How's it going in the kibbutz? A nice life, ha? You suffer a bit, but, in return, the idealism, the romanticism!"

Zalmen mumbled and made a gesture with his head. Ben Yishai gathered that Zalmen was no longer a kibbutznik, and proceeded to change course: "Nu, that's it? Done with the kibbutz? Why didn't I know earlier? Between you and me: that's a business for young fellows, but not for serious people. You know, when you grow up, you look to serious matters . . . Shulamit, come here, we have a guest!"

Shulamit came in quickly with a surprised look. Recognizing Zalmen, she cried: "How are you, Zalmen?" and warmly shook his hand. She assessed him closely and declared with a contented ease: "So you've grown up, ha? Sit down, Zalmen, I'll bring you tea right away. Have you seen our kids yet? Poke inside the kitchen, and you'll see them!"

At the kitchen table sat a couple of healthy, rosy-cheeked children; an eight-year-old boy and a six-year-old girl. Shulamit pointed at the boy: "See, his name is Amnon, what a genuinely Israeli name, eh?" The two children, noticing the stranger, turned shy and quiet. They were full by now and wanted to play. She forced them to stay at the table while complaining to Zalmen about the maid, who had left over an hour ago already, and still hadn't come back: "Why are there even maids here in Tel Aviv? They just do a little sweep around the house and then run off . . . !"

The children played and made a racket. The little boy, Amnon, latched on to Zalmen's feet and neighed like a horse. The girl, Shoshana, climbed onto his shoulder. Shulamit got angry and yelled at the girl: "Are you going to eat or not? I'm going to call an Arab already!"

Little Shoshana got scared and began to eat. She knew Arabs were thieves who snatch little kids. The children often overheard conversations in the house: people were mad at the neighbor, Dina, who hired an Arab woman to do her laundry; about how Mr. Shlomovitch, who has been in the country for only three years, has an Arab in the building in the center of Tel Aviv; how other Jews pride themselves on never buying vegetables from Arabs. Once, after hearing all those stories, little Amnon, together with a couple of other young boys, beat up a little Arab boy who was gathering trash in the Tel Aviv streets and chased away his donkey. The Arab boy wept so much that Amnon himself began to sober up . . . When the children were done eating, Zalmen went into the other room with Ben Yishai to talk business.

"Work? What? There's not enough work in the village? It's, as you know, the greatest sin for our people," Ben Yishai shook his head, "that people abandon our most important post, the village, and come into the city. Why, the essence of a people, its base, as you know, are the farmers, the village people!"

Zalmen was silent. Unexpectedly, Ben Dor arrived. He greeted the others and promptly took out a booklet, inspected long calculations, and checked the accounts. He had arrived in the city a few months earlier and started a business with Ben Yishai: They provided sand and gravel to the Tel Aviv construction sites. There was a lot of building construction in Tel Aviv, and so a great need for sand to make concrete. The business had grown and required more and more workers to dig the gravel, which they called *zifzif*, at the beach, and more camels to transport the sand from the sea to the highway.

Ben Yishai was able to buy as many camels as his heart desired. The camels were not organized. As for workers, he wasn't allowed to exploit them, as was explicitly stated in the statutes of the Histadrut. And Ben Yishai was a loyal member of the organization. What can you do, though? It is necessary, after all, to hire workers. So, Ben Yishai created a collective, a *kvutse*, with Ben Dor, and registered it with the Histadrut. A collective may, as is well known, hire workers. So they named the collective "The Flying Camel" and hired workers.

The gravel was dug at the beach. They quickly filled up the holes with water; the barefoot workers routinely came down with rheumatism. They were all members of the Histadrut, like Ben Yishai, but they earned only thirty piaster a day. The camels didn't have any idea that they were working in a socialist collective—they carried the gravel, shook their chins and humps, and grabbed full mouths of prickly cactus leaves in the process. Ben Yishai and Ben Dor were pleased.

*   *   *

Shulamit put her kids to sleep and came into the salon. She sat down near Zalmen, gave a sweet little sigh, and uttered softly and with love: "This is what it's like to become your own boss, with a house, a budget, kids, worries." Ben Yishai took out a cigarette, lit it, inhaled, and said to Zalmen: "Nu, good. Tomorrow I'll speak with Avraham Greenberg about bringing you on to work. He's a construction entrepreneur. With me, you understand, there's a kind of collective. . . . The Histadrut supervises . . . We're not permitted to hire workers just like that . . ."

Comrade Gamzu and Comrade Katz

1

Moshe Gamzu carried all the responsibility for the campaign "In Favor of Jewish Labor" in Tel Aviv. In the morning, Gamzu headed to the Histadrut House by the beach. There, he verified the list of the volunteer and conscripted workers who had gone to the picket lines that day. Then he went to his office and began writing an article for the Hebrew Socialist newspaper:

"Betrayal of the national idea! Two Arabs work at the contractor Zilbershteyn's building. Doctor Greenfeld is building a house with pure Arab zifzif! On Baal Shem Tov Street, the stones for the foundation of the yeshiva under construction were brought by Arab drivers. The lemonade maker Vitman is buying ice from an Arab factory in Jaffa . . ."

Gamzu tried to focus on writing his article, but the telephone continually interrupted him. His number was known across the entire city. A couple of days earlier, the Histadrut had published a call: "Every member who sees an Arab working should immediately telephone comrade Gamzu, telephone number 363. Roaming picket lines will immediately show up to that location. We are calling all citizens of the first Jewish city—workers, merchants, store owners, and contractors—to take part in the struggle for Jewish labor." Moshe Gamzu's work was therefore very challenging, demanding a lot of concentration, devotion, and energy. It started with Shabbes: Arab shoe shiners set up, free as birds, polished Jewish shoes, and brought the money from the Jewish city to Jaffa. Jewish policemen had even established protocols, but it didn't help at all—savages who act as if it doesn't matter . . . ! During the week, ragged Arabs arrived, dressed in sacks, and worked all the various jobs for a pittance: carried sacks, loaded trucks, pushed wheelbarrows, and did all the hard labor.

The picket line let a small group into the city center, and the rest into the surrounding alleys.

2

Katz was a bricklayer. He always worked for the building contractor Avraham Greenberg. But that day, he didn't go to work: The Histadrut required him to participate in a picket line. He was a bit annoyed, because he already paid twenty piaster a month to the "Fund for Jewish Labor," but nevertheless he went out. On Ferdinand Lassalle Street, he spotted an Arab taking down a barrel from a wagon. The barrel was large and heavy. The Arab positioned the barrel on his back, uttered a moan, put it back on the wagon, and again tried to put it on himself. His face twitched and his knees trembled. He decided, after this task, to buy bread and a bit of halva to gobble down. He directed another stare at the barrel, bent down, placed his back underneath, and stretched out his hands to his back to grab the edges. Katz ran over to him and gave him a shove: "What are you doing?"

"I'm working."

"No work is needed. Get lost!"

The Arab shot a terrified look around. Meanwhile a couple of other guys showed up from the picket line and surrounded him. The porter understood what was going on—he lowered his head and slowly walked away, mumbling under his breath.

Not far away, in Halutzim Alley, Shimoni—who had recently arrived from Poland—spotted an Arab shoveling sand. So he ran over to him and tried to grab the shovel from his hand. But the Arab didn't let him. He extended his naked chest and stared with a pair of fiery black eyes. Shimoni shoved him with both hands, and the Arab fell on the concrete. He got right back up, held his bruised knee with his hand, and screamed: "*Walla, haram!*" (I swear by God: It's a sin!)

Jewish porters and wagon drivers came over from nearby. School-children walking home from school stopped to watch. Workers looked down from a nearby building. The crowd was shoving to get to the front and shouting: "They think it's 1929!"

"Why are you standing there? Slap him silly and get rid of him!"

The rags hanging down from the Arab's wide pants were sprayed in blood. He tore off a piece of his trousers and placed it on his wound. A Jewish policeman arrived from the back. He arrogantly pushed through the crowd, inquired what had happened, and hit the Arab with his short club: "Scram!"

The Arab workers hid in the corners and waited for the pickets to disperse. Then they crawled out and searched again for a way to earn a few coins.

* * *

The next day, there was a large convening of a couple hundred men at the seacoast Histadrut House. Kitzis took the opportunity to speak and said briefly: "Comrades! We don't need to talk much. The principle of conquering labor is the holiest principle of the Labor Movement. We need to take action." Moshe Gamzu says we have to educate the drivers! They run transportation all over the city! That's even worse than the restaurants that sell Arab meat. Because meat you eat up once and that's it, but the houses will remain for years . . .

The zifzif workers were for the most part simple people and didn't even understand Hebrew. Besides, they were worn out from working, so they sat dozing. When the discussion turned to specific picket lines, Monyek got up and cried out: "Comrades, the Arabs are also workers; they also want to live!"

The whole crowd sensed right away where this was coming from. They all raised their heads. Ben Yishai said: "Listen to this guy! If the Muhammads work, you'll lie nine feet under . . ."

"Comrades!" Monyek continued, "the joblessness stems from the capitalist order, and not because of Arab workers . . ." He wanted to say a lot more, but they didn't let him. "Throw the Communist out, the pogromist!" they shouted. Monyek was thrown out. Picket locations were chosen to protect the Jewishness of the zifzif, and the convening adjourned.

3

Zalmen carried bricks to the third floor of Mr. Azrieli's building on Ahad-Ha'am Street. There was a lot of construction recently in Tel Aviv and the tempo of work increased steadily. The entrepreneurs took on new projects, one after the other. The workers toiled at a rapid pace to make it profitable for the entrepreneurs to build new buildings—and for the rich Jews from abroad to build houses in Tel Aviv. The work was hopping. The bricklayers dunked the mortarboards in clay, splashed the clay on the wall, laid bricks, and shouted to the dark-skinned workers: "Clay! Bricks! Clay! Bricks! Fa-s-te-r!"

Zalmen put thirteen heavy concrete bricks on a chair, put the load on his shoulder, and stepped onto the stairs. At first, he had tried to think of something to make the three-floor march easy on himself; later, however, his brain became blunt and empty. It occurred to him that he was trotting like a donkey, not thinking about anything: up-down, up-down . . . The bricklayers made jokes at the expense of the "green" one: "Work Zalmen, work! The faster this land gets built up, the sooner we get to go back home!"

At noon, they ate on the lot. The workers, who had brought little packs of food, peeled eggs with filthy hands, spread butter on bread, gnawed quickly, and lay on the sand to sleep. In a matter of minutes, the entire group was snoring and emitting a sharp odor of sweat and breath.

A young man in a white suit woke them up, handed out cigarettes, and offered a light. The crowd wiped their sleepy eyes, inhaled the smoke, and looked at their watches. The young man cleared his throat, fixed his tie, and started talking: "See, fellas, you should only smoke these cigarettes, from the firm called 'Redemption.' Because you need to know that these particular cigarettes are made with one hundred percent Jewish labor. And these cigarettes are the only ones."

The men were still half asleep and didn't listen to what he was saying. The young man distributed another couple of cigarettes, repeated what he'd said, and left. One worker suddenly yelled: "Fellas, one o'clock!" The crowd slowly got up, stretched, gave some big yawns, and began to climb the steps. Around three o'clock, a driver arrived with a full truck of bricks. A couple of barefoot Arabs jumped down from the cab and began to stack the bricks by the gate. There was some agitation in the building. Katz walked down the steps and approached the car.

"Listen carefully," he said to the driver. "Today you're being given leeway, but if it happens again, you'll be driving back with the bricks."

Zalmen was standing right next to him. He couldn't help himself. "Katz," he turned to him. "Just look at the Arabs' faces; you can see they're dying of hunger!"

Zalmen waited for Katz to burst out yelling but Katz was silent. He stood sullenly by the wall, laid bricks, and, from time to time, directed silent glances at Zalmen. When the worker Greenfeld yelled "no more work," he quickly grabbed his trowel, wrapped his sweater around his shoulders, and asked Zalmen: "Where are you going? Downstairs?"

"Yes."

"Good, we'll go together."

For a while he was silent. Suddenly he burst out: "You're still green and don't understand the local conditions! Trust me—I also would have liked for the revolution to come. I hate the rich and the factory owners; what? Am I not a worker? I don't know what's going on? But here in this land, I want to work. I wandered across the globe, I was driven out of everywhere, I was a foreigner everywhere, a leper, a yid, a devil, impure. I want to have at least one corner of this earth where I can lay my head. And if the Arabs are allowed to work, then we won't have a resting place here, either . . ."

Zalmen wanted to reply with something, but Katz interrupted him: "I'm not one of those fools who babble nonstop that conquering labor is socialism—no, that talk is hypocritical. I've heard it thousands of times already, that if you want to be a Zionist, you must banish the Arabs from the workplaces, because there isn't any other option. So, what am I supposed to do, hang myself? Listen up, Zalmen, I'm telling you seriously: In the Histadrut building you can talk about whatever you want: about strikes, about revolution, about the blood-sucking capitalists. There's only one thing you've got to keep silent about: the Arabs . . ."

He turned and left through an alley and disappeared.

4

Katz walked home with fast strides and in good spirits. The first floor—
he was thinking—would be constructed with pillars, so that later it would
be possible to build an additional floor . . . and when the crash comes,
there will be a few pounds of rent money coming in to earn a living. Why
not? Haven't I suffered enough? Am I a green halutz? Isn't it time for me
to have a slice of home?

Katz was still a young man when the Ukrainian Cossacks had flooded
Jewish Ukraine with blood and fire. The pogroms tore through like a
storm, shattering, killing, and ruining everything. There was a time when
he fled with his father to a village and hid for three days in a haystack.
When he emerged, gaunt as a shadow, he had lost his father.

He wandered through the ruined villages, begging for bread, and looking
at the blood-stained walls, the tear-filled red eyes, and the faded, lowered
heads. He crossed the Polish border, lived for a while in Germany, then in
Vienna, and in the end, left with a group of khalutzim for Palestine. During
the events of 1929, he was in Tel Aviv. News arrived from all across the land
that Jews were being beaten: slaughtered in Hebron, molested in Tzfat,
shot in Jerusalem . . . The streets were full of people: distributing weapons,
sharpening sticks, delivering horrible news, and preparing themselves.

He was in a mixed neighborhood. From afar he saw Arabs attacking
a car, dragging a tall, broad-shouldered man out of it, and killing him
by striking his head with eucalyptus sticks. On the white freeway, the
red stain of blood sparkled, reminding him of pogroms in Ukraine. Half
an hour later, he and a few other guys went into an Arab home in the
neighborhood. An old woman and a couple of young children cried and
pleaded for mercy. He ran into another room where a tall, seventeen-year-
old Arab stood in a corner, pressed against the wall, as if he were trying
to push himself between the bricks, to save his life. Katz fired and left. A
pair of fearful eyes gazed at him and a guttural scream sliced through the
air like a butcher's knife . . .

It was a summery day. By the window sat Katz's young daughter,
laughing in the sun. He washed his hands, and as he was stroking his
child's head, he whispered: "You'll have a home . . . you'll have a home . . ."

More on Children in the Jewish City

1

As spring began, the trees bloomed on Rothschild Boulevard, and the wintery, cloudy sea turned blue. Mazalah the Yemenite whitewashed her mistress's spacious rooms in the heart of Tel Aviv and sewed a dress for herself, till late at night, for the upcoming Purim carnival. And the secret agent, Samberg, began arresting Communists in honor of Purim and May Day.

Monyek had washed up thoroughly after work, when Samberg entered the room and yelled: "Hurry up! Get dressed and come with me!"

"Why? What have you got on me?"

"Faster, faster! We'll talk at the police station."

About ten men were already waiting in the commissioner's office. Samberg, with a couple more policemen, led them away to the investigation's judge and submitted the complaint: "This group endangers the population's well-being!"

The judge issued a temporary, seven-day arrest warrant. But there wasn't a jail in Tel Aviv. That was its pride: "the only city in the world without jails and without brothels!" The brothels were in Jaffa and at night, Tel Aviv residents snuck out there through dark alleys; and a jail—quite a large one—was also in Jaffa. So Monyek and the other fellows were sent to the Jaffa jail. And nobody spoiled the Purim celebration: Cars and trains came from all the remote colonies, tourists came from faraway cities, and in the morning, journalists began describing the carnival, which was scheduled for noon. The masked players stretched along packed streets and depicted biblical scenes. In the evening, the city was drenched in light. On balconies, orchestras played *Am Yisrael Chai!* (The

Jewish People Lives!) Worker-boys circled in horas and sang: "Arabs labor in Petah-Tikvah." Even the young sons of rich fellahin joined the circles and danced with everyone. Affluent Jews and tourists from abroad nodded their heads saying: "What youth, what fire!"

A few days later, the carnival ended. The Yemenite Mazalah took off her white dress and hid it in the pile of rags until next year's Purim. She went back to frying fat cutlets, carrying out night pots from under the beds, all the while humming the adapted couplets that were sung at the street carnival. The tourists left. The Tel Aviv merchants were back on Herzl Street trading dunams, and the small nine-year-old Yemenite, Yohanan, who had attracted so much attention with his curled peyes and fiery little eyes, went off to the Caucasian Neighborhood, because very early the next day, he had to go back to work in the factory.

2

The Caucasian Neighborhood lay in a deep pit on the edge of Tel Aviv. By day you could see the carts transporting the garbage from the Tel Aviv streets, as well as the dilapidated little barracks, crowded together, where the Yemenite, Bukharan, Caucasian, and Kurdish Jews lived, up to ten people in a stuffy box. The little one, Yohanan, slept with his seven young brothers and sisters on a floor full of holes in one of the ragged little barracks. At dawn, his mother left for the women's day-labor market, at the edge of Carmel Street, where a large crowd of Eastern women—from eight-year-old girls to sixty-year-old wrinkled grandmas—shouted, with Middle Eastern accents, in all the languages of the world, to the red-cheeked ladies: "*Spanji, ya-madam!*"—"Cleaning, mistress-dear!"— "*Gnädige Frau!*" They stayed there until the afternoon, waiting patiently; maybe the Master of the Universe will still have mercy and a lady will need a helper for at least half a day. Across, on the corner of Shenkin Street, his father stood with a spade in his hand among a crowd of men who had gathered from all corners of the city, hoping a supervisor would rush over needing to hire several pairs of working hands to build a roof. At nine o'clock, his father laid away his spade, put a thick sack on his shoulder, secured it by wrapping a thick rope around his hips, and squeezed in among a bunch of porters near the small steps of the large pharmacy called Fatherland, at the corner of Allenby and Benyamin Streets.

* * *

By now, little Yohanan had been working for a couple of years at a metal factory, where he'd been earning a whole five piasters a day. Every morning, he found it hard to get up from his warm bed and run to the dark factory, where, among the groans of sawing and planing machines, he notched large, heavy pieces of steel. On that day—after Purim—waking up was even harder than usual: the springtime sun, which had shone for several days, had dried out the mud in the lower block, and the humid little barracks filled up with the pit's damp, steamy air. At dawn, when it cooled down, rain—the year's final one—lashed the barracks and poured in through the perforated roof onto the wide floor's cots, on which lay almost a dozen children. The water poured down from all the surrounding hills into the "hole," causing a flood. Yohanan's head was still spinning from the Purim dancing and hora circles. He hastily put on wet shoes and damp socks, grabbed a bit of bread and olives, and ran off to work.

3

When he walked home after work, the happy springtime sun was still shining. He enjoyed the green fields and the groves that bloomed on both sides of the road. Yohanan was attracted to the freedom, to the fresh air—far from the stinking pit—and suddenly he had a thought: *Maybe I won't go home at all? I could sleep outdoors!* The idea filled him with a sudden joy: no more oppression, no more barrack, no more machines! Food? It would work out somehow . . . !

He turned toward the sea, walked happily through the long streets, and settled on the sandy beach, which was covered with half-naked, sunburned bodies. He stayed there for a couple of hours, gazing at the radiant young men and women, hopping around in swimsuits free as birds, doing gymnastics, playing tennis, and swimming far into the loud sea waves. Late in the evening, when it got darker, and embracing young couples arrived from the city to lie on the warm sand, he sensed a strong pull in his heart and remembered he didn't have anywhere to eat. He went up to the sidewalk and strolled between the lit-up beach cafés and crowded terraces, toward the Carmel Market.

The market shops were already closed, and the produce carts had long since disappeared. Children, most of them Yemenite, were climbing on the hills of scattered bits of straw, digging rotten apples, stale tomatoes, and bitten bananas out from the depths. Yohanan turned to a pile without thinking too hard and began searching. The digging children greeted him with an angry grumble and a displeased glower. Yohanan, rummaging with his fingers, continued sweeping quickly through the bits of straw and tossing rotten fruit into his mouth.

4

By that evening, Yohanan already had made peace with the other boys and joined their group. Together with his partners, he packed fruit into a large sack and then went off with them to their apartment. The children walked through the sandy alleys of the Yemenite quarter, cut through the mixed Jewish-Arab neighborhood, Neve Shalom, and stopped near an almost deserted ruin.

"We're living here for now," one of the kids explained to him, "but the bastards are planning to build here. Well, we'll have to look for a new apartment." One by one the boys crawled through a narrow hole that led inside a cellar. A short boy, whose chubby belly looked like a samovar on his small, skinny feet, dragged a pack of rags and empty cement sacks out of a corner and spread them out on the floor. The group sat down on the prepared bed. An older boy, eleven years of age, with a large hat that fell over his ears, pulled a pack of cigarettes from his pocket and dispensed them among the crowd. The flaming cigarettes sparkled in the darkness of the cellar. Yohanan swallowed the smoke and felt happy. He began to hum that famous Yemenite song:

Hodu ve-shabhu le-Tel-Aviv
Ki hi lanu me'od khaviv
Me'od khaviv

Thank and praise Tel Aviv
we love her,
you must believe

All the children joined in, getting carried away with the catchy melody. Yohanan woke up in the morning when the sunrise shone through the windows and holes into the cellar. The children lay around, dressed in long, raggedy pants, wide, unbuttoned jackets, and large hats that hung down. Early on, a loud sound came from the alley above: a donkey bellowed, an old Arab hawed and cursed, and a barefoot fellah, loaded with two cases of vegetables and grapes, announced his merchandise.

The children got up lazily, yawned with wide-open mouths, and scratched their heads viciously. When the early risers sat by the bag of fruits and began chewing hungrily, the rest of the group suddenly woke up, got to their feet, and began grabbing at yesterday's gathered leftovers. Before they left, Hananiah the coach driver announced to the new guy: "We're going to the market now. Anything you can grab, you take: bread, fruit, herring, raw meat. You can gobble down as much as you want, but the rest you gotta give to the treasury."

The children walked back through the alleys. On the way, they met more groups of kids as they crawled out of their holes and rushed into the market. Carmel Street was already full of people, yelling as loud as they could, with shiny fruits winking from their baskets and suspended fish and calves looking downward with rolled-up eyes. The children mingled among the dense crowd, lurked near the carts, hid under the store shutters, and lay in wait for a moment favorable for snatching something. Yohanan was agile and learned quickly. When he was standing hiding behind a cart of grapes, a young guy pulled him by the sleeve and yelled: "Yohanan, get out! Levy is around! He's catching kids and taking them to the police."

Yohanan resolved to fight till his last drop of blood rather than fall into Levy's hands. Whenever that goat-beard, Levy, showed up at the market, he disappeared into a side alley and reappeared in another corner of the market, as if he had popped out of the ground. He kept going like that for weeks, eating scraps, sleeping in burrows, and staying out of police custody. Until the police came to him.

The Jewish policemen with the Hebrew letters on their hats surrounded the market and conducted a raid of the children. Many children disappeared into the side alleys. But, forty children, Yohanan among them, were captured. He, together with the rest of the large gang of ragged, barefoot, filthy children were marched through Binyamin Street and Rothschild Boulevard to the police station. All the children were gathered on the roof of the police station, photographed, and given a lecture from a respectable woman—the chair of the department for social welfare at the Tel Aviv City Council. She let them know that "decent children have to live with their parents, learn in school, or go to work"—and then they were dismissed.

5

Monyek was still in jail, and every week he was led to the judge to lengthen his sentence. Monyek's camel was noble, as all camels are. When he stopped getting proper care, after Monyek's arrest, he up and died. He was left lying on the coast of the blue sea, and jackals celebrated a magnificent feast over his corpse through white, romantic nights. Monyek's little son, Len, walked around confused: His father hadn't come home; his mother was worried. Lately, milk and bread had also become rarities at home. Len was scared to ask his mother about it, because as soon as he mentioned his father, she would immediately pull a handkerchief out of her pocket and begin to wipe her eyes. The neighbors' children pointed at him shouting: "Your daddy is a thief . . . He's sitting with all the thieves and Arabs in jail . . . They get whipped there with iron rods . . . and his camel croaked . . ." He ran inside the house, lay on the bed, and wept bitterly.

A Leap Across Generations

1

Just as the muddy, Jerusalem dusk fell and united the sticky mud of Shaarei Rachamim Alley with the thick, wet darkness, various people began to arrive through the back door into the two wide basements in that corner of the city. They growled—each one individually—right after stepping over the threshold: "Why do we come here so much? In the end, they'll 'allocate' this apartment!"

Leybl arrived first. He stormed inside like thunder, glanced one last time behind his back, and immediately asked: "Is there something to grab?" He approached the cabinet and pulled out a piece of hard bread, half of a tomato, and a couple of salty olives. He swallowed it all in one gulp, lay flat on the wide bed, and just a minute later, filled up both large rooms with a cyclical, whistling snore. A little later came Yankl "sheygets." He stood in the middle of the room, shook the water from his hat and trousers for a bit, scrubbed the thick layers of clay from his shoes with a large wedge, and asked Motke: "Anything to eat . . . ?"

More guys arrived, hungry and weary. Motke lit the primus and listened to the conversation at the table. Yankl "sheygets" argued stubbornly: "The Jewish Yishuv is reactionary through and through. We must rely on the Arab masses!"

The discussion continued. The primus made a sound and the teapot began to boil. Motke glanced at his watch and went to put on his leather jacket. "It's time to go fetch Hanke," he thought. The door opened and Berl "Siberianik"—a tall guy with a big head, walked in the room. He sat down with a bang and began to recount: "As you know, the Histadrut announced a strike of all the professionals building the water reservoir in the colony of Romema, until they fire all the Arab workers and hire Jews instead. Well, all the Histadrut members weren't at work; only our guys were there. Now they're saying that we're strike breakers . . . We must issue a call to the Jewish and Arab workers . . ."

2

A soggy winter evening lay over Jerusalem and covered the city, including its narrow alleys, jagged rocks, and randomly scattered houses, in wet darkness. Motke ran through twisting nameless streets in a thin, prickly rain. Below, breathed the Old City: ancient walls, peaked towers, mosques, and churches making their distinctive marks on the cloudy sky. From afar, small fires glowed from the new garden neighborhood, Rehavia: Zionist officials and English judges played cards, drank coffee and whiskey, and listened to music there. Nearby, in jam-packed Yemenite houses, mothers put their children to sleep—eight people in one tiny little room.

He ran along the edges of deep quarries, walked through dark yards and water-filled ditches, and came to the wide, English, officials' neighborhood, Talbiye. He stood by the door of a high wall, from which radio voices emerged, and waited for Hanke. Memories flitted through his head, still preserved and intact, of bygone Jerusalem days. He had arrived here right after leaving the kibbutz and worked for sixteen piaster a day. He sat on the wet ground all day rubbing the concrete floors and wall edges with a stone, until teeny-tiny, glimmering mosaic stones peeked out. The wet stone, which he continually dunked in sand, made holes in his fingers. A harsh wind blew through the large open windows and splashed thick raindrops onto the workers sitting on the floor together, with bandaged fingers and trembling from the cold. In the evening, he stayed alone in his small room, which had a view of the little square stone yard. The landlady spoke Arabic and Ladino. The drinking water from the "hole" was turbid and tainted. Hanke's letters arrived saying that she intended to leave the kibbutz soon.

Once, acquaintances took him off to a "meeting." And then, on that same day, Motke moved into the recently rented, new apartment, which consisted of two large, empty basements. The walls were pockmarked with holes from bedbugs, and a tall bed stood in the corner, making the rooms seem even creepier.

Underground life had begun. The neighbor, Hershel, an older, single man with a toupee, barely left the house. He sat at his small table for full days writing proclamations and open letters. Until recently he hadn't had a room at all and slept at various people's homes, wandering from room to room, never knowing where he would sleep in the evening, and then showing up in the middle of the night in an unfamiliar guy's bed.

Motke used to go to the gate of the Old City, buy a piece of meat from an Arab for cheap, and bring it back to the house. As a primus hummed in the middle of the large room, Hershel put away his pen, warmed his hands by the fire, and inhaled the smell of the meaty soup into his wide-open nostrils. He relished every spoonful of food, sucked out the bone marrow, and, shaking his head, turned to Motke: "Believe me: Ten years living in basements is no small thing . . ."

After eating, he asked Motke: "would it be possible for you to go nearby, to the third street on the left, to the second floor, and ask whether or not a letter has arrived for me?" He had a female acquaintance who was sick with tuberculous in a hospital in Tzfat. She was from whom he expected letters. And, when Motke returned emptyhanded, he would always say: "Weird, I was supposed to receive a letter and didn't! You didn't receive anything either . . . ? No one writes letters anymore . . ."

3

Of the two rooms of the basement apartment, one was dark, and the other sat on a limestone slope, with a view of the tall mountains and wide fields. The basement was located at the edge of the city and opened to an old Jerusalem alley. Women sat there on the ground, leaning on houses and thresholds, with their children's heads on their knees, inspecting, with nearsighted eyes, for lice, and crushing them with great delight in their dark nails. Young women talked secretively about female topics and received wise advice from old women. Nineteen-year-old girls, who had never had any romances or read any novels, lowered their eyes with embarrassment and blushed from their own sinful thoughts when they saw a young man from afar.

In the mornings, skinny yeshiva boys ran through the alley, shaking their fur hats and their long peyes, looking around, and filling the air with wild wails and sad songs. Jews who were living on charity money from abroad hung around the large yards of the different distribution agencies, conversed about Torah matters, and recited Psalms for a strong drink. Small children with tzitzis hanging out from under their long, black coats and ringworm blooming under their hats ran with large Talmud volumes under their arms into their *kheyder* classrooms. Hasidim in long, black coats ran around like poisoned mice. Women sat at storefront thresholds, calling out to customers and quietly cursing, all while washing their hands.

Before the Sabbath, women and girls walked with empty tins to the two ditches from which the entire alley drew water. In winter, the rain streamed into them, mixing in the mud and filth from the surrounding hills; filling the ditches so that people drank from them until Shavuot, when worms began to flourish in the muddy waters. On Shabbes, the entire alley squeezed inside the small synagogues, where people mostly fought and pushed on account of the couriers, who had traveled to Polish shtetls to solicit charity-box money, but had deposited most of the money into their own pockets.

In the evenings, a couple of fellows went down into the basement apartment. They brought "little packages," and held meetings. The basement lived in peace with the alley. The storeowners were even pleased: "Sure, they're halutzim, but they help sales nonetheless." In the alley they knew that when it comes to praying, halutzim are part goyim and don't pray. But one time, right as they were in the middle of writing a proclamation, an older Jew in a long, black coat dropped inside and yelled: "Jews: we're missing one person for minyan; come quick!" At first Hershel was scared. He shoved the proclamation under the table and muttered: "Eh . . . but we don't have hats . . . that is, we do have hats . . . but just today those hats went missing . . ."

4

Hanke arrived. Papers lay scattered in every corner, and the mud that people had tracked in from the clay fields to the back door was a couple centimeters thick. It was just like a fair: Fellows lay on the beds, discussing, smoking, and spitting. People drank tea from one cup, and while bathing, dunked their soapy fingers in a tin can of clean water. A couple of days later, she moved in completely. She was a bit confused and couldn't adjust to her new life. In her head, she still heard the kibbutz bells ringing. She stood for long hours by the window, gazing outside.

For weeks, a rain cloud hung over the neighborhood and covered the mountains, the forest, and the fields in black. During hard rains, deep mud shut the basement off from the surrounding world. At night wind howled in the valley, in the mountain caves, and through the forest trees. During that time, Hanke wrapped herself in a thick fabric, leaned against the walls, and sang sad Russian songs.

A few weeks later she got "organized" and joined work in the "operation." Every evening, she ran to "connections" and carried "packages." But at night, an uneasiness overwhelmed her: The group of men who hung around the basement—most of them "underground" people—looked at her with eager, hungry eyes, which both offended and irritated her. Once, when she and Motke were home alone, she said out of nowhere: "Here, everything seems different than on the kibbutz . . . You know that I didn't love you there either. But there I was more independent . . . It occurs to me that here in the city, my boyfriend will also be my husband . . . It won't be you . . . I'm saying this to you so you won't have any illusions . . ." Motke thought that despite their long acquaintance, she was still strange and closed off to him. He sat and looked at her quietly, and some kind of odd feeling of fondness and admiration swept him away.

5

Meanwhile, Hanke got a job with a Jewish-English family in the affluent neighborhood of Talbiya. She did housework all day and spent her nights in the basement apartment. Motke used to come to pick her up. One rainy day, Motke stood waiting for a long time near her house, contemplating Hanke and himself, and didn't sense that rain was falling slowly all over him. The droplets soaked through his clothes and trickled over his body . . . He only woke up when Hanke came out, took him by the hand, and called out: "Heavens, you're wet!" And she wiped the water from his face.

Her voice was soft and smooth as silk. Motke was very moved. Only now did it occur to him that he rushed around for two hours every evening, in the rain, for this particular girl. He backed away from her, so as not to get her wet, and was silent. They ran fast under the pouring rain, holding each other's wet hands. Arriving at the basement, Motke pushed open the door with his foot and did not budge from the threshold. Hanke took a step forward and turned pale. Across the room, on the bed, sat an unfamiliar person with a long beard and moustache, looking at them. All three were silent for a while. Finally, the foreigner asked in English: "Are you Motke?"

"Yes, I am."

"Hershel told me to stay here," the foreigner said, pronouncing the name "Hershel" in a funny way. Hanke ran to the other room to change. Motke made tea. They spoke at length: "An Englishman?"

"No, an Arab, from Syria."

He was the first Arab Motke was able to trust. Motke shot questions at him, not waiting for any answers. Motke himself couldn't believe that here, right in front of him, was a person who had grown up in the traditional, feudal Orient and suddenly, leaping over generations of development, from Muhammad to Lenin, had fallen into a world of ideas more progressive than those of capitalist Europe.

6

Karem, the Arab with the beard, lived in the basement from that night on. For weeks straight he didn't go out to the sunshine. After the meal, which usually ended up around 5:00 PM, Hershel turned on the lamp and crawled into the other room. Motke and Karem cleared the plates to a corner—they always got washed by the next day before breakfast—smoked cigarettes, and dove into conversation. Over the couple of weeks of living together, they had become very good friends and told each other every possible thing.

Karem was born in a Syrian port city. His father was religious and in his later years, even respected the sultan and couldn't believe that in Istanbul, Muslim women walked around without veils. There were many important people in his family. As a child he often traveled out to the rural areas and saw how the fellahin lived out there. When he got older, his father sent him off to a French high school in Beirut. There, he joined a nationalist student circle and threw rocks on the tramways during the transport strike that broke out against France. From then on, he'd gone through a long evolution, becoming aware of imperialism, revolution, and the unity of the colonial peoples and the world proletariat, until he arrived at his present convictions.

He didn't know any women. He had been in love with one girl back in Syria, but she was always veiled. He had come to Palestine to work among the Arabs. But he quickly had "failed," and because of a "conspiracy," had shaved his beard and temporarily disappeared into the "basements." At first, life in the underground seemed like a dream to him: The Jewish guys from Poland and Russia, whose burning discussions and lengthy histories of revolutions, wars, and movements lasted through stormy nights, as rain slammed the windows, and the wind wailed in the attic holes and over the noisy woods. They mixed in his imagination with the Syrian city of his birth, its pious, faithful, veiled women and its Arab mosques. Motke, for his part, explained to Karem about pogroms and anti-Semitism, Hasidism and Zionism, and why the Jewish workers had come to adopt the "conquest of labor."

"Understand?" he said once in conclusion. "I'm an anti-Zionist, but I understand the tragic situation of the Jewish people, which has spurred this kind of movement. And you, Karem, as long as you work here, you have to understand it too."

* * *

A knock on the door interrupted their conversation. A fellow they knew, who was followed inside by an unfamiliar movement man, said something in Hershel's ear and disappeared. The stranger remained. This new guy, who was similar to an Arab, spoke bad Russian. He was an Armenian. A little later, a blast of cold damp wind barged in, together with two girls, soaked like cats: Hanke and Dora.

The basement cheered up. The large room filled up with the sounds of speaking: Yiddish, Hebrew, Arabic, Russian, Polish, French, and English. Everyone talked; everyone felt revived. Outside, the storm still rained and whistled. Prickly drops banged against the door and windows. Karem quietly began to hum an Arabic song:

A daughter of a fellah
Sitting under an apple-tree . . .

"Sing about the Jewish cobbler boy," Motke requested.
"No," he got embarrassed. "I don't know Yiddish that well."
But the girls pleaded with him, and he relented and started to sing that Yiddish song, with his pronunciation, mixing something of an Oriental sadness and trilling into the melody.

Metvin, Metvin, af dayn keyver
Veln mir shteln a monument
Un af im vet shteyn geshribn,
Metvin iz geven a held

Metvin, Metvin, on your grave
We will put a monument
And on it will be written,
Metvin was a hero

The Yiddish words came out a bit distorted in his mouth. Above, in the alley, stood the distribution agencies and yeshivas. Not far away, in the Old City, minarets, the Temple wall, and churches rose, and here, in the basement, an Arab from Syria was singing a song about a Jewish cobbler boy from a faraway land, who was murdered in the struggle for the liberation of oppressed people—a song that had been carried into and sung in all the prisons of the Near East.

7

The sun shone all around; spring had arrived even to the old walls of Jerusalem. The clouds dissolved, and the basement windows reflected greening mountains and blooming trees. Passover approached, and Jews began to prepare for the holiday. The alley bubbled with activity. Women scrubbed and kashered, cleaned off the filth from the entire year, and whitewashed the cockroach holes from the previous summer. Religious Jews carefully observed the Shmurah Matzah, young girls became kneaders, the yeshiva students rocked back and forth over the old holy books and suppressed sinful thoughts that the spring sun had awoken in them. The droves of fellahin prepared to go to pray at the grave of the holy prophet Musa and there to ask Allah for rain in the winter, for the olive trees to bloom well in the spring, and for the young lambs to be successful.

The cool room was bustling. Dora and Hanke worked nonstop: They created "connections," carried "little packages" from "camp" to their room, and from their room to "points." To keep from provoking suspicion, Dora carried the "little packages" in a matzah box from the Manischewitz factory. The neighbor women did wonder: "What are those girls getting so many matzos for? They won't eat it all up until Shavuos!" In the evening, pious wives struck up conversations with their husbands: "They're kind of strange girls, already grown yet unmarried . . . ! And at night single men hang around there . . . That's surely inappropriate . . ." The pious Jews didn't take it much to heart. They tugged their little beards and thought: "Whatever; they help the sales nonetheless! Well, so what if it's not so appropriate?—Doesn't really matter! Sinful women have always been present in the world; even our forefather Jacob's daughter-in-law Tamar was a sinful woman . . ."

The action began a couple of days before Passover, which that year fell at the same time as the pilgrimage to "Nabi Musa." From all over the country, guys came to "work." They lay in tiny little rooms, in basements and attic flats, in all the remote corners of the city, and waited. When the "little packages" came in, they filled up their pockets and went off to the nearby villages, mosques, cinemas, and cafés. Later, all the remaining fellows snuck back secretly to their rooms in the attic apartments, packed their pockets once more, and returned to the alleys and villages.

Motke had been running around all day. In one room, there were a couple of men across from him who rose from their "work" and yelled: "Motke? Would you look at that, it's really him!" Motke looked in the corner, where they were lying, and recognized tall Theo and Shimon. "What're you doing here?" he asked them, shaking their hands.

"Oh, you see, they sent for us, so we came!"

"And you're not afraid?"

"Afraid? When there was a need to starve in the swamp and get malaria and rheumatism, didn't people go then . . . ?"

Motke kept running. He came home late in the evening, worn out. Hershel greeted him with a sad face and, as soon as he got in, announced: "You still have a fair bit of work to do today! The fellas failed to complete the job. There's no one left . . ."

Motke threw himself on the bed: "I'm gonna take a short nap, regain my strength a bit . . ."

*　*　*

Late at night Motke left to go to the "point." He walked through twisting, snaking, narrow alleys, ran uphill and downhill, and nearly suffocated in the huge crowds. Oriental Jewish families were sitting on the floors of stone courtyards to celebrate the Seder: Old women in Turkish shawls, gray grandpas in long, striped black coats with fezzes on their heads, young scrubbed and combed girls, and legions of very small children sat on divans, in circles, rocking calmly and murmuring, with a sad melody, about the miracles of Egypt, of Jewish liberation. From the nearby yards wafted the murmur of Yemenite and Bukharan Jews, who were reading the Haggadah with a trilled Oriental melody. The large springtime stars sparkled above, a mild wind blew, and he felt a clarity in his heart: a different liberation . . . a true one . . . a united one . . . of all the oppressed . . .

*　*　*

In the darkness of night he delivered the little package to a young Arab, who quickly disappeared.

"Plowed-up, Raw Earth"

1

It was still early dawn when several cars drove up onto the soft ground of Wadi Hawarit. The rubber tires sank deep into the sand and left wide tracks behind them; the motors moaned and pushed forward with all their might. In the first car, half-sleeping English soldiers sat on wooden benches. On a high mountain with planks was a group of kibbutzniks holding boards. The third car was almost empty: A couple of gentlemen reclined on upholstered seats, smoking thick cigarettes. A tractor followed them from behind, panting and trying to catch up to its nimbler comrades, and yet, lagging even further behind. The front car's drivers looked back with concern, and slowed down. The noisy caravan drove into an empty, sandy valley. Someone stuck his head out from the last car and yelled to the driver: "Stop; these are the fields!"

The cars stopped. The guys poured out. The surveyors set up their machines, looked at the carts, made marks for the fellows with the boards, and talked among themselves. Finally, one of them said: "You can go up to plow." The wide, sandy valley suddenly began to revive. The English soldiers sat on the hood of the car, drank coffee from thermos bottles, and warmed themselves in the sun. A couple of them napped. The kibbutzniks swiftly tossed the wooden boards and metal rods out from the truck and applied themselves to the task of building a barrack. Shortly thereafter, the first wall was ready.

Ignatz walked around like a poisoned mouse, trying to help, not knowing what to do, and finally standing by the wall, opening his eyes wide, and mumbling: "There, the first wall of our first home on our own land is ready!"

Shloymke "jamus" patted the tractor, poured in oil, and opened up the first garden bed. The boys stood up straight and fixed their eyes on the white plow as it dug into the sandy earth and lifted large, yellow heaps of clay to see the light of day for the first time. Far on the horizon, some people showed up. Through the clear dawn air, bare feet, white, wavy shawls, and wide, black pants became visible. Here and there, black, thin-legged goats and fat, red-colored sheep emerged from the yellow sand. The sad cling-clang of the herds and the barefoot people slowly came closer. They approached from all sides. The English soldiers rose up and tapped their rifles. The boys picked up their pace and rushed to knock together the barrack walls.

*   *   *

With a roar and a clatter, the tractor floated over the wide, flat field. The yellowish brown garden expanded and grew longer. Shloymke pressed forward. The black tents in the middle of the field didn't budge. A thin, tall woman with long, disheveled braids lifted a curtain from a hut, carried out a bundle of branches, and made a fire. Inside, five small children, in short, dirty shirts that didn't cover their bellies, gathered by the exit. They noticed the group of foreigners and stayed on the tent's threshold, afraid. A hairy dog circled between their little feet, cowardly lowering its tail. An older woman stood up, uncovered her breast, and picked up a small child from a little pillow in the corner. The child latched onto the full breast, dunked his little head into her warm body, and drew out his mother's milk with clenched lips.

The tractor hummed like a large iron cockroach and circled around and around. The sandy square around the tents became even smaller and smaller. The young ones stood by the raised curtain, following their curious little eyes around the malevolent wonder surrounding their home, and chewing on the sticky bread their mother had handed them.

2

The shepherds and their herds came very close, positioned themselves by the bank of the plowed field, and watched. The sheep spread all around. Several goats, noticing the torn-out roots, stretched their chins, sniffed in the air, and ran over the plowed heaps to the moist, tasty grasses. The boys had completed putting up the walls of the barrack. Ignatz uttered: "The Bedouins are already leading their herds onto our land!" He strode over to the soldiers and spoke a few words with one of the older ones. An Arabic translator immediately yelled out to the Arabs: "Ya, shabab, take the goats away from their plowed field!" A tall shepherd trilled: "What? Is this the first time we're pasturing here? My great-grandfather pastured here!"

"If you pasture here, you'll get a large fine. Yallah, get them out of here!" The herdsmen didn't move. The officer spoke quietly, and a soldier got up and pointed a rifle at a goat, which stood with its head bowed, feasting on the tiny leaves of dogtooth grass. A small shepherd jumped on the clay heaps and began to drive away the goats.

* * *

The tractor had come right up to the tents. It circled like a black bird, casting its shadow on the tents' mats, and crawled forward, stabbing the edge of its plow, like sharp nails, into the last strips of land. Shloymke held the wheel with both hands and turned the machine past the hut. The right wheel drove over a rope and tore up a slab of earth. The rope whistled in the air, and the sheet fell and hit the woman, who was holding the child, in the shoulder. The nursing child lifted his head from her breast and burst into a wailing cry. The Bedouins stood leaning on long sticks, gazing with sharpened chins and wide-open eyes; even the English soldiers stopped napping and rose from their spot. The translator spoke briefly with the officer and then stepped over the plowed rope and said to the women: "You must free up this area. Take the children away from the tents!"

"Have you no fear of Allah whatsoever? This is our field!" screamed the first woman. She pulled her children closer to herself and, pointing to the tent, said: "Take a look! As you see, we don't have anything; these few sheep are our only livelihood. What will we live off of now?"

The translator got flustered. He spoke quietly: "It's a lost cause; this won't help at all! Maybe later there will be a trial. For now, leave without making trouble."

"Where should we go? In the past, we could wander from field to field. But now, everything is plowed and planted . . ."

The translator turned around. The English officer turned to the boys: "You've got to attach the tent to the tractor and OO-F-F-F . . ." he gestured with his hand. The boys watched silently. Ignatz wrinkled his forehead and began speaking quietly, as if to himself: "When there's no other way . . ." A couple of workers hopped over the plowed rope with their heads down, lifted the torn rope, and tied it to the plow. The tractor gave a roar and shook the earth.

<h1 style="text-align:center">3</h1>

For a while, the women watched everything going on with eyes wide open. Suddenly they grabbed their children's hands and threw themselves down on the wide-open garden bed, right under the tractor wheels. The old ones tore the hair from their heads and wailed: "Save us, save us, brothers! Foreigners are bringing death here!" The children rubbed their naked bodies onto the hard clay heaps and wailed bitterly. Their dog walked in circles and barked. The frightened sheep ran all over the field, and the ringing of their bells could be heard throughout the distance.

The fellahin jumped from all directions toward the tent. Several soldiers with rifles in their hands immediately ran across the garden beds and surrounded the tractor. The fellahin stopped running, still crouched forward. A couple of policemen began dragging the women, with their children, out of the garden bed. The old one clamped her feet onto the heaps, waved her hands, and cursed: "A curse on your god! Destruction to your home!"

A young Arab stepped out of the mass of fellahin and hurled himself toward the policemen holding a heavy stick. A soldier lifted his rifle and pointed it at his chest. The Arab crouched to run ahead, but an old fellah grabbed him by the shoulder and pulled him back: "Leave it now, Rasheed! Allah will avenge our honor!" The policemen evacuated the women from the field. The old women limped over the garden beds without ceasing their curses. From behind, the crying children ran after them. The tractor moved and dragged the tent with it. The belongings of the expelled residents remained on the empty piece of land: a dirty coffee ladle, a broken clay pot, a couple of soggy cushions and mats. A while later, the workers tore the other tent apart.

The People Are Getting Restless

1

When he woke up early in the morning, Mustafa's head was still full of the words and concepts he had heard at the cell meeting late the previous night: "class struggle" . . . "concentration of capital" . . . "imperialism" . . . "markets" . . . "raw goods" . . . "proletariat" . . .

He jumped out of bed, washed up, and looked outside through a tiny window. The house stood on a mountain. Before his eyes, the sea stretched wide and far. At the port's new brick buildings, it was still quiet; only the excavator, which dug twenty-four hours a day, moaned. Shadows rose toward the right, on the sand between the palm. The Bedouins who slept there were already up to go to work. At a nearby mosque a muezzin started singing. His drawn-out voice mixed with the crackle of the machine and poured over the roofs of the mountain houses: "*La eylo, eylo Allah . . .*"

The fresh clarity of the cool dawn overtook him completely. Ahead of him lay an entangled slice of life: a kilometer-long stone breaker in the waves, iron-and-concrete port structures, tall ship chimneys, petroleum flowing in large metal ponds, and thousands of ragged fellahin and Bedouins, just rising from their sleeping spots on the sand and heading out, with bundles of pita and onions, to find some day labor for a couple of piasters.

He ran out of his room, jumped down the steps, and felt an unbounded energy within himself. In the street, a colorful mass of people passed by: urban workers in wide, oriental pants with European jackets on top; newly arrived fellahin in long, striped coats, with wide shawls on their heads; and Bedouins from Transjordan with braids, white, clenched teeth, and wide-open eyes, overwhelmed by the mechanized urban noise and machine-like pace. Hunched and carrying food wrapped in scarves, they slowly poured into the harbor and the office of the Iraq Petroleum Company, which hired workers. Mustafa flowed into the teeming masses.

A sizable crowd already stood at the Iraq Petroleum Company. The gates were still closed. The crowd of workers stretched out on the pavement, sitting down on nearby staircases, smoking, and patiently awaiting their destiny. Mustafa sat down near a group, smiled around, and asked an older fellah: "Where do you come from, uncle?"

"Oh, from far, very far." The fellah looked with some suspicion at the young fellow in urban dress.

"No work, huh?"

"No rain—no bread. Hunger rages in the villages."

"And why does hunger rage?"

"*Min Allah* (it's from God)." The fellah raised his finger to the sky. The people nearby shuffled their feet over the pavement, stretched their rag-clad bodies, and listened attentively to the conversation.

"But here in the city there's a lot of bread. They just don't want to distribute to the poor."

"*Moosh baaraf* (I don't know)," the old fellah shrugged.

"You see," Mustafa pointed at the small sign with the three letters I. P. C., "with the money they have, you could plant every field in the world."

"*Koolshi min Allah* (everything is from God)." The old man pointed stubbornly at the sky. The circle of people around Mustafa became even more crowded. The Bedouins, suspicious of his urban foreignness, looked at him with mocking eyes and drank in his words. He sat among a company of desert people and told of a land where every person has something to plant and something to eat.

2

The clock chimed 6:30. Mustafa quickly said goodbye to the crowd and ran off for the port, where he'd been working for quite a while. Throughout the port area, work was surging. Machines roared and human hands were on the move. The large excavator dug into the ground by the stone walls. On the other side, at the coast, they poured earth into the water and set concrete to flow in and dry out a piece of the sea where they wanted to build merchandise warehouses. Long rows of containers had been arriving nonstop from the Atlit quarry, traveling far into the sea on the wide breaker, and casting thousands of cubic meters of rocks into the water to lengthen the walls.

Young Bedouins bashed stones. Fellahin spread hot tar over the nearly completed portion of highway. Two rows of workers carried a thick, heavy pipe on their shoulders. They wriggled under the heavy load at the front and back, their knees bent and blood dripping from their bare, trembling feet, as they stepped over the jagged rocks. A supervisor followed them from behind with a stick in his hand and urged them out of habit: "Yallah! Yallah!" A couple of dockhands sang in a sad, monotone voice to the rhythm of the shaking rows of people: "*Yallah, Muhammad la bakshish . . . Ya-ll-ah Mu-h-a-m-m-ad . . .*"

A tall, blond Englishman in a black striped suit walked through, accompanied by a fat, dark-skinned Arab engineer in European attire with a red fez on his head. The Englishman glanced at the workers around him, spoke with the engineer, and continued walking. At noon, he entered a small restaurant near the port. It was empty there, as most of the workers ate on the sand and not outside on the street. Mustafa ate a heavily peppered salad and looked at a newspaper. Across the whole front page, in a black frame, was a headline in large words:

"Last Bedouins Deported from Wadi Hawarit! Anyone with a Beating Arab heart, come to the Conference in Jaffa." He ate up his food and returned through the port gates. A group of surveyors set up their tools and began to measure out a new place for a military port where the English battleships docked.

3

When it got dark, they put aside their work. Groups of workers crawled behind the newly built buildings, lay flat on the sand, and slept there until the next morning. The train from Atlit spat out workers from the quarry. Fires were lit in the night cafés. The first prostitute-dancers arrived. The whole mountain of patched-together Arab workshops below spilled light toward the villas on top of Mount Carmel. Mustafa ran off to the house and changed quickly. The landlady delivered a letter to him. He left, began to climb the mountain, and read by the lamplight. His father had written:

"My dear son, Allah should protect you from Satan, from bad people, and from sinful deeds! Spring is coming soon. The last rain will fall in a couple of weeks. Even so, I don't think you need to come home, because there won't be any work near us. I don't think we'll plow this spring. The government demands taxes, plus the fine it imposed on us. And Khadj Ibrahim also demands the money that we borrowed from him to pay that fine. The sum, together with the interest, adds up to half of our land. If they auction off our land, we'll end up with nothing. So it's better for us to sell it ourselves. But we don't have the heart to give our land away to the foreigners. What do you think, my son? Certainly we won't do any plowing, because by harvest time the land surely will not belong to us . . ."

Mustafa didn't finish reading. He felt like screaming to his father: "You see? They took it from us anyway, like from Abu Khalil . . ." But his father was far away . . . Mustafa stood for a while, deep in thought. His heart howled in pain and fury; suddenly he snapped himself out of it and walked off in hasty strides.

On the mountain, a person was standing and pretending to examine the trees. He whispered to Mustafa: "to the right, behind the tenth tree . . . on the path below . . ." Mustafa walked down a narrow stone path and encountered a couple of seated people. One by one, moving like shadows, more members arrived, and the meeting began. People spoke of the situation in the country, about the strategic position that England was rushing to construct, and about the land that was being stolen from the Arabs. Mustafa asked to speak and said: "The Effendis sell the land to the Zionists and bring English soldiers to expel the fellahin. Near us in Khaldia, for example, Shukri Effendi destroyed the entire village in order to build a palace for himself and plant a large grove. That's why they are good friends with the English and with the Zionists. Only the poor fellahin and the workers are truly against the Zionists and the English."

Shmulik noted something in the dark on a piece of paper, and then he got up to speak: "The struggle of the oppressed peoples in the colonies is a progressive struggle, even when it's being led by elements who are themselves reactionary, because this is a struggle that weakens the imperialists, sharpens the crisis in the cities, and radicalizes the masses of workers there." Shmulik spoke for much longer, and everybody listened carefully. The meeting lasted till late.

4

Ragib El-Husseini was the secretary of the Muslim prayer houses. He controlled their property accounts, which belonged to the mosques and to the Waqf, and he paid the salaries of Al-Aqsa's sextons. He was planning to write a book about the heretics who say that the legends of the Koran had been completed before Muhammad's time. But lately, black shadows had invaded the land and brought Ragib El-Husseini many worries: The infidels had bought up the holy land of Palestine, the youth had stopped fasting for the long fast of Ramadan, the Bedouins had become less pious, and the fellahin had rebelled and didn't want to pay the third of the harvest from the Waqf-fields. The Bedouins of Wadi Hawarit, who had been expelled from their land, asked for help, and the fellahin of Khaldia asked for a loan to pay their debts; if not—they threatened to sell their land to the Jews. He told this to his uncle, the Mufti Khadj Amin El-Husseini. The Mufti Khadj Amin El-Husseini, who was often a guest of the high commissioner, and used to receive his frequent invitation for lunch, was very upset by these events and compiled a "Holy Letter to the People of Faith."

Many peasants, poor and rich, assembled at the mosque of Qantura. Even the shepherds from the southern area came, even though they had already been landless for a while. Ragib El-Husseini spoke for a long time about the fatherland and at the end took out the holy letter. "It's written in the Koran," he preached, "that any land, which Omar subjugated with his sword, belongs to the Prophet and to his heirs—the Sultans! And the Sultans are, as you know, the heads of the people of faith. From there it is derived that only people of faith may occupy land in Palestine, and not infidels. And anyone who sells land to the infidels violates the Koran and is a sinner."

He straightened up and concluded in a thick voice: "Allah will punish the sinners in the afterlife. And as they walk across the thin hair, which stretches from this world to the world to come, Satan will give them a shove, and they will fall into the burning fires of hell . . . and in this world, they will be excommunicated from the congregation of the faithful. You must not allow them into the mosque to pray, you must not bury them in the cemetery of the faithful, and you must not give your daughters as wives for their sons . . ."

The fellahin listened silently. On the way to their huts, they talked among themselves: "So who's going to pay the government taxes?"

"And how are people going to get the money to cover their debts?"

"And who will give out seeds?"

The Effendis became even more distressed. Something was stirring among the impoverished fellahin. "A terrible fate hangs over the land," one person said to the other, "and it is un avoidable . . ."

"There's got to be something to do: The fellahin are rebelling. They are going to bring a catastrophe to the land . . ."

"The youth are also rebelling. In those Jaffa cafés, that young guy Issa El-Issa incites the young Arabs against us old folks and demands that they come out against England." The Effendis had become nervous and tense. A fear flashed in their eyes: "The people are getting restless . . ."

The Assassination Attempt

1

The train to Haifa glided between clay villages, verdant groves, plowed sandy fields, and gray mountains. Here and there a camel shook its hump, or a donkey scampered. Tall slender eucalyptuses, wide-branched olive trees, and piles of boulders marked borders between villages and landowners. The repetition of yellow-gray colors cast the whole area in one sad monotone. Locked among naked rocks, the landscape warmed itself lazily under the fading sunbeams as spring ended. Near Binyamina, the scenery suddenly revived. The fields and mountains burst into happy conversation, every tree wore outstanding attire, and every wadi received a unique look and a special color.

Motke wiped the small window and scanned the familiar clefts: Right there is where the Kabara swamp used to lay like a black stain in which you could crawl up to your belly in mud. Now it's flat as a table; cut through with wide canals to suck the wet from the depths and direct turbid water into the sea. Only in a far, remote corner, did tall wild grasses still rise, concealing the stagnant swamp waters. Out there, crystal water flowed in long concrete culverts over the solid, dry shell of earth. A worker slowly paced across a field. He lifted steel bolts and lowered them, dug ditches and filled them. Near the closed bolts, water flowed over concrete rails, rolled into open garden beds, encircled young, fragile sprouts, and sunk into the thirsty earth. The paved road snaked over hills and valleys, sticking its tongue out into the soft sands, and, after its rinsing in the winter rains, glittered like a crystalline stripe of water. And there, mature trees rose in the orchard, which had been planted with sweat in the burning khamsin days.

His eyes didn't catch any people up and about, only tiny dots moving here and there among grape vines and plowed garden beds. That's where he used to stroll with Khayim at dusk . . . And under those wild carobs is where they kissed nervous young girls . . . That same tall palm tree still overlooked both the young colony and the ruins of the old Arab village. The camp emerged in his vision; the people, and the sadly dissolved dreams, the drifting, lost days, with the smell of the smoky kitchen, the communally entangled nights, Shloymke's outpouring of melodies . . . On the left, a square of white, concrete little houses had grown with red roofs and green window shutters. A long row of scaffolding marked the line of a newly constructed street.

Motke gazed, gazed, and suddenly shuddered: "What a horrible strangeness! It's being built, it's being built . . . and it all is totally foreign and far off for me . . . I lived in all this so recently—and now, I've got nothing to connect me to this life, this life which is erupting so powerfully and sprouting from every small clod of earth and every blade of grass . . ." He stood that way for a while, alone and sadly staring, until two people's conversation woke him up from his reverie. A chubby woman in glasses argued feverishly with a young engineer: "It's a safe place . . . It's a bit unnerving there now with the Bedouins, but once they run out of food, they'll go away . . ." He kept listening to the conversation: "A flat roof is absolutely necessary," said the woman. "Guests will be able to stroll on the roof and look out at the waves in the sea . . . And I already have a name for the villa: Tel Galim (Hill of Waves)."

The train cut through a mountain, sped between flat fields, and then it went through an Arab village: again, clay huts, little groups of men, tall girls with jugs on their heads, smoky fires, black-clad women, and barking dogs. The chubby woman looked through the window and moaned: "There are still so many Arab villages in these regions . . ."

* * *

Motke arrived in Haifa late at night. He wandered the streets and alleys for a long time, until he found, in a remote yard, the "house" with all the specified features. He climbed up steep narrow steps. He knocked and immediately heard a series of barefoot steps and a quiet whisper. After a quarter of an hour of knocking, a sleepy girl in a nightgown opened the door. She stood on the threshold of the tiny little room and examined him with curiosity. In the sole bed a guy lay wrapped in a blanket. Motke stood in the middle of the room a bit confused. The girl lay down on the edge of the bed, covered herself with the blanket, shed the nightgown, and yelled at him: "What are you standing there for? Take your clothes off and find a spot by the wall." The guy stuck his head out from under the blanket: "You must be hungry, yeah? In the cabinet down there, there's some bread and sausage. You can finish it."

The next day at noon, he left for the shuttle car to Alfiya by the regular route. Driving down from the Nazareth mountains, he glimpsed the springtime valley, blooming within the mountains' confines, and clearly displaying its remote settlements. People worked the fields on both sides of the road: tractors with chains climbed up hills and down into dugouts; sweaty mules dragged plows; girls in wide, fluttering pants stretched out on garden beds, tearing out wild grass; herds of cows pastured and ran away from the noisy tractors with their frightened-animal eyes. In the hills, long-legged water tanks lifted their round heads over the tightly packed cluster of barracks and houses and conversed in a silent language with their close friends the storks.

2

That evening, when Motke arrived in Alfiya, Rasheed and Abed were standing and waiting for a car on a small bridge near Haifa. Abed, an older Arab in peasant clothes, was too nervous to stand and had sat down on the bridge's concrete railing. Small taxis flew by quickly, honking loudly and disappearing over the zigzags of the road. It began to get dark. A cool mild wind blew in from the sea. In the port, a siren thrummed. A cargo car packed with English soldiers drove by; the nearby cement factory whistled the end of the workday. When he heard the whistle, Abed stood up, raised his hand to his face, shielding it from the day's last sunbeams, and looked up to the white mountains of Yajur: "the whistle means the Yahud are leaving," he told Rasheed, "but our people will stay at work another good couple of hours. I worked there too after the land was lost.

Our people work like mules and earn a fifth of what a Yahud does. At one point they decided to form a *jamia*, an organization, and the Yahud promised to help. But then, the Yahud didn't strike with us . . ."

Rasheed wasn't listening to him, but at those last words he groaned: "asking the devil for help!" A truck drove in. The Arabs paid up with the driver for eight piaster each and jumped up on the load of sacks. Abed patted his belly and tucked his feet under himself. The car moved. The road was full of holes and rocks. The car shook and jostled the people. Abed continued patting his belly and quietly saying his prayers. It became pitch dark. The car's large eyes cast light beams onto the road. From both sides of the road, rows of trees flew madly by. Rasheed looked outside and leaned over to Abed: "Recognize this valley?"

"My eyes still see, thanks be to Allah! My entire childhood took place here, and you think I wouldn't recognize it? In the summertime, people used to go from one edge of the valley to the other for water!" He got up, gripping the truck bed with both hands, and looked around. Black fields lay on either side. Small villages, bunched together, winked with small illuminated windows. A tardy tractor drove back home.

"See there?" Abed pointed at an illuminated hill far away. "That's where I was born. Then they expelled us and built a colony on the hill. So, we moved away westward, to the mountains, and plowed the valley by foot. Then the Effendi sold the land, and there wasn't any food in the mountains. Afterward, we lived for some time in Kmat, until the Yahud started building a city there . . . so we wandered this way, with our belongings on our mule, from one piece of land to the next, until there was nothing left . . ."

After a couple of hours of travel, the car pulled over in the middle of the road, between rows of houses, and the driver yelled: "Afula! Hop off!"

Rasheed and Abed remained on the road. "Should we head over now?" asked Abed.

"No, it's too early. There're a lot of cars around. We should wait a couple of hours."

They spotted a little wrecked house in a field and walked toward it. It was an old Arab house. It was stinky inside. Abed scraped off his shoes and sat down crossed-legged in a corner. Rasheed leaned on the wall and lowered his head. Suddenly he woke up as if from a nap: "Do the tools work okay?" Abed tucked in his long jacket and pulled out a couple of short iron pipes from a deep pocket. He tapped and sniffed them and brought them up to his eyes.

"Everything works fine," he answered quietly. "The wicks haven't budged." Rasheed bent over, took the little pipes in his hands, and stroked them with his fingers.

"Are you're afraid of dying?" he asked.

"No!"

"Afraid of hanging?"

Abed trembled: "Does it take a long time to die . . . ?"

In a nearby house across the road, a child was weeping. They both perked their ears and listened: "And I'm not going to have any kids . . ." Rasheed suddenly said, just like that.

"So should we go back?" Abed asked.

"Back . . . ? Back where? There isn't any back! In our swamp, there are planted flowers growing now. In Wadi Hawarit, there are saplings sprouting in the sand, and in Haifa, they're building a port for container ships, to flood the entire land with fire. Back where . . . ?" He looked outside. No fires burned in the surrounding windows. He got up: "We need to go!"

3

They walked at night, past the mountains' black shadows. It was quiet and dark. Abed was walking in the lead. Rasheed asked him: "Are you just guessing?"

"I can walk here like it's midday. I know every little path. Pick up your feet and don't disturb the bushes." They went down the mountains and entered a vineyard. The little trees stood lined up, tied to long wires that stretched from one corner to the other. Crouched under a dense vine, they looked out at the nearby village, a couple hundred meters away.

In the high windows of a brick house, a fire was still burning. Its glare shone on the sky and on the nearby houses. The yard was surrounded by barracks and houses, except for the side facing the garden, which wasn't built up. Downhill on the left stood long brick stables. A chain clanked in the silence—a cow torn from its trough—and a horse neighed. A person's heavy steps clomped across the yard. Abed bent down: "The night watchman! Lower your head!"

Rasheed lay flat on the ground. They heard their hearts beating and the noise of the little branches. The steps became distant and disappeared at the other end of the wall. They moved ahead, jumping from one little tree to the next. On the side, tractors, crop machines, a harvester, and many smaller tools stood under a roof held by four poles, and large, empty wagons sat in each corner. Rasheed and Abed crawled on all fours for a bit to leave the vineyard. They stood up next to a barrack and began moving along the walls. Rasheed whispered: "Gimme!"

Abed handed him a pipe; he lit a match and looked inside a window. By the weak light, Abed noticed that Rasheed had turned pale. "What?" he asked.

"Nothing . . . A kid is there . . . inside . . ."

"Light it! Give me a light!"

"Let's keep going, to another window . . ." At that moment, a door creaked, and a figure stood on the threshold. It was Motke, the one who had come here with a "little package," stepping outside for fresh air. The dogs wandered across the yard, circling the shadow and barking. The match in Rasheed's hand was on the verge of going out. Abed swiftly pulled another small pipe out of his pocket and pushed the wick to the flame. A small, green fire sparked and sent forth a small flame into the night. A windowpane clicked. Footsteps ran off into the mountains.

Blood in the Streets

1

The rumor traveled from village to village and circulated across cafés, mosques, and *madhafahs*: "It's starting already . . . ! In Jerusalem there's fighting in the streets, in Haifa they're throwing stones at the police, and in Nablus they're shooting soldiers and government buildings from the rooftops . . . They're going to drive out the Ingleyz and take the land back from the Yahud! . . ."

Young Arabs dragged revolvers and rifles out from under piles of hay, as well as old pipes, and tested the sharpness of their *shibriya* knives. Small children cleaned rusty bullets. Middle-aged fellahin weighed heavy eucalyptus sticks in their hands. Women wailed and asked Allah to have mercy. And by Wednesday all the villages knew that on Friday, they'd be brawling in Jaffa.

Mustafa arrived in Jaffa Friday morning. As soon as he arrived, he noticed the tense expectation that hung over the city. Jaffa was on strike. The noisy old-fashioned carriages, which shuttled constantly between Jaffa and Tel Aviv, stood abandoned on the street corners. The coachmen had nothing to lose. In any case, everyone rode the large, red buses, and they barely made enough of a living to buy the oats to feed their animals. So they left their horses in their stalls that day and encouraged one another: "People will go to the mosque and from there—to the government building!"

The shops were closed. The poor, bankrupt shopkeepers had been glaring hatefully at the growing Tel Aviv storehouses and their gold-draped vitrines for a long time, and for weeks now they had been preparing for the demonstration. The boatmen pulled their boats up to the coast, not transporting the halutzim, who came on large whistling ships. They took their long paddles in their hands and went out to the alley near the mosque. The carpenter and cobbler shops, and the tile factories, whose doors opened to the streets and always roared with banging and knocking, stood shut. The lemonade vendors, who constantly rang their brass bells, yelling: "ice-cold, ice-cold!" with a trill, had also vanished. Even the tall porters, dressed in sacks, hadn't shown up. A small, barefoot newspaper vendor ran in the middle of the street and yelled in a little, squeaky voice: "Abu Jelda shot down twelve English airplanes. Soon, they'll shoot down the rest here in Jaffa!"

He banged his foot on a stone and disappeared, limping, into a narrow alley. In the center of the city, the stores and factories were also closed, but those streets were lively and deluged with a mass of fellahin, streaming in from every corner.

2

Mustafa walked among the crowd and searched for familiar faces. A hand grabbed his shoulder: "*Ahalan wusahalan*, Mustafa! You're here, too?"

"*Salam aleikum*, ya, Abed! Are there a lot of folks from the village?"

"'A lot?' so many—half the village! Anyone who could travel has come . . . but we thought you would stay in Haifa."

"They're going to be in Haifa too! But everyone is coming here today." The crowd stayed put where they were. From the back, people pushed and yelled: "Move!—what's the holdup there?" A young Arab stepped back and said: "They're looking for weapons! The Ingleyz are looking for weapons!" and slipped into a side alley. Armed soldiers stood on the street corners, searching passing fellahin. They angrily watched the masses as they streamed in nonstop, patting down the pockets of their wide pants and asking them furiously: "Where are you all heading?"

"To the mosque, to pray!"

When people suddenly get the strange urge to pray, it's not possible to do anything with them; certainly, the Ingleyz had nothing against the fellahin praying . . . but why should they need to bring revolvers and the clubs they call *nabuts* to their holy prayers? The governor of Jaffa understood the nature of this prayer well. He issued an order forbidding all demonstrations and cautioned the police to be prepared. Policemen drove around in large trucks and gathered up stones from the streets around the city hall and the mosque. Soldiers installed barbed wire across all the alleys leading to the government building. Armed patrols kept watch over all the neighborhoods day and night. They brought machine guns and large transports of munitions from the Jerusalem barracks. Airplanes flew all over the country and reported a lot of movement in the villages and in the Arab cities.

*   *   *

Tel Aviv remained on the sidelines and lived life serenely: In Beit-Ha'am people discussed the Hebrew prophets, on Herzl Street they speculated on construction lots; Sabbath observers smacked the young people who smoked cigarettes in the middle of the street, and writers prepared to celebrate the eight-hundredth birthday of the Rambam. At the stock market, people even reported that they had recently acquired new lands: They had finally won their legal case against the fellahin of Infiat near Hadera, and purchased a part of Wadi Kubani, establishing a foothold in the south, in the area of Beer Sheva, where until now there hadn't been any Jews.

*   *   *

Armed policemen and soldiers stood on every corner. At the large Clock Tower Square, across the alley from the mosque, stood seven upright rows of soldiers with rifles in their hands. Behind the ground troops, armed cavaliers sat on horses. They awaited the demonstration.

3

After prayers, the worshippers exited the mosque, went through the narrow alley, and headed toward Clock Tower Square. Musa Kazim Pasha, the elderly chair, walked in the first row, surrounded by the important people of Jaffa. Musa Kazim strode step by step. Behind him, the youth impatiently shoved each other; they were followed by a mixed crowd of fellahin, shopkeepers, workers, women, and children. A wave of red fezzes and white shawls secured to heads by black agals crashed against the gray walls of the alley.

Suddenly, two Arab officers and an English representative shoved through a small door in the nearby prison to get to Musa Kazim, blocking his path. "Honored sheikh," one of the officers began in Arabic, "your life is important to us . . . but it is endangered here in the throngs . . ."

"I'll die for Allah and for the fatherland," the old man answered stubbornly. His escorts repeated these words, and, as they were repeated from mouth to mouth, his words spread like a wave through the streaming masses.

"No, sheikh!" interjected the second officer. "Allah gave you long years and you have to protect them . . . come with us . . ." They grabbed his hand and forced him toward the door of a government building. At first, the old man didn't let them; but then he surrendered. His escorts followed him and disappeared through a brick door amid a noisy storm of yelling and wailing. Now the youth were moving forward in a hurry. Boatmen from the port marched in the first rows: hale young men, tall as pine trees, with giant oars in their hands. They trembled under the load and sang an old Arabic battle song. The shoving masses sang along shouting: "The faith of Muhammad depends on the sword!"

* * *

Mustafa marched in the first row, among the fishermen. Ahead of him, he saw rows of armed soldiers and officers standing on the sidelines coldly staring without blinking an eye. Behind him, several young Arabs from Khaldia walked, singing and yelling with enthusiasm. Saeed kept elbowing forward, blasting the Ingleyz, their God, and their ancestors with harsh curses. The unrest on the square intensified until the crowd became a glowing, moving mass, trembling like a storm. The passive indifference of the officers provoked them even more, and a roar, mixed with curses and demands, erupted from thousands of wide-open mouths: "Sons of bitches!"

"Give us back our land!"

"A curse on your father's fathers!"

"Long live free Palestine!"

Saeed couldn't hold himself back any longer; he bent over, grabbed a stone that was sticking out of the pavement, and threw it at the soldiers. The soldiers didn't budge, but one of the officers turned to face the rows of soldiers and quietly and apathetically ordered: Fire! The drawn rifles fired callously into the crowd.

* * *

The noise on the square transformed into roars of fear and anger, muting the moans of the injured. The masses retreated and pushed into the narrow alley of the mosque. From there, however, new throngs streamed out, blocking the way. These throngs collided with those throngs. People fell and got trampled by those who were fleeing. An older Arab went off to another alley and, with great momentum, jumped up on a fence. His wide, low-hanging trousers got caught on the barbed wire, and he was stuck hanging and wailing to Allah and some merciful people for help. On the square, many injured people lay strewn about. The pavement was covered with red splotches and rivulets of blood. Several people screamed in agony; others twitched in their last, dying convulsions.

* * *

The square became empty for a time. But right after the initial fear, the youth, shuffling along the houses, returned to the square and began constructing a barricade: They dragged small tables and bottles from the cafés, gathered stones and porcelain dishes, lugged iron bars out of the homes, and tore up the pavement.

The soldiers marched forward, intent on dispersing the crowd. A tall fisherman, hiding behind a pillar, made a swift move, brandished his long oar, and unleashed it on an officer with all his might. The officer twisted, grabbed his left hand, which had cracked under the bang, and fell. An Arab soldier ran up, raised his gun with both hands, and lowered it down on the fisherman's head. The fisherman fell and a stream of blood gushed from his head.

Mustafa ran inside a café, grabbed a marble table cover, covered himself with it like a shield, and marched forward. He got pushed against an injured person, and his heavy covering fell out of his hands and shattered on the pavement. Mustafa fell on his knees and spotted Saeed in a puddle of blood. Young Arabs ran by, picked up the pieces of marble, and hurled them at the soldiers.

*   *   *

There were brawls all over. The Arab youngsters fought bitterly—They tore up parts of the sidewalk and stones from the pavement, attacked armed soldiers with their bare fists, and ran at cocked gun barrels. Bottles, windowpanes, pieces of furniture, and stones flew across the square. From the surrounding windows, older men and women encouraged the fighters and cursed the soldiers.

The exhausted Arabs retreated from the square, which was now covered with injured people, and waited with stones in their hands by the entrance of the mosque's alley: On the third floor, a balcony door opened, and a wide wooden bed, made up with pillows and blankets, soared down onto the soldiers' heads. A pillow exploded and a cloud of feathers covered the bloody square.

4

At dusk, Saeed was lying in the state hospital by the seacoast. Bandages pressed against his throat and legs. He tried to turn but couldn't. Heat flashed in his head, and he fell slowly into a hard, leaden dream. Disoriented, he looked out at the round dark sea, which lay before him, and instantly recognized a familiar scene: the little houses of his seacoast village, the sun setting under a red horizon, and watermelon-laden boats rocking on the silent waves. They were the watermelons from the first time he traveled to the city with his father to sell them. He felt good and began singing a song. The Arab policeman, who stood guard at the hospital door, felt anxious from the dying man's song and whispered a silent prayer . . .

Hanke and Mustafa

1

Shiny sunbeams penetrated through the tiny windows, which were situated low, level with the small stone courtyard, and created a white spot in the middle of the small, dark room. Hanke lay in the shadow of the bare, stone wall, half stretched out on the bed, leafing through her journal:

I/13

Every evening, I run through the alleys, carrying "connections." Jerusalem alleys, stone houses, foreign people, Yemenites, Sephardim, Caucasians, monks, Englishmen, and priests—but what am I actually doing here, in all of this? I, Hanke, daughter of a dry-goods shopkeeper, am going to make the revolution of the Lifta fellahin . . . I'm going to revolutionize the Orient, these crowded little Arab villages, by calling for the uprising of the East against the English military bases in Singapore and Hong Kong, against the City of London, against Deterding . . . Isn't that strange!

III/13

I can't be alone in my room any longer; it's horrendously sad for me here between these walls. Motke comes occasionally. What do I have still in common with him?

III/18

I'm still living with Motke. It just seems straightforward and understandable. It's something like the old way of life with a legal husband whom you don't love, but you live with him anyways.

IV/2

I read today what I wrote a bit ago about fellahin, revolution, and imperialism. I wrote nonsense. It's actually so simple: I'm a worker and I'm fulfilling my obligation. And it's really the same everywhere—in Shanghai, Honolulu, or Jerusalem. I'm just a brick in a large building, a small piece of dust in the hundred-million-person sea that's called "The Orient."

IV/15

I've been alone for many weeks now. Because of Nabi Musa, no one is allowed to come to me. I don't meet anybody—I only see someone when I'm taking or delivering "connections." Everything here seems so foreign.

V/20

They arrested Motke. The accusation itself is horrible. I'm overwhelmed by it, and I must stop writing. They do, after all, sometimes hang innocent people . . . I can't even go to see him. What does he do all day in prison? Why is our life turning out so strange?

V/25

I haven't written for a long time. V. comes over often. We've been "living together" for many weeks now. It's straightforward and regular: He comes several times a week and stays till late. No, I'm afraid to tell the truth, even to myself: He is a stranger to me now, like he used to be! He doesn't feel anything toward me. Why does it upset me so much?

V/29

Motke is still in prison. There's not even any news about his trial. No one knows anything.

2

Hanke put away her notebook, picked up a thick book from her bed, and tried to read. But it didn't work: She was very weak and hungry. The words swirled before her eyes and melted together into one large blob. She put away her book, got up, and left the room. She walked through several winding alleys out to Jaffa Street and turned back down King George. It was a bright day. Bright light poured over the stony city. The streets lay open and awake, and in the clarity of daylight they seemed even emptier than they were. Passing Hanke were several rabbis in fur hats, a worker, and a donkey, loaded with jugs of water. The heat intensified her weakness and she could barely stay on her feet. Where should she go? How could she get money for lunch?

She stood for a while near the cooperative restaurant, expecting someone she knew, someone from whom she could borrow money. Workers entered and exited; they rushed to eat up and run back to work. All the faces were unfamiliar. She left through different side alleys to go to Dora's apartment. Maybe she could get a meal at Dora's . . . ?

She walked through a narrow alley, went up the steps, and then shoved her hand inside, under a closed door. The key wasn't there but, in the room, someone moved. Hanke pushed the door open and went inside. On a made bed, in a corner, lay a tall, brown-skinned guy. He got up and inquisitively looked at Hanke. She took a step closer to him and asked, smiling: "You're Mustafa, right? I saw you once with Zalmen."

"So you're from the same kibbutz?"

"From the same one. You're living in Jerusalem now?"

"Temporarily. I had to get away from Jaffa just now." He lowered his head and sat down on the edge of the bed. Never in his life had he seen such deep blue eyes. Her bright gaze confused and dazzled him. Hanke turned around, went to a cabinet by the wall, and began looking through it. She had her back to Mustafa, so he was able to look at her more boldly. The round lines of her tall body and its movements invoked a silent, desirous tremble in him—and it embarrassed him.

"Do you know if there's anything to eat here?" Hanke asked, turning her head to him. Again, he noticed her eyes. They cast light and awoke a disquiet. She was very pale and seemed unsteady.

"I don't know," he jumped up, "but I'll run down to buy something!" With one leap he was down the steps and out in the street. The unfamiliar uneasiness didn't leave him. The image of that girl followed him. He returned to the room with a pack of food, still feeling confused. He approached her tentatively and sat down across from her. Hanke took out plates and forks from the cabinet and made a salad.

"OK, come and eat!"

"Thanks. I'm full."

"No, you'll eat, come! I won't eat by myself!" He took the spoon in his wide palm, attempted to eat with it for a bit, and laid it back down. He cut up thin slices of bread, folded them into cups, scooped pieces of salad with them, and put it all in his mouth. Mustafa looked at Hanke, who was swallowing her pieces of bread with tomato, and wondered why she ate so simply. Suddenly, he asked: "You probably read a lot of books, huh?"

"I used to read a lot. Now—less. I don't have the time or peace of mind."

He was curious whether this girl had studied a lot and understood world affairs. He started asking her about different subjects. Hanke had, meanwhile, finished eating and begun to wash the dishes. His eyes followed the movements of her fingers as they rubbed the decorated plates. Hanke finished washing the dishes, wrote a few words to Dora, and put out her hand to Mustafa: "You'll come over sometime, yeah? Dora knows my address." And she ran down the steps.

3

A jumbled storm tore through him and shook him up. He felt a seething as he had in the instant when he discovered classes and class war, like that first time he comprehended that the large gray mass in the cities and villages could elevate themselves to the level of human beings. "Here is a woman who doesn't wear a veil and looks me straight in the eye, a woman who is a free person, not a livestock sold for a hundred pounds to work and sleep with, a woman to love . . ."

* * *

He turned over in bed, irritated by an intense longing. An uneasiness settled in, haunting him sweetly, an uneasiness that purified and elevated him. He sensed something new, a new light dawning in him.

Ben Yishai Builds a New City

1

In Germany, Hitler came to power. At the large assembly at the People's House, the greatest Hebrew poet, Malkin, said: "Hitler is God's messenger; he is a staff in the hand of the Almighty! Now the German Jews will repent and build the Land of Israel . . ."

Ben Yishai went to the gathering with his wife. Shulamit had tears in her eyes. Ben Yishai applauded for a long time. The next day, he went to his neighbors and announced: "From now on, an apartment of two rooms with a kitchen will cost eleven pounds a month. The Yekkes (German Jews)," he added quietly, "love large apartments, and they pay even higher prices." Mr. Aron, the owner of house no. 63, on Rashi Street, decided to build two more floors on top of his building and then evicted all the residents. When his neighbor, Frume the seamstress, went to look for an apartment, she found a taped note: "One room with a kitchen, for affordable prices," the new owner, a small Jew with a belly, said: "It's an affordable apartment, for poor people, four pounds a month . . ."

"Four pounds? You know my husband is a barber who makes 7 pounds a month in total!"

"What can I do about it? Did I tell your husband to be a barber? No fooling, the workers are all swindlers nowadays." He put on a pair of glasses to examine his female client and noticed her advanced pregnancy. He immediately cried out: "No . . . no . . . no . . . I don't rent out to people with kids! You must understand," he urgently began to explain in a soft tone, "I have nervous neighbors . . . American Jews . . . I can't rent to people with kids . . ."

*   *   *

The first ship of German refugees arrived and with them began the big "boom." Posters hung in the streets of Tel Aviv: "Give friendly greetings to our persecuted brothers!" Shopkeepers read the posters and charged the German Jews even more money. "Stupid Yekke," they would say. "They usually have brains . . ." On Herzl Street, the store owners took to downing double portions of ice and washing it down with fruit juice. On every street, they installed scaffolding, built new houses and additional floors, sweating nonstop. The speculator Greenshteyn announced in the newspapers: "A new colony is being built, by the name of Kiryat Dvora near Tel Aviv. (His wife's great-grandmother was called Dvora.) Building lots for low prices." Many workers and store owners paid money to buy lots. A week later, when they traveled to see their lot, it turned out that there wasn't any land there . . .

*   *   *

The price of land rose throughout the entire country. Tarsis Effendi couldn't resist the temptation of the high prices and auctioned off the village of Jalil for the debts that the peasants owed him. Some of the fellahin didn't want to leave the land and went after the foreign plowmen with a hail of stones. The police came and arrested twenty fellahin. They were sentenced with a two-year prison term.

Yakobson, the *Tarbut* teacher, arrived in a ship full of halutzim and with an ocean of enthusiasm. When he spotted a palm tree, he cried: look, palm trees do indeed exist in this world! I thought they only grew in the Bible. He was delighted with the Hebrew signs. At night, he strolled with his shtetl's secretary of the Jewish National Fund. They saw a building where concrete was being poured by electric light. The workers, tired and dirty, could barely stand on their own feet. The secretary pointed at the building and said: "Thus is our land being built! What enthusiasm!" The Tarbut teacher quietly whispered the blessing of gratitude, *shehehiyanu*.

2

The coffee was too hot, and Ben Yishai burned his tongue. He set the warm cup aside and began leafing through the newspapers. He went through several pages like that, then stopped on the last page and scanned through the various compact announcements: "Jews, settle in the city of your Fathers! Hebron awaits its Jewish children. Purchase lots near the Cave of the Patriarchs." "Buy lots on the mountains between Hebron and Jerusalem. Ill people will travel there from all over the world to heal their lungs, and jobs will be plentiful."

That's where Ben Yishai got angry and yelled to his wife: "It's all a lie! On the mountains there's not even a single tree. You can't plant trees at all there because the mountains are bare cliffs!" Ben Yishai was furious! They beat him to it! He scanned through several more announcements, and while sipping the cooled-down coffee, said to Shulamit in the kitchen: "The speculators of Nalewki have invaded our poor fatherland like a gang of flies. They are selling our holiest ideals by the pound and by the ounce!"

3

It was still quiet in the "heart of Tel Aviv." In the newly finished houses, which were a mixture of styles and colors, the shutters were still lowered. Only a few young Yemenite women passed by, stooping under heavy baskets of vegetables and dairy products, and several groups of boys and girls headed to the sea. Closer to the city center, the streets became livelier and louder: Half-naked workers sweated on buildings, drivers unloaded sand from large vehicles, respectable Jews walked to Herzl Street, and formally dressed tourists rode in taxis, to look at building lots. Every step of the way, from the large display windows, from cobblers' shacks, from soda stands and herring shops, announcements, both printed and penned, looked down from above: "Purchase building lots . . . ! In the new city, Lloyd George . . . in the new colony, Sara's Tent . . . among the villas at Blue Sea . . ."

The corner of Rothschild Boulevard and Herzl Street was already bustling with people and hollering. The exchange market was operating in full force: beggars, small speculators, homeowners who lived off rent money, and leaders of contract collectives filled up the avenues, reclining on benches, and standing around in circles under the tree shade, talking, yelling, and making hand gestures. "Well, what's the big outrage?" argued a middle-aged man with a fair bit of gray in his beard. "There's buying, there's selling, and Jews make a living! What good is the Land of Israel for, if not for making a living?"

"But they're stuffing the Arabs with money, stuffing them," interjected a thin little voice belonging to a young man in his twenties. "They're making the Arabs rich!"

"Me, I bought a piece of land on my very last dime," called a man with a frightened voice from a corner. "It turns out my lot is somewhere on a rock."

A German Jew tried explaining his trouble: "I wanted to see my land right away; the sellers stared at me with their big eyes: 'What? You're going to travel to look at your lot? But it's dangerous to lay a foot there! The Arabs stab anyone who comes.' So, I asked them: 'So, how will you build there?' They answered: 'P-s-s-s, you still aren't familiar with our Land of Israel! In a few weeks, there will be several cities and a couple of colonies established there, and you won't see any Arabs around.'"

4

All of a sudden people started running. The exchange market rose and fell willy-nilly all over the street. In the great panic, people screamed: "What happened?"

"Is there a fire?"

"Where's Magen David Adom ambulance?"

An elderly Jew calmed down the crowd: "Nothing happened. There's no fire. A bunch of idle boys came down to King Solomon Bank and are making trouble there." There was a big commotion at King Solomon Bank. Workers in paint-speckled clothing, young women holding children by the hand, cobblers in leather aprons, and shopkeepers stood by the door and growled: "They should give the money over to us and go gobble up their land . . . !"

"We toiled and saved up, saved up and toiled, hoping to buy a little house. We see a sign: 'A New Neighborhood to Be Built Near Tel Aviv'; so we say: 'Good, for now we'll buy a plot, and then later, when we save up a bit more, we'll get to building . . .'"

"A pox on their insides . . ." a young woman interjected.

"There's no road and no water . . . they just sold us sand from a desert . . ."

"This is the bank where we deposited our money . . . give us our money back! . . ."

"They sold us the land that belongs to an entire Arab village without even notifying the village. Just like as if we were in Tel Aviv and they would sell us the streets of New York . . ." The crowd kept standing and making a racket at the bank entrance until noontime—and at the end, left with nothing.

5

At midday, Ben Yishai was so absorbed in his thoughts he didn't even notice that his cutlets were burned. Right after the meal he met up with Ben Dor and told him: "The speculators are destroying this country. Something's got to be done!"

"Clearly we can't just sit with our hands on our laps. Everyone else is raking in gold and we should stay quiet?"

"Would it even be possible to build that kind of a new neighborhood in Tel Aviv, something like its own city, a garden city, let's say, so that each and every Jew could actually own his own estate, like it is written in the Torah . . . ?"

"Is it possible? Sure it's possible; you just need to want it. There are lands around the old agricultural school Mikveh Yisrael, valuable lands . . . gold . . . !"

"But that's so far from Tel Aviv . . . ?"

"I know! But we can call it 'extended Tel Aviv.' What, Tel Aviv can't expand just like New York? And then our new neighborhood will be right in the middle of the city . . ."

So right then and there they came up with the plan together: Every family will have a house with a garden and six dunams of land. You can live reasonably on six dunams of land. For now, we will announce only 20,000 such lots . . . When things improve, with God's help, we'll expand the city!

"Now that's what I call 'development!'" Ben Yishai beamed with joy at the plan. "That's how to build up a country: with momentum, with volume! We'll chop the wings off of all the speculators, who are trying to become rich at the expense of the People! A very own a house and a very own garden . . ."

Ben Dor had already become accustomed to his partner's long speeches, so he nodded his head while thinking about other things. Ben Yishai became ecstatic and began breaking down his theory of building cities for him: "A city is like a wheel; once it begins to turn, it keeps on turning. Take, for example, Tel Aviv: a Jew made a little soda factory, and he hired a worker. The worker needed to have an apartment—another Jew built a house with apartments; he hired construction workers . . . Add to it the rise of a Grabski in Poland and a Hitler in Germany—and the city is growing like yeast!"

6

A week after that conversation, Ben Yishai was so busy he was in over his head: He had purchased three hundred dunams of land in the area of Mikveh Yisrael; prepared for printing, on quality paper—in Hebrew and English—the plan for the new colony, with its city park and city theater; and issued brochures in the name of his newly founded company, *Even Yisrael*, about the new garden city. But Ben Yishai was not only thinking about the Jews already in the Land of Israel. He knew that there were millions more Jews in exile who longed for a piece of land; they were just very poor and couldn't afford such a pleasure. He solved the problem: They'll pay in installments! And that same week he called a press conference for all the newspapers of the Jewish diaspora in the offices of his company *Even Yisrael*, where he gave—along with tea and cake served by Shulamit herself—a short speech:

"Our company has been built on solid foundations. And the bedrock of the People are the workers and farmers. We, the 17 million Jews (let's hope that our Jewish tribesmen in Russia aren't also already lost to us) have enough wanderers! Therefore, our company has decided to build a colony for Jews as a garden city, where they will be occupied with productive work. Here you have our plan: for now, only 20,000 families. We won't rush . . . slowly but surely . . . and to make it possible for every Jew, even the very poorest, to be part of the colony, we're offering the lots on an installment plan: 1 pound a week . . ."

7

In a few weeks' time, Ben Yishai's speech had been printed in the Jewish-diaspora newspapers around the world in giant capital letters: "A New Garden City of 40,000 Families in the Land of Israel!" And emissaries traveled out to all the countries where Jews lived, to recruit shareholders and colonists.

The only difficulty was collecting the money: Should it be deposited in just any bank? That's not a good enough plan since Jews want everything, as you know, snip-snap, on one foot, and this kind of thing drags on: the rest of the land has to be purchased, and then it has to be apportioned . . . And what should be done when they demand their money back? That's why a dedicated bank is necessary to hold the deposits. But Ben Yishai couldn't found a bank by himself, because according to the law, the bank had to be completely separate from the company that purchased the land. So he came up with a new idea: Shulamit would establish the bank!

A couple of days later, workers hung a large sign over a newly finished building on Ahad-Ha'am Street: Bank Tarshish, Ltd. To this bank, Jews from the entire world sent their pounds for the colonization company, *Even Yisrael.*

"The Cedar of Lebanon" and "The Future of Our People"

1

The Hebrew Writers' Union had split years ago, and for many years now the artists gathered in two clubs: the older artists in the café called The Cedar of Lebanon, and the younger in one called The Future of Our People. Both cafés were located on Allenby Street, far away from each other. There were no major differences to speak of between the older and the younger writers. In Palestine, social conflicts, land disputes, national uprisings, and strategic plans were all quite intertwined, but the Hebrew artists weren't writing about it; they understood that those topics reeked of politics—and politics, as is well known, is the opposite of art. They occupied themselves only with explorations of the deep, spiritual essence of man, so they concentrated, strolling from one café to the next, on the soul of the individual person.

In the café Future of Our People, they ate nonkosher meat and smoked cigarettes openly on the Sabbath. In the café The Cedar of Lebanon they didn't eat meat at all—they satisfied themselves with sour milk of Jewish production and smoked their cigarettes in secret while going to relieve themselves, as people do, so the smoke wouldn't be detected. The rabbis issued a declaration against The Future café, where clashes with pious Jews also occurred, but the revolutionary writers held their ground and continued to eat nonkosher cutlets in the heart of the Jewish city.

When the question arose of sending picketers to the Jewish groves, and the unions of doctors, lawyers, and teachers sent their delegates to picket, the Writers' Union also united. All the writers gathered in

The Future of our People and sent out pickets to prevent the Arabs from working.

2

In the two cafés, journalists from various countries also hung around. Zibulski, a journalist from Poland, worked nonstop, and especially during the Purim season when he had to write long expansive articles about Meir Dizengoff, the mayor of Tel Aviv, who rode on a white horse at the head of the carnival; about the joyous workers, who continually danced hora in the streets; and about the Yemenite maids, who were invariably chosen as the Queen Esthers. Throughout the year, he wrote about the young generation of Jewish farmers, the Hebrew prophets' ideals of the workers' communes, and the Arab villages, which had become rich from Jewish money.

Lerner was an American journalist who wrote for a Yiddish socialist newspaper in New York. It wasn't as easy for him as it was for Zibulski: His articles had to be both Zionist-leaning and radical-progressive; they had to discuss the poverty of the fellahin, as well as raise a loud voice against speculation and brokerage. He praised the communes and criticized not allowing the Arabs to work. He wrote about the economic revival of the Jewish People and scorned the fuss made about the handful of Jewish farmers, while all the new arrivals stayed in the city and Tel Aviv was just shop after shop.

His task, which was to please everyone, was a tough one. And in The Future of Our People they decreed: He's a Communist, a loyal member, and that's all . . . But here's where the real story begins:

One day, when he was sitting in his room at his desk, holding a pen in his hand and smoking a cigarette, thinking about what to write for his newspaper, there was a knock on his door, and a young woman entered. She stood at the threshold and asked: "Is this where Lerner lives?"

"Yes, here!" he got up.

"I came here to invite you for a talk at a workers' group." The girl was Hanke. Lerner shoved his hands in his pockets and didn't take his eyes off her for a few seconds. Hanke blushed, lowered her head, and stood still like an accused person. Lerner was already twenty-nine years old. But his thickly wrinkled face made him seem a couple of years older. On the end of his nose sat a large pair of glasses, supported by long, silvered temples on his tiny little ears. From under the glasses peeked out tiny little eyes and a small wrinkle in the right corner of his forehead, which gave his face a constant cynical grin. In America, Lerner used to have a girl, Mary. He loved her very much and took her with him on his trips to foreign countries. On one of those trips, he met with a good-looking young industrialist, who ended up taking that girl from him.

"Don't be sad," she told him as they were parting ways. "Life is messy and full of surprises . . ." Lerner was sad though, and for a long time.

3

Hanke felt his probing gaze, but she quickly returned to her senses and asked for the second time: "So, do you have time tomorrow evening?"

Certainly, he had time! He offered her a cigarette and began talking like an old acquaintance: "So, is this how it is? You all are wasting your short lives in this remote corner . . . ? Across the entire world, great historical events are taking place, and here you are making a fuss in a spoonful of water thinking that you're accomplishing who knows what . . . !"

His speech offended Hanke at her core. The "entire world" had been her weak spot throughout the years, but the words of this person, whose pointy nose and cynical grin suggested untrustworthiness, angered her. She shot back: "Nonsense, who lives in the 'entire world?' A worker in New York can only live on his own block and struggle in his own factory."

"Yeah, but what about the horizons? Everything here is so small and miniature, without any prospects . . ."

"It's got the same prospects as anywhere else in the entire world! Every place is important, and of course you can't know which is more important and which less . . ."

"No, no," he answered back firmly. "There are countries where you see the goal clearly and fight directly for it, but what do you envision here in this country?" He went to the desk, pulled a large stack of American newspapers from a drawer, and addressed Hanke: "See this? Cotton, sugar, crops—this is what has an impact on history, not your proclamations that you distribute in some village, ninety percent of which get lost. A stock-market crash on Wall Street has more impact on the fellahin of Palestine than all your propaganda." After a moment of silence, he said to her: "You can take these newspapers. I'll come pick them up. Can I come to you . . . ?"

Hanke understood what he meant and replied: "No, it's impossible, no strangers are allowed in my room." They parted ways, and Lerner escorted her to the door. When she had already walked away a bit, he tossed out at her: "You can talk to me informally . . ."

4

Several weeks passed. Lerner came to Hanke's every evening, but someone was always there: sometimes Mustafa, sometimes Dora, and sometimes other, unfamiliar people. He barely went to Café Ruth, where the journalists gathered, wrote even fewer articles, and became very impatient. Once, he went to her very early and found her still lying in bed. "I missed you very much," he told her with a trembling voice.

"What's the big deal," she answered apathetically, shutting her eyes again and sticking her head under the pillow.

"But you're never alone!" he began with a pleading voice.

"Why should you need me to be alone . . . ?" she laughed in his face. Her stubbornness upset him. *She's playing with me*, he thought, and lost his courage—*I've got to speak plainly with her*. But he did not speak plainly with her right away. He put it off day after day, and resolved, "you have got to be alone with her sometime, totally alone . . ."

* * *

Mustafa kept coming. But he had become quieter and sadder. He was certain that Hanke loved Lerner because he was very learned and knew so many things. At night, when Lerner gave his long speeches, he shoved himself in a corner and shrunk to become invisible.

A Chapter in Which Two of Our Heroines Get Married—and the Next Steps of Motke and Zalmen

1

No one came to her room all evening, and Hanke and Lerner sat alone talking until late. Mustafa hadn't come over for a couple of nights now. Lerner was pleased and spoke with a revived voice. Hanke lay propped up on her elbows, looking over Lerner, but not listening to his words. She felt sad spending that evening alone with him, and even his profound words didn't move her.

Lerner looked at his watch and noticed that it was already half past midnight. *Certainly no one will come at this hour*, he thought. *You've got to talk seriously with this girl now.* He pushed himself toward Hanke and took her hand. Suddenly, they heard quick steps above, running down the stairs and clopping on the stone. Dora stormed into the room, and while catching her breath uttered: "It's so late, and I still don't have a place to stay tonight!"

"So, you'll sleep here."

Lerner got up with a sour expression on his face, said goodbye, and left with a heavy heart. The girls made the bed and began to undress. Hanke suddenly felt the need to ask about Mustafa. She tried to ask in an indifferent tone: "Is he staying in your room for a long time?"

"It's still unclear, but probably longer. He shouldn't step out of the house and make the neighbors suspicious . . . Ach, you drove him nuts!"

Dora suddenly turned red. The girls stood, undressed. They looked at their naked bodies for a while. *She loves him,* Hanke thought, adjusted her nightgown, and stroked her own white, femininely curved hands, which shone in the dark. They jumped into bed, cuddled under the blanket, and fell asleep instantly.

2

Dora slept at Hanke's for a couple of weeks straight. They avoided talking about Mustafa, and the topic became like a wall between them. Lerner continued to come over every evening, staying until late. His impatience grew: Many times, he stayed until the young women went to bed, then he looked, confused, at the two bodies in their bed and told himself, as he walked home: *I have become an old fool . . .*

One time, Dora didn't come to bed. Hanke had been looking nervously out the window, listening to the passing steps, and feeling more unsettled every minute. A silent agony languished in her heart: *She's not coming . . . she's staying with him . . .* Hanke tried calming herself down—it's practically all the same to her—but the feeling of sadness didn't go away. Lerner decided to take advantage of this opportunity. He glanced at his watch, bent over her, and quietly uttered: "For a long time I've been wanting to speak with you . . . Understand, there's not really any plan here . . . and there's not really any point for you staying in this land forever . . . We'll both leave . . . We can even go tomorrow to the American consulate about papers . . ."

Hanke wasn't surprised by his offer. Her eyes wandered across the room, and she suddenly pushed him away: "Drop it, let's go!"

Above, on the pavement stones, steps sounded and then disappeared into a side alley. Hanke rose and dragged the cover from her bed: "well, I'm going to bed," she said, slapping her pillow. "It's about time I slept alone for once!" She laughed in his face brazenly. Her free attitude bothered him. He ran around the room, gulping one cigarette after the other. Hanke was standing barefoot and waiting. He went to the door, gestured with his hand, and left. When Lerner was gone, she threw herself on the bed, shoved her head into the pillow, and wept deeply, bitterly: It isn't possible to escape one's destiny . . . I've got nothing against Dora . . . I'm destined to suffer and to cause suffering . . . I'll suffer with him, and I'll suffer with a different person . . . That's how it always goes with me . . .

3

She woke up in the bright of day and looked outside. All around, the world was shining, and the sky was blue. Impatiently, she waited for the evening. She even worried that perhaps Lerner was offended and wouldn't come. She ran around the room, then stood at the window, and yelled out into the empty void: I'm going . . . immediately . . . tomorrow . . . !

Lerner arrived late, his head bowed. He sat down at the edge of the sofa and was silent. Hanke lifted her head haughtily and asked: "so, when are we going . . . ?"

Lerner thought she was mocking him and became even more furious. Hanke pulled him toward her and stroked his arm. He grabbed her fingers and began to fondle and kiss them: "Do you truly mean it? Really and truly?"

"Of course . . . !" and she stretched her whole body and began to caress him. He embraced her with trembling hands and whispered with choked and broken words: "No, no one will come here now . . . We're both here now . . . Tomorrow we'll go to the consulate . . ." She laughed in his face. Impatient as he was, he threw himself on her. Hanke slightly struggled for a while longer and later gave in to his solid hands.

4

Each morning, just after waking up, while he was still lying on the floor wrapped in the rough, prickly blanket, Motke relived "that night" all over again in all its details: the kibbutz playroom, the kitchen, the dark courtyard, the dogs' barking, and the sudden thunderclap from the edge of the village. Then, everything was a blur: naked people ran from the barracks weeping and screaming, asking him questions from all directions, and he didn't know how to answer. Later, they found the briefcase with the proclamations . . .

He stubbornly analyzed every tiny detail, trying to dig the images out of his memory of people and things in those last hours before "the end." Over and over, he pieced together the course of events, as if quietly hoping that somewhere, in a corner of "that night" the secret source of his confusion lay hidden. He thought through the contingencies a thousand times, to lessen the fateful outcome. He paced the room, reliving that dawn when the police came to begin their investigation: "They shot right after he left?"

"Yeah, right after."

"Did he have time to run to the barrack?"

"No . . . but maybe . . ."

But he was calm. A pale calm ruled over him through and through. Everything around him was pale: the sky, the houses, the people. Three months had already passed, and each day the same: the same cell, the same thoughts, and the same strip of world visible through the small window on the other side of the stone wall. Only on Friday was there any difference. He was brought to the city, held in a waiting room for a long time, and then asked endless complicated questions. The investigation tormented and exhausted him, but even so, he waited impatiently for this day: He saw streets and people. He spoke and heard human voices. He even enjoyed the intensely sorrowful feeling that overtook him when he returned, because he longed for change so strongly.

5

In the depths of his consciousness, he didn't believe he would be hanged. He closed his eyes and tried to imagine how he would look hanging from the rope. But that wasn't death yet. His hanging body still had a connection to living thoughts. A commotion in the yard shook Motke out of his thoughts. He knew it was time for *khakure*, when the prisoners could walk the yard, and he climbed out the window to look down below. He only saw white, shaved heads circling around the wall. Soon the heads disappeared. After the *khakure*, a key turned in his door. He thought he would be taken to walk the yard, which he used to do alone, after all the other prisoners, but the supervisor gestured to him: "Get dressed, you're going to the city!"

Motke quickly put on his shoes. In front of the investigative judge, he was first asked standard questions: "Were you in Binyamina?"

"Yeah."

"Worked in the swamp?"

"Yeah."

"Did you knew the Arabs in the area?"

Motke contemplated for a while, trying to remember the Arabs in the area. But the swamp reminded him of the kibbutz, and an ocean of memories flooded his brain; images came and went and didn't let him focus his thoughts at all on any specific thing. The judge pierced him with an interrogating look and didn't take his eyes off him. Suddenly, a side door opened, and two policemen led in a young Arab in chains. The judge glanced at the two prisoners and asked Motke in a severe tone: "Well, do you know him?"

Motke stared a while at the tall, dark-skinned Arab and answered: "No, don't know him."

"And do you know him?" the judge asked the Arab. The Arab shook his head no, without opening his mouth.

"Speak!" the judge yelled. "Do you know him?"

"No!"

They stood across from each other for an extended time. The young Arab hung his head low. Motke looked at him and searched for a connection between this group member, the murder in Alfiya, and the Kabara swamp. Suddenly, something flashed through his mind and his eyes lit up. He remembered the history of Kabara that Zalmen had told him once: An old fellah died because they took the water from his well; his grandchild found him eaten up by mice in the withered garden. Could this be his grandchild . . . ?

The events began to run through his brain very quickly: I came, of course, to Binyamina to dry out the swamp . . . that is why the old fellah died . . . that is why his grandchild went to Alfiya to shoot people . . . that is why they arrested me . . . And he could see the whole tied and tangled knot. After the interrogation everything went quickly: he hadn't been asked much and was sent straight back to his cell. He felt his fate spinning out of his control, manipulated by strangers, and that things were constantly happening behind a screen so he couldn't see them clearly.

A couple of weeks later he was transferred to the general cellblock for political prisoners. He got updated there immediately on everything: At the demonstrations in Jaffa they had arrested a fellah, who had sewer pipes in his pocket. The investigation revealed that the pipes were full of explosives. They compared them with the bombs that had been thrown in Alfiya, which revealed they were the same sort. After lengthy investigations, the fellah admitted he had participated in the Alfiya attack and gave up another friend of his, a young fellah, Rasheed, from the Binyamina region.

Motke stood by the little window of his prison cell and gazed intently at the outside world. From the newspapers that had been smuggled into the prison, Motke had learned about the course of the investigation: Rasheed stubbornly denied it, but his friend, the fellah, revealed every detail about the preparation and execution of the attack. The court had taken the defendants to the Jezreel Valley and reenacted the drama at the very spot. Rasheed's guilt was proven beyond a reasonable doubt.

6

Even before Rasheed's trial ended, Motke was sentenced for distributing literature. Motke got three months imprisonment and after that, expulsion from the country. The courtroom was full of people. From the attack onward, the press had been full of details about the murder and about the Communists. The streets were full of talk about Motke. People shook their heads: "It's shattering to think that only yesterday he was a halutz . . . !"

One evening, a supervisor entered and smilingly said to Motke: "*Fradj*, Free! Get dressed and come to the office!" Motke turned pale. He got dressed quickly, and in confusion, swapped his shoes with his jacket sleeves, quietly shook his friends' hands, and ran down the steps. In the office, the policeman smiled at him, the iron door opened, and he stood, a free man, beyond the thick prison walls.

7

He looked around. He was standing on a blank block in Jaffa. In the side alleys, gramophones screeched. Several young Arabs with tall fezzes passed by. A soldier with a rifle patrolled along the wall. Where should he go? He slowly paced through the Jaffa–Tel Aviv streets, searching for familiar faces along the way. All the faces were strange. Nobody noticed him. Herzl Street was bustling. Large windows glowed with light. Couples strolled, drank lemonade at shiny kiosks, and laughed happily. He went down along Allenby Street: Where will he go now . . . ? Suddenly he spotted the bus to Jerusalem and hopped on. He pushed his head out the window and looked at the passing fields, small villages, and tall, rocky mountains.

As soon as he arrived in Jerusalem, he ran off to what used to be Hanke's address. The lady who owned the house looked at him with bewilderment: "What? She hasn't been here for a long time . . . She was sent to prison . . . !" He continued wandering around the dark alleys, looking into the Yemenite courtyards, where families were sitting on stony steps and conversing. The surroundings were dark and gloomy. He felt good in the evening's sadness. It got late. The people gradually disappeared; the yards closed. He was still wandering aimlessly and gazing at the stone walls. He counted the alleys, made mistakes, turned back, and cursed this city that had no numbers or names for its streets and houses.

8

For an entire night, he walked around the dead, stone city. He still must see her, see Hanke . . . In a couple of days he'd be deported, and might never see her again . . . In the middle of the night, small fires began to glow in the houses: Old Jews wailed the destruction of the Temple. Police guards clopped on the pavement in pairs. And the racket of their boots echoed across the alleys, mixing with the wailing of the old people. Bodies dressed in rags moved across dark ruins and unfinished buildings: Arab workers from remote villages and camps crawled out from under their tatters and looked outside to check if it was already time to get up and go look for work. When it became light out, Motke paused his wandering by a cellar that had two windows facing a yard.

Motke entered the yard and softly knocked on the window. A sound of knocking fingers woke Hanke; she got up and looked around, astonished: There was a man's suit laying there, wrinkled, and a pair of men's shoes stood in the middle of the room. Then she noticed Lerner, who lay next to her, snoring. The fingers knocked again on the windowpane. She raised her head and noticed the silhouette of a man. Her eyes played tricks on her: Him? Now? . . . She adjusted her nightgown, opened the door, and yelled: "Motke?!"

Motke quietly stepped inside and noticed a strange man, who tossed the blanket from his head with both his hands and looked frightened and weary-eyed. Motke was so tired he could barely stand up. Hanke spoke, fiddling with her shirt: "See, Motke, I married a journalist, and I'm leaving for America tomorrow . . . We'll have a large apartment, nice furniture . . . I really only made a pointless detour: Even if I hadn't gone to the kibbutz, I probably would have done the same thing I'm doing today anyway—right after high school or at university . . . It's impossible to run from your own destiny . . . !"

9

At noon, Zalmen took a nap on a sand hill in the shadow of the unfinished building. A worker pulled out a newspaper from his small lunch basket, quickly scanned the foreign telegrams and political articles, and having surveyed the Palestinian news section for a while, shouted: "Take a look at what's going on!"

Several workers, who were semisnoozing nearby, raised their heads: "What?"

"Something about an Arab with a Jewish girl! Take it and read: 'A search for literature in a suspicious Jerusalem apartment; a midnight raid found them both lying in bed "according to the laws of Moses and Muhammad"' . . ."

The crowd laughed. Zalmen didn't respond at all; he took the newspaper and immediately saw Dora's name: It's certain, he mumbled to himself; it's Dora and Mustafa. He was ashamed of himself. A sinking feeling suddenly took him over and gnawed at him. A free man shouldn't feel jealousy . . .

After lunch, he impatiently carried the bricks on the steps, knocked over a couple of chairs in his path, and almost split open a worker's head. In the evening, he washed up quickly and took a car to Jerusalem.

The women's prison was in Bethlehem. Zalmen ran off to the Jaffa Gate, where the neighborhood's cars were idling. It was already dark. The Old City's walls rose darkly with its towering Migdal David. In the middle, on the dirty steps of the narrow tunnel-alleys, children played, and young porters ran around with baskets on their shoulders. On the terraces of the nearby cafés several old, reddened women sat with gramophones spinning sadly. Old people with red fezzes on their heads smoked hookahs and looked apathetically toward the skies. Zalmen felt a deep sadness blow over him, as well as a smell of rotten apples, burned chestnuts, and an old, musty past.

10

The car had a couple of Jewish women traveling to Rachel's Tomb and an old Russian monk, who had come down from Constantinople to see the birthplace of Christ. The Jewish women were constantly scratching themselves and picking lice out of their clothes one after another; the monk looked around with blind eyes and kept mumbling incomprehensible prayers. The earliest Zalmen could see Dora was the next day at noon. They spoke through the prison bars. To the side a former postman stood and listened; he had been sentenced for stealing money and then elevated in prison to a semiofficial. Dora smiled, but, noticing Zalmen's sad eyes, turned serious. She placed her hand on Zalmen's fingers, with which he held onto the bars, and said: "Nu, don't be sad!"

"I wanted to see you . . . so much to see you . . ."

They didn't know how to begin talking and stood silent. The guard turned his head: "You have one more minute left!"

Dora began talking at a fast pace: "I want to stay here in this country . . . I'm fed up with dragging myself around and wandering . . . I love him, Mustafa . . . and hey, you've got to settle down somewhere . . ." She stroked his fingers. The minute was over.

*   *   *

When Zalmen got out of the car in the Old City of Jerusalem, a person in civilian clothes detained him: "Come with me! You're under arrest!"

Before a Storm

1

When the guard of the Akko prison, Schubin, received a letter for a convict, he would coincidentally pass by the political prisoners' cellblock and mutter to the convict Ephraim: "Give a look at this letter and tell me what it says . . . I've just forgotten my glasses . . ." He would say this every time, even though everyone had long known that he couldn't read or write . . . When he brought a letter for Zalmen, he handed it over to Ephraim to read, "because he just forgot his glasses"; everything must go in its order, and according to discipline . . . Zalmen grabbed the letter quickly. It was from home. He recognized his father's tall, constricted letters:

> To my dear son, may his light shine: First, we're all healthy. We should hear the same from you. And second, we may all possibly come to the Land of Israel shortly. Because God, blessed be He, has helped and enabled us to purchase a property semi-free, by paying one pound per week. It's with the Even Yisroel Association. And the money we're paying is secure because we've deposited it in Tarshish Bank. And they say that, God willing, in a couple of months, they'll begin to plant. So please go there and see precisely where our lot is located . . . and we'll have the privilege to see each other soon enough . . . and the Redeemer shall come to Zion . . .

Zalmen didn't finish his letter, because Schubin came back running with an alarm: "Guys, pack up your stuff and get going! They arrested a whole mess of fellahin. Sorry but you'll have to spend a couple nights in general housing . . ." Zalmen got wrapped up dealing with his things and didn't leave his cell as the new prisoners were led in. Locked in chains in twos, bent over with bowed heads, they stood along the walls. Most of them limped, and had bandaged heads, and black eyes. Several gray-haired elders could barely stand on their feet. Moaning, they leaned against the walls, dragging each other along with them. Zalmen went up to a young fellah: "Why did they arrest you?"

"They were brawling. One half of the village against the other."

"Why?"

"Over a piece of land. Just yesterday they were all sharing. . . . But today they say that it's theirs . . . And then, there were fights in the Haifa prison. A dozen policemen or so came in and beat everybody up . . . hit them over the head, backs . . . right in their eyes . . ."

Schubin saw Zalmen and went to get him out. He dragged him through the corridor by the arm, out into the large yard with the criminals. Mahmed, a political prisoner walking near Zalmen, defended the fellahin: "When they have so little land . . . The villages are packed with landless fellahin . . . they're always fighting: for a field, a well, a tree, for a little spot of pasture . . ."

"I know . . . I know where the fights come from," mumbled Zalmen, touching his father's unfinished letter in his pocket.

2

At noon, the prisoners were evacuated from their cells. They lined up and walked around a pond in the middle of the yard: their noon stroll. Afterward, a policeman yelled: "on your knees!" And every prisoner got down on his knees and waited for the English commander. The commander walked past the kneeling bunch, stared coldly in every direction, and turned back to his office. The policeman handed out food: thin little pieces of bread and tiny pots of slop. The group remained kneeling the whole time.

After eating, Zalmen hung around the yard and looked at the prisoners. He stood beside a tall young Arab, who stood out from everybody else in his long pink shirt. "Why is he wearing such a thing?"

"He got 15 years . . ."

"15 years . . . ? For what?"

"He raped some daughter of a rich Ingleyz, a young girl . . ."

Zalmen noticed someone among them with his hand chained to his foot. "And that guy, what's he in for?" he asked.

"He raped a man . . . a forty-year-old man . . ." The chained one, a healthy young man with the muscled neck of an ox, stared at the ground, not uttering a word.

"And that one's in for taxes. He couldn't pay up so he got locked up. A few are doing time for theft: They didn't have anything to eat, so they went into other people's fields. Then there's also some who got into fights with the Sayoni (the Zionists); their land got sold off, they didn't want to leave, and they got into fights."

3

In the corridor, heavy steps echoed. Through the bars, the prisoners spotted armed policemen standing in a line by each door, with guns in their hands. "What happened?"

Someone ran to the window, shoved his head through the bars, and yelled: "They're taking him to be hanged!"

The crowd jumped up from their spots and hung on the windows. Zalmen looked out through the dusty windowpane and noticed a slim Arab in the yard, dressed in red, being escorted by two policemen, the prison commander, and a civilian. "Who is that?" he asked.

The prisoners watched with tense stares and were silent. Only the old man answered quietly: "That's Rasheed . . . They say he threw bombs . . ."

Zalmen now recognized Rasheed's figure and his walk. He walked step by step, as if he were strolling by himself. The policemen and the commander behind him moved slowly and silently, like at a funeral. A deadly silence dominated the entire prison. Breathing was the only sound. In all the surrounding windows heads hung looking down at the yard, at the prisoner in red. Suddenly he stopped, raised his head to the walls, and yelled: "Allah will be with you, prisoners!"

"Allah will bless you," they whispered in the windows. Rasheed, with his escorts, disappeared into a small door of the fortress. The prisoners focused silently on the windows for a while, looking at the empty yard. Then they sat back down on the floor. On the door of the prison, a flag fluttered.

"Already dead!" muttered one of those who had been looking outside.

Silence dominated the whole afternoon in the cells. Even the guards walked on tiptoe and didn't slam the doors. An old prisoner in Zalmen's cell said: "He's told to go on the stairs. And he doesn't know which one is death. And when he gets to that one, it's C-R-A-S-H . . . He falls through, and the noose on his neck . . ." The old man placed his hands around his own neck and stuck out his tongue. The crowd around him, in the half-dark cell, stared with wide, frightened eyes.

4

Evening fell. Darkness covered the brick prison fortress and crawled into the corners of the cells. Prisoners who were not allowed any more time out in the yard walked to the "zones"—large clay pots in the corners—and did their business there. A sharp stench spread across the cells. Zalmen looked through the window into the oncoming night: A dark sea churned and washed the yellow-sanded shores of semicircular Haifa Bay. Across from it, the mountainous city shone with all its multistory buildings. Hundreds of red flames sparkled in the port. A ship emerged from the mountain, slid like a shadow over the water, and disappeared behind the horizon.

On the Haifa seashores, hundreds of workers had put aside their labor: boiling-hot tar and heaps of stones for the highway, the chisels and hammers of the quarry, long pipes and iron wheelbarrows—and headed to their resting places: the wide strip of sand amid the port's large, unfinished camps. Barefoot, with torn, baggy coats, they ran like desert birds between the stilled machines and the unfinished facades and sat down in circles to eat their suppers: thin, burned pitas, with ground, salted weeds. Afterward, they lay down in their spots, where their snoring was muted by the sound of the sea waves. Mustafa sat down near a group, took some of their bread, and began quietly: "You build so many houses but you end up sleeping outdoors!"

"The will of Allah! There was no rain, so we came from our faraway villages to earn some money so we could eat!"

"So, Allah wants some people to go hungry and others to amass gold?"

5

Two policemen passed by, leading a civilian. Mustafa went silent. He looked at them and recognized Motke. The policemen led Motke up to the ship and submitted his papers to the captain. When the ship whistled for departure, a wind began to blow. The quiet, broken sea suddenly rose and flung itself with a deafening sound at the shore. The calm waves grew, carrying themselves with momentum over the stony walls, slamming back with a slap, and with newly increased force, flew into a new onslaught.

The wind strengthened, digging into the depths of the sea, and producing giant waves, which wriggled with wide-open, foamy mouths, ready to destroy the shadowed, stony barriers. Secret forces were swimming from hidden abysses. The entire sea, far on the horizon, hurled itself like a wild animal, roaring, and rambling forward.

A storm was in the air.

APPENDIX
Prologue: With Happiness and Song

*A prologue translated from the Yiddish Press**

Kibbutz Aliyah in Poland already had a couple of years of history behind it. Its people had wandered through many hakhshara training programs, worked in sawmills and for nobles, gone as seasonal laborers to the countryside, and waited for their travel certificates, due any day. We will begin, however, from its last hakhshara, in Mosh, because from there, the kibbutz had to depart directly for Palestine, and we will indeed begin its story with that evening, when twenty-year-old Sara appeared in the late afternoon in the small hut that stood in a remote corner of the shtetl of Mosh.

Sara stormed like thunder into the small, overcrowded room and immediately created a fuss around her. That same evening, she threw off her coat, her dress, even her blouse, and remained in a pair of men's shorts and a thin tricot sweater. And she walked around in these clothes until she left. She never entered her room through the door, instead first thrusting in her naked feet and full hips, then her distinct, compressed breasts, and finally a head covered with a wave of hair, from which peeked a pair of giggly eyes.

---

* *Folksblat*, July 24, 1936, 3; *Folksblat*, July 26, 1936, 4. Parts of this prologue were integrated into the novel with some modifications.

Having arrived and changed her clothes, she immediately began to speak about tomorrow's work: She doesn't want to work in the kitchen, she doesn't want to work in the laundry—she's not interested in any female job! She wants to join the guys to do the hardest jobs. She spoke, looking at the distraught crowd of young guys. It was dirty in the room. Semidressed girls, tired after a long day's work, were lying on the floor, napping. In the corners, among dusty duffle bags, torn work clothes, and old socks, young guys were lying on straw mattresses and blankets, scratching themselves. No one remembers that there is allegedly water there, and that one should wash . . .

Next morning Sara ran off to the guys' jobs: pumping water and mixing clay. In the evening, after work, she flew inside the house like an unslaughtered rooster with an emergency: "Oy, my heart, my heart . . ." With a messy head, semiclosed lips, and eyes shut, she threw herself onto a straw mattress in the middle of the room. A turmoil, people running about. Guys brought water, they rolled up her tight tricot shirt, and placed water on her snow-white breast. The guys scanned Sara's naked feet and the calm motions of Hanke's elastic, smooth body. Almost all the rest were small-towners, overworked, with thick-skinned hands, exhausted faces, and tired eyes. At night, however, all the girls were irritated. Over the small, stuffy room, after the lamp was turned off, a reserved sob had been hanging, broken up by quiet moans and whispers.

People were sleeping pressed like herring, twenty people on a twelve-square-meter floor. On the straw sacks, which at nighttime had been spread over the entire room, guys and girls were lying, one next to the other. It was the "revolution." In the small towns, months earlier, their leader, Ignatz, had spoken in one breath about asceticism, the art of the body, and the spirit of the New Man. The girls gazed at him then with dreamy glances and sang hearty songs by the pale flames of downturned lamps.

People came and went. Students arrived from the University of Warsaw, graduates of the Hebrew High School of Bialystok, and children of shopkeepers and artisans in small towns. No one knew the number of people in this place; no one counted the arrivals and the departures. The kibbutz had been working on the construction of a large building. People were carrying blocks, mixing clay, and handing bricks. But no one knew exactly what they were working on. Several people said that they were building a large whiskey factory, others: a mental institution or even an asylum for alcoholics . . .

Zalmen loved his work on the building. During the day he walked calmly along the twisted, swaying scaffolding, treading up and down with heavy blocks on his shoulders, and enjoyed looking down to the ground from the fourth floor to see how the brick walls were growing and rising. He gazed with respect at the broad-shouldered Polish workers who were laying bricks and blocks with no rush, throwing trowels of clay, drinking beer in the middle of work, and napping at noon with a smile on their lips.

"They are surely not holding discussions for entire nights," he thought with jealousy. "Here are true workers! And we'll also become like them, there in the Land of Israel . . . We, sons of small shopkeepers and *Luftmentshen*, will strike roots there in its land and in its labor . . ."

But at night, on arriving home, he was overtaken by a sense of despair. His head spun from the amount of flesh pressed against the floor. Before going to sleep, standing half-naked, he tapped his head with both hands, to see whether his hat fit, and only then lay on the straw mattress. "Are you crazy?" his neighbor asked him. "Why are you sleeping with a hat on?"

"What should I do? I've lost three hats already. You know I can't mix lime without a hat. It's enough that I have to search for my socks for an hour every morning." Zalmen again tapped his head with both hands and, sure his hat fit well on him, he wrapped himself in the blanket and closed his eyes. But he didn't fall asleep. The previous hakhshara training programs began to intermingle in his head, mixed with scenes of his dream future. He remembered his first hakhshara, in the sawmill of Kudelich: He had come to work in that sawmill right after finishing high school. His mother cried; she wanted him to become a doctor: "For so many years I withheld food from my own mouth, cared for you in a foreign city, so that you would become a sawmiller?" But he bit his lips and left.

By then, he had already given everything to the commune: "I've liberated myself of money, of possessions, of any trace of private property. And in the Land of Israel, they will create for the first time the true commune on dry fields and plowed, raw earth . . ." There, in the hakhshara in Kudelich, it was clean everywhere: both in the room and among the people. Three months he'd been sleeping near Dora and never touched her at night. Only on the Sabbath, in their free time, would they read together and kiss . . .

It's been a month since Dora left with her workers' group for the Land of Israel, and he hasn't received a single letter from her. What was happening there . . . ? His eyes blinked rapidly. Half dreaming, he noticed thousands of halutzim in quarries and hakhshara programs. This halutzim song began humming in his head:

> From Klosowa till Shachriya,
> "Oy, what are we hearing from you?"
> We are preparing to make aliyah
> "And we laugh at you . . ."

> פֿון קאָסאָווע ביז שחריה
> אוי, וואָס הערן מיר פֿון אײַך
> גרייטן מיר זיך צו דער עליה
> און מיר לאַכן פֿון אײַך

Life in the hakhshara went on: People came and left. Among the arrivals was Khayim. He was a teacher in a small town somewhere, and suddenly he had decided to make a radical change in his life: "changing from end to end," he said to Ignatz, who came to pick him up from the train. He wore glasses and had a wig on. Ever since his first day he had generated suspicion among the young crowd: What's a person with a wig doing here? A former teacher? He was sent away to some workshop, and all day he scrubbed polished tables with a rag.

He came from work in the evening. In his small room it was messy and dark, as usual. In the corner, on the bed—the only bed reserved for the sick—lay a girl with fever, due to what kind of illness, it was unknown. This girl, tall and thin, with a pair of glasses on her pointy nose, was dressed in a white nightgown that flashed like a light beam in the dark room. The guy, chubby with red hair, freckles, and foolish eyes, lay dressed in these clothes: a green shirt with epaulets and rough, dark-blue trousers.

Both were covered up with a white bed sheet. That was the hospital of the kibbutz. When people passed by it, they remembered that sick people lay in this room, and whispered: "sh . . . sh . . . sh . . ." and scampered on the tips of their toes.

"Nu, how do you like it here?" Ignatz asked Khayim.

"But I hadn't yet considered how it'd look. Only now is it all becoming clear."

"Outward appearances shouldn't frighten you. We carry within ourselves a great human message . . ." "Redemption of people and society! We must always reveal the points of light that illuminate and lead us to our goal . . ."

Sara was sitting on a duffel bag, gazing intensely at Ignatz. She felt he was descending into an abyss, delivering from there the true meaning of life. Shaul the poet was also sitting nearby. Also, Hanke was stretched out on a straw mat. Here was the spiritual little chamber of the "point," which hosted discussions and singing almost every evening. Ignatz spoke passionately and at length. His eyes were glimmering, throwing off sparks. He gestured with his hands and gazed into the distance, as if over the heads of a big mass of people. Later, with closed eyes and swinging heads, they dreamingly crooned a mellow version of *Avinu Malkeinu*, and very late, after midnight, over the darkened huts of the shtetl, and over the snowy fields nearby, they sang a tune of Siberian prisoners:

Din-don, din-don
A sad bell is ringing . . .

A few days later, Ignatz spoke about "Hunger and Love in Literature." The crowd was lying half asleep on straw mattresses, listening. Zalmen pushed himself into a corner and wondered: Seriously, what's the point of talking so much? If Ignatz had gone to work construction, he surely wouldn't have been speaking so much . . . Sara listened to the long, muddled sentences and understood very little. Suddenly, she sensed Khayim's gaze sliding over her body. She bent her knees, pulled her skirt way down, suddenly turned red, and ran out of the room. The next day, she met Khayim, looked deep into his eyes, and began speaking. That same evening, they sat on a suitcase, speaking quietly. Khayim said: "I came to turn my life around. I came here. I was hoping that amid it all," he gestured with his hand over the room, "I would meet someone. And now I think I have." Sara listened with her eyes to the ground. They were alone now, even though in the small room around them, tens more people lay and sat.

These were cold nights. People were sleeping in their clothes. The straw mattresses lay pressed together, and the blankets were in disarray. Khayim's straw sack lay near Sara's. When it turned dark, he reached out his arms between the tangled blankets, fumbled in the cold, and touched Sara's warm hand. He quietly rolled toward her and kissed her fingers. Later he freed himself from a pile of blankets, leaned over Sara, and kissed her eyes and hair. Sara lay calm, as if asleep. Only her head swung back a bit, and her breathing got faster. Suddenly, she trembled, gave Khayim a look with a pair of big, wide-open eyes, and thrust herself under the blankets.

When Khayim woke up the next morning, Sara was already not lying on the nearby straw sack. He scanned the room with his eyes and spotted her standing by a window. The windowsills were frozen. Through the thin layer of ice appeared flying snowflakes, driven by the wind. Sara stroked the hardened frost flowers from the window. She turned around for a moment and their eyes met. Her face was pale, and in her gloomy eyes was a still sadness. At night, Sara lay curved, her head deep in her pillow. Khayim, as usual, was sleeping nearby. Sara couldn't fall asleep for hours, but she remained tucked in and immobile until late. Only when it began to dawn did she pull out her head, remove hair from her face, and look around.

A pale light had been creeping into the room's darkness, spreading a dark shine over the conjoined bodies. Things swirled in her head as in a nightmare: the room, the sleep, the filth, and the talk about "hunger and love." Later, she suddenly thought: I'm twenty years old. And she touched sleeping Khayim with her hand. Khayim woke up, unsurprised. He slid under the pile of blankets, hugged her, and whispered quietly: "my Sarenke . . . little Sarenke . . ."

Sara lay with her eyes shut, and without resistance she gave in to the movements of his fingers' undressing her. Suddenly she sensed her hot body laying naked among so many young guys. She trembled lightly and bit her lips, like a sharp pain had slashed her organs. Afterward, she embraced Khayim with her arms, kissed him for a long time on the lips, until she was out of breath, and quietly whispered: "q-quieter, sh-sh-sh."

It was quiet in the barrack; only the heavy breathing of several tens of wide-open mouths filled the sweaty air. Suddenly a soft moan punctured the silence, and a broken, suffocated squeak tumbled out like a bird that had been shot down. It turned quiet again, and someone woke up, raised their head, and fearfully asked: "Who's there?" and fell back to sleep. The pale dawn became clearer. On the frozen windowsills, elaborate ice flowers sparkled. A wind whistled in a cold chimney, and millions of snowflakes let loose in a wild dance between heaven and earth.

Zalmen worked constantly at the construction site and could barely stand up he was so tired in the evening. Ignatz went out to work only for several days. He was too weak to carry bricks, and he couldn't even keep up at mixing clay. He therefore stayed in his house and, for hours, paced around the room with large strides, deep in thought. In the evening, he held talks, led casual conversations. Ignatz was known in the movement. He had grown up in turbulence: The poverty in the shtetl and the hunger of the nearby Belarussian village had caused him distress. He eagerly devoured life and wanted to devour everything. He passionately read Bialik's poem "In the City of Slaughter," wept in secret over the Kishinev pogrom, and recited for weeks, for all his friends, Jasienski's lyrics about the peasant uprising in Ukraine. Ignatz spoke about everything with enthusiasm, discussing about all kinds of topics with the same holy glance in his eyes. On the eve of Yom Kippur at the hakhshara, he sang the sad Kol Nidrei melody, as well as a revolutionary song of the Narodnaya Volya. He propagated free love devoid of any familial constructs and spoke enthusiastically about the Christian ascetics of the desert. On the question of labor, he was a lefty: "We will organize with the Arab workers, and together with them—that is our path!"

The entire kibbutz knew Ignatz was waiting for "his girl," Anda. The commune washed a shirt with a small standing pitcher. Mira found somewhere a pair of intact women's stockings and made them into socks. Even a clean handkerchief was prepared for Ignatz. In the evenings, he trotted around in his room on the narrow strips of earth between the straw mats and sang, starry-eyed. Ignatz went to pick up his girl from the train. Sara joined him. She had recently become more serious and occasionally even threw on a long dress over her manly short pants. She still gazed passionately at Ignatz and looked into his face when he spoke. It was snowy early in the morning. They held each other's hands, skipped, and laughed like children. Ignatz didn't speak now of intellectual matters, just casual small talk. Far from the village, he hugged Sara and kissed her.

Anda arrived. She was thin and flexible like a sapling and had green catlike eyes, which lit up at night, and tiny, solid breasts that reminded people of green, unripe apples. Close to her, Ignatz walked slowly, as if she were made of glass, spoke softly, and gazed at her dreamily. In the evenings, he sat next to her on a straw mat, held his head low, and was fervently silent. He dragged together several blankets, made a place for her to sleep, while he went off to lie down on the other end of the room. Every morning, he jumped out of bed and, wrapped in a bedsheet and wholly shivering from cold, gazed at the sleeping girl.

Khayim left. He had decided to stay another half year in Poland, as a teacher, and only then go to the Land of Israel. Ignatz, who had a lousy spot by the window, lay on the empty straw mattress next to Sara. One night, Sara woke up, sensing a cold hand stroking her fingers. She was frightened for a moment but very quickly noticed it was Ignatz, and she looked at him with a surprised, curious stare. Ignatz reached for her hand, kissed the tips of her fingers, and whispered softly: "I myself don't know what's going on with me . . ."

Sara pulled back her hand, her voice sounding hurt: "And your girl?"

"I don't know, perhaps this is stronger . . . stronger than everything . . . ! Ah, life! Life!"

Every morning, Anda cast gloomy glances at the corner where Ignatz slept next to Sara. In the evenings, she would disappear for entire hours and return with red, defeated eyes. Ignatz strolled with long strides across the small room among the straw mattresses, held his head low, and smiled sadly to himself. In the small, dark room, people whispered: "It will turn into a tragedy at some point!"

"And, most importantly, it will begin in the Land of Israel, when Khayim arrives at the kibbutz . . ."

"One tragedy? Two at same time!" And indeed, shortly thereafter, someone told the whole group: "Sara is depressed . . ."

Ignatz was speaking one evening among a fatigued bunch: "We live in a stressful century. The thousands of currents that cross our souls . . ." At this point, Zalmen interjected and said: "People lie in the mud and bark at the moon . . . !" And that very idiom remained on the kibbutz for many years.

* * *

Finally, the travel certificates arrived. People began preparing for the trip. Every day, guys and girls traveled home, to pack laundry and clothes that their mothers had prepared and to catch a last glimpse at the exilic shtetls that they were about to leave for good. Sara and Ignatz left together, with the first group. Standing on the threshold, Ignatz turned around, toward the room, and said: "See you in the working, socialist, communal Land of Israel."

Zalmen didn't leave until a few months later; he went home only two days prior to his departure. His mother was walking around with teary eyes, rummaging in the closets, and constantly placing new items in his suitcase, which had been standing for three days straight in the middle of the room. She had been washing, patching, sewing buttons, and quietly moaning until late at night. About half of the shtetl came out to the car in the morning of his departure. His mother kissed him, and her voice broke out in sobs: "I won't ever . . . ever . . . ever see you again . . ."

At the station in Warsaw, it was all hustle and bustle. Young people made a circle and danced a hora. Several people were singing Hatikvah. The train moved. The halutzim stood by the small windows, gazing at the vanishing station lights, and singing: "*Mir geyen in land / mit freyd un gezang* / We're off to the land / with a joyful band."

GLOSSARY

Aliyah (Heb.): lit. ascent; Zionist term for the immigration of Jews to Israel.

Asuan (Arabic): brothers.

A Night in the Old Marketplace: title of I. L. Peretz's polyphonic modernist Yiddish drama (1907).

Bakshish: bribe (from the Persian; also used in Turkish).

Baron: short for Baron Edmond de Rothschild (1845–1934), a wealthy Jewish benefactor of early Zionist settlements in Palestine.

Bialik, Khayim Nachman (1873–1934): renowned Hebrew Zionist poet. He wrote the influential poem "In the City of Slaughter" in the aftermath of the Kishinev pogrom (1903).

Birobidzhan: the proposed Soviet, Yiddish-speaking Jewish autonomous area on the far eastern end of the Soviet Union, decided in 1928, officially declared in 1934.

Hashish: a drug produced by cannabis, usually consumed by smoking (from the Arabic).

Halutz/Halutzim: lit. pioneer/pioneers; Zionist settler(s) in Palestine.

Khawadja (Arabic): Mister.

Chuppah: wedding canopy used in Jewish weddings under which the ceremony is taking place.

Conquest of Labor (Heb. *kibush ha'uvoda*): a campaign in the 1920s–30s by Zionist settlers to force Jewish employers to hire only Jewish workers.

Conquest of Land (Heb. *kibush ha'adama*): refers to possessing land for Jewish settlement in Israel/Palestine.

Davar: a Labor Zionist Hebrew newspaper (1925–96).

Deterding, Henri (1866–1939): founder of the oil company Royal Dutch Shell and its general manager until 1936.

Dunam: Land measurement. One dunam is equivalent to 0.25 acres.

Effendi: a title of nobility in the Ottoman Empire.

Emek (Heb.): valley, here often referring to the Jezreel Valley.

Ehrenburg, Ilya (1891–1967): a well-known Soviet writer of Jewish descent.

Gedud Ha'avodah: lit. Labor Battalion; a Labor Zionist group founded in 1920 for the purposes of labor, defense, and the settlement of Jews in Palestine.

"Going sitting": participating in a sit-down strike, here for the purpose of the Conquest of Labor.

Grabski, Władysław (1874–1938): Prime Minister of Poland in the 1920s. He took anti-Jewish measures in economic areas, which led even well-to-do Jews to leave Poland, including for Palestine, which became known as the "Grabski Aliyah."

Fellah/Fellahin: Arab peasants.

Hajj: the annual Islamic pilgrimage to Mecca.

Hakhshara (Heb.): a training program organized by the socialist-Zionist Hashomer Hatzair organization in Europe to prepare its members for their pioneering, communal new life in the Land of Israel, working as agrarians on a kibbutz.

Hallel: a Jewish prayer recited on holidays to praise and give thanks. It consists of Psalms 113–18.

Hankin, Yehoshua (1864–1945): nicknamed "the redeemer of land," a Zionist responsible for the purchase of land for Jewish settlement, largely from rich Arab families.

Hashomer Hatzair (Heb.): lit. the young guard; a Labor Zionist youth group founded in 1913 in Galicia, Austro-Hungary. Inspired by Marx, Freud, and Herzl, among others, it founded kibbutzim in Palestine and, later, Israel. See a lengthy discussion in the introduction chapter.

Hatikvah (Heb.): lit. The Hope; Israel's national anthem since its founding in 1948, it was written in 1878 and sung in Zionist circles even before the state's creation.

Hejaz: the Western part of Saudi Arabia that includes the major holy Islamic cities and Muhammad's birthplace.

Histadrut: The General Union of Hebrew Workers in Palestine. In mid-1960s it dropped "Hebrew Workers" from its title and replaced it with "Workers."

Hora: circle dance that came to be associated with halutzim, originally from the Balkans. "They often involve circular formations, quick turns, hops and jumps, and stomping." (Yael Horowitz, *"Everything You Have Is Yours?":* Israeli Folk Dance and Building a Zionist National Culture," unpublished paper, 2023).

Ibn Saud (1875–1953): King of Hejaz in Saudi Arabia.

"In der sokhe ligt der mazl-brokhe" [In the Plow Good Fortune Is Found] and **"Dort vu di tseder"** [There Were the Cedars]: popular songs of the time, written in Yiddish and German in the late nineteenth century, that became widespread in Zionist circles, whether in their original or in Hebrew translation. "Sokhe" was by Elyokim Tsunzer, and "Tseder" by Yitshak Feld.

Ingleyz: the English (in Arabic pronunciation).

The Internationale: the Soviet and socialist anthem, originally written in French in 1871 by Eugène Pottier and set to music in the following decade.

Issa El-Issa (1878–1950): the publisher of *Falastin,* the first Arabic daily in Palestine, which was sharply against British rule and Zionism.

Jamia: (Arabic) an organization, here, of workers.

Jasienski, Bruno (1901–38): a Polish Communist poet of Jewish origin. His poem "A Note on Jakub Szela" depicted a peasant rebellion against serfdom led by Szela during the mid-1900s.

Jeddah (Arabic): a foremother in Islam, and a large city in Saudi Arabia.

Jewish Agency for Israel (Heb. *Hasochnut Hayehudit*): Zionist organization established in 1929 to encourage immigration of Jews to Palestine and then the State of Israel.

Kamionka: a town in Poland.

Karl Marx, Dr. Herzl, and Trumpeldor: three major figures in the history of Labor Zionism. Yosef Trumpeldor (1880–1920) was an early halutz who was immortalized for his sacrifice. Theodor Herzl (1860–1904), an Austrian Jewish journalist, was the visionary of political Zionism. Karl Marx (1818–83) was a prominent German political thinker of Jewish descent whose father converted to Christianity when Karl was a child. The author of *The Communist Manifesto* (1848), Marx is considered the father of Communism and was also popular among socialists in this period.

Khamsin (Arabic): dry, desert wind.

Kibbutz: a Zionist communal settlement founded on the basis of collectivist ideals, beginning in the early twentieth century.

Kitab (Arabic): Muslim religious school.

Kol Nidrei (Heb.): lit. all vows; the best-known prayer of the Yom Kippur service.

Kushan: bill of land ownership (from the Turkish).

Kvutse (Yiddish; Heb. *kvutza*): lit. group; another word for a kibbutz or a smaller version thereof.

Lermontov Mikhail (1814–41): A major Russian Romantic poet.

The Life of Klim Samgin: an epic four-volume novel by Russian socialist-realist writer Maxim Gorki (1868–1936), completed in 1936.

The Love Parade: a musical comedy film from 1929 and the first "talkie" directed by German Jewish director Ernst Lubitsch (1892–1947). I could not find the film *Only You I Love*.

Luftmensch (Yiddish): Yiddish; an impractical person, lacking in steady income, dreamer.

Madhafah (Arabic): a living room dedicated to receiving guests and drinking coffee.

Minyan: the quorum of ten male worshippers needed for Jewish prayer.

Mosh: the name of the training campground of Hashomer Hatzair in Poland, short for moshava (Heb. agricultural settlement).

Muezzin (Arabic): the man in a Muslim community who does the call to prayer.

Musa Kazim Pasha (1853–1934): the leader of the Arab Executive Committee in Ottoman Palestine. When the British took over under the "Mandate," they never recognized the group, and it was disbanded in 1934.

Mukhtar: a village bureaucrat appointed by the Turks to be in charge of a specific Arab village.

Muscovites (Arabic): lit. from Moscow; Russians.

Nalewki: a central street in Warsaw, mainly populated by Jews at the time of the novel.

Narodnaya Volya: a revolutionary anti-czarist organization, founded in 1879 in Russia.

Nashashibi family: a dominant Arab family in Palestine.

Oneg-Shabbes: lit. "pleasure of the Sabbath"; a celebration to mark the beginning of the Sabbath.

Pitshich: a town in Poland.

Productivization (of Jews): an ideology adopted by European Zionism that argued that Jews not being engaged in manual labor (in agriculture or industry) contributed to anti-Semitism. As a solution, Jews should be trained in agriculture and trades in various locations, including the Land of Israel.

Radziner Hasidim: a Hasidic dynasty founded in nineteenth-century Poland, known for its radical doctrine.

Ramadan: the holiest month on the Muslim calendar, characterized by fasting during daylight hours and an often-communal after-fast meal.

Revisionists: members of the right-wing Zionist movement called "Revisionist Zionism," led, starting in 1923, by figures such as Zeev Jabotinsky (1880–1940) and Uri Zvi Greenberg (1896–1981).

San Remo, conference and resolution: post–World War I (1920) conference in San Remo, Italy, where the winning powers divided the former Ottoman territories, including the British Mandate over Palestine (1920–48), and the implementation of the Balfour Declaration.

Sayoni: Zionist (in Arabic pronunciation).

Shabab (Arabic): youth or young people.

Shekhina: divine presence in Jewish thought, associated with the female aspect of God.

Sheygets (Yiddish, derogatory): young gentile man or impudent boy.

Shock worker: a term from the Soviet Union for a worker whose group exceeded production quotas and was assigned to a particularly urgent or arduous task.

Shomrim (Heb.): lit. guards; people belonging to the Labor Zionist youth movement Hashomer Hatzair.

Smocza Street: a street in Warsaw that was predominantly Jewish before World War II.

Tabu: registration of land ownership (from the Turkish).

Tarbut (Heb.): lit. culture; the chain of secular Hebrew-language schools. in Eastern Europe during the period of the twentieth century between the two world wars.

Wahabism: a fundamentalist interpretation of Sunni Islam, founded in the eighteenth century in Arabia.

Yahud (Arabic): Jews.

Yekkes: nickname for German Jews in Israel and elsewhere.

Vertinsky, Alexander (1889–1957): a Russian artist and singer.

Zamarin: the old Arab name for Zikhron Yaakov, an early "Baron" Zionist settlement close to Haifa.

Zifzif: a type of sand commonly used for construction in Israel/Palestine.

ABOUT THE AUTHOR

HANAN AYALTI (pen name of Khonen Klenbort, 1910–92) published many works in Yiddish and Hebrew, including *Boom and Chains*, originally published in Yiddish in 1936. Other works translated to English include *No Escape from Brooklyn* (1966) and *Yiddish Proverbs* (1963). He was born in a small town in the Russian Empire (now Belarus) and immigrated to Palestine in 1929. After four years, he fled to Paris due to his activism and published this novel a few years later. He came to the United States in 1946.

ABOUT THE TRANSLATOR

ADI MAHALEL teaches Yiddish studies and modern Jewish culture at
the University of Maryland, College
Park, and at the YIVO Institute for
Jewish Research. He is the author
of *The Radical Isaac: I. L. Peretz and
the Rise of Jewish Socialism*. His work
focuses on modern Jewish literature
and film with an emphasis on com-
parative approaches across linguistic
and cultural-political contexts.

Printed and bound by CPI Group (UK) Ltd, Croydon, CR0 4YY

16/11/2025

14773350-0001